THE CAFÉ OF INFINITE DOORS

THE CAFÉ OF INFINITE DOORS

ZARA MARIELLE

NEW YORK

Cover design by James Iacobelli
Cover images by Getty Images: Catalin Daniel Ciolca (glass), Matt Anderson Photography (door) and Shutterstock.com: benchart (door detail), Bill45 (knocker), Dancake (clouds), Ninell (feathers)

Union Square & Co.
Hachette Book Group
1290 Avenue of the Americas, New York, NY 10104
unionsquareandco.com
@unionsqandco

First Edition: April 2026

Union Square & Co. is an imprint of Grand Central Publishing, a division of Hachette Book Group, Inc. The Union Square & Co. name and logo are registered trademarks of Hachette Book Group, Inc.

Print book interior design by Marie Mundaca

Library of Congress Cataloging-in-Publication Data has been applied for.

ISBNs: 978-1-4549-6127-7 (paperback), 978-1-4549-6128-4 (ebook)

Printed in Canada

MRQ-L

10 9 8 7 6 5 4 3 2 1

To my mother, Barbara,
who would have been so proud.

AUTHOR'S NOTE

The ancient Scotland chapters in *The Café of Infinite Doors* are very loosely based on existing mythology, particularly the Celtic figure of the Morrígan, a goddess of death and battle who sometimes takes the form of a crow. I humbly ask forgiveness from any historians or academics for the artistic liberties I've taken.

Likewise, though the characters in these chapters would have been speaking Scottish Gaelic, I have used a slightly "Scottified" version of modern English, in order to keep the dialogue more relatable to contemporary readers. May the linguists among you forgive my transgressions.

CHAPTER 1

Long Ago

Before mortals captured time and partitioned it into years, there stood a stone village nestled between a loch and a wood. In that village was a hut, and in the hut writhed a woman, naked upon a bed of straw.

The hut shook with her raw screams, primal terror mingling with low, whimpering moans, begging for the end to come. Sweat clung to her feverish skin, her tunic discarded in a pile on the earthen floor. At the foot of the bed, an unshakable midwife knelt, whispering encouragement as she squinted between the woman's legs. Her ancient eyes scrutinized the turmoil.

"Mistress," said the midwife's young apprentice, who'd been twisting her apron, muttering prayers to the gods. "Are ye quite sure the bairn can be born this way? Can we nae try again to turn it?"

"I've told ye, lass. 'Tis far too late to fret about that now. It shall be born feetfirst or nae at all."

The girl looked almost as pale as the suffering mother-to-be. "But is it nae dangerous?"

"Aye, 'tis indeed." The midwife gritted her teeth, masking her temper for the sake of the poor mother. Her patience with the trembling apprentice had long worn thin, for since the contractions had begun, the sun had already set and now the moon had nearly completed its arc across the night sky. Despite their herbal remedies and ritual chants, and the massaging of the stomach to nudge the bairn into position, the mother's wretched agony stretched on and on. The midwife pushed her exhaustion to the back of her mind, knowing it was selfish to think of her own aching back when another woman's life was in peril. "Offer her comfort," she hissed at the apprentice, more to get her out of the way than anything else.

The apprentice scurried behind the mother and began to massage her shoulders with timid fingers, but at that moment another contraction shook the mother, who released a bleat so piteous that the girl recoiled in terror. When her eyes landed on the windowsill, she froze.

"Mistress, look!"

"What now?" The exasperated midwife followed the girl's gaze to the stone window ledge, where there perched a raven. Its feathers were glossy and black, eyes shining like polished stones as it observed the scene.

"The bairn," the girl whispered, wide-eyed. "Do ye think it belongs to the goddess? To the Great Winged One?"

"We've nae time for your superstition, lass!" Furious, the old midwife shoved the girl aside and lay her own gnarled hands over the woman's clammy skin.

"But, mistress, ye said there was nae father, and the legend says—"

"'Tis nae time for fairy tales. Now, watch for the feet! Make sure they dinnae get caught!"

The bird's gaze followed the midwife, its focus burrowing into the back of her cloth-wrapped head, but she swept the sensation aside. Goddess or nae, the mother and child were both in peril.

"Be calm, brave thing!" the midwife urged the suffering woman, pressing her tired hands downward and feeling for the shape of the babe within. The mother's panting breaths were becoming faint, the babe refusing to shift from its unnatural positioning. "We shan't let ye die on this night!" Conviction rang in the midwife's practiced words, masking the danger lurking ahead. For the old midwife was all too familiar with the fragility of life, of the narrow ledge separating it from death, and how easy it was to tumble down one side rather than the other.

Another contraction racked the mother, her weak frame spasming as she whimpered. The midwife muttered a prayer as she clasped the mother's hand. When a ripple of movement shifted beneath the stretched skin of the woman's belly, the apprentice peered between her legs, gasping.

"They're coming, mistress! At last, the feet are coming!"

"I can see that, lass!" The old midwife squeezed the mother's sweating hand. "What did I tell ye?"

The latter responded only with a strangled sob, her face pale and mottled as trampled snow.

"Nae! Stay with us now, and push!" the midwife cried, silently commanding the spirit of death to stand back. With a heart-wrenching moan the woman convulsed. "Push! Ye can do it. The bairn is but a moment away."

"She's out to her waist, mistress!" the apprentice cried. "Great Winged Goddess, 'tis a lass!"

"Aye, so she is. Now, watch how I guide her shoulders." To the mother she half begged: "Ye must be strong, now. Yer daughter is almost out!"

The mother screamed as her pain crescendoed, body shuddering with one last, desperate push.

In a torrent of blood and fluids, the midwife's gnarled hands guided the bairn outward into the world. The gods had heard them.

The midwife laughed, the delirium of fatigue taking over as she cradled the healthy, wriggling new babe. The apprentice sprang to action now—too late to be useful, but relief softened the midwife's annoyance—and severed the cord with a sharpened blade before busying herself with the tying of the knot.

"Ye did it." The midwife squeezed the mother's hand, admiring the squirming bairn. "Did I nae tell ye 'twould be all right?"

But the triumph was short-lived.

As the lass began cleaning the bairn with boiled loch water, the midwife tended to the new mother, whose panting grew fainter by the second. The rush of fluids spilling forth from her loins had not slowed, and now blood pooled in the straw beneath her. The old midwife could almost see the gnarled hands of fate gripping the poor mother's neck. Ignoring the ache in her back, she spun on her heels, snatching up a bundle of rags to staunch the bleeding. When she hobbled back, what she saw halted her in her tracks.

There were solid pieces within the flood of the afterbirth. The old woman squinted, picking up one of the delicate objects: a fragile thing—thin as the edge of a leaf—speckled in pale blues and grays.

It was an eggshell.

CHAPTER 2

Marceline squirmed in her chair, tugging at the hem of her dress as it rode up her thighs. The restaurant around her buzzed with conversation, waiters weaving between tables with glinting trays balanced over their heads, pools of candlelight illuminating strangers' faces. Marceline soaked it all up, giddy at the prospect of a rare evening away from the apartment—in San Francisco's trendy Marina District, no less. Across from her, Baxter pored over the menu, frowning at the choices.

He glanced at her. "Stop doing that."

"Huh?"

"Moving around like that."

"Oh, sorry." She knew better than to tell him it was the dress, that it was shorter than she was comfortable with, that she'd never have chosen it for herself. In her mind, the topic was filed under the *avoid* heading, and anyway, she should be grateful he cared enough to choose clothes for her. That he was even still attracted to her at all. "What are you having?"

"Steak." Baxter slapped the menu closed. "You?"

"The fettuccine Alfredo looks good."

"Treating yourself?" He raised an eyebrow in that way that made Marceline blush. She shrugged. Baxter would have preferred for her to order a salad. Surely their five-year wedding anniversary was special enough to merit carbs, if just for one meal.

"Should we get a nice bottle of wine?"

"Better not. What if you're pregnant?"

Marceline tensed. She'd hoped the topic wouldn't come up again tonight. "Bax, the test was negative," she said, as gently as she could manage. She braced herself as her husband's angular jaw tightened a fraction.

"They're not always accurate. There's still a chance—"

"We'll try again next time I'm ovulating. I promise."

"That's what you said last month," he mumbled.

Marceline looked away, trying to shake the guilty feeling this topic conjured. She knew it wasn't her fault she wasn't pregnant yet. But a part of her suspected it was. Perhaps if she wanted it more, the way he did, she could will a baby into being. Perhaps her secret fear of having to shepherd a child into a world she'd barely experienced herself was manifesting as some sort of metaphysical contraceptive—

No, no. She put a stop to the familiar train of thought before it could gather speed. She would not let this ruin the evening.

"You look nice, Bax." She smiled. It wasn't a lie. The shade of his button-up made his stormy eyes pop, the sleeves partially rolled up to reveal strong forearms, though the tip of his crude tattoo still protruded. Baxter hated that black X scrawled on his skin—a souvenir of some drunken night of teenage shenanigans. Marceline didn't mind it, though. After all these years, it had grown on her.

Not that she'd known him then. Baxter had been twenty-five when they'd met—seven years older than Marceline. Her high school friends had teased her about dating an "older man," as if he were some hunched, white-haired grandpa with one foot already in the grave. They'd been blown away when they'd seen him: this tall, broad-shouldered prototype of manhood. None of them could believe a frizzy-haired, toothy dork like Marceline had managed to ensnare someone like *that* as her first boyfriend. They'd been even more shocked when he'd married her six months later.

"You look nice too." Finally, he smiled back. She basked in it—Baxter was serious by nature and his genuine grins came few and far between. Suddenly, the itchy discomfort of the too-tight dress seemed a minor price to pay for an evening out with her handsome husband.

The waiter came, and Marceline was careful not to seem too friendly as Baxter ordered their food and wine, for the waiter had a dimpled, boyish grin, and she couldn't risk Baxter's jealousy. Not tonight. Tonight, there was something she'd been planning to ask him. She needed him in a benevolent mood. Was now the right time? She felt reluctant to break the spell. Maybe the topic would arise naturally. And if not, she'd mention it during dessert. He might be tipsy by then, and more willing to negotiate—though it could also go the other way. The last thing she wanted was to create conflict, but this had been on her mind for a long time, and it couldn't wait anymore.

Baxter's good mood persisted as the food arrived. Marceline savored the creamy pasta as she listened to him recount his day at the call center. He'd had to reprimand one of his "minions" (his word, not hers) who'd been loudly crunching on a cereal bar while on a call. She made sure to laugh in all the right places. Seeing him chatter away was a rare treat. Almost like being back on that sun-filled terrace of their honeymoon suite in Palm Springs—the only real vacation he'd ever taken her on. Although he'd promised if she gave him a child, they'd celebrate with a trip, possibly even out of the country this time.

He'd consented to ordering a few glasses of wine, and the alcohol had loosened him. Marceline giggled at each anecdote, waiting for the right moment. It wasn't until the waiter asked if they wanted dessert that she realized the evening would soon be over. But even as she opened her mouth to broach the topic, her courage evaporated.

She set down her wineglass. “Bax, do you mind if I use the bathroom?”

“Don’t stray,” he half joked. She laughed and stood too fast, almost toppling into the table. How she loathed wearing heels! She put one foot in front of the other, trying not to tug at the dress hugging her hips as she navigated away.

Their waiter passed as Marceline skirted the perimeter of the room.

“Ladies’ room is there.” He pointed behind her, dimpled grin contrasting with the formal black of his uniform.

She averted her eyes. “Thanks.”

Once in the restroom, she locked herself in a stall. She needed a moment. Sitting on the toilet seat with her eyes closed, she cradled her purse. What if Baxter said no? The likelihood of that, she realized, was high. Could she carry on as before? The thought conjured a lump in her throat as she unzipped her purse and rifled for the little square of notebook paper. Unfolding it over her knees, she reviewed the bullet points, though she’d long since memorized them. She read through it once, twice, three times, then folded it again.

If only she had someone to give her advice. But there was no one. Her high school friends had receded into the unreachable depths of the past, and her beloved grandmother was dead and gone, as was her father. As for a mother, hers had run off when she was a baby.

There was no one else left.

She shook her head to dislodge the loneliness, focusing instead on her breaths until the moment had passed.

When she emerged from the stall, so did another woman, from the one next to her. Marceline smiled at her as they washed their hands side by side. The woman—who was middle-aged, with cropped hair and a conservative pantsuit—nodded, her eyes slipping downward to Marceline’s own outfit.

“Oh, these aren’t my clothes,” Marceline blurted.

The woman jerked up, halfway through squeezing soap into her hand. "Sorry?"

"I just saw you looking at my clothes. They're not mine. Well, they are, but I didn't choose them. My husband did."

"Okay...?" The woman's forehead creased in mild confusion. She went to rinse off the soap.

"I mean, it was nice of him. It's not that I'm not grateful, but personally I like dressing for comfort."

The woman gave a quick smile as she pulled a paper towel from the dispenser and wiped her hands, already heading for the door.

"Can I ask you something?" Marceline blurted again. Absurd as it was, the idea of this stranger leaving the bathroom made her feel even lonelier than before.

"Me?" The woman paused, though there was no one else present.

"Yes. I'm sorry, I know it's a little weird. It's just—you have a job, right?"

"Yes..."

"I figured. What is it you do? Would you say it brings you fulfillment?"

The woman looked uneasy. "Um, are you trying to pitch me something?"

Marceline backpedaled. "No! Sorry! God, this is coming out all wrong." She cringed, all too aware of the sweat dampening the underarms of her odious dress. "I guess I'm just taking a survey? But a survey of one, and you're the one who happened to walk in, so... wow, I'm really messing this up, aren't I?"

The more Marceline babbled, the higher the woman's eyebrows rose, until she looked genuinely concerned.

"Hey, relax. It's okay. I guess I have a minute." She cleared her throat, visibly uncomfortable. "I'm a software engineer. And it's fine? It's not my passion, but I have a healthy work-life balance. Time for hobbies and whatnot."

Relief tempered Marceline's nerves, if only by a fraction. There was something so alluring, so luxurious, about the concept of hobbies. She'd often imagined herself backpacking through Europe or learning to paint, or— No, no. She had to focus. She straightened. "And do you have a husband?"

"I have a wife," the woman said. "She's an accountant."

"Right. So, there's no single breadwinner at your house."

The woman gawked at her in bewilderment. "Breadwinner? This is the twenty-first century. I think we've evolved a little beyond that concept." Her creased forehead and probing eyes made Marceline feel like an exotic beast in a cage.

"Oh, for sure," she conceded, blushing. Obviously, she knew Baxter was a little old-fashioned in his beliefs, and yes, those beliefs were a bit restrictive, but she was trying her best to open his mind. She didn't know many other people in real life anymore, but TV had taught her that there were all sorts of possible dynamics between couples. Surely, they could find one where they were both happy?

Desperate to push past the discomfort, Marceline persisted. "And what about the division of labor at home? Do you both do housework too, in addition to going to work every day?"

"We both do our part." The woman glanced down at the silver watch on her wrist, then back at the door, almost longingly.

"It's our five-year anniversary," Marceline offered. "My husband and I are celebrating. That's why we're here, at dinner." *Please don't leave*, she silently begged.

"Ah. Congratulations." The woman's hand moved to the door handle. Then, quite suddenly, a serious look pinched her brows, as if something had clicked within her brain. She let go of the handle, lowering her voice: "Is he hurting you?"

"What?"

"Your husband. Do you need me to call the police?"

"Oh no! God no," Marceline guffawed. Baxter was grumpy, yes, but he wasn't one of *those* men. "I just need to practice something."

"I don't understand."

"Tell me if this sounds good, please." Marceline pulled the folded piece of paper back out and began to read, gripping the thin paper between her fingers. "'Number one: Financial security. If we both have an income, we'll be able to provide for the baby easier . . .'" The stoic line of Baxter's mouth materialized in her mind.

"Are you pregnant?"

"Oh no. Definitely not. I mean, he wants me to be, but no, not yet."

"I don't understand. You're planning to have children?"

Marceline flinched at the directness of the question. "Sure, eventually. But this is more about the job."

"I see." A grave look crossed the woman's face, making Marceline feel like this stranger knew something she didn't. The look bothered her, but she returned her focus to her list. Just when she'd been longing for someone to listen to her, this woman had appeared. She had to take advantage of the situation.

"'Number two: Overtime. If I had a job, you wouldn't have to do overtime so often.'" She glanced at the woman for confirmation.

The woman crossed her arms, watching Marceline almost broodingly.

"'Number three: Coworkers. If I had coworkers to chat with, I wouldn't act so needy when you get home every day.'" Baxter's disapproving face flashed in her mind again, and when she looked up, the woman's eyes swam with pity. Sweat dampened Marceline's hands, wrinkling the edges of the paper.

"Did he call you needy, honey?" The sudden compassion in the woman's voice splintered through Marceline like lightning. "Listen, I don't know your situation, but you're not needy just because you're missing human company. Everyone needs to interact sometimes."

Marceline swallowed her discomfort. "I kind of am, though. We both agreed it's something I better work on."

When the woman put her hand to her heart, an avalanche of shame crashed over Marceline. She'd wanted someone to listen to her, but she hadn't anticipated being looked at under a microscope either. As if every relationship didn't have its flaws! She twisted the paper between her fingers.

The woman reached out and squeezed Marceline's shoulder. "You'll do great." When Marceline dared tear her gaze away from the floor, the jarring pity still lingered in the woman's eyes. "I wish I could help you more, but I'm in the middle of a company dinner. Remember to be strong and say exactly what you mean. Don't take no for an answer. Okay?"

Marceline swallowed. The woman was clearly trying to be nice, but she didn't know Baxter. "Thanks," she mumbled, staring down at the pointed stilettos pinching her toes. "Thank you for listening."

The woman patted her on the shoulder and left.

The shame lingered, constricting Marceline's chest. Her gaze skidded to the mirror in front of her. She looked how she felt: frumpy and desperate. The dress had ridden up her thighs again, hugging her body in all the wrong places. *Snap out of it*, she told herself, tugging it down again. *It's your anniversary.*

Taking out a cracked compact, she dusted powder over her freckled pallor and forced a smile at her reflection. Not so convincing, but the woman was right. All she could do was her best.

She was halfway back to the table when someone tapped her shoulder.

"Miss!"

Marceline turned, finding herself face to face with the waiter and his boyish grin. Her eyes darted away. She kept walking.

"Miss! You dropped this."

She glanced behind her again. He was holding out a piece of paper. Her list. Shit! She could almost feel Baxter's glare drilling into her back from across the room.

She snatched the note away, mumbling a hurried thanks.

By the time she approached the table, she was trembling.

Even through the hum of conversation and soft classical music, the scrape of Marceline's chair seemed to resonate across the room as she sat, cowering under her husband's steely gaze.

She started to babble: "I'm sorry, Bax, the pasta didn't agree with me, but now I'm feeling bett—"

"Not. Here." His voice was strained, ice frosting his irises.

An awkward titter rose from within her. She gripped her spoon and went to dip it into the glass tumbler of chocolate mousse awaiting her. The edge of the spoon hadn't even skirted the surface when Baxter banged his wineglass down on the table.

"We're leaving. Go wait in the car."

He threw the keys at her and she caught them, sneaking a longing look at the untouched mousse. It would have been her last dessert for a long time.

Thick sheets of rain saturated the darkness as she bent her head against the downpour, ambling out of the restaurant as fast as her impractical heels allowed. The cold prickled Marceline's bare arms as she hurried toward the car, trying desperately not to think of the impending explosion of Baxter's anger. If she'd only ignored the waiter, they'd still be in the warm restaurant, enjoying a pleasant evening.

By the time she reached the shelter of the car, her hair clung to her face in sodden clumps. She shivered, drumming a nervous rhythm into the dashboard of the battered Civic until the sudden appearance of two black, shining eyes startled her out of her mind.

She flinched, then released a nervous laugh. It was only a bird. A great black raven, perched on the hood of the car. It peered at Marceline through the windshield, eyes round as polished beads.

What was it about ravens appearing during her moments of deepest distress? Her grandmother's funeral, for example, had been swarming with ravens. Once, Marceline had confessed to Baxter that she liked imagining the birds were sent by her grandmother from the beyond. After all, the kind old woman had loved scattering birdseed around the yard outside her trailer. The fanciful confession had annoyed Baxter, who hated birds. She'd even seen him try to chase a raven, once, in the parking lot of their apartment complex. The episode had bewildered Marceline, who'd by now learned to keep such musings to herself. Anyway, it was just a comforting thought.

Marceline's heartbeat began to slow as she stared into the bird's black eyes. Perhaps something would distract Baxter from his rage. Perhaps he'd realize it was all a misunderstanding. She clung to this irrational hope until the bird took off in a flurry of wings, along with any notion of temporary security.

Across the street, her husband stepped out of the restaurant. She shrank into the passenger's seat as he crossed, scowling. When he swung open the door, a burst of frigid wind slapped Marceline in the face. Baxter snatched the keys from the dash and started the engine.

All of this without so much as a glance at her.

The car shrieked as Baxter swerved out of the parking space and onto Chestnut Street. A cluster of college students under an awning—she could tell from their SFSU sweatshirts—turned their heads, jarred by the sound. Marceline watched them through the side mirror, wondering if they knew how lucky they were. She would have loved to spend four whole years learning and making friends. Perhaps she could even have done a semester abroad to somewhere wildly different, like Ecuador or South Africa or Denmark. But that would require her to be a student first, and Baxter had felt education was too expensive, so the best she could do was stream travel shows and educational programs all day while she cooked and cleaned.

The car sped through a puddle, a murky tidal wave crashing over her view. The water dripped away, students shrinking into the distance.

Desperate to ignore the tension, Marceline leaned back into the passenger's seat. Outside the warm car, red-and-yellow puddles of light blurred the dark pavement, and traffic hummed, rain splashing in torrents. She was keenly aware of Baxter's white-knuckled grip on the steering wheel, his knit-together brows, his eyes staring resolutely ahead.

It was fifteen minutes before he uttered a sound. And when he did, his voice was so brittle it made Marceline want to dissolve right into the upholstery.

"Show it to me."

She wrung her hands, daring to glance at him, but his eyes were still glued ahead. She hated conflict. It scattered her brain, making her feel flustered. "Wh—What? Show you?"

"Don't play dumb with me, Marce. That goddamn paper. What was it, his phone number?"

"Paper?" Something clicked in her brain. The note she'd written to herself. He was referring to the scene with the waiter. She released a strangled laugh. "That? That was mine. It was nothing—"

"I saw him hand it to you. I'm not blind."

"No, I mean, it had nothing to do with the waiter, it was just—"

"Then fucking show me."

Her mouth hung open. "You want to see the note?" Now was *not* the time to mention her carefully planned arguments.

"Did I stutter?"

"No. No, you didn't. I will. I mean, I am. Wait..." She jolted into action, rummaging through her purse, her fingers shaking almost violently. Had she even put it back in here? She couldn't remember, couldn't focus. Why was there so much stuff in her goddamn purse? The longer it took her to find it, the more suspicious it looked. But there had to be a shopping list, or a receipt—anything she could show him instead.

"I'm waiting," Baxter snarled, interrupting her frazzled thoughts.

"I can't find it, but I swear it's—"

The car emitted a deafening screech as Baxter stomped on the brakes. Marceline jerked against her seat belt, then slammed back into the seat. The line of cars behind them released an angry chorus of honks.

"Get out."

She blinked, too shocked to speak. Outside it was still pouring, and the time on the dashboard display read 9:16. Half the streetlights were out, and except for a handful of shady characters crouching in doorways, not a single pedestrian had braved the downpour. She wasn't familiar with the San Francisco neighborhoods, since she couldn't drive. She and Baxter lived twenty minutes south in a low-rent area of the commuter city of San Bruno. He'd never taken her south of Market Street.

"Baxter, please. I have no idea where we are—"

"Either you prove the note was nothing, or you find your own way home." He cringed, clutching his forearm through his shirtsleeve, as if his tattoo was burning him.

"But I don't know where I put it..."

"Fine." He unclicked her seat belt. She gaped at him, and he looked stonily back at her.

Behind them the car horns continued to blare. Someone shouted a string of insults out the window, but Baxter ignored them. Marceline sat frozen in her seat. These were the moments she hated the most—when he was unreachable in his anger. But he'd never abandoned her before. She put a trembling hand on his sleeve. If she could just make him remember this was *her*, his soulmate, his partner in life...

Baxter shook himself free. "Go!"

Tears sprang to her eyes and a knot of fear unfurled in her stomach as she stepped out of the car and into the rain.

CHAPTER 3

The Honda sped away, leaving Marceline shivering on the sidewalk. Within seconds she was soaked to the bone, the synthetic fabric of the minidress clinging to her skin. She blinked, wiping a soggy strand of hair from her eyes just in time to be sprayed by a burst of filthy water from a speeding truck. Shocked, she shrank back from the street, tottering in her heels.

How would she get home? Her panic expanded, frenzied thoughts cluttering her mind. If only Baxter would buy her a phone—but who would she call? She trembled, exposed both to the elements and the sinister eyes she was sure were watching her from every doorway as she paced the filthy sidewalk.

Shielding her eyes, she wandered to the end of the block until she found a pair of street signs. Folsom and Eighth Street. It meant nothing to her without a map. A block or so to the right, cars zoomed across a freeway overpass. Was Baxter driving down that freeway now? No, impossible—he was trying to scare her, that's all. He would never leave her.

She cradled her purse. There was nothing inside save a few crumpled dollars left over from her grocery allowance. No driver's license or phone or credit cards. Still, holding something seemed to help.

Marceline scanned the street for an empty doorway—any outcropping that might provide shelter while she waited for Baxter to return. Across the street she saw a bus stop awning. Shivering, she braced against the downpour, heading for the crosswalk. When the light turned green, she bent her head, hugging herself with goose bump–covered arms as she set one unsteady foot in front of the other. The judging eyes of the drivers stopped at the intersection prickled her skin. Part of her wanted to turn and ask them for help, but she knew better than to approach strangers.

The stilettos pinched her toes, and her feet pulsed with pain by the time she reached the other side. There were fewer lights here. More sinister shapes loomed, blurred by darkness and rain. Pressing on toward the bus stop, Marceline did her best to harness her fear. To focus on her destination rather than the fact that she was vulnerable, a woman alone, scantily clad in a questionable neighborhood on a dark, rainy night.

She made it to the bus stop and ducked inside, anxious for shelter, for a schedule explaining how to get home—just in case. There *was* one, but it had been half ripped from the scratched plastic wall, a mess of graffiti rendering its remains illegible. STOP OUT OF SERV, flickered the digital marquee above it.

Shit.

Marceline leaned against the shelter's interior wall, face crumpling. She shoved her hands over her mouth to keep the sobs in.

That's when the car pulled up.

"How much?"

The deep voice startled Marceline, who stiffened, terror flaring across her nerves. Between the blur of tears and rain, she could hardly make out the driver's face—only a smear of gray—was he wearing a suit?—topped by shadowy dark hair. The car itself was obscured, too, but its low, angular body signaled expensive, sporty connotations.

"Come on, don't be shy."

Marceline shrank farther into the wall of the bus stop, wishing she could vanish into it. Any response she might have given lodged dryly in her throat. *Please go away*, she pleaded silently, gaze locked on the puddles at her feet. *Please go away, please go away...*

"Let's get you out of the rain," the man said. A second later, the sound of a car door opening sent fear zinging up her spine.

That was what did it—that sound.

One moment, she was paralyzed by fear. The next, she was sprinting into the street as fast as her accursed shoes would let her. Cars honked and swerved as she dove between them, careening across the street without a backward glance. She needed to get far, far away, and quickly! Was he following her? Impossible to tell over the furious Klaxons, the dizzying thud of blood in her ears.

An alleyway yawned open before her, and without a second thought she darted inside—only to trip on something solid. She flailed, trying to steady herself against a brick wall and instead landing directly on top of her obstacle: something damp, soft, and moving. Something alive.

"Get off me, bitch!" A pair of rough hands shoved her away, and Marceline scrambled to escape the huddled figure in a sleeping bag she was now splayed over. She launched herself off him, only for the heel of her damn stiletto to get stuck in a pavement crack. Her ankle erupted with pain as it twisted beneath her, sending her plummeting into a dumpster. The huddled figure shouted after her, a string of vicious, guttural swears clattering in her head. *Shelter*, she thought, frantic. *I need shelter.* She emitted a whimper, searching for a refuge, a haven.

And then, she found it.

A shining point in the darkness. The eye of a raven, lurking in the shadows. The bird turned, beak pointing across the alley like an arrow.

Pointing to a door.

It stood a mere five feet away at most. Its details hit her all at once: the carvings in the oak, the brass knocker in the shape of a fierce-eyed bird, turned green with age. Above it, a stained-glass transom, glowing orange and gold. How hadn't she seen it? It stood ajar, warm light shining inside like an invitation.

Pouring her last ounce of strength into her legs, she half scurried, half limped up the three steps toward the door.

It opened to receive her. The trash-strewn alley melted away, replaced by a sudden, blinding glare of golden light.

CHAPTER 4

Long Ago

The midwife, the apprentice, the mother, the babe. Four generations of women entangled in one primal drama, the violent battle waged within a mere instant upon that thin ledge, the one separating life from death. A drama complicated by a foreign object, the incomprehensible presence of this shattered artifact, the eggshell in the afterbirth.

None of them were aware of another human presence in the room. Only the raven's glossy eyes fixed upon her: the mother's firstborn child, barely five years old, peeking out from beneath a mound of straw.

Bronagh was her name, and she had no interest in mysterious eggshells, nor in her newborn sister. From her low vantage point, her eyes searched for only one thing: her mother's gaze. But when she found it, it was already half empty. A helpless panic spread over the girl as the shocked midwife stood over her mother, gnarled hands clutching the blue fragments to her chest like a talisman. Bronagh began to tremble as her mother's eyes rolled in her direction, staring at the space between them, empty of life.

Her fingers twitched once, twice, and then not at all.

"Mama!" Bronagh screamed, bursting from her hiding place and throwing herself over her mother's limp body. The apprentice gasped.

"Out," the midwife cried, eyes widening at the intruder. "A deathbed is nae place for a child!" She dropped the eggshell into the folds of her shift.

The apprentice passed the newborn to her mistress and lunged for the five-year-old, who clung to her mother's breast, sobbing as the warmth of life seeped away. After a struggle, the apprentice managed to snatch the frantic child.

"Shh, shh," she crooned as she hauled the screaming child out of the hut. "I'm sorry, 'tis the way of the world. But ye have a sister now. She'll be yer new family—may the Great Winged Goddess protect ye both."

The words meant nothing to Bronagh. She didn't care about the gurgling babe. She only wanted her mother, but that horrid, vacant gaze was seared in her mind. It was the same glazed look of the wild boar the menfolk brought back from the hunt.

The heavy door of the hut shut behind her, wood scraping against stone, triggering a flurry of feathers as the raven took off from the windowsill. Bronagh sank into the dirt, watching the bird disappear into the clouded sky.

The sun crested over the distant trees, bringing its pale halo to kiss the fading night. Bronagh gripped her knees. A long, anguished moan—the sound of a dying creature—arose from her depths. For though she didn't yet have the words to express the feeling, deep within her young heart, she knew. Knew that the one person who had loved her was gone, that she would spend her life searching to regain that warmth. That the search would be fruitless.

Like the raven in the window, her old life had flown away. She would never find it again.

CHAPTER 5

Marceline crashed into the hardwood floor, blinded by the pain in her ankle.

"Lu! Come quick," a masculine voice called. "She is hurt!"

The raven hopped to where Marceline lay twisted on the floor, pausing inches from her face. It must have swooped in right after her. It peered down its beak at her, head cocked.

"Where—where am I?" Something large and solid blocked her view. She recoiled: it was the body of an enormous man. "Don't hurt me!" She tried to scramble to her feet, but collapsed again, moaning. How had the sports car man followed her inside? Her mind jumbled with flashing images—darkness and rain and pavement—only half aware of the soft light and flickering warmth surrounding her.

"Hurt you? God no," this other man exclaimed. He was huge, well over six feet tall, a T-shirt stretched over a wide belly. Potentially Hawaiian, with tan skin and smiling brown eyes. But just because a stranger had a kind face didn't mean they were safe. Marceline's eyes shot to the door. "It is closed by key," the man said, then backpedaled: "I mean to say, we do not force you to stay. Just, whoever pursues you cannot enter." His speech was oddly assembled, its flavor foreign—vaguely French, except for the trill of heavily rolled *r*'s. He winced, mimicking Marceline's cringe as she pushed herself into a sitting position, as if he too could feel the flaring pain. "What were you doing alone beneath the rain?"

She opened her mouth—but where to even begin? The evening's events pressed down on her like a curse, conjuring an overpowering urge to melt into tears. But before she could utter a sound, a second person was standing over her. A woman.

"And dressed like ye stumbled out of a dance hall, too." She, too, had an accent—a thick, rolling one. Scottish? Marceline gaped at the woman, too shocked to be offended. She stood about as tall as the man, but the resemblance stopped there, for she was bone-pale and willow-thin, clad in a long dress and draped with gauzy scarves that flowed around her like wind.

"Nobody says *dance hall* any longer, Lu," the man chuckled. "We call them clubs now."

The woman dismissed the comment with an eye roll, peering down at Marceline. It occurred to her how she must look: soggy, disheveled, and stuffed into a too-tight dress.

"These aren't my clothes," Marceline mumbled, heat rising to her cheeks.

The woman raised an amused eyebrow, eyes burning black against her ghostly complexion. "'Tis nae my problem how ye dress yerself. Wear a badger skin for all I care."

Marceline stared. The woman's age was impossible to guess. A thick, dark pile of hair coiled high on her head, stray pieces jutting off at odd angles—no, not hair. Feathers, Marceline realized, startled. Long, glossy, black feathers, growing straight out of her scalp.

What in the world?

"Lu, maybe allow her to inhale before you commence judging her outfit? She is soaked and freezing," said the man, who seemed to be in his late twenties or early thirties. With a grunt, he crouched to Marceline's level, observing how she clutched her ankle. "And injured too. Here, let me help you."

He leaned in and wrapped an arm around her, but Marceline did not move, so transfixed was she by the woman's feathered mane.

"You will acclimate to her." His soft touch nudged her out of her stupor. Marceline winced as she put weight on her ankle once more.

She leaned against him as he guided her toward a chair near a fireplace full of flickering embers. His body hummed with warmth beside her. Marceline hadn't been this physically close to any man other than Baxter for—well, ever, she realized. She tried to ignore the twinge of foreboding as she sank into the bulk of his side. At least the softness provided a momentary distraction from the hot pain in her ankle, from the cramping of her other calf as she hopped on one foot, from the torrent of thoughts like *Baxter would flip if he saw you right now.*

Together, they shuffled awkwardly across the room and to the chair.

Now that she no longer lay in a tangled heap on the floor, she took in her surroundings: A half-dozen little square tables. A long wooden counter with a shiny chrome espresso machine and glass pastry case. In the corner, a large potted plant wilted on a side table, and a rustic stone fireplace spilled heat like a warm embrace. A trio of African masks hung above the mantel. Was this a café?

Despite the odd assortment of artifacts from around the world, the stone walls reminded Marceline of the quaint English cottages she'd seen in travel documentaries. A warm yellow glow permeated the room, though she could see no light source, no window or lamp. In fact, even the stained-glass transom she'd noticed from outside had disappeared, replaced by the smooth gray stone of the wall.

What an unusual place, she thought, gawking as the raven swooped upward to join an assembly of mismatched companions; she spotted a blue jay, a sparrow, two pigeons, and—her eyes widened—something that looked like a massive vulture. She'd watched enough nature shows to know these species did not flock together. The birds stared back, as interested in her as she was in them. While the larger birds roosted in the rafters, the smaller ones perched on what looked like a long, curved branch—no, a rib! The enormous skeleton of some gargantuan, finned beast swayed from the beams above, rocked by some sourceless breeze.

Perhaps "unusual" had been an understatement.

"Welcome." The man extended a hand. "I am called Sylvan."

Shyly, she shook it, continuing to gaze around her. The place seemed to be open, judging by the one customer sipping from a steaming mug at the table closest to the fireplace: a hunched, white-haired old woman, manipulating a protractor over a vast scroll of parchment covering the entire table.

"That is Kilda," the man—Sylvan—said. "She is a cartographer. She has been appearing here since much longer than I have, although I found this place only one year ago. It's quiet right now, but customers have tendencies to arrive in clumps because of the time zones. Am I conversing too much? I enjoy when newcomers arrive. It makes things shake."

Marceline made a stilted sound, unsure how to respond. The time zone thing felt like some sort of bizarre joke. Yet despite her confusion, her soaking clothes, and her dripping hair, she could feel her shoulders relaxing. Like the rain upon her skin, the trauma of her evening had begun to seep away, giddy warmth spreading through her in its place.

"And ye worried *I* was going to overwhelm her?" The feathered woman smirked, her hand on Sylvan's shoulder. When Marceline noticed the woman's fingers, she almost fell out of her chair. They weren't fingers at all, though one of them did bear a thin, silver ring.

They were talons. Long, curved talons.

They had to be some sort of bizarre fashion accessory, Marceline rationalized. Right?

The woman's coal-black gaze lingered on Marceline, as if unsure what to make of her. Marceline fidgeted. She was used to being visually assessed, but usually it was Baxter doing the assessing. Not that he meant any harm by it, but... Oh! Baxter! Shit. Marceline's stomach twisted at the thought of him. What would he do if she wasn't there waiting when he returned?

"My husband—"

"—can wait," the woman interrupted. "Now hold still." She brandished a rag and stepped behind the chair, before aggressively toweling Marceline's dripping hair.

"No, you don't understand, if I'm not there when he comes back, he'll—"

"Sylvan, make her a warm brew. She's shivering." She pointed a talon at the fireplace, and with a *whoosh*, flames flared from the embers, climbing the charred logs. Marceline gaped, first at the newly roaring fire, then at the avian appendage that had apparently revived it.

"What would you desire?" Sylvan asked. "Tea? Coffee?"

"Oh. Uh, tea?" Marceline made sure not to look at his face. Baxter wasn't here, but a five-year habit was hard to break.

"Get her something to wear too," the woman ordered.

"Relax yourself, Lu," Sylvan said. "One thing at a time!"

"Your name is Lu?" Marceline gave a timid smile, trying to get a feel for the stoic woman behind her. Her actions were kind but her manner stern, and Marceline wasn't sure what to make of the combination.

"Lu*cretia*," the woman corrected. "Sylvan insists on giving everyone nicknames."

"She opposed Lucifer and Lieutenant, so Lu is the result," Sylvan called from behind the counter. "She selected the dullest one."

Amusement nudged the corner of Marceline's mouth. "Nice to meet you, Lucretia."

"Indeed." The feathered woman punctuated the word with another tug at Marceline's sopping locks. "We expected ye much earlier. What happened?"

"Expected me?" Marceline tried to turn her head, but Lucretia swiveled it firmly forward again.

"It is not as if she had an appointment," Sylvan called over the clatter of mugs and the whistle of an old-fashioned teapot.

"Still," Lucretia countered with another yank at Marceline's wet hair. "I could have been doing other things."

"You *were* doing other things."

"Nae the point," Lucretia muttered. In a daze, Marceline let her head jerk from side to side as the feathered woman continued to towel her off. How was it possible these people had known she was coming? She hadn't even known it herself.

While the tea steeped, Sylvan set a cardboard box at Marceline's feet. "The lost objects. No haute couture in here, I fear."

Marceline reddened again. "Oh. These aren't my clothes," she said for the third time that night, tugging at the minidress. "I didn't choose them. My husband—"

"Aye," Lucretia interrupted, her voice soft. "*That's* why yer here."

Marceline twisted in her chair, unnerved by the woman's knowing tone. "I'm sorry, I don't understand. Who do you think I am?"

"Marceline Sapnis. Dinnae ye tell me I'm wrong."

Despite the warmth of the room, a shiver danced up Marceline's spine. They knew her name. Not only that, they knew her *maiden* name, the one Baxter had told her to forget. She was Marceline Grone now, he'd said. Now and forever. She'd known better than to argue.

"How..."

Sylvan gestured vaguely at the rafters. "The birds."

"The . . . the birds?"

"You must have perceived them around." He sifted through the box's contents. "Would this go well on you?" He held up a complicated gown fit for a Shakespearean production.

"Honestly, Sylvan, she's nae going to a ball," Lucretia chided.

"Well, the selection is restricted." He kept rummaging. "This one?" He brandished an oversized beige trench coat. "You can remove your wet belongings and wrap it around yourself. You will appear like a blinker—"

"Flasher," Lucretia interjected.

"But it is better than remaining iced and waterlogged." Sylvan chuckled, and Marceline found herself smiling too. She stood, testing her ankle before taking the garment.

"Where can I change?"

"Storeroom." Lucretia pointed behind the counter. Beneath the layers of gauzy scarves, swirling blue patterns snaked up her arms. They were beautiful tattoos, much more elegant than Baxter's crude X.

"Lu! Do not dispatch her there yet. She will never return!"

"What's in the storeroom?" Marceline asked.

"Definitely not a ghost." Sylvan's sheepish eyes darted toward Lucretia. Marceline gave a stilted smile, not understanding the joke. "Why do you not change behind the partition?" Sylvan gestured toward a Japanese-style three-panel divider in the corner, near the wilting plant.

Marceline headed behind the screen. But as she began peeling off the soggy dress, the hiss of whispers caught her attention. She paused, half undressed, straining to listen.

"Why the ferociousness?"

"There's a shadow about her. A faint stink of evil."

"Evil? Her? Come on, Lu. It is impossible."

"'Tisn't, I can see it. It surrounds her—a dark aura."

"Perhaps she stepped in some evil out on the street?"

Lucretia ignored Sylvan's jest. "I cannae be sure she's safe. Nae until I check Falkirk's mind."

Were they talking about her? And who was Falkirk? She pulled on the coat. Baxter always mocked Marceline's awkwardness, but she didn't think she was evil. If anything, the hushed observation made her more anxious to please these strange people who'd saved her from a fate she didn't want to contemplate.

Something sharp nipped at Marceline's thigh. With a startled yelp, she leapt away from the potted plant—no longer wilting, but instead rearing its many stalks, each of which featured a leafy green head, complete with snapping jaws.

Marceline screamed as the largest head lunged at her, latching its teeth around the hem of the trench coat. She yanked the coat away. The plant did not let go. Momentum sent her tumbling backward, crashing half naked into the partition. She toppled with it to the ground.

Startled, Lucretia and Sylvan gaped at her. Sylvan's tan face deepened to ruby red. He turned away. Marceline realized why a fraction too late.

She scrambled to pull the coat over her exposed breasts. "The p-plant!" she babbled. "It's—it's alive!"

"Technically, all plants are alive," Lucretia informed her.

Sylvan, however, gasped, eyes still averted. "Oh, droppings! Did she harm you? We have neglected to feed her today."

"Feed her?" Marceline stared from Sylvan to the feathered woman.

"The plant. I call her Maia, after my niece," Sylvan shared. "She is the fiercest eight-year-old the world has ever seen. I am considering perhaps giving the lesser heads separate names soon, so if you construct any ideas—"

"Too much detail, lad," Lucretia interjected.

A slightly hysterical giggle burbled involuntarily out of Marceline as she clambered to her feet, wincing at the pain in her ankle. She shifted her gaze to the old woman in the corner, who still hadn't looked up from her parchment. A pigeon was now perched on her head and had made a nest in the cotton-like mass of the woman's white hair. Behind her, one of the African masks above the mantel winked.

This wasn't where she'd expected her night to take her.

A dazed giddiness overtook her brain as she sank into a chair, hugging the coat around her body. "I'm dreaming, right? None of this can possibly be real..."

"Real? For the love of Nature, why are ye people so obsessed with what's real and what isn't?" Lucretia looked exasperated.

"*You people?* Here we go..." Sylvan smirked. "You must forgive Lucretia, she does not depart much."

"Hilarious," Lucretia shot back. "All I'm saying is reality is limiting, and I'm bloody tired of..."

Sylvan groaned, his eyes glittering with mischief. "Not *that* can of worms."

"What have I told ye about bird jokes?"

"Come on, that one was clever! No, Falkirk?"

The raven, who'd perched upon Lucretia's shoulder, gave an underwhelmed squawk before taking off. Marceline startled as he landed on her lap, nestling his shining black head against her. A thin gold cuff glinted, looped around one of its legs.

So, the raven was Falkirk? And Lucretia could read its mind? Marceline's head swam, bits of her evening blurring together. She stroked the bird in her lap, taking comfort in the texture of its glossy feathers. What would have happened to her if this bizarre place hadn't appeared out of the blue?

"We are overwhelming her, Lu." Sylvan threw Marceline a sympathetic smile. "I know this is abundant to take in. For the sake of simplicity:

no, you do not dream, and—oh, excrement! Your tea!" He scrambled back to the counter. "Why do you not sit by the fire?"

Marceline gave a weak nod. She limped toward the stone fireplace and sat, not taking her eyes off the plant in the corner, whose largest head was gnawing on the edge of its ceramic pot. She hardly noticed the steaming cup Sylvan placed before her until the tantalizing, spiced aroma taunted her nostrils. She took a sip. The light, soothing flavor was just what she needed to collect her scattered thoughts. Sylvan and Lucretia watched her, as if waiting for her to speak.

Finally, she did.

"What is this place, exactly?"

Lucretia hesitated. Sylvan tugged pensively at a short lock of his wavy black hair.

"It is . . . a place to repose, you could say. Or *not* repose." He gestured to the old woman, Kilda, who muttered to herself as she pored over her parchment, the pigeon pecking at her scalp.

"That's a horrible way to explain it," Lucretia chided.

"Blame your own translation spell." Sylvan yanked a dish rag from his back pocket and swatted her with it. "You attempt it, if you can do better."

"Nae thanks."

Sylvan rolled his eyes. "Okay." He offered Marceline a warm smile. "It is a place to do what you cannot usually do. Or be who you cannot usually be."

The warmth of Marceline's cup seeped into her hands. "I don't understand."

"Listen," Lucretia cut in. "Do ye like yer life?"

The blunt question took Marceline by surprise. "Do I . . . ? I mean, of course. I have a roof over my head, and . . . and a husband who loves me . . ."

"He left ye alone in the street."

Marceline blinked. Had she told them that? "Well yes, but..." She wanted to explain Baxter's behavior, but she had no clue where to begin.

"But?" Lucretia pushed.

Marceline swallowed, searching for an answer. "Well, I mean, my life's not perfect. Baxter's been through a lot, and he copes by—"

"I did nae ask for yer husband's psychological profile. Do *ye* like yer life?" Lucretia's black eyes glittered, piercing through Marceline, sharp as arrowheads.

She shrugged meekly. "I wouldn't mind a little more freedom..."

"Well, there ye go. That's why yer here."

It was a vague explanation, yet the words rumbled deep inside her stomach, resonating truth. To these people, these *strangers*, she wasn't just Baxter's wife. Here, between these four walls, maybe she could become a person unto herself. Even as the thought rose inside her she felt guilty for having it, but there it was, true as her own name.

"By any chance"—Marceline chose her words carefully—"does that mean you're hiring?"

CHAPTER 6

It was still raining when Marceline stepped out of the café's warm glow and back into the dark alley, but she was no longer afraid. She knew the raven, Falkirk, was watching from the shadows. Now, instead of fear, her veins pulsed with a new sensation: a fizzing warmth filling her like helium, lifting her from the inside. She was familiar with the adrenaline rush that rose within her whenever Baxter was in one of his moods, as well as the swell of love she felt when he wasn't, but this was nothing like either. Instead, it was like she'd been launched into a new and exciting world, a world she wanted to explore. That she *could* explore.

Despite Lucretia's hesitancy, she'd been invited back for an interview. She just had to prove she was worthy and then get Baxter on board. If she could do those two things, life would soon be different.

She'd have somewhere that belonged entirely to her.

Rain pelted her skin, soaking through the wretched dress once more. Sylvan had tried to convince her to take the coat, but she'd refused. She couldn't anticipate what Baxter's mood would be like when he returned, but one thing was certain: showing up wrapped in an unfamiliar coat—a man's coat—wouldn't help. It didn't matter, though. She felt impervious to the rain now.

She was still buzzing with excitement when a car pulled up in front of her. The window rolled down. "Marce?"

"Bax!" She stiffened at the sight of him. Somewhere in the back of her mind hid the awareness that she should be furious. But she wasn't—she couldn't be, not while she felt so relieved. He'd come back for her, in the end. She'd known he would.

Baxter's mouth pressed into a thin line, expression impossible to read, blurred by rain and darkness. "Get in the car."

She did, busying herself with the seat belt so as not to look at his face, her heart palpitating with fear of what she might find there. Just because he'd returned to her didn't mean she was in the clear. She focused on the time on the dashboard: 9:41. Surely, she'd spent more than twenty-five minutes in the café, hadn't she? The man in the sports car, the raven, the tea...All of it must have taken two hours at least. The only logical explanation was that the car's clock must have randomly stopped.

Marceline adjusted the air vent, desperate to recapture some warmth. If Baxter was still angry, the animosity could carry on into the night. She hated the thought of anything tainting the strange and improbable magic of her evening.

Besides, a part of her worried that if she looked into his eyes, he'd see it all. And he wouldn't like it.

"Marce." Baxter's voice was barely a whisper above the swipe of the windshield wipers as his hand wrapped around her wrist. "I hate the thought of losing you."

Relief rose within Marceline as she dared to look at him. His pale eyes shone with intensity, the scarlet glow of brake lights glistening within them as he stared at the street ahead. She swelled with tenderness. She could feel how sorry he was. Underneath it all, he was only jealous because he loved her so much.

She grabbed his hand. "I'm sorry I scared you." It wasn't Baxter's fault he overreacted sometimes. He'd experienced so much suffering from such a young age, how could he not be sensitive? It cost her nothing to apologize if it meant they could move on.

"I was driving in circles. I couldn't stop picturing you with that damn waiter. It was awful." His fingers trembled in her palm like he'd been the one stuck outside, rather than sheltered in the safety of his warm, dry car.

"Shh. I know, baby." She disentangled her hand to stroke his knee, but when her fingers brushed the fabric, she stopped, realizing it was wet. "Bax, is that mud?"

Her husband's posture stiffened, his jaw clenching as she took in his wet hair, the mud caked into the outfit he'd so carefully donned before dinner. A faint alcoholic tinge lingered in the air between them. Had he gone drinking? While she was—as far as he knew—out on the street?

How had he even had the time?

"Honey?"

"Don't." The sudden harshness of his voice staunched any further questions, and Marceline swallowed the familiar frustration of being kept in ignorance. He shut down when he was hurting. She knew that, in theory. And yet she couldn't help but wonder if other women's husbands acted similarly evasive. Was it a guy thing? Something she'd just have to cope with forever? Her hand twitched as Baxter's fingers interlocked with hers. Forever was a long time.

Baxter stared at the road, turmoil radiating off him so feverishly that Marceline felt it as if it were her own. She hadn't known him as a kid, but these moments were like a trapdoor to the lonely, unloved child still living within him.

And so, she forgave him, the way she had always forgiven him.

Hand in hand, they drove in silence, out of San Francisco and onto I-280, curving around industrial complexes and into the hilly suburbs and off the exit ramp until at long last they entered the maze of their apartment complex.

When they arrived, Baxter got out and circled the car to open her door. Marceline gripped her ruined shoes in one hand, pressing her weight against him as he helped her up the stairs, his body a hard wall of muscle against hers. A few hours ago, she'd been pressed against another man, the sensation altogether different. She brushed off the guilty thought, afraid Baxter might somehow read her mind. Whatever she'd felt then was only the relief of being saved from a scary situation.

Now, that desperation had evaporated. Their warm bed awaited, and Baxter would use his body to show her how sorry he was.

And soon, she'd find a way to get back to that café, to discover its secrets, to become a part of it.

Later that night, when Baxter made love to Marceline, it felt like an act of revenge.

Afterward, when they lay entangled beneath the bedroom ceiling's lone, bare light bulb, catching their breath, Marceline's mind drifted back to the café. She smiled. It had been like inhaling pure oxygen after years of breathing pollution.

"That good, babe?" Baxter purred in her ear. He rolled off her and onto the mattress, slick with sweat. The desperation he'd shown in the car had been unloaded, and he was starting to act like himself again.

"Amazing," she said, to please him. If she wanted to take advantage of his good mood, she had to do it now. But it had to sound natural. Spontaneous.

"Do you think it worked?" He nibbled at her ear.

It took a moment for her to connect the dots. After all the drama of the night, the Conception Question had faded to the back of her mind.

Time to proceed with caution.

"I hope so," she lied. She turned to face him, twisting the sheets around her body to shield her from the chill seeping through the windowpanes. "Bax, I've been thinking. About when the baby comes."

Her husband's lips parted into a smile—a real one that made her heart stutter with guilt, love, or both. He reached out, tracing the contour of her shoulder, her breast. Even in the frigid light of the fluorescent bulb, he was beautiful, all angular lines and twisting muscle.

"I was thinking," she stalled. How to start? She thought back to her list, which had caused her so much trouble tonight, and so much joy, too.

"What, babe?"

"Well, we'll need more money, when it comes." She was careful to use *when* rather than *if*. "If I got a job, maybe just a part-time one, it would make our life easier. I'd like to contribute, and you already work so hard..."

His hand dropped to the mattress. The smile faded. "Haven't we talked about this before?"

Marceline bit her lip. "Sure, a while ago, before we were trying...I mean, it's different now." For the first time since she'd left the café, all her fears and anxiety came flying back like magnets to metal. They rumbled, twisting her gut from within.

"You'd have to take time off for maternity leave anyway. It doesn't make any sense."

"Sure, but if I already had a few months of income saved, we could use it on—on a crib, or a stroller, or baby clothes..."

Baxter's frown deepened. He rolled away from her. "I don't think so."

"Baxter. I—" She caught herself. Telling Baxter she was lonely wouldn't help. He believed he should be enough for Marceline, and it bothered her that she couldn't believe it too, no matter how hard she tried.

"Make me a father, and we'll talk about it. When the kid starts school, maybe."

Marceline's heart sank. The enchantment of the café, the unexpected feeling of belonging, the passion of the intercourse she and Baxter had shared moments before—it all seemed to fade into mere memory.

She shifted, widening the span of mattress between them, eyes drifting over the mostly empty white wall. Baxter had said he'd let her paint and decorate, but it never seemed to be in the budget. Now it was five years later, and she'd gotten used to the blankness of the room. Aside from the cherished light-up globe on her nightstand, the only decoration was their wedding picture.

She'd spent so much time staring at that photograph that it had faded into the background. Now she focused on it. There she was, eighteen years old in her white dress, beaming up at Baxter, so strong and handsome and serious. Picture-perfect. What wasn't contained in the frame was the sadness she'd felt that her father couldn't be at the wedding, that her grandmother had died less than a year before, dumping her life upside down. She'd been Marceline's legal guardian for most of her life, since her father had been a long-distance trucker who spent most of his time driving 18-wheelers back and forth across the nation.

Marceline bit her lip, dwelling on the resentment she'd harbored toward her father for not approving of Baxter—resentment she should have harbored toward Baxter for making her choose between them. Less than a year later, her father had died of a heart attack, taking any hope of reconciliation with him. She'd wanted someone to blame, but Baxter was her only remaining family. Even her friends had dropped out of her life one by one, scared off by his protective streak. Baxter was all she had.

Her cozy life in her grandmother's trailer with its snickerdoodle scent, their spontaneous outings and game nights and silly songs—all of that was over. Now, she couldn't imagine life without Baxter.

Would she have found her way in the world if she hadn't met him? Bumbled forward, lonesome and ungraceful and lost, eventually finding someone just as uncouth to stumble into love with? Or perhaps she'd have created her own adventures, alone. Stuffed her whole life in a suitcase and ventured off into the world, unencumbered by anyone else's opinions about how her life should be.

Either way, her father still would've died.

Perhaps choices were a mere illusion, a comforting lie that made people *feel* autonomous. If that were the case, what did it matter that she had no opportunity to make them? Guilt burned in her chest. She felt vile and unfaithful in her late-blooming resentment toward Baxter.

And yet, here he was telling her no. Again. It didn't matter how much she longed to become part of the café, as she'd already felt it becoming a part of her in those few short hours—or minutes—depending on how one saw it. Baxter's answer was the final answer.

Wasn't it?

Leave him, she remembered her father saying, during those tense, secret phone calls before his heart attack. *I know you're in love, but he cut you off from your family. He won't even let you drive. This isn't the life I wanted for you.* He'd continue to give reasons until Marceline couldn't take it anymore and hung up. It had happened again and again, until the calls had stopped.

She'd thought he was avoiding her—but no, it turned out he was dead. She'd found out four months later from a distant cousin who'd tracked down her number to tell her, before promptly disappearing again. Marceline was so devastated she'd confessed it all to Baxter, and given the circumstances, he'd forgiven her for lying about staying in touch with her father.

No, Marceline thought, *I'm not going to leave him.* Even with her father gone, she continued to repeat it like a mantra. *I'm not going to leave him. I'm not going to leave him.*

Baxter had begun snoring beside her, his whole body rumbling like a beast at rest. Marceline pulled open the nightstand drawer and unwrapped a pair of earplugs, stuffing them in her ears. That Baxter should be able to sleep while her mind spun in dizzying circles felt like the greatest injustice of all.

No, she thought, *I'm not going to leave. But just this once, I am going to make my own choice.*

* * *

The following morning, Baxter stamped Marceline with a kiss and left for the call center. As soon as the door creaked closed behind him, Marceline rushed to the window, heart jackhammering as she waited for him to drive away. Her list of chores was a mile long, but if time at the café played the same trick as it had before, she should be able to return early enough to do it all without Baxter suspecting a thing.

As soon as Baxter's car left the parking lot, Marceline ran to the kitchen table. Her husband's laptop sat open between their dirty breakfast dishes. Hurriedly, she reconstructed the password she'd managed to glean after various instances of inconspicuous cleaning behind him, neck craned. They'd argued repeatedly over her unsupervised internet use, and each time, Marceline had reminded him that she was a grown woman, not a child. It was pointless. Baxter was flexible as a block of concrete.

The laptop lit up and Marceline exhaled. Feeling like a petty criminal, she opened a search engine and typed: *how to act in a job interview*. It was hard to focus with one eye on the door, but she did her best, reading through article after article and jotting key words like *transferable skills* and *fast learner* on a Post-it, even as her confidence dimmed.

Setting the Post-it aside, she racked her brain for ways to make herself sound employable. She'd only ever had one job—helping the lunch ladies in her high school cafeteria—and the only requirements had been agreeing to wear a hairnet and withstanding harassment from her peers.

When at last she'd compiled a meager list, Marceline looked up a map of San Francisco, scouring the intimidating sprawl of streets until she located Folsom and Eighth. Her triumph was short-lived—according to the results, there weren't many buses heading in that direction from San Bruno. The BART train ran regularly, by contrast, but she'd have to walk twenty minutes to the station. Could she manage it with her ankle still weak from the night before? The train also required a special pass that had to be loaded with money.

Money she didn't have.

She chewed her lip, mulling over her predicament. The bus was cheaper, yes, but not free. She could scrounge up the fare today, but what if they hired her? How would she return? Would it be okay to ask for an advance? She exhaled, long and deep. At least she had a roof over her head. And a husband who loved her, even if he had a funny way of showing it.

She rummaged through her purse, and—guiltily—through the pockets of each of Baxter's jackets, collecting a grand total of six dollars and nine cents. It was enough. She checked the directions again. The bus journey would take an hour and a half, and she had less than ten minutes to get ready.

Stumbling to avoid putting weight on her still-weak ankle, Marceline pulled off her ratty nightdress and wrestled on some clean jeans and a powder-blue cardigan with embroidered flowers that she loved, although Baxter thought it made her look like a retiree. She had to make a better second impression. After all, if she didn't do well, she'd be back where she started, a prisoner in her own life.

No, she thought. This is no time for self-sabotage.

She shook the grim thought out of her mind before it could take root and slid covertly out of the apartment, feeling as if unseen eyes were watching her as she limped down the hallway and pressed the elevator button. The doors opened. Panic spasmed through her at the sight of a tall blond man waiting inside. But he was much older than Baxter and had a handlebar mustache. She gave the man an awkward smile, reeling with relief. In all the years he'd worked at the call center, Baxter had never returned home unexpectedly. He sometimes called in the middle of the day, though. Would he buy it if she said she'd taken a nap?

She ambled across the parking lot and the street to the bus stop, and despite the dull pain in her ankle, arrived as the bus was pulling up. She was painfully aware of her apartment window glaring down at her like an inanimate spy. Nervously, Marceline smiled at the driver and copied the passenger in front of her, slipping coins into the slot. She lamented their loss as they jangled away.

She scanned the bus for an empty seat, fending off school bus memories of bad smells, gossip, and wads of gum tossed at her head. Today would be different, she decided. Today would be an adventure. A risky, forbidden adventure, but if she played her cards right, she'd be rewarded with more adventures.

It was a chance she wasn't willing to lose.

CHAPTER 7

Long Ago

The rough exterior wall of the hut scraped Bronagh's back through her clothes as she brought her knees to her chin. A child of five has no concept of time, but all the same, it felt to Bronagh like she'd been waiting alone outside the hut for hours by the time the midwife hobbled out, wiping her bloody hands on her tunic.

"What are we to do with ye?" she sighed, her weathered face peering down at Bronagh, who merely continued to stare at the ground, picking apart blades of grass. The old woman prodded: "Do ye have any other family?"

Bronagh shook her head. She was aware other children had fathers, but the word *father* felt ungainly, foreign on her tongue. She'd heard of grandparents too, but of them she knew even less. Her entire family had consisted of one loving person. It had been more than enough.

The midwife gave Bronagh a rough pat on the head. "Fear not. We'll find some solution or another."

Soon after, four gray-faced druids came for the body. Bronagh's throat tightened as she watched them, unable to believe that the limp, linen-wrapped shape they carried was her mother. She stared after them, hardly noticing when the midwife's apprentice followed them out of the hut, cradling a squirming bundle.

"She's so bonny, mistress!" the younger girl said to the midwife, beaming down at the bairn.

"Aye," the midwife agreed, turning away from Bronagh to peer at the babe. "That she is. A miracle. I must take her to the chief at once. He must know what we've witnessed." She pulled the fragments of eggshell from her tunic, her gaze pensive, before tucking them away again. Then she frowned, eyes swiveling to Bronagh once more. "Take the wee lass to the Hut of the Unclaimed."

"Aye, mistress." The apprentice beckoned to Bronagh, who shook her head. The apprentice spent a few minutes trying to coax the girl before growing frustrated and heaving her over her shoulder with a grunt.

Bronagh did not struggle. She simply hung there, letting herself be carried away from the only home she'd ever known.

The apprentice deposited Bronagh at the hut where the other orphans resided. The stooped crone whose lot it was to wrangle the children sighed at Bronagh's arrival.

"I suppose we ought to find ye a corner to sleep in," she muttered. "As if it were nae crowded enough."

That evening, the chief's ceremonial horn howled throughout the village. The irascible orphan-mistress corralled the ragged children toward the raised platform in the village center to hear the news. Bronagh followed, her little legs dragging through the haze of shock and fresh grief. If she'd known of the chief before, it had made no impression upon her young mind. Her small world had contained only her mother.

And yet, she found herself here, gathered among a rough crowd of strangers, all shoving and muttering and straining to hear the fur-draped man on the wooden platform. She longed for her mother's arms, still unable to believe she could be gone forever.

"This is a glorious day," the chief announced, his voice rising above the crowd. Bronagh could scarcely see the top of his elaborate headdress through the mass of villagers, yet the words seared the edges of her heart.

Her stomach churned, floored by the possibility that adults could tell such blatant lies. Today was *not* a glorious day. Today was the day her mother had died.

Yet, the chief continued: "Today, for the first time in almost two hundred years, the Great Winged One—Goddess of Battle and Bloodshed—has borne a daughter through a mortal surrogate."

A collective gasp swelled from the crowd, followed by a tide of murmurs. Bronagh stared at her feet. She did not know what a surrogate was, and she didn't understand why she was here. Nothing made sense. It felt to her as though one of the giants from her mother's stories had stomped all over her life and torched the remains, leaving only smoldering ash.

The chief went on to announce that his council of druids would anoint the bairn with sap from the sacred oak, and a village-wide feast would be held on this day every year henceforth. On and on he went, each word eliciting a flurry of excitement from the crowd. Bronagh stopped listening. There was no point trying to understand the inexplicable. Instead, she let the ashes of loss settle over her, still as stone.

A loss that only grew as the years wore on.

Gone were the lullabies, the kisses and clapping games. Gone was the warm bed of furs where she and her mother had slept side by side. Between fighting for a corner of scratchy blanket with which to cover herself at night and scrounging for potato scraps to gnaw upon during the day, her world became a bleak haze of loss.

Later, she learned that the cozy hut she'd lived in with her mother—with its bouquets of dried heather hanging above the hearth—had gone to her newborn sister, where she resided with a rotating staff of wet nurses. Sometimes in the village, she caught glimpses of the child. Quill, she'd apparently been named, after a glossy feather found on the window ledge when she was born. A posse of servants followed her wherever she went.

"Is it true she's yer sister?" other orphans would ask. "Why is she dressed in such fine furs when ye've only got rags like the rest of us?"

Bronagh had no answer. As much as she'd tried to forget it, she'd seen Quill come out of her mother with her own eyes. And yet there were those in the village who claimed that because Bronagh's mother had merely been a birthing vessel for the goddess, the two were not related at all.

They certainly didn't *feel* related.

Bronagh was ten the first time Quill approached her. Already she was working as a laundress, for the orphan-mistress had made it clear it was time to earn her keep if she wished to continue sleeping in the Hut of the Unclaimed.

Bronagh was lugging a basket of soiled linens almost as heavy as herself to the loch's edge, when the five-year-old popped out from behind a tree, startling her.

"Hello," Quill said, gazing at Bronagh with wide eyes. Shifting from foot to foot, she fidgeted with the hem of her elaborately embroidered shift—a more beautiful garment than anything Bronagh had ever worn, or even washed for someone else. "Eilidh says ye're my sister. Is it true?"

Bronagh took a wary step back. "Who's Eilidh?"

"My nursemaid." Quill pulled a cloth-wrapped packet from within her skirts. "Do ye like butter cake? I've brought ye one."

Bronagh hesitated, eyeing the treat. She had half a mind to refuse it out of pride, but her stomach grumbled in protest at the mere thought. She snatched it, unwrapping the square and cramming the cake in her mouth. The buttery crumbs left a decadent taste on her tongue. Had she ever eaten something so rich?

"I can bring ye more if ye like. Ye really are my sister, aren't ye?"

Bronagh licked her lips, already missing the sweet taste of the cake. Like everything, it had been too good to last. "Nae. I'm naebody."

At this, Quill frowned. "But Eilidh said—"

"Yer Eilidh's a liar," Bronagh snapped. When Quill's little pink mouth drooped into a pout, she felt a pang of remorse.

"She is nae," the child argued. "She said we came from the same womb, and 'tis nae yer fault yer life is wretched and mine is charmed, because nae everyone can be divine. Do ye know what a womb is?"

Bronagh blinked, trying to digest all this at once. The nursemaid was only confirming what Bronagh already knew, and yet to have it relayed to her by a child—and a spoiled one at that—made her stomach twist from more than hunger pangs.

"Do ye?" Quill repeated, scrambling closer. "I think 'tis like a sleeping pallet, but for bairns."

"Aye, that's it." Bronagh had no desire to explain what little she understood of female anatomy to a child—much less one who'd called her "wretched."

"Why are ye carrying that basket?" Quill asked.

"'Tis laundry."

"Can I help?"

Bronagh stared at the girl. "Why would ye want to?"

"For fun." Quill beamed. "Or we could play a game! I have all manner of dolls. I've got a big one with red hair, and another—"

"Quill!" A frantic nursemaid emerged from the trees and barreled toward them, panting. "There ye are! In the Goddess's name, I've been looking everywhere." The heavy-bosomed woman scrambled toward them, red-faced, skirt held aloft so she wouldn't trip. She stopped short when she saw Bronagh.

"Eilidh!" Quill shouted. "Bronagh *is* my sister, isn't she? Tell her 'tis true."

The nursemaid shot Bronagh a suspicious glance, lunging to grab Quill by the wrist. "Come on now, ye cannae be playing around with just anyone. 'Tis nae proper. Look at the state of yer boots!"

"Eilidh, tell her!"

"Hush, child," the nursemaid scolded, tugging the girl away. "The druids will gut me like a stag and sacrifice me to the Winged One if they hear I've let ye run around in the dirt with rabble and castoffs."

With that, she ushered the girl down the path toward the village.

As Bronagh stared after them, the gray haze of ash that had dusted over her life seemed to thicken. The child had meant well, and yet the fierce wave of grief washing over Bronagh was overwhelming. She clutched her basket, reeling with pain, for suddenly it felt as though she were losing her mother all over again.

Her stomach gave an ominous gurgle, and a moment later she was retching chunks of butter cake and bile into the grass. Bronagh whimpered, wiping her mouth on the back of her hand. She should have known it would be too rich for her malnourished body. And yet, for Quill, it had been nothing. A mere snack, likely baked just for her.

Over the next few months, Quill tried to approach Bronagh again and again. Each time she appeared from nowhere, bearing random gifts: a whittled bird a villager had given her, a necklace of carved beads, a loaf of bread. But each interaction left Bronagh more shattered than the last, forcing her deeper and deeper into the cave of her own sorrow. Eager as she was, Quill represented everything Bronagh would never have, everything she'd lost. For before Quill, Bronagh had been a much beloved child, coddled and kissed, bathed and fed with care. Quill's arrival had taken it all away.

Quill's arrival had killed her mother.

CHAPTER 8

Marceline settled into the hard plastic bus seat and began studying the Post-it note. Or trying to—it was impossible to focus until they finally rounded a corner, leaving the apartment complex well out of sight. Finally, once they'd merged onto the interstate, her heartbeat calmed. Outside, shopping malls turned into rolling hills covered in rows of shabby houses like crooked teeth, the buildings gradually becoming bigger and more commercial, the sidewalks wider, cluttered with tents and shopping carts overflowing with garbage bags.

When the scrolling marquee above the aisle announced her stop, Marceline disembarked. The wind whipped her hair as she stepped onto the sidewalk, hurrying to the spot where Baxter had left her. The area looked less sinister by day, though still not picturesque.

Shivering, she sped up. She had to focus. Now, where was the café? She walked a few blocks, but nothing stood out, so she tried the other direction. When at last she found the sketchy alley, the overflowing dumpster made her stomach turn. This was it. The place she'd run to, after the man in the sports car—no, no! She breathed through the remnants of panic, gripping her purse against her abdomen.

There it all was: the intricate, carved door with its fearsome raven-headed knocker, the stained-glass transom glowing like embers against the shadowed wall.

Her fingers tingled in anticipation as she climbed the stoop and grasped the knocker. Exhaling, she thumped it against the tarnished brass plate.

The moment the sound faded away, an onslaught of second thoughts broke loose in Marceline's mind. Was this place truly worth risking her husband's wrath? Was it too late to reconsider? The wind whistled, nipping through her thin cardigan. More than likely, it was all too good to be true. The hallucination of a wet, shocked, shivering mind.

"Don't you chicken out," Marceline muttered. She reached for the knocker once more but no sooner had her fingers grazed it than the door flew open. She leapt back in surprise, heel landing halfway off the top step, but a clawed hand darted out from the doorway and caught her sleeve, tugging her forward.

"Ye're lucky I'm quick," Lucretia quipped. "I wouldnae have followed ye down the steps."

"Oh, right." Marceline fumbled, recovering her balance. "I mean—thanks."

In a blink, Lucretia receded inside, tucking her talons under crossed arms. She looked every bit as impressive as before, with her statuesque stance and intense, furrowed gaze. Except for an outrageously colorful tunic and clashing paisley scarf, she had all the allure of a vampire. A tall, pale creature, hugging the shadows.

"Well, get yerself inside. How's the ankle?"

Marceline was about to respond, when it occurred to her that despite hobbling around all morning, her pain had now vanished. She paused, marveling. "Excellent, actually."

“Aye, good,” Lucretia said, distracted, shutting the door and bustling away toward the counter. “We’re beginning a ritual. I’ll have to ask ye to please not make a peep.”

“What kind of rit—?” She abruptly stopped as Lucretia held a talon to her lips. Marceline winced. She’d been in the café less than a minute and already she’d managed to blunder. Baxter always said she was a chatterbox.

She mimed zipping her mouth closed and followed Lucretia, who went to fill a hammered copper teapot at the sink. Was she supposed to help? Or should she give Lucretia some space? She didn’t want to appear desperate. Although, Marceline reasoned, she actually *was* desperate. Why else would she have defied Baxter’s wishes and come from so far?

Realizing she was in the way, Marceline stepped back and absorbed the details of the café a second time, eager to reaffirm to herself that no, she hadn’t invented it all.

On the wall above the mantel, one of the African masks raised an eyebrow at her. Someone had brought out a vintage record player, and the potted plant in the corner—Maia, Sylvan had called her—was bobbing her many carnivorous heads to the sounds of Elvis Presley.

Lucretia wove through the tables toward the fireplace, where she hung her kettle above the dancing flames. Overhead, the great skeleton swung from the rafters, though with significantly fewer birds perched on it today. The old woman, Kilda, still sat near the fire, Falkirk the raven perched upon the shoulder of her oatmeal-colored sweater. Two more customers occupied their own separate tables: a freckled man reading a leather-bound book, and a tan child humming to the music and scribbling on a sheet of paper, colored pencils scattered around her. When something nudged her shin, Marceline looked down to see a white chicken pecking at her shoelaces.

She turned her attention back to Kilda, and to the sprawling parchment that covered most of the old woman's table. Sylvan had called her a cartographer, so she supposed the parchment must be a map, though it didn't look anything like the stacks of folded and laminated guides her father had kept in his 18-wheeler, which had so fascinated Marceline as a child. Instead, it looked like an antique newspaper, only scrawled with inky symbols, crisscrossed lines, and strange markings, rather than neat rows of set type.

When would the interview begin? Marceline wondered. The longer she waited, the more nervous she felt. She repeated the speech she'd prepared in her mind: *I am eager to learn, and I follow directions well, without ever complaining. I'm not afraid to get my hands dirty.* (That line had been inspired by the toilet bowl she'd have to clean later, at home.) *I am punctual and trustworthy, and—*

When Lucretia brought her talon gracefully to her side, dimming all the lights and music in the café with the gesture, Marceline suppressed a gasp. *Incredible,* she thought. If the other customers noticed this change in ambiance, it didn't faze them, but Marceline fell into silent reverence at the air of mystery blanketing the room. Magic—happening before her very eyes.

A shriek pierced the newfound silence, and Marceline tensed. But it was only the copper kettle. The high-pitched whistle faded as Lucretia removed the pot from the fireplace and brought it to the cartographer's table. The latter had pulled her parchment to the side to make room for a wrought-iron perch on a stand, a mug, and a frilly tartan potholder.

"Falkirk?" Lucretia called, pouring the steaming water into the mug until it was almost overflowing. Though the music had ceased, the coloring child continued to hum the tune of "Blue Suede Shoes," her thin warble punctuating the hush as the raven alighted onto its perch.

A low voice rumbled beside Marceline as something soft brushed against her side, sending a rush of warmth to her cheeks. "Did it commence?"

She fumbled for an answer, but Lucretia looked sharply toward her, aborting Marceline's unchosen words so all she could supply was a timid shrug. She'd wondered whether Sylvan would be here again, only because he'd been so welcoming. It was nice to have an ally.

Lucretia set the kettle down on the potholder and sat across from Kilda, who waited, hands clasped in her lap. The two women exchanged a nod. Then Lucretia looked to Falkirk, and they too exchanged a nod. Finally, the raven swiveled its glossy black head in Kilda's direction, and they exchanged yet another nod. Everyone was ready. But for what? Marceline watched, enraptured.

The raven leaned forward from its perch, tilting toward the steaming mug as if about to drink. Then all at once, it plunged its head into the hot water with a dramatic splash.

Marceline gasped and spun toward Sylvan, who'd remained at her side, arms crossed. Apparently amused, he smirked down at her, a tiny dimple appearing in his cheek. His dark eyes shifted to where Marceline's fingers dug into his bicep. Her cheeks burned hotter than ever as she released him. But why was no one else shocked? How was the poor bird breathing? Wouldn't the scalding water kill it? For what felt like a dozen slow minutes, Lucretia and Kilda stared solemnly at the creature with its head submerged in the steaming mug. Then, Falkirk's dripping head reappeared. The bird gave a little shake and returned to his perch, unperturbed.

Puzzled, Marceline snuck another peek at Sylvan, who patted her shoulder as if to say, *Don't worry, this is all completely normal.*

The old cartographer pulled a handkerchief from her pocket and dabbed at the damp, ruffled raven. But her attention remained fixed on Lucretia, who now raised the mug to her lips. She gulped its entire contents down without pausing. When she set the empty mug back on the table, it clattered against the silence.

Lucretia closed her eyes, the stern lines of her face softening into serenity. Every part of her radiated stillness, save for the light twitching of her eyelids. Indeed, if not for the straightness of her posture, she might have seemed asleep.

Then her eyes flew open. A crackle of blue electricity flashed over her pale skin in a map of lightning-filled veins, making her swirling blue tattoos writhe like convulsing snakes.

"Bottles on shelves," she gasped, eyes so wide her dark irises were bordered in white.

"The same ones?" the cartographer asked. It was the first time Marceline had heard the old woman speak. Her voice was gravelly, the accent guttural and rolling—and not entirely unlike Lucretia's, though not quite the same, either.

"Aye."

"And outside?"

"Snowdrifts."

"City or countryside?" Kilda seized a marbled fountain pen and began jotting notes in the margins of her map.

"Lake," Lucretia frowned. "Nae, a village. *Beside* a lake. Frozen over."

"Any signs?"

"Aye." She squeezed her eyes shut again, talons pressed to her temples. "Cyrillic."

"Russian? Ukrainian?"

"I know nae." The lightning blazing over Lucretia's tattooed arms had begun to flicker and dim.

"Go back. Quickly, before ye lose it."

Scowling with renewed concentration, Lucretia complied, eyes still shut. The lines vanished from her face once more, replaced by that electric flash, duller this time. Marceline watched, fascinated, wishing she could see what Lucretia saw.

"Pen!" the birdwoman demanded, eyes suddenly flickering open.

Kilda tossed her the fountain pen and Lucretia wrote something on the edge of the map in halting, careful script. The older woman craned her neck to look.

"Aye, Russian. It says, 'no fishing without a license.' And was there a portal?"

Lucretia's lips tightened as she thought. "Aye... a boat. With a hole cut into the bottom."

"Fascinating." Kilda took the pen back and scribbled the information down on her map. "Anything else?"

"Nae." Lucretia slumped in her chair. "Nae, 'tis gone." The glowing veins had subsided into her skin, leaving her looking tired and haggard.

"'Tis nae matter. We'll try again soon, dinnae ye fret." Kilda smiled, a thin silver ring flashing on her gnarled finger as she patted the feathered woman on the shoulder. Marceline blinked. She thought she'd seen Kilda's wrinkled skin smooth over for a moment, her eyes burning bright with youth. She wondered what other strange illusions she'd witness before the day was done.

"Of all places, ye had to choose the largest country on the planet." Lucretia's weary tone was directed at Falkirk, who squawked indignantly. "I know, 'tis nae your fault." She reached out, caressing the bird with what looked like her last ounce of energy. Then, with a dejected wave of her taloned hand, music and light flooded the room, usurping any last inkling of the occult in favor of the cheerful pedestrian hum of the café, the husky crackle of the Elvis record spinning on its axis.

The ritual appeared to be over, yet Kilda still scribbled away on her map, stopping occasionally to peer at specific parts through a magnifying glass. After a while, she sighed and tucked the tool into the white nest of her hair, behind her ear.

"Let's get some rest," the old woman whispered to Lucretia. The gentleness of her voice constricted Marceline's heart with a sudden longing for her own dead grandmother.

Lucretia threw Kilda a tight, tired smile. "Aye. Perhaps that would be best." She stood, Falkirk flying to her shoulder, and wandered back toward the counter. When her eyes swept over Marceline, she paused, as if remembering her presence. "Show her around, Sylvan, will *ye*?"

"Certainly, Lu."

They watched her slide behind the counter and disappear through the gauzy curtain Marceline assumed led to her private office. Kilda rolled up her map and hobbled after her.

As soon as Lucretia had disappeared, Marceline turned to Sylvan. A million questions danced on the tip of her tongue, but if life with Baxter had taught her anything, it was that people didn't like being bombarded with questions. But Sylvan didn't seem overly concerned. "You should observe your expression." His mouth twisted into a bemused grin. "You appear as if you could faint."

Flustered, Marceline looked away. Was he making fun of her? It was hard to tell, with the strange way he spoke. Cheeks burning, she shut her mouth—which she hadn't realized had been hanging open. If she wanted the job, she was going to have to impress him, and quick. She couldn't bear the thought of being turned away.

"Hey, it is usual to feel overwhelmed by this all," he said. "I certainly was. It is not every day one deviates to a magical establishment. No?"

"I guess not," she conceded. But how had *he* ended up here? And how long ago? Also, what *was* that ritual they'd just witnessed? The questions piled up, but her lips remained locked.

"Do you need to perch?" Sylvan gestured to a chair, and she deduced he was offering her a seat. His kind tone reassured her, if only by a sliver. Maybe he hadn't been mocking her after all.

She shook her head. "I'm okay."

"Indeed?" Sylvan cocked his head like a puppy. "Your face appears to have many questions."

Marceline stared at him, trying to think of something that would make her sound intelligent or perceptive. All that came out was: "What just happened?"

Sylvan headed toward the counter, ushering her to follow. "Where even to commence? You witness many bizarre occurrences here. After a while, it all feels pedestrian." He shooed away a stork as it tried to casually saunter its way behind the counter.

Now the floodgates were open, the questions spilled out in a torrent.

"But—do they do that all the time? And why? Have you ever asked? What happens if they don't do it? And the raven—Falkirk—is he okay? Was Lucretia possessed? What does she see?"

"Whoa, deaccelerate!" Sylvan chortled, taking a brown apron off a hook and handing it to her, then grabbing a much larger one for himself. "One thing at a time!"

"Sorry," Marceline mumbled. He'd given her an opportunity to ask *one* question, and she'd acted like a total freak. Shame burned her cheeks. "I know I'm kind of a lot."

"What? No!" Sylvan's forehead creased, perplexed. "I do not intend to criticize. Stop apologizing for your existence."

"I'm sor—" She caught herself, biting her lip. "I apologize—"

The dimple reappeared as he grinned. "We can work on that. So, let me attempt to explain..." He paused, thinking. "I do not know the ritual's precise purpose, but it is frequent. Once a month, maybe."

"Why?"

"They seek portals. Not the ones that arrive you here, but to somewhere else. Somewhere threatening, if Lu's mood indicates correctly."

"Portals?" She had the sudden feeling she'd been dropped into a science fiction movie.

"You know, enchanted doors." He shrugged, gesturing toward the café's entrance. The stork tried to sneak its way past his leg, and Sylvan waved it away again. "Out! Employees only!"

Enchantment. Yes, at this point there was no denying it. The truth had been flapping around her head since she'd first entered this place. She ruminated, letting it sink in as she watched the stork wander away, resigned.

Sylvan observed her, as if to assess how she was taking this news. "So, from where do you come?"

"Oh—" The swift change of subject jarred her. "Just around here. I grew up in my grandma's trailer out in East Bay. Hayward."

"The east of which bay?" Sylvan bent to pick up the chicken that was pecking at his sneakers.

"This one," Marceline insisted, equally flummoxed by the chicken as she was by his strange brand of humor. "San Francisco."

"Oh!" His eyes lit up. "I have always wished to visit there."

Marceline gave an awkward little titter, before shutting her mouth. What was she doing, joking around with strange men?

If Sylvan noticed her hesitation, he ignored it. "But see, that is the enchantment." He scratched the chicken beneath its wattle. "For you, the door arrives to San Francisco. For me, it arrives to Papeete. The portals open when you need them the most, and then they remain. Then they are like scabs that do not close unless you forget them."

Marceline peered at him, searching for clues that he was messing with her. "Papa who?"

Sylvan's face split into a grin once more. It was lopsided, she noticed, the dimple appearing only on his left cheek. "Papeete is the capital of Tahiti, in French Polynesia. Where I was born and reside, since always.

Well, technically an adjacent district, in Faa'a. You would enjoy it. We have a lychee tree behind where we reside. Do you appreciate lychee?"

"I…"

"Foolish query. Everyone appreciates lychee."

Marceline gawked at him as if he'd told her he lived in a time-share on one of Saturn's rings. "You're… you're serious?" She'd seen footage of Tahiti in travel documentaries, but she was quite sure it was thousands of miles away, and not behind the door she'd just entered. She gripped the counter, feeling like some giant spatula had descended from the sky to scramble her brain like an egg.

"Utterly."

"Like, five minutes ago you were on the other side of the globe, and now you're here?"

"Correct."

"But how many doors are there?"

"Oh, infinite," Sylvain said, gesturing emphatically with the arm holding the chicken. The latter gave a squawk, so Sylvan set it down. "The possibilities never culminate! A door can appear anywhere, at any time, so long as there is a person in need, and a bird to guide them." Apparently sensing her bewilderment, Sylvan paused. "You are sure you feel serene? Do you need some moments?" He squeezed her shoulder.

She flinched, and Sylvan withdrew, confusion flickering over his face. Marceline cursed herself. *Obviously* he'd meant it as a friendly gesture. She opened her mouth to explain, but somehow, articulating her Baxter-based anxiety felt like a monumental task—one she didn't have the courage to tackle.

"How did you learn English?" she asked instead, hoping they could ignore the moment.

"I did not." He grinned, and relief lapped at the edges of her nervousness. "Not beyond random elementary sayings."

"But you're speaking it now." Now that she understood he wasn't mocking her, she had to admit chatting with someone so easygoing was a breath of fresh air. The thought triggered a sobering jab of guilt.

"Lu enchants the café so everyone can comprehend each other," he explained.

She nodded. "Right. That's why you sound..." She trailed off, reddening as she struggled to complete the thought without coming off as rude.

"Like a thesaurus in a blender?" His eyes twinkled. "A quote from Lu. Ironically, since she is responsible. From my view, you all converse in highly amusing French."

"I'd love to learn other languages." Marceline allowed herself a shy smile. "When I was a kid, I had a dream of visiting every continent. I still have this globe my grandma gave me. It lights up like a lamp. I watch a lot of travel shows too. There's one that features a different destination every week, and the host, this guy with a big mustache, he interviews locals about their favorite spots and foods and—" Realizing she was rambling, she bit her lip. Her gaze drifted to the door, trying to imagine all the different types of scenery that might exist behind it. Egyptian pyramids, the canals of Venice, the ancient temple of Angkor Wat... "I don't suppose if I stepped through, I'd be able to..." She trailed off again when Sylvan shook his head, looking apologetic.

"The door only returns you to where you came from. It is pitiful, I know. If you observe someone else using the door, you will only see swirling darkness."

It took a second to realize he meant that it was a pity. She gave a wistful sigh of agreement. It would have been nice. "And what about Lucretia and Kilda? Are they able to pop over to Scotland whenever they like?"

"Kilda can, yes." He stuffed his hands in the pockets of his apron, shifting his weight as if he felt suddenly uncomfortable. "Lucretia does not depart." Marceline waited for him to say more, but he didn't.

Shame crept up her neck, heating her cheeks. "I said something weird, didn't I?"

Now it was Sylvan's turn to look bewildered. "Pardon? No, not at all."

"Can I ask one more question?"

"I fear your limit is achieved."

Marceline blinked. "Oh . . ."

"I joke." He grinned. "There is no limit on questions."

She released a stilted laugh, feeling slightly ridiculous. "Okay. So, Lucretia . . . is she, like, a witch?"

Sylvan smirked. "Lucretia is . . . Lucretia." His gaze flickered over Marceline's shoulder, but when she turned, there was only Falkirk, perched on the edge of a chair, fixing them with an intense gaze. "I adore her, but even I do not know all her secrets. Come, I will instruct to you the espresso machine."

"Um, Sylvan," she began, remembering the reason she was even there. Nothing in her covert research spree that morning had prepared her for magical rituals, and this all felt strangely informal. "Is this part of the interview?"

The dimple returned to his cheek as he smiled. "There is no interview. Lu was tugging your leg. The truth is, this job is not a *job*, precisely. You can work if you desire, or just repose . . ." he said, looking awkward as he brushed his glossy black hair out of his eyes. Marceline braced herself for bad news. "But there is no compensation."

"You mean it's not paid?" She frowned. "So, it's like volunteer work?"

"Effectively. Does this impede your desire?"

Marceline thought. It would have been nice to have an income. Besides, when Baxter eventually agreed to let her work here, he'd require proof she was earning enough to help with the kid. *Possible* kid, she thought, bracing herself against the uncomfortable twisting in her stomach. Hadn't that been one of her main arguments? Still, she couldn't deny she wanted—no, *ached*—to learn everything she could about this strange and wonderful place.

"No. It's not a dealbreaker." She hesitated, wondering if it would be unwise to say more.

"But . . . ?"

"Well, it's just, I can't get here without a bus pass, so I was hoping to buy one with my earnings."

"The door does not lead to your backyard or your closet?"

Marceline shook her head.

"Droppings." Sylvan made an awkward face. "Well, I will mention it to Lu. Do not worry, we will resolve the conundrum."

This time when Sylvan grinned, Marceline did too, hardly able to believe her luck. "Really?"

"Really. So, you are in acceptance?"

Joy bubbled through her body as she grinned, clapping her hands over her mouth to stifle a childlike squeal, too excited to feel embarrassed now.

Sylvan grinned back at her. "Great." He extended his hand. "Congratulations, Marceline Sapnis. You own the job."

"I own the job," she repeated, half in disbelief. His palm was soft, fingers warm as they enveloped hers in a handshake. A cloud of sweet euphoria expanded within her, soft edges pushing aside the guilt tied to her maiden name, the guilt of lying to her husband. There'd be plenty of time for guilt later. Now it was time to celebrate. She'd found a job.

No, not a job. More than that. A new life—one she couldn't wait to discover.

Tension crept back into Marceline's body as she climbed off the bus, crossed the street and then the parking lot, and let herself into her apartment building. What if today was the day Baxter had come home early? Her shoulders stiffened as she rode the elevator; they'd practically fused to her ears by the time she unlocked the apartment. It wasn't until the door popped open to reveal an empty living room that her breath unhitched. Still, she proceeded with caution, checking the bedroom and bathroom too. She was safe.

She trudged to the bedroom and flopped onto the bed, letting her mind travel back to the café and the bizarre ritual she'd witnessed. She was no closer to understanding what it all meant, but she felt privileged to have been allowed to watch it unfold. Remnants of wonder fluttered through her as she spun the globe on her nightstand with one lazy hand.

And yet, a certain sadness bloomed on the periphery of her wonder: Apart from her secret calls with her father, Marceline had always told Baxter everything. Her hopes and dreams before they'd married, the trivial occurrences in her day afterward. But this—this was huge. And she couldn't tell him.

She released a sigh so deep, it resonated to the four corners of the bare bedroom. *I* will *tell him*, she told herself. *And when he sees how happy I am, he'll come around.* She frowned resolutely at their wedding picture on the wall. *Yes, I'll tell him.*

Just not yet.

CHAPTER 9

Long Ago

Bronagh picked at a discarded bread crust as she stacked the stoneware plates, glancing about to make sure no one had seen. The Feast of the Goddess's Daughter was already over, the sky darkening across the long table piled with dirty dishes and empty goblets, yet Bronagh's stomach rumbled. Despite the skinned boar whose bones clung to the spit above the bonfire, there had been nothing left but a meager handful of boiled parsnips by the time she'd finished serving. Hunger gnawed at her insides as she lugged dishes to soak in a barrel. The surface rippled, reflecting the pale moon in its soiled loch water.

Already, the rest of the villagers had clustered around the raised platform from which the bard crooned a devotional chant to the Winged Goddess. Like every year, Quill had been ushered upon the stage to receive praise, in the place of honor beside the chief himself. Warm firelight licked the grave faces of the druids behind them, their beards trailing to their belted waists.

Bronagh glowered, watching Quill fidget in her seat—a piece of furniture carved with swirls almost as elaborate as those on the chief's throne. The child picked at the garland around her neck, squirming the way only an eight-year-old could. Lowering her eyes, Bronagh cleared the table, shivering beneath her thin shawl. It was bad enough the village had dedicated an entire feast to her sister every year on her birthday, but why should she be forced to attend? Did no one care that to Bronagh, this was a day of mourning?

Applause and murmured blessings arose as the bard took a deep bow, harp in hand. Bronagh wished she could sneak off to the Hut of the Unclaimed for some solitude before the other orphans returned, but the stern brows of the lesser druids guarding the festivities told her it would not be worth the effort. One of the gray-faced men caught Bronagh's eye and scowled, waving her toward the group gathered by the platform. She kicked at a rock, giving in to the anger she'd been harboring all day. It churned in her stomach, mingling with hollow hunger as she inched forward reluctantly to join the crowd.

The bard called the midwife to the stage. The village's previous midwife, the one who'd overseen Quill's birth, had long passed on to the Otherworld and been replaced by her apprentice, now a married woman of twenty-one. It was strange to think how back on that painful night the apprentice must have been no older than thirteen—Bronagh's age now.

"The Great Winged Goddess attended the birth," the midwife swore to the crowd, a fanatical gleam in her eye. "She was there in her raven's guise!" She unwrapped the fragmented eggshell pieces from their cloth with reverence, among murmurs of awe. The midwife rambled on, and when she was finished, the villagers broke into applause worthy of a miraculous revelation, as if this were not the same tale they'd already heard eight years in a row.

The festivities dragged on for hours—songs and poems, tales and blessings. The chief bragged that he'd lain a tribute of fresh milk at the squirming babe's feet. Bronagh picked at her threadbare hem, tracing circles in the dirt with the toe of her boot. Trying to focus on the firelight licking the villagers' upturned faces rather than her sister's wriggling form, or the way she picked apart the wildflowers of her garland, petal by petal. It was as if Quill had no idea these honors were for her—no, worse than that—as if she knew, but didn't care. As if it were normal to be held in such reverence. A nuisance, even.

To the dismay of the druid beside her, Quill had shredded her garland and was now attempting to escape from her chair. He quietly wrangled her back. Oblivious, the chief tapped his bejeweled fingers against the armrests of his throne as the bard struck up another tune.

Disgusted, Bronagh looked away, fighting the reaching claws of emptiness she was so used to by now. A fierce desire to hurl a rock at the stage gripped her, but she swallowed it down. The druids were quick to punish any transgression against the goddess with a ritual sacrifice at the foot of the sacred oak. Any attack on Quill would be considered an affront to the goddess herself.

Now that she thought of it, aside from the chief and his druids, Quill was the only person in the village with no reason to fear such a violent fate. Even those who worshipped other gods—harvest deities, gods of the hunt and of the loch, spirits of the river and woods—tread cautiously when the goddess was invoked. For the Queen of Ravens—Mistress of Death and Battle, She of Many Names—was known to be merciless.

At last, the moon rose high and round in the inky sky, and the festivities came to an end. The druids exited the platform in a procession, led by the chief, Quill trailing sleepily behind him. The villagers dispersed, some to their huts and others to bestow upon Quill last-minute offerings. Bronagh scoffed, watching her sister shift from foot to foot as villagers swarmed around the procession, bowing low before her.

Bronagh dragged herself to the Hut of the Unclaimed. Relief washed over her when she found that the other orphans had not yet returned. As she smoothed her straw pallet in the corner, her mind drifted to her mother. She no longer remembered her face, she realized with a searing pang. The fierce longing that lived coiled in her gut seized her from within. If Quill hadn't been born, her mother would still be here.

"Bronagh?"

She flinched at the timid voice. It was rare anyone addressed her by name. Yet there stood Quill in the doorway, still clad in her festival tunic, her black hair a mess of tangles around her wilting wildflower crown. It seemed she'd escaped her admirers.

"Can I sleep beside ye tonight?"

Bronagh's lips tightened. It had been almost two months since her sister had last tried to approach her. "Ye have yer own hut. A far nicer one."

"But 'tis lonely." The child pouted, casting her eyes to her boots. "And my nurse snores. Besides, 'tis my birthday."

"Nae." Bronagh fixed the eight-year-old with a hardened gaze. "Nae, this hut is for mortals. Go home, Quill."

The beginnings of a whine broke her sister's voice: "But—"

Bronagh erupted. "Who do ye think would be punished if the so-called divine child were found sleeping amongst us *castoffs*?" Still sharp, the nursemaid's brutal words three years hence prickled in her mind. "The chief would have my head on a platter. Now be gone!"

The child's bottom lip trembled. "But, Bronagh, ye never let—"

"I said be gone!" Resentment bubbled under her skin as she shooed the child away, then turned her back to spread her rough blanket over the straw. She did not turn again until both the soft thud of Quill's footsteps and her faint sniveling had receded into the night.

As the years passed, Bronagh did not soften. Things only grew worse as Quill became a teenager, and, adding insult to injury, blossomed into a beautiful young woman with hair as black as night, while Bronagh remained haggard and dour.

Still, even Bronagh could see Quill bore the whispers around her like a yoke, sighing at the careful courtesy of the village wives, the cautious avoidance of the menfolk. Often, Bronagh witnessed her disappearing into the forest alone, only to reappear hours later, brooding. Nobody dared question these sporadic retreats. Whether Quill liked it or not, the villagers respected her.

As for Bronagh, she was not *dis*respected, no. Worse, she was forgotten.

Things might have been different. Despite the question of parentage, the two girls were similar in many ways. Both were quiet, shrewd, and solemn—Quill, because no other child dared play with her, and Bronagh, because she wrapped resentment around herself like a winter cloak.

Both were lonely.

But no amount of coaxing or bribery could persuade Bronagh to love her sister. In the end, Quill's desperate attempts ceased. Bronagh was unreachable. In her eyes, Quill's birth had been an act of murder.

And goddesses or not—sisters or not—murderers must be punished.

CHAPTER 10

Before Marceline had hurried out of the café the day before, Sylvan had given her a quick introduction to the espresso machine, in all its shiny, chrome glory. Though Marceline wasn't much of a coffee drinker, she'd surprised herself by being able to spout random facts about coffee production, thanks to a documentary she'd once watched called *The Origin of Single Origin*. Sylvan had been visibly impressed, and Marceline would be lying if she denied the small swell of pride she'd felt at his reaction.

Later that evening, she'd been dreamily chopping cucumbers when Falkirk surprised her by showing up outside her kitchen window, a bus pass clamped in his beak. Marceline had been simultaneously delighted and alarmed by the raven's presence, since Baxter was due to arrive home from work at any minute. After a quick, one-sided conversation on Marceline's part, the bird departed, the payment of a bag of peanuts swinging from his beak. Relieved and a little giddy, she tucked the bus pass—her ticket to freedom—into her apron pocket.

She was still buzzing with the novelty of the visit when, five minutes later, Baxter came home. The sudden click of his key in the lock made her snap to attention. He'd barely stepped into the living room, and already the energy in the apartment had changed.

A cursory glance at his face confirmed her fears: Baxter had had a bad day.

She ran to grab his coat. "Hey, baby. How—" She course corrected, determining too late that it might be better not to ask. "How do you feel about tuna casserole? I'm warming it up now."

Baxter looked at her, and Marceline noticed he was breathing hard, almost as if he'd run up the stairs instead of taking the elevator. "Did you have a guest?" A storm was brewing in his gaze.

She flinched. "A guest?" The idea was so absurd she had to laugh, but it was a tense, stilted laugh. "Of course not." Who did she know who would come over? She had no friends, and for all her efforts at small talk, their neighbors kept to themselves.

He continued to study her, before his gaze skirted past her, darting around the room as if to verify it was indeed empty. "Okay," he said, dropping his keys in the bowl by the door. His hair was disheveled, like he'd run his hands through it and not bothered to smooth it down again. He took a single step into the room, before changing his mind and whipping back toward his keys, scooping them up again. "I'm going out," he announced, his voice deep and stony.

"But, Bax! The casserole…"

The door shut. He'd already left.

Marceline stared at the door, stunned. What in the world? After a moment of bewildered paralysis, she realized she was still holding his coat. With a sigh, she hung it up.

Only then did she spot the black feather on the floor.

Her breath hitched. "A guest." Baxter couldn't have meant Falkirk, could he? But no, it was absurd. Having a bird stop by for a visit was a little unusual—fantastical even—but it wasn't worth having a jealous rage over, was it? And anyway, it was a moot point. Falkirk had already gone by the time her husband arrived. Unless Baxter had seen the feather and found it somehow suspicious?

Marceline sighed. There was no telling what had set Baxter off, but thinking about it was making her anxious, so she resolved to look on the bright side: At least she'd have a few more hours alone to daydream about the café. That was something, wasn't it?

Lucretia let Marceline in with a distracted "Evening," then stalked back to the table she'd apparently been occupying.

"It's morning for me," Marceline replied, stifling a yawn. Sylvan was not yet present, and since no one jumped to offer her any instruction, she timidly followed Lucretia to the table.

"Aye, same difference." Lucretia sat down, unfolding a newspaper.

"Oh, thank you so much for the bus pass!" Marceline loitered awkwardly beside the table. She didn't want to assume she was invited to sit down.

"Hmm?" Lucretia squinted at the newspaper and frowned.

"The bus pass? The one Falkirk brought me?"

"Did he now?" Lucretia scowled at the paper like it had personally insulted her, then turned the page. "Well, I only hope he didnae steal it off some poor sod." She turned the page again. "Blast it!"

Marceline flinched at the exclamation. "What's wrong?"

"This bloody paper! Every time I look away, or even so much as blink, the content bloody changes! 'Tis driving me mad. I cannae get through a single article."

"Oh." Marceline blinked. "Um, where did you get it?"

"Kilda brought it earlier, before she left to deal with a leaky roof. Helps me keep up with the old homeland." Lucretia shook the paper, emitting a frustrated grunt.

Marceline leaned over to have a look. THE SCOTTISH TIMES was printed in heavy black lettering across the top. She started reading an article about a craft fair happening in Edinburgh: "This coming

Sunday local artists will gather in front of St. Giles's Cathedral to—" Deliberately, she blinked halfway through the sentence. "—what your colleague doesn't know won't hurt her. Simply dispose of the offending sandwich—" Amused, Marceline blinked again. "—although, if Mr. MacLean wants to entice any voters, he must take a bolder stand on the policies that—"

"Why's it doing that?" Marceline asked.

Lucretia shrugged. "Cursed, I assume. By whom or what, I've nae idea, but 'tis doing my bloody head in!" She shoved the newspaper across the table. Immediately, a blob of bird poop landed on it. "Ugh." Lucretia looked up to the rafters, where a snowy owl perched, looking thoroughly unrepentant.

Marceline stifled a giggle. "You must spend a lot of time cleaning up after the birds."

"Nae. Only *my* birds can enter, and they all know to do their business outside. They're supposed to, anyway." She glowered at the owl.

Marceline watched the bird fly off toward the fireplace. "Tell me, what's Scotland like? I'd love to go there one day." She pictured its location on her globe lamp, recalling a travel documentary she'd watched once—images of shaggy reddish cows roaming rolling green hills dotted with crumbling old castles and . . . Her thoughts snagged. "Hey, is the Loch Ness monster real?"

"She is, aye," said Lucretia. "Though she'd nae appreciate being thought of as a monster, the vain creature."

Marceline gave an uncertain laugh. She was still wrapping her head around the concept of magic and all its implications. "Can you tell me what it's like there? I want to know everything."

"Everything? 'Tis a tall order."

"Just something, then. What does the air smell like? When you touch the buildings, can you *feel* the history beneath your hands?"

Lucretia snorted, but a certain sadness lingered in her coal-dark eyes. "I couldnae tell ye, I'm afraid. It's changed so much since I was there. Sometimes Kilda shows me pictures and I hardly recognize the place."

Marceline frowned, taken aback by the birdwoman's sorrowful tone. "You never go back at all? But how long has it been?"

"Haven't ye got anything better to do than interrogate me?" Lucretia huffed, crumpling the soiled newspaper into a ball before walking off to toss it into the fire, where it ignited in a burst of turquoise flames.

Marceline followed her. "But Sylvan goes home to Tahiti all the time, and he said Kilda goes to her village in Scotland. That little girl"—she pointed to a child stacking blocks into a tower—"told me she lives in an orphanage in Mexico. Can't the door take you back there whenever you want?"

"For Nature's sake, would ye like to know how heavy my flow is too?"

"If it offers me some insight, then sure," Marceline countered, surprised to be reunited with her long-lost snark.

"Ye've got more bite than I thought." Lucretia's black eyes glimmered with amusement. "There's hope for ye yet."

A saucer of dead flies gripped in her talons, Lucretia gravitated to the corner where Maia the Venus flytrap bobbed in her pot, growling and asserting dominance over her lesser heads. Determined to get an answer, Marceline trailed after Lucretia. Why did she have to be so elusive?

The plant's heads hissed, fighting over the tiny, winged corpses the feathered woman sprinkled over them with a pair of tongs. Lucretia tutted as Maia shoved her other heads out of the way, viciously snapping her leafy jaws.

"I can't even picture you outside of here," Marceline said, watching. "What with your general, uh, birdiness, and everything." Falkirk, who'd perched on top of the espresso machine to watch, shot Marceline a look, as if to say, *Birdiness? Really?*

Lucretia snorted, amused. "I promise ye, I'm naewhere near as interesting as ye seem to think." She dumped the rest of the flies over the plant with a sigh, plopping the tongs into the sink before turning to Marceline, hands on her hips. "I'll answer one question, and then nae more. Will that satisfy ye?"

Marceline nodded, her thirst for answers overtaking the guilt of having annoyed Lucretia.

The feathered woman took a deep breath. "Nae, I never leave the café. I can't." She rounded the counter. "Now, make yerself useful and wash the dishes."

"Wait, never?" Marceline gestured toward the curtain she'd seen Lucretia disappear behind so many times. "So, that's not your office? It's where you sleep?"

"Aye," Lucretia said.

Marceline stared at her boss, welling with sympathy. She knew what it was like to feel trapped. But at least she could accompany Baxter on errands sometimes, not to mention the monthly rummage sales his work organized. And, though she wasn't supposed to, she'd found a way to come here, too.

She turned on the tap and fished for the sponge, thoughts tumbling around in her mind. Even a place as magical as this could feel like a prison if you weren't able to leave. Marceline had managed to sneak out of her own prison, but all that stood in *her* way was a single human. What forces were keeping Lucretia here?

"So, you're, like, trapped by magic?" The question would have sounded utterly foolish a week ago. Regardless of the cause, there was probably little Marceline could do to help this woman who'd offered her shelter in her time of need.

"That was yer one question, I'm afraid." Lucretia plucked an already dry dish from the rack and wiped it distractedly before shoving it in the cupboard.

"I'm being nosy, aren't I," Marceline mumbled. "Baxter says I don't know when to be quiet."

Lucretia turned back toward Marceline and for the briefest of seconds her eyes softened. "Sounds like that man has a lot of opinions about ye. Dinnae ye think it might be time to stop assuming he's right?"

Marceline stared at Lucretia. "Well, he knows me better than anyone."

"And what about yerself?"

Marceline gave a stilted laugh. "I can't be objective about myself. I *am* myself. I don't understand."

"I think ye do." Lucretia gave Marceline a knowing look.

Marceline stared at the soapy dish in her hand. Was it possible Baxter was wrong about her many faults? She spent more time with him than anyone else. Well, until recently. She scrubbed at the dish, unnerved.

"Oy!" Lucretia reached over and playfully flicked some soapy water at Marceline's face with her talon. "Are ye all right, lass? Ye've gone all pale. I did nae mean to launch ye into an existential crisis."

"I'm fine." Marceline forced a smile far more cheerful than she felt. "Just thinking."

"Listen, all I meant to say was ye have plenty of good qualities that ye dinnae seem aware of. I know I've been teasing ye, but what if ye thought of yerself as curious, instead of nosy? Curiosity is a lovely quality."

"But not with you."

"Aye," Lucretia confirmed with a sardonic snort, drying another dish. "Exactly. Nae with me."

Sylvan arrived roughly an hour after Marceline, looking ponderous and withdrawn as he tucked a golden feather—she assumed it was some sort of key—into the pocket of his shorts. He brightened when he saw her. "Marsupial! You are ready for more coffee education?"

"Marsupial?" The cheer in his smile nudged Lucretia's comment about Baxter and his judgment to the back of Marceline's mind. "You gave me a nickname?"

Sylvan grinned. "It took me eras to create a fine one. Easier than Kilda, though. For her, I compiled only Kilowatt or Killed-a-Man—she did not approve that one, though."

The tingle of delight she felt overwhelmed her. "Well, thanks... Silicone? Silk? Silver...guy?"

"We will workshop this," he teased.

"If everything you say is being translated from French, how do puns work?"

He cocked his head in that puppy-dog way of his. "Very smart magic, I assume."

They resumed their coffee lesson, moving on from shot pulling to milk steaming.

"You have a dairy talent. You are still nurturing it, but soon it will be obvious," Sylvan said after Marceline botched her third pitcher of foam. She blushed, knowing he was only being kind, but appreciating the lie all the same. "Me, at school, I was not a rapid learner. I did not enjoy it, then. Except art. If you can imagine, I used to walk around with a foolish vest, spotted with paint. On purpose." He snickered at the memory. "I believed it offered me an interesting look, even if it was too warm and I always perspired in it."

Sheepishly, Marceline nodded as she cleaned the steam wand. "I wasn't cool either," she confessed over the noise. "I used to pull around one of those rolling backpacks."

"Ha! Like a stewardess?"

"Yes, exactly!"

He refilled the pitcher with milk so she could try again.

As she did, Marceline tried to imagine Sylvan decked out as a high school stereotype—a goth, or a band geek, or a skater—before shutting down the thought. Sylvan's life was none of her business. What would Baxter think if he saw her bantering with another man?

"You are all right? Your expression changed." The worried timbre of his voice sent a flurry of remorse into her stomach.

"Yes. No, I'm sorry. No." Discomfort clawed at her throat. "I'm a freak. Sorry. Baxter says I was born with my head in the cl—" Lucretia's comment from earlier interrupted the thought. Could she be right about Baxter's opinion not necessarily being correct?

"Your husband?" That look of concern on Sylvan's face was too much.

"Could we not talk about him?" she blurted, then backpedaled. She'd been so desperate for a social life, and yet here she was, snubbing the first person to show her an inkling of consideration. "Oh my God, I'm sorry, I just—"

"Marceline, please do not apologize."

"I'm sor—" She caught herself, biting her lip.

Bemusement glimmered in the rich brown of his eyes. "I do not judge you. It is a hard-to-banish habit. Trust me, I know. Anyway, we will not compost you for saying the wrong thing."

"I know *you* won't." She squirmed, glancing toward the curtain that led to Lucretia's private quarters. She'd disappeared behind it to rest, or maybe to brood. Though Marceline believed the feathered woman's analysis of her self-esteem issues came from a good place, she couldn't shake the feeling that her presence was a nuisance to Lucretia.

"Do not be anxious about her. She is . . . prickly. Like a pineapple. But if you wait long enough for her to, uh, ripen, you will find she is abundantly sugary inside."

"A pineapple?"

"Maybe the café does a bad translation. It is not a perfect metaphor." A blush bloomed over Sylvan's tan skin. Was it possible he was as awkward as she was, underneath his lighthearted demeanor?

The warmth of the café tingled inside her. "It's great." She smiled down at the milk in her pitcher. "Hey, it's less lumpy! Maybe I do have a dairy talent."

"Of course you do. I do not say such things faintly." Sylvan grinned. "Do you wish to observe something?"

Swelling with pride, Marceline let herself be whisked into wonder as Sylvan showed off the improbable designs he could conjure in the foam, using a stirring stick as a paintbrush: a sea turtle, a duck, and even a perfect likeness of Lucretia in profile.

"It's so lifelike," Marceline marveled. "You *are* an artist."

"Thank you." He pushed a black lock behind his ear. "I used to be better. I had an entire studio of paint. Well, a shed. I suppose I still have it. I do not use it now."

"Really?" Marceline's eyes lit up. She'd always wanted to make art, but supplies were expensive for a hobby she'd drop once she realized she wasn't any good. At least, that's what Baxter had said. She frowned at the thought. Painful as it was to acknowledge, Lucretia had a point—Marceline's husband consumed quite a large percentage of her brain space. What if she didn't need to be good at art? What if she simply needed to enjoy it? The idea felt revolutionary. She looked at Sylvan, reining in her focus. "Why did you stop?"

In a flicker, the smile dropped from Sylvan's face, and Marceline sobered. She knew what pain looked like. Baxter's more fragile moments had made her deeply intimate with the feeling. It tore her to pieces, seeing good people tormented by the things that had hurt them. And Sylvan was a good person, she was sure now. She didn't know him well yet, but she could tell.

"It is a meandering story."

"Stop showing off, will ye?" The interjection came from behind them, and they turned to see Lucretia emerge from behind her curtain. Her feathered locks were ruffled, pillow creases marking her cheek.

"Speak of the demon," Sylvan declared, banishing any trace of sadness and showing the birdwoman her foam portrait.

"Ach, what superstitious nonsense," the feathered woman quipped. She raised her brow at Marceline. "Are ye half decent with the machine yet?"

"I'll need a lot more practice—"

"Nonsense," Sylvan cut in. "She is natural."

"Good," Lucretia said. "We do things properly here. 'Tis nae Starbox."

"It is 'bucks,'" Sylvan corrected her.

Lucretia shot him a skeptical look. "Nae, I'm quite sure 'tis 'box.'"

Before Marceline could get a word in, the two of them were bickering. She watched them, bemused. They were so different, yet their interactions were so comfortable, so easy. She felt a tiny drop of envy land inside and ripple through her. What would it be like to have that kind of friendship? Her thoughts traveled to memories from her school days—of sticky ice-cream fingers and endless games of Pictionary. She hadn't been the most popular girl in school by a long shot, but she'd had a handful of good friends. Where were they now?

"I'm telling ye 'tis 'box'! How could a buck brew coffee? They dinnae have opposable thumbs!" Lucretia was shaking a dishrag at Sylvan now, apparently having forgotten her earlier annoyance.

Realizing the time, Marceline tapped Lucretia on her blue-tattooed arm, interrupting. "I should probably go soon."

Lucretia ended the debate with a final glare at Sylvan, before turning to Marceline. "Nae yet, lass. I think ye ought to visit the storeroom."

Sylvan shot the birdwoman a surprised look. "So soon?"

"Aye. Best get it over with."

Bewildered, Marceline looked from one to the other. "The two of you were talking about the storeroom when I was here before."

"Strong memory." Sylvan's brown eyes roved over her, as if to gauge her readiness, then glanced at Lucretia again.

Although his hesitation made her uneasy, she felt eager to prove herself. She mustered her courage. "I'd like to go in."

Sylvan turned to Lucretia, forehead creased in worry. "Can I not accompany her, at least?"

"The two of ye cannae fit in that tiny space. Let the lass go alone, Sylvan. Dinnae treat her like a bairn. Anyway, she'll want privacy."

Marceline did her best not to be rattled by the cryptic exchange. "I'll be fine," she said, despite the ominous roiling in her gut.

"Ye see?" Lucretia clapped her on the shoulder. Marceline winced at the scratch of talons through her sweater. "Go on and grab us some espresso beans. They're in a big plastic tub."

Sylvan's unease was palpable. "Good luck," he said to her, his tone grave.

Marceline swallowed the lump in her throat. She figured Sylvan meant to be reassuring, but the idea that luck would be necessary only increased her foreboding. She smiled weakly, tiptoeing toward the door.

Trying to hide her trembling, Marceline opened the storeroom and stepped through. "Is there a light in here?"

"No," Lucretia and Sylvan said in unison, but they sounded faint, as if they'd been suddenly separated from her by a thick pane of glass.

Shivering, Marceline kept one foot wedged to allow a slice of light to seep into the dark space, which looked the size of a generous walk-in closet. Palms clammy, she scanned the gloom, searching the multitude of obscured objects. She could just make out the shape of a white tub resting on the shelf opposite her. Analyzing the distance, she cringed. She'd have to remove her foot from the door to reach it.

She took a breath, preparing to spring forward, grab the tub, and run out again before the door swung closed. But no sooner had she moved her foot than the door slammed shut, plunging her in darkness. Her panic swelled as she groped for a handle. Then her eyes fell upon something shimmering in the corner. A cold sensation flooded her core.

Two luminous eyes gazed back at her.

Marceline's throat tightened with a scream too scared to emerge. A voice filled the space—familiar yet alien, kind yet cold.

"You deserve better," it whispered.

The scream came unstuck, tearing through Marceline's throat. She threw herself at the door, clawing until she found the handle. Scurrying out, she let the door slam behind her.

"Ghost!" she shrieked, sprinting as far from the door as she could get. "It wasn't a joke—there's really a ghost in there!" She rammed into a table, grunting in pain.

Sylvan winced. "You are okay?"

Marceline nodded as she clutched her throbbing leg. Her eyes darted back to the storeroom door, and she tried to banish the chill of the creature's words. She deserved better. Better than what? What exactly did the ghost know about her? And how? Did Lucretia tell her? She trembled, racked by fear and confusion.

Lucretia regarded her coolly, arms crossed. "Well, that's done, at least. Calm yerself, lass. 'Twill get easier with time." She offered Marceline a brief pat on the back. "Now, we'll see ye tomorrow, won't we?" She strode off without waiting for an answer.

Still shaking, Marceline tried to blink away the afterimage of the ghost's luminous eyes as she gathered her coat and purse. How could anyone here concentrate knowing what horror lay a few feet away? She'd felt like her skin had flipped inside out, leaving her exposed and naked before this creature that had seemed to know so much about her life.

In a daze, Marceline said her goodbyes and headed for the door, anxious to quell the eruption of feelings whirling beneath her ribs. She was about to cross the threshold when Sylvan caught up to her.

"Wait! You are all right, yes? You are sure?"

"Yes. Totally. Super all right." Marceline nodded, her continued trembling betraying her.

"I..." He looked suddenly bashful as he lowered his voice. "I want you to know that the ghost is not a human. It is only energy. A manifestation of what lives already inside of you."

"In me?"

"In anyone who visits it. It scared me too, the first time I met her—or him, in my case. But the ghost only says what already lives in your heart. It showcases what you would prefer to ignore."

Marceline clutched her purse, trying to wrap her head around this. If this was true, it meant somewhere deep inside, Marceline believed she deserved a better life. The idea carried so many destabilizing implications that she shied away from it, shivering. "What did the ghost say to you?"

Sylvan cleared his throat and tugged at the hem of his shirt, his gaze dropping to the door. "Do not worry about me. Like I said, I only wished to check you are fine."

"I am." She smiled, but in her mind the ghost's eyes trailed over her face, detecting the lie.

Marceline had no time to dwell on the ghost incident when she got home. She was well into her list of chores—having already folded laundry, ironed Baxter's work shirts, and moved on to the kitchen—by the time Baxter swung the door open, surprising her. She gasped, dropping the bowl she was drying so it shattered against the ugly linoleum.

"Baxter! You startled me!" she exclaimed, hesitating between picking up the shards and running to take his coat. As a result, she stood paralyzed in a half crouch, bouncing nervously between both ideas.

"Keep that up and we won't have any bowls left."

Marceline bit her lip, straightening. "How was work? I missed you." She went to turn off the nature show on tropical birds she'd chosen because it reminded her of the café.

Baxter said nothing. Instead, he remained planted in the doorway, looking serious and tired and handsome in his tucked-in dress shirt. One of his arms hid behind his back, an inconspicuous pink blossom peeking out from behind his shoulder.

He'd brought her flowers.

"Oh, Bax!" Her stomach curdled as he held the bouquet out like an offering. She took the flowers, burying her nose in them and inhaling the sweet, unmistakable aroma of her own guilt. She'd spent the day trying to detangle his opinions from her thoughts, and here he was, simply trying to make amends. "They're beautiful. What's the occasion?" she asked, still hiding behind the bouquet, lest Baxter notice the muddled emotions parading within her.

A shadow passed over his face. "Do I need an occasion to bring my wife flowers?"

He took the bouquet back, thrusting it onto the table, then pulled her in with such passion that her forehead banged into his sternum.

Was this about their anniversary night? Did he still feel remorse about leaving her on the street? She almost wished she could bring herself to regret it too, if only to stifle the sense of duplicity nagging beneath her breastbone.

Eventually he released her, patting her cheek like one might do to a child. He slid his jacket off, handing it to her with a deliberate look, as if to remind her she was slacking in her duties. "What did you do all day while I was gone?"

She jarred at the question, noticing how he seemed to hold her gaze even as he sank onto the sofa and reached for the remote. Did he know? No, of course he didn't. How could he? She hung the jacket on the hook. "The usual," she said, bustling back to the kitchen to look for a vase. "How was work? Get any donors?"

"Barely. Half my guys don't give a shit. It's just a paycheck to them. Assholes."

He paused, as if silently cursing his employees. The call center, GrownUpsCare, was a nonprofit that offered resources to foster children across all forty-eight continental states—a mission that meant more to Baxter than his colleagues could ever know.

"What's with you? You seem nervous." When he turned, his gaze was still probing her. Marceline's heart stuttered. She made an effort to slow her pace, hating how easily he could read her. "Me? Nothing. I missed you, that's all."

He raised an eyebrow. "So you said." With a sigh, he leaned his neck over the back of the sofa so he was staring at the ceiling. "I'm starving, Marce. What's for dinner?"

The rapid change of subject brought a flood of relief. "Oh, I hadn't thought of it. There should be some chicken left."

"What else could you possibly have been thinking about?"

The relief vanished as quickly as it came, giving way to a flicker of indignation. For someone who supposedly knew her better than anyone, Baxter seemed shockingly unaware of her interior world. She stifled the instinct to say something sarcastic—a habit he'd all but trained out of her—and instead shrugged, trying to brush it off.

"Whatever. Chicken it is." Baxter dismissed the question, closing his eyes for a moment, before turning on the television.

Local news hummed in the background as Marceline swept the remains of the broken bowl and began preparing dinner. When she finished, she called Baxter to the table. They sat in silence, Marceline glancing at her husband between bites. His handsome face was lined with stress, tired eyes hovering over her shoulder as he scraped food around his plate. Beneath the table, she balled her napkin into a sweaty clump. Yes, she could admit she let his opinion of her carry a lot of weight. But life wasn't easy for Baxter, either. And now his wife was keeping a major secret from him.

But the more time she spent dwelling on it, the more suspicious she'd look. Pushing the chicken breast around her plate, she racked her brain for something to talk about, imagining what would happen if she set her fork down and blurted it all out, right here, right now.

"So, you didn't do anything noteworthy today?" he asked again, his gray eyes suddenly pinned on her in a way that—once more—sped her pulse up several notches.

"No?" She fixated on her wilted pile of broccoli, painfully aware of the drum-and-bass cacophony in her chest, thumping to the tune of *he knows he knows he knows*. "Well, I did use that new detergent. The winter pine one. More chicken?"

"No, it's dry. But you'd tell me if something was going on, wouldn't you? You wouldn't *lie* to your husband?"

"Bax—Baxter," she stammered. "If this is about that waiter, I told you—"

Baxter's nostrils flared as his fork landed next to his plate with a *clang*, cutting her off. She squirmed in her chair, regretting her words. *Why would you mention that?* she raged at herself. *How stupid can you be?*

"I thought we were past that one." Invisible daggers punctuated each word. "I brought you flowers, didn't I? Can't you just fucking drop it?"

"I'm sorry!" Marceline abandoned her massacred napkin and scrambled around the table to rub his back. "I'm sorry, baby! You're right, it's over. I need to get over it." She massaged him through his shirt, wondering how he'd managed to turn the tables on her. She hadn't mentioned the restaurant incident—or her subsequent abandonment—since the night it happened. "And the flowers are so, so lovely."

"Not every guy would put up with this bullshit. You realize that, don't you?"

"I do! I'm so grateful for you, Bax."

"You don't *sound* grateful."

"I am! Of course I am—" She grasped for a way to fix this, and in a sickening flash, the answer came to her. The words clung to her throat, but she pushed them out, like a fraud. "You're the perfect husband, and we're going to have the perfect baby."

The statement hung in the air, and she wondered if he could hear her duplicity echoing through the tiny apartment. Then, at last, his shoulders relaxed under her hands, and Marceline's breathing came easier.

"That's right." The remaining tension dissipated with an exhausted sigh. His hand fluttered up to grip her fingers. Flooded with relief, she buried her face in his golden hair.

Still, the ghost's probing eyes drifted through the back of her mind, its voice echoing in her ear: *You deserve better.* Lucretia would agree.

"It's been a long day." Baxter pulled Marceline's hand to his lips, kissing it softly. "But I'm home now. Let's make a baby tonight."

CHAPTER 11

Long Ago

Bronagh enacted her revenge upon Quill in a hundred small and secretive ways: spittle in her oats, stinging nettles hidden within the straw of her bed, undergarments turned sticky with pinesap.

This last act had been easy to achieve, since Bronagh was now forced to spend every day with Quill. Two years ago, at the age of thirteen, the younger girl had begged the chief's council to let her work as a washerwoman alongside her sister, rather than sit idly and do nothing. This had enraged Bronagh, who wanted nothing to do with her. Besides, it didn't take a fool to notice how lightly soiled the garments in Quill's basket were, compared to the sweat-and-shit-stained scraps in Bronagh's.

The more the villagers favored and coddled Quill, the angrier Bronagh became.

Often in the evenings, families gathered around the firepit and listened to the bards sing songs and tell tales of the gods. When an elder recounted the well-known tale of the warrior who offered the head of his enemy to the Great Winged One, everyone shivered, averting their eyes so as not to look at Quill. The latter picked at the hem of her tunic, pretending not to hear, but Bronagh's lip curled at the bolt of inspiration.

When the menfolk returned from the next hunt, bloody and triumphant and lugging a slaughtered boar, Bronagh made use of her near-invisibility and pilfered the head of the beast while the butcher sharpened his knives. Hiding the grotesque thing in her washing basket, Bronagh crept to her sister's empty hut, snuck inside, and tucked the head between the luxurious furs of Quill's bed, topped with a crown of twisted heather.

That night Quill's horrified screech rang throughout the village, inciting chaos. Every man, woman, and child close enough to hear sprang into a frenzy. Like crazed animals, they clawed at each other's throats, yanking fistfuls of hair. A savage urge filled Bronagh's head. She plunged to the ground, beating it until her fists bled.

It was no secret that the Winged One's scream could spark havoc. When at last the chief managed to restore order, a brief and horrified census revealed four villagers had been wounded. As the dazed victims were taken to the healer, Quill stood by, wrapped in her furs, moonlit face twisted with shame.

Bronagh crept within earshot as the chief approached her sister, bowing far too low. "O Daughter of the Great Goddess—if, if I may call ye thus—"

"Quill will do."

"Aye, Quill"—he looked profoundly uncomfortable using her given name—"let it be known that I mean ye nae offense, but might ye explain what provoked yer panic?"

When tight-lipped Quill led the chief into the hut, half the village followed, crowding the doorway. A chorus of gasps erupted at the sight of the severed boar's head laid out upon the straw. The mottled meat had begun to smell, flies swarming its empty sockets, the heather crown still perched atop it at a ludicrous angle.

"Who would dare do such a thing?" the chief demanded.

A scandalized murmur rose from the villagers. Bronagh skulked at the back of the huddled group, hiding her satisfaction.

"If anyone knows the culprit, I demand they step forward," the chief cried over the din.

"'Twas her! I saw her take it!"

Bronagh froze as the crowd turned to her. Who had spoken? Scowling, her gaze fell on a snot-faced youth whose finger pointed at her like an arrow. The butcher's lad. Perhaps she'd not been quite as invisible as she'd thought.

"How dare ye!" Bronagh protested. "I would nae *dream* of disrespecting the child of a goddess!"

But it was too late. Already the murmurs swelled like a tide around her.

"But of course, 'tis nae surprise."

"She's always been jealous."

"See how she blushes?"

"As clear an admission of guilt as any!"

The chief's voice rang above the others: "Ye'll be punished for this."

"Aye," a deep and gravelly voice concurred. It was the High Druid, first advisor to the chief, looking most ridiculous with his long beard half tucked into his rumpled nightshirt. "The Mistress of Death and Battle demands a sacri—"

"Nae!" When Quill's voice joined the cries, the others faded around her.

"B-but, Goddess," the chief babbled.

"Quill!" the girl corrected him, jaw set. "I'll hear nae more. 'Tis a mere question of harmless rivalry amongst sisters. I'll nae have her punished."

"Divine One," the High Druid boomed. Bronagh thought she detected a jealous glimmer in the chief's eye when the crowd shifted to listen. "Surely such a disrespectful act ought to be punished? She should be sacrificed to the Great Winged One, as an example."

"Sacrificed? My own flesh and blood?" Quill's eyes flashed. "How dare ye even speak of it?"

The old man shut his mouth, bushy eyebrows rising into his wrinkled forehead. No one had ever spoken to him thus. "Are ye quite sure?" the chief tried.

"I shall nae be questioned." Quill's imperious tone made her seem far older than fifteen in this moment. She usually never made demands—which struck Bronagh as an egregious waste of power—so this rare behavior provoked the chief to grovel in a way that might have otherwise been comical.

"The Child of the Winged One is merciful indeed," someone exclaimed, sparking a chorus of agreement.

"Enough," Quill muttered. "Leave me be. The hour is late."

The villagers dispersed in whispering clusters. Offering his respects to Quill once more, the chief too took his leave, along with the tight-lipped druid.

But Bronagh remained where she was, fixing her younger sister with stormy-eyed intensity. That she'd narrowly escaped being disemboweled at the foot of the sacred oak seemed irrelevant. Her revenge had backfired. She'd wanted to frighten Quill—to show her she would not grovel, the way others did. Instead, she'd been revealed as a villain.

When Quill returned her sister's gaze with an embarrassed shrug, the hatred rumbling through Bronagh's heart was pure as death itself.

CHAPTER 12

Despite the ever-present whisper of the ghost in her mind, Marceline soon fell into a routine at the café, training herself to stay as far from the storeroom as possible. She focused instead on perfecting her barista skills and familiarizing herself with the sleek chrome espresso machine and all its trappings, supported by Sylvan's patient coaching.

As the end of her second week neared, Marceline was determined to concoct the perfect cappuccino before having to return home for a long, café-less weekend. The prospect of staying away for two days straight made her shoulders sag, but she tried to ignore the feeling and focus on the present.

Sylvan let her in, greeting her with a smile that thawed the foggy chill of the grimy alley outside. Lucretia, too, gave a nod of acknowledgment before returning to her task of meticulously dusting the entire perimeter of the room with a single one of her own feathers. Falkirk perched on her shoulder, surveying her work like a foreman.

Marceline took an apron from the peg and slipped it over her head. "What's she doing?" she whispered to Sylvan, pointing her chin toward their muttering boss. Three customers were present, none of whom seemed bothered when Lucretia shuffled past their tables, murmuring unintelligibly. The African masks above the mantel exchanged bemused looks as the birdwoman swept past them and toward the door, where she dragged the feather over its wooden surface like she was painting it.

"Protecting us." Sylvan shrugged. "She enacts it each week."

"From what?" There was a manic frenzy to Lucretia's movements—the same desperate energy that Marceline had witnessed during that kettle ritual.

"Who knows? It is better not to exacerbate her when she does this."

Having apparently finished, Lucretia stuffed the feather into her gauzy tunic and turned toward Marceline. "So, ye keep coming back. I thought Sylvan would have scared ye off by now."

"Me?" Sylvan asked. "For what reason?"

"Just yer face," Lucretia teased, cupping his cheek with her talons.

"Rude!" Sylvan put a hand to his heart, feigning shock.

"I like your face," Marceline said without thinking. Her own words startled her. Why didn't she think before she spoke? What would Baxter say? *No! It doesn't matter*, she chided herself, though the thought tied her stomach in knots. Cheeks burning hot enough to combust, she backtracked. "I mean, as far as faces go. I'm no face expert. I mean, I have one, obviously, but I don't have a degree in faces or anything—"

Lucretia's amused smirk heightened Marceline's embarrassment. "Nae, please continue. Where might one acquire a degree in faces? This is fascinating."

Sylvan tugged his T-shirt, smoothing it over his belly and fiddling with the hem. "Be kind," he told the feathered woman. He jammed his hands into his pockets, embarrassed. "Also, thank you," he mumbled to Marceline.

If one could die from awkwardness, Marceline would have expired on the spot. "Cappuccino!" she practically shouted. "Anyone want a cappuccino? I can make them now. Oh—you know that."

The feathered woman let out an amused snort. "Very smooth transition. Have ye thought of composing speeches?"

Sylvan cleared his throat. "Lu is not *actually* an asshole, Marsupial. She only masquerades."

"Am too," Lucretia quipped, throwing Marceline a subtle wink before pausing, her eyes going momentarily out of focus. Marceline threw a perplexed glance at Sylvan, hardly daring to look him in the eye—not after what she'd just blurted. "Kilda will be here in five minutes, and she'd like an Earl Grey with a dash of cream," Lucretia said, alert again. "Can ye boil some water, Marce?"

"Oh yes, of course."

"Grand. Ye can do some sweeping afterward. If ye need anything, feel free to ask Sylvan and his lovely face."

Marceline blushed furiously as the feathered woman strode off to fill the bird feeders.

"Um. Yes. So." Sylvan shifted his weight, making a valiant attempt at ignoring Lucretia's teasing. "You know where everything resides, yes? Kilda prefers loose-leafed."

Marceline nodded and turned toward the shelf that held the teas. "How does Lucretia know when Kilda's coming and what she wants?" she asked over her shoulder. After their mortifying moment, it was easier to talk to him without eye contact.

"They have a relationship of telepathy. Or so I believe."

"Oh." Of course, she thought, amazement overtaking her embarrassment. Why wouldn't they?

The space behind the counter was narrow, and Marceline focused on ignoring the absurd tingling she felt when Sylvan's side brushed lightly against hers, as he reached for the cupboard near the tea shelf. "Feces! Not again," he exclaimed.

"What?" Marceline turned. Sylvan was holding the teapot—a ceramic, single-serving one with cheerful flowers painted on it—and shaking it upside down.

"Remove yourself, pest!" He slapped the bottom of the pot with his palm, and a gray shape the size of a wine cork clattered to the floor. The creature craned its ugly face upward and gave them the finger before disappearing in a crack of smoke. "Tea goblin," Sylvan muttered, shaking his head. "Rude bastards. They consume the tea and deposit their foul, sticky saliva in all places, then collapse like tiny sleeping drunkards." He gave a heavy sigh. "I will wash this. You can please boil water?"

Marceline was filling the kettle when the door burst open and Kilda hobbled out from the swirling black void, leaning on her polished wooden cane. With a cheerful wave, she closed the door behind her, tucking the golden feather hanging around her neck back into her sweater. Another key, Marceline suspected. Would she eventually be bestowed with such an honor? She watched Kilda disappear behind Lucretia's private curtain, then reemerge, rolled-up map tucked under her arm. Slowly, she headed for her regular table by the fire and set up camp.

Marceline poured cream into a tiny pitcher, arranging it on a tray beside the teapot and matching cup. "Can I bring it to her?"

He chuckled. "You do not need to ask this."

"Oh, right." She reddened, forcing an overconfident demeanor. "I *will* bring Kilda her tea, then. I'm 100 percent qualified and definitely won't trip and fall and spill everything."

"You see? You are learning. What is the expression? Impersonate until you transform."

Marceline hid her smile. *Fake it till you make it* was what he'd meant, but she liked his version better. She was about to tell him as much, but even the thought triggered a hailstorm of questions in her mind: *What are you doing? Are you flirting? You can't flirt with other men!*

Before her silent spiraling could develop into a full-blown tornado, she lifted the tray and began her halting journey toward the corner table. Despite the birds squawking overhead—including a very vocal parrot who only seemed to know German profanity—Marceline inched forward, keeping her eyes glued to the pot so as not to spill the steaming tea.

She reached Kilda's table and set down the pot and mug a safe distance from the unfurled parchment, exhaling in relief. "Sorry to disturb you. Your tea."

The cartographer lowered her spectacles to the edge of her nose. "Ye dinnae disturb me, child."

Marceline hadn't been called a child in a long time. With a stab of distant grief, her grandmother's face swam into her mind. She shook it off, fidgeting beside the table. She'd briefly introduced herself to Kilda but had yet to have a real conversation with her, mostly due to the look of intense concentration the old woman bore whenever she worked on her map—which was to say, always.

"Sylvan said you're a cartographer?" Baxter's voice invaded her head, accusing her of asking too many questions, but she couldn't help herself. Her curiosity was a chronic, lifelong condition, and there was no cure. Anyway, Lucretia had said curiosity was a *good* thing.

"Aye. 'Tis a strange thing, identity." Behind her glasses, the old woman's owlish eyes sparked, her smile twisting the network of wrinkles around her mouth. "Do have a seat."

Pleased, Marceline pulled out a chair. She'd been curious about Kilda since the night she'd stumbled into the café. After all, she'd never met a cartographer.

One lifelong side effect of Marceline's desire to travel was a fascination with maps. As a child, she'd spent hours poring over the atlas in the school library. Now, she examined the cartographer's complicated creation, surrounded by meticulously laid-out tools: a ruler, three sharp pencils, and a tall, curling quill—one of Lucretia's, it seemed—resting in a pot of warm brown ink that caught the room's light like a jewel.

"I do confess," Kilda said, filling her teacup, "there are days I'm nae convinced 'cartographer' still fits. But who amongst us hasn't held a hundred different roles, and borne a multitude of appellations?" She added a dash of cream.

Marceline nodded sagely. Maybe in the past she'd been a granddaughter, and even a daughter, however part-time. She'd been a student and a friend too. Now, she was only a wife.

The realization soured in her.

Kilda took a thoughtful sip. She closed her eyes a moment, then opened them, fixing Marceline with a pointed stare. "Ye brewed this yerself, didn't ye?"

"Oh. I just boiled the water. Is it all right? I can make you a new one."

Kilda set the mug down, peering at Marceline like she could see through her skin, until a serene smile bloomed on her face. "Ye have a good heart. I can tell from the flavor."

Marceline willed away the absurd instinct to cry. "You can?"

"Aye. Now, as I was saying, there are similarities between what I once did and what I do now. After all, maps allow us to see what is ahead. But what cartographer is so skilled as to know *all* that lies ahead? 'Tis an impossible task. And yet, I persist, for the greater good. Would ye like a tea cake?"

"Sorry?" Marceline blinked as the old woman fished a squashed, foil-covered lump from the pocket of her thick sweater and handed it to her. The thin silver band on her gnarled ring finger glinted. "Oh. Um, thank you." Marceline picked at the red-and-silver foil. "Is it tea flavored?"

Kilda released a gravelly titter. "Nae. Ye're meant to eat them at teatime."

"Oh." Marceline took a tentative bite, the chocolate-and-marshmallow flavor bursting in her mouth. "Thish ish—" She chewed and swallowed, embarrassed, then tried again. "This is delicious."

"Indeed."

Marceline snuck another glance at the parchment spread over the table. "So, this is your map?"

It didn't look like a map at all. It had longitude and latitude lines like her globe at home, but instead of going straight up and down and across, they curved unexpectedly, sometimes looping and tangling together like lengths of yarn after a kitten attack. Shaded orbs that might have been planets overlapped, connected by arrows that curved in dizzying directions, often splitting into two or even three distinct pathways. Ancient languages, runes, and hieroglyphs were scrawled every which way, and some parts had been so furiously scribbled over with layer upon layer of ink that they were saturated in darkness.

"Aye. And a right pain in the arse, some days. Here, have another."

Marceline accepted a second tea cake from Kilda's pocket, wondering how many sweets the old woman was hiding on her person. "How does it work? The map, I mean."

"That, I'm afraid, is a question I'm nae equipped to answer."

"But didn't you make it?"

"'Tis more of a collaborative effort. Alas—or perhaps thankfully—I've nae way to visit what it is I am mapping." Kilda blew on the surface of her drink. "That's why the birds go in my stead. I can only hope their memories constitute an accurate description of what *is*. Perspective is a fickle thing."

The answer hadn't brought Marceline much clarity. She prodded, "But what inspired you to start?" She had trouble picturing the eccentric cartographer in the mundane world outside the café.

"'Twas the raven."

"Falkirk?"

"Nae, his great-great-great-great-great-great-grandmother."

"That's a lot of greats."

"They dinnae live as long as we do." Kilda took another sip, gaze shifting to where Lucretia was once again muttering and dusting the perimeter. Without being prompted, Lucretia flinched, locked eyes with

Kilda, and raised an eyebrow. The old cartographer nodded and turned back to Marceline, chuckling softly. "Ye best make yourself comfortable if I'm to start at the beginning, child."

All at once the light in the café dimmed, leaving only a pool of amber encircling the old woman like a spotlight.

Marceline gasped, the sound engulfed by a sudden, omnipresent hush. Shadows entrenched the crinkled web of lines around Kilda's eyes as she fondled a stray thread on her green tartan shawl.

"Let me start by saying, child, that I was never one to go against the grain," she began, a wistful note crackling in her ancient voice, a brogue rumbling like thunder over distant hills. "Even as a bairn, my complete lack of rebellion puzzled my parents. I grew into womanhood quietly, without a scrap of adolescent turmoil, plowing steadily forward on my narrow academic path."

A rush of warmth signaled a presence at Marceline's side: Sylvan, pulling up a chair.

The cartographer took another thoughtful sip of her tea. When she set the cup back down, a shiver danced down Marceline's spine. The cream in her cup had dispersed, revealing a reflection swimming over the surface—one belonging to a much younger woman. One with smooth skin and sharp eyes, which shone behind those same rounded lenses.

"I was the first lass admitted into Glasgow University's new cartography course, in 1963. The field suited me, for my desire to travel the world was preceded by a more practical desire to first understand every inch of it on paper. Alas, my parents saw university primarily as a hunting ground for suitable lads. They made no secret of their disappointment that I never once brought home a beau."

Marceline snuck a look at Sylvan, who gazed at the cartographer, enraptured, as he nibbled on the corner of a croissant pilfered from the pastry case. When he sensed her looking, he gave an embarrassed smile and tore the pastry in two, handing her half. She was thankful for the shadows concealing her blushing cheeks.

"In my third year, I moved to a women's dormitory. 'Twas then that I began to emerge from my shell—one Saturday night after winter exams. And that, child . . . children"—Kilda nodded at Sylvan—"was the event that started it all."

The cartographer took another sip. When she set the mug down again, the reflection rippled into a new image: two twin beds beneath a low-peaked roof. The surface blurred, the angle changing to reveal two girls. One leaning into a mirror, applying lipstick, the other—young Kilda, again—engrossed in a book.

"I owe everything to my dear roommate, Jeanie. My intention had been to continue onward to postgraduate studies. She, however, was less than studious. She was better suited for consuming her own weight in whisky and being a merciless flirt."

"Intelligence of a midge, by the sound of it," Lucretia quipped. She'd paused her dusting to seat herself on Sylvan's other side.

"Dinnae be jealous, love, we were merely friends." Kilda slid her wrinkled hand across the table to rest atop Lucretia's talon, and for a flash of an instant the cartographer's face shifted, shining as young and fresh as the image in the mug.

Marceline stifled a gasp of delight, her gaze trailing from the silver band on Kilda's now inexplicably youthful hand to the one on Lucretia's sharp talon. How hadn't she realized the two were a couple? Probably because Kilda seemed to be at least in her seventies, while Lucretia—youthful as she looked—had apparently been around since the dawn of time.

Kilda released Lucretia's hand, shattering the illusion of youth. Ignorant of Marceline's epiphany, she continued. "'Twas after my last winter exam that I finally gave in to Jeanie's nagging and agreed to accompany her to a party. Like Mother, Jeanie was hellbent on procuring me an eligible lad. One who might nae be put off—in her words—by my utter disregard for fashion." Kilda chuckled. "In truth, a part of me did long to let loose, just that once.

"Determined that I enjoy myself, Jeanie plied me with drink after drink. I'd always avoided substances that impeded my higher faculties, yet I daresay I found drunkenness rather freeing, as two decades of self-imposed pressure lifted from my shoulders. *Liberation*—that was the word people were using. Until then it had seemed purely theoretical. Now, as I explored the blurred, joyful faces around me—candlelit, long-haired lasses decked in wildflowers, young lads wreathed in curling smoke—'twas almost enough to make me lament the years of my youth I'd bypassed in pursuit of knowledge.

"I drank on, and the world began to shift. The colors in the room—somebody's bedroom, filled with smoke and pillows and patterns—burst before my eyes, lines swimming together, separating to reveal glimpses of doorways. Doors to secret worlds, free from the confines of geography. Doors I ached to open. Unsteadily I stood, stretching like a tower into the billowing clouds of pungent smoke, reaching toward the nearest shimmering portal that hung above the windowsill. But as I approached, it vanished. And instead, there perched a raven."

As if on cue, Falkirk landed upon Kilda's shoulder, settling in to listen. Kilda turned her head, speaking directly to Falkirk as she reached up to stroke his glossy feathers. "The raven's eyes radiated intelligence. I lowered my gaze in deference. And then, the bird spoke to me, its voice echoing within my skull, clearer than my own thoughts. Nae a croak or a squawk, but instead, a warm, feminine voice. She said: *The portal has gone.*"

Marceline flinched, alarmed. It was not Kilda who had quoted the words, but another voice, this one ringing inside her own mind. She peered over at Sylvan, who returned the look. He'd heard it too.

"Yes, my children," Kilda confirmed. "'Twas just so she spoke. I was stunned as ye are now."

The voice in Marceline's head, the voice of the raven, continued to relay Kilda's tale. *"It has gone, but 'twill return. For there are many portals, concealing many realms. Some offer wanderers protection, and others we must protect ourselves from. Yours is an astute and nimble mind. Will ye endeavor to help us search? Will ye dedicate your gifts to mapping the unknown, so we may protect ourselves?"*

"Understanding I'd been born for this task," Kilda said, "I accepted at once. The candlelight around the raven burned brighter, yellow pools of light bursting before me, obscuring my vision. When they faded, the bird was gone. And yet I knew she would return."

Falkirk nipped at the wild white cloud of the cartographer's hair, before taking off to settle on the skeleton hanging from the rafters. Kilda's eyes remained on Falkirk as she spoke.

"A week later, in my advising professor's office, I announced my plans to change my thesis topic to the mapping of unknown worlds. How naive of me to believe the stuffy old goat would understand my vision!" A spark of anger traversed her face as she glared into her mug, where the reflection of a stern man with a pompous mustache now floated. "How foolish, to divulge my sacred task to such small-minded dunces!" Kilda spat the words out. "My professor advised me to return home and rest, grumbling that this was what came of letting women pursue higher education."

"The man was a fool," Lucretia scoffed.

"Ye're nae wrong, love. Thus, I understood that university could offer me nae more. That evening, I packed my trunk and caught the train home. By then my parents were in poor health, and I dedicated my days to their care, as I waited for the raven to return. Then one morning, I awoke to find her perched on my windowsill, beckoning me to follow her. I tore outside after her, barreling into the brambles, heedless of the nettles stinging my bare feet as I neared the thicket at the far end of the garden. When I saw it, I stopped short. There it stood: the shimmering portal I'd seen all those months before. And that, my dear children, is how I found the café."

Marceline dared not move a muscle, so captivated was she by the reverberations of Kilda's words against the silence.

Lucretia sighed. "Where would I be, had ye nae accepted the call?" The two women exchanged a look, and Marceline averted her eyes, overwhelmed by the private tenderness of it. A pang of longing bloomed. *You deserve better.*

"So." Marceline cleared her throat, choosing her words carefully. "You sent the raven to entrust Kilda with the map project? Why?"

When Lucretia tensed, Marceline wondered if she should have stayed silent.

"Not all realms are cozy and welcoming," the birdwoman said darkly, and for a moment, she looked exhausted, the way she had after the kettle ritual. Marceline's gaze traveled to the storeroom door, shivering at the thought of the ghost lingering beyond it, but when Lucretia caught her, she let out a bitter laugh. "Oh nae, lass. Much worse than that." She shook her head, as if dislodging whatever demons had settled in her thoughts. "Anyway, I believe we've wasted more than enough of Kilda's time."

With that, Lucretia flicked her talon in the air, and all at once, light returned to the café with a crescendo of background noise—squawking birds and crackling fire, the low warble of an Edith Piaf record. She threw a pointed look toward Sylvan and Marceline.

"And the two of ye! I dinnae pay ye to lounge about, listening to stories."

"Factually, you do not pay us at all," Sylvan countered. "Thus, we are free as birds."

"What did I tell ye about bird jokes?" Lucretia smacked his side with her rag before heading away to the counter.

"Aye, there's still so much work to do," Kilda muttered to no one in particular. She reached for her protractor, gazing thoughtfully at the map as it seduced her back into her own mind, whirling with theories and portals and memories, and doors to dark, dangerous worlds.

CHAPTER 13

Long Ago

Bronagh and Quill were crouched at the edge of the loch, washing bundles of clothing, each in their separate worlds. Bronagh had fallen into a deep meditation on the injustice of life—even deeper than usual, for tomorrow was Quill's sixteenth birthday, the sixteenth anniversary of Bronagh's beloved mother's death. At midnight tonight, Quill would join the druids for their secret ritual at the sacred oak—only the gods knew what that entailed—and the following evening, the village would erupt into a whirlwind of festivities. Already, people had begun ambushing Quill, offering her sweet cakes and other gifts. For the sixteenth year in a row, not a single word of sympathy would be uttered in Bronagh's direction.

Knee-deep in her own sour thoughts, Bronagh glared at the midmorning sun rippling on the surface of the loch, seeing no beauty.

She heard a splash.

Startled, she turned toward her sister, who was scrubbing garments several paces away. Or she had been, a moment ago. Now, she lay face down in the shallows, splashing up a frenzy, her basket overturned on the shore.

Bronagh frowned at the scene. What madness was this? Her so-called divine sister had long ceased her pathetic attempts to catch Bronagh's attention. Had Quill been suddenly possessed by some malevolent spirit? Was she going to die? And was Bronagh going to let it happen? She contemplated these questions, lip curling.

"Great Goddess!" a voice exclaimed behind Bronagh. Annoyed, she turned to see Loic—a village lad who'd recently sprouted into manhood—dropping a cloth bundle onto the grass and sprinting into the shallows to rescue her flailing sister. Bronagh eyed the bloodstained scraps strewn on the shore. He'd likely been bringing them the soiled gear of that morning's hunting party.

Bitterly, she watched Loic grab Quill around the middle and drag her to shore as she jerked and flailed and almost clocked him in the jaw. Leave it to her sweet, divine sister to gain the sympathies of a strapping young man merely by splashing about, Bronagh thought, disgusted. Panting, Loic rolled Quill onto the grass, flipping her onto her back. Quill's vacant black eyes rolled back into her head.

The image of Bronagh's dying mother flashed through her mind, triggering a fresh slash of anger. Aye, she thought. She *was* quite capable of letting Quill die.

"In the Goddess's name, why do ye nae run for help?" Loic's reprimand startled Bronagh out of her contemplation.

She sprung to action despite herself. "Forgive me, it seems I've taken root with shock—"

"Go!" Loic roared.

Bronagh scurried off down the path leading back to the village. But as soon as she'd moved beyond the tree-lined bend, she slowed her pace. Did the lad imagine he could gain the Winged One's favor with his heroic act? Or was Loic yet another of her sister's silent suitors, who courted her only in their dreams, believing themselves unworthy? The thought sparked rage in her heart. Her sister was bonny enough, she conceded dryly, but what divine favors had she ever bestowed upon the village, save accidentally inciting riots when frightened? Bronagh herself was twenty-one already—almost past the marrying age—and not a single lad had yet approached her. She gritted her teeth. Despite her deliberate slowness, the ring of stone huts was already coming into view. She hurried her pace, realizing she had to at least *pretend* to be concerned.

The first person Bronagh came across was the blacksmith, hammering away at an axe over his forge.

"Help!" Bronagh cried between ragged panting, as if she'd sprinted the whole way.

The blacksmith squinted at Bronagh as if she were some crazed intruder, though they were in fact the same age and had grown up a dozen paces from each other.

"'Tis my sister," Bronagh wailed. "Something's amiss with Quill. She's by the loch."

"Great Goddess!" The blacksmith dropped his half-formed axe into the dirt and ordered his apprentice to mind the forge, before sprinting down the path. Bronagh jogged behind him, ruminating about whether anyone would spring to action if *she* were the one in peril.

Halfway to the loch, the blacksmith almost plowed into Loic, who'd managed to swing a waterlogged Quill over his shoulder despite her spasming limbs.

"Let me help ye!" The blacksmith lunged forward to grab Quill's jerking legs, his biceps straining with force. Loic shifted his position, anchoring his arms under Quill's. They staggered back toward the village, Quill swinging between them like a slain stag.

Bronagh trailed after them all the way to the chief's hut.

"Call for the healer at once," the chief barked at Bronagh, before ushering the boys carrying her sister inside and slamming the door.

Outraged, Bronagh stared at the door, tempted to ignore the order and return to her washing. Only the fear of the possible consequences stopped her. With a sigh, she went to retrieve the healer, before stalking back to the loch, seething.

There she spent the rest of the day glowering and scrubbing garments so hard that by the time she was done they looked even more tattered than before.

For hours, rumors circulated like the frantic beating of wings around the village. Whispers that ravens had been dropping dead, and that druids had analyzed their entrails, finding prophecies of great and terrible changes nestled in their rotting corpses. Whispers of how Quill's sudden illness was surely related to such events.

Then, just before nightfall, the chief emerged from his hut and blew his horn, announcing the cancelation of both the ritual and the feast. Women who had begun cooking days before grumbled, while disappointed bards put away their harps, songs unsung.

When the chief summoned his council of druids, a tremor seizing his hands, the whispers turned to worry.

In the Hut of the Unclaimed that night, Bronagh tossed and turned. Despite the snores echoing around her, she couldn't sleep, the thick anger stewing inside her preventing it. Finally, she tossed her threadbare blanket aside and hastened to dress herself, before stalking out into the cobalt night.

Smoke rose from the chief's hut, reaching its ghostly fingers into the sky. Bronagh prowled toward it, evading the notice of the muscled guard barring the entrance. Silent as a spirit, she crept behind the chief's hut and hitched her skirts, searching for a foothold in the stone. Restraining a grunt, she hoisted herself upward and began her arduous, vertical journey to the roof.

With only the light of the moon to guide her, Bronagh managed to clamber to the top. Clinging to the thatch, she took a moment to catch her breath, before approaching the smoke hole at the center of the roof. She had to pull her apron up to shield her mouth and nose from the twisting gray smoke, willing herself not to cough as her watering eyes peered down into the hut.

The blazing fire threw dancing shadows over the gloomy walls of the chief's abode. At its center, Quill lay upon a bed of straw strewn with luxurious furs. Beside her knelt the chief, dressed in his ceremonial helm. From her smoky, bird's-eye view, Bronagh could see the gleam of his balding head through the open top of the headpiece.

The healer bent her wizened body over Quill's, rubbing a salve into the girl's now-relaxed limbs. In a ring around the trio, half veiled in shifting shadows, sat the druids, networks of wrinkles carving dark trenches into their cheeks and beneath the hollows of their eyes. Each indistinguishable, save the High Druid with his fur-lined hood, agates woven into his long beard.

But these men didn't interest Bronagh. She returned her gaze back to her sister. Even through the thick curtain of smoke, she could see the fire reflecting off the whites of Quill's eyes, lending them an eerie air of alertness, though her lips muttered a nonsensical stream of sounds. Bronagh turned her ear toward the smoke hole, straining to make out her sister's words.

"The hordes..."

The words rose through the smoke as Quill's head lolled back and forth, on the edge of consciousness. What followed was mostly too low to hear, but Bronagh managed to pick out a few more words: "...they come..." and "...my mother's favor..." These last words spread tension across Bronagh's back.

The druids shifted forward, straining to hear. Then the High Druid stood, striding to the bed. Leaning on his staff, he knelt beside Quill, speaking to her in a low voice, though each word landed like a stone: "Shapes and shadows have been spotted from atop the cliffs, on the horizon stretching over the coast, O Daughter of the Raven Queen. Are these the hordes ye speak of?"

"...with my mother's key the invader enters..." Quill muttered feverishly, triggering a swell of whispers.

Bronagh had heard enough.

Clinging to the thatch, she shivered, goose bumps rising on her skin. She'd seen more than enough proof of her sister's power. As a child, Bronagh had smashed bird's nests and hidden behind trees just to watch Quill's healing hands make them whole once more. She'd witnessed how the birds—ravens mostly, but other birds too—flocked overhead whenever Quill was near, and how they sometimes perched on her shoulder, whispering secrets into her ear. Despite these proofs, Bronagh had refused to believe it. Now, as she clung to the smoky thatch of the chief's hut, her face twisted in rage as she confronted the bitter truth: Her sister had the gift of prophecy. She truly *was* special.

And Bronagh was not.

Bronagh reeled, slapped with a fierce urge to escape this accursed hut, where her own inferiority rose with the smoke, clogging her throat and stinging her eyes. But she had to hear the end of the prophecy. Lightheaded with rage, she slid away from the smoke hole and took a desperate gulp of air in a wretched attempt to clear her head, before crawling back to glare down upon her sister—ears straining over the spiteful thud of her own hammering heartbeat.

All at once, Quill's bloodshot eyes sprang open. With a strangled sound she sat up. Gasps rang around the room as the druids collectively flinched and the old healer recoiled in shock. Even Bronagh found herself anchoring her grip to the thatch so as not to lose balance.

"I must go," Quill announced, wild-eyed, gaping at the faces surrounding her.

"But, Daughter of the Goddess—the...the prophecy—is there more?" the chief stuttered his bafflement. The High Druid's forehead knit into a patchwork of worry.

"I remember nothing," Quill snapped with uncharacteristic ferocity. She rose from the bed, pulling the furs around her, clearly bothered by the thinness of her undergarments before these strange men.

"Are ye quite sure you're well?" The healer wiped her hands on her apron.

Quill didn't answer. Instead, she searched the bewildering crowd until her gaze traveled upward. Before Bronagh could duck away, their eyes met. Shock loosened her grip, her startled cry ripping through the night.

Bronagh flailed, plummeting off the roof and onto the hard ground. Her leg crumpled beneath her with a painful *snap*.

Gripping her shin against waves of pain, Bronagh prayed no one had heard the crash. Her prayer went unanswered—unsurprisingly, for the gods had never shown her any favor before. Seconds later, the guard came running, followed by a gaggle of baffled druids rushing out of the hut.

"Who's this?"

"That laundress. The sister."

"Was she listening?"

"The council is a private matter!"

Darkness and pain blurred their faces, but she distinguished the chief's helm pushing through the group, accompanied by the High Druid and Quill herself, who was still clutching the furs tightly around her.

The shocked chief opened his mouth, but instead, it was the voice of the High Druid that boomed out into the night: "Ye have breached the secrecy of the council." He glared down upon her. "'Tis a grave offense. Ye'll be punished accordingly."

Bronagh could only wince in response, as white-hot pain burst through her leg.

"Leave her," Quill muttered.

"I dinnae need yer pity, *Goddess*," Bronagh snarled. Being sacrificed to the gods seemed a welcome relief, compared to this miserable life.

"I care nae," Quill snapped back. "I did nae ask to be who I am, nor do I know why ye treat me with such disdain—"

"Someone has to," Bronagh retorted. Quill sighed, spearing her with a look of pure disappointment as she knelt beside her.

Bronagh made to shift away but only managed to groan, gritting her teeth as Quill placed her cool hands over the exposed skin of her leg, muttering a string of whispers that sounded more like the rustling of leaves than words. The whispers wriggled their way into Bronagh's bones, making her writhe.

The pain vanished.

Suspiciously, Bronagh stared down at her leg. She tested its movement. Not a glimmer of an ache. A shiver traversed the whole of her body as her kneeling sister shot her that same sad smile she'd given her so many times.

Without a word more, Quill rose. Furs bundled around her, she turned and walked off toward the forest.

Nobody dared follow her.

Bronagh's heart hardened as her sister's form grew smaller and smaller, one more layer of rough stone encasing whatever last glimmer of humanity remained within. For once again, Quill had positioned herself as goodness incarnate, branding Bronagh a foe for all to see. The pain in her leg may well have vanished, but now her entire body filled with a hot, bubbling fury that consumed her soul as her sister vanished into the trees.

CHAPTER 14

When Marceline entered the Daly City community center that Saturday, a familiar man with a clipboard directed her to a far table beneath the basketball hoop. Smiling shyly at a cluster of fellow volunteers—they were easy to recognize, with their matching logo-inscribed T-shirts, which Baxter liked to describe as "jaundice yellow"—she wove her way to the table, where a half-dozen cardboard boxes already awaited her.

Baxter's office held the rummage sale fundraiser every month, and as much as he complained about the extra commitment, Marceline knew he'd never miss it. The cause was too important to him, too personal.

For her part, Marceline loved the rare social opportunity the event provided. Or rather, she had until recently. Ever since she'd begun frequenting the café three weeks ago, extended time with her husband made her nervous—especially since he'd started questioning her about her day more and more often.

At present, Baxter was still outside, unloading donations from one of the trucks, which meant Marceline was safe from her own lies-by-omission, at least for a few more minutes. As soon as he was finished, though, he'd come over to her table, and they'd spend the day side by side until the event ended at around three. It was only ten now. She eyed the door as she set her purse on one of two folding chairs, hoping the turnout would be large enough to keep him distracted.

She reached for a box at random, prying it open with a tad more force than necessary. The box ripped down the side, spilling an avalanche of fabric to the floor. Marceline forced herself to take a calming breath before bending to pick a tiny onesie out of the heap. Children's clothing. Scooping it all back onto the table, she surveyed her merchandise. *All of it* was children's clothing. Had Baxter arranged this, or was it merely a random occurrence? Suspicious, she began folding the items into neat piles.

Despite his complaints, Marceline knew how much Baxter cared about his job. Often, when he acted especially strict, Marceline made a point to tell herself that he was ultimately a good man. Why else would he spend forty-plus hours a week in a windowless call center, overseeing a dozen indifferent team members for so little pay? Thanks to the efforts of people like Baxter, foster children across the country had access to school supplies, clothes, and suitcases. But then again, she wondered now, could a man still be good, even as he controlled and belittled his wife? How much goodness was enough to cancel out the bad?

"Are you Marlene?"

Marceline flinched, whipping her head toward the slim woman who'd appeared beside her.

"Oh, whoops, didn't mean to startle you," the woman laughed. "Just wanted to give you a cashbox." She handed over a battered aluminum container, her hot-pink nails glinting. She was probably in her fifties, though her shirt was knotted to reveal several scandalous inches of tan skin and a bejeweled belly button.

Marceline took the box. "Oh, thank you." She thought of correcting the woman about her name, but that ship appeared to have sailed, because the lady kept talking.

"I'm Shelby," she said, making herself comfortable in the chair beside Marceline's. "Started fostering a few months ago. I've got a thirteen-year-old girl and a nine-year-old boy right now. Siblings. They're in here somewhere." She waved a hand toward the other tables arranged throughout the massive space. The event hadn't yet started in earnest, though a fair number of early bargain hunters had begun trickling in. "Do you have any?"

"Foster children? Oh, no." Marceline's cheeks flushed, dazzled by the woman's larger-than-life energy.

"You should try it. I mean, it can be hard, emotionally, but it's also so, so rewarding. Hey, is Baxter your husband? Talk about a tall drink of water!"

Marceline laughed uneasily. She never knew how to respond to such comments.

"I'm serious!" Shelby's kohl-smeared eyes crinkled in the corners. "You're one lucky lady. That strong jaw. And what is he, six-foot-two?" Marceline had no time to answer between questions. "Have you been married long? Come on, spill!"

A surge of middle-school slumber-party nostalgia taunted Marceline as she tucked a rogue strand behind her ear, blushing. "Five years. We met at an arcade. I used to go there after class with my high school friends, and he worked there."

"Well, if that isn't the most wholesome thing I've ever heard. Was it love at first sight?"

Marceline paused. Was it? She had no other experiences to compare it to. She remembered that queasy, fluttering feeling, the tongue-tied panic she'd felt when he'd first spoken to her, her damp palms in the face of his gray gaze... "It must have been," she said finally. "I think I was in shock. I'd never had so much as a peck on the cheek, and suddenly this handsome boy—no, this *man*, was asking for my phone number... I was sure it was a joke. Later that night, he called me. My dad didn't usually live with me, but since my grandmother—"

Her throat tightened and she changed course. "Well, anyway, Dad was the one who answered the phone. He was so furious! *Who is he?* he kept asking. *Why haven't I heard about him?*" She stopped short, realizing she was sharing far too much.

Shelby didn't seem to mind. "Typical father. I'm sure he warmed up to him in the end, though, didn't he?"

"Well—"

"What are you ladies jabbering about?" Someone clapped Marceline on the shoulder, hard. She straightened like an arrow in her folding chair.

"Bax! You scared me."

"Just keeping you on your toes, babe." He planted a kiss on her cheek. "Who put you in charge of the cashbox, and what were they thinking?"

"It's fine, I can manage."

"Don't worry, I got it." He pulled up a chair on her other side, sliding the box over.

"Cool tattoo." Shelby pointed to Baxter's forearm. In one agitated motion he rolled down his sleeve, which had ridden too far up. How he'd gotten ahold of a long-sleeved version of the GrownUpsCare shirt, Marceline wasn't sure, but she wasn't surprised, either. He never showed his right forearm if he could help it. Somehow, Shelby didn't notice the tension. "What does it mean?"

"It means I was a dumb teenager who made bad decisions," Baxter half growled. "Could you see how they're doing over in kitchenware? Will looks like he needs help."

Dismissed, Shelby left, leaving a faint sadness in her wake. Marceline had appreciated the company. She gave the older woman a discreet wave.

"You're welcome, babe." Baxter tugged Marceline in for another kiss.

Marceline picked at a loose thread in her jeans. "I thought she was nice."

Baxter snorted. "Jesus, Marce, you'd trust a rattlesnake if you thought it had smiled at you." He slid a protective hand between the small of her back and the chair.

When the sale officially started, crowds began filing in through the double doors. Marceline sat idly by while Baxter handed change to customers, chitchatting and smiling. Every so often, he'd pick through the contents of the table, setting aside a tiny sweatshirt or a pair of miniature sweatpants. The growing stack under the table made her uneasy, but she tried to ignore it. Instead, she watched her husband, marveling at the Jekyll-and-Hyde difference between public and private Baxter.

With the customers, he was that same, charismatic golden boy, the one she'd met all those years ago. Before she'd known about the dark trauma festering inside of him, the pain poisoning his dreams. She'd learned all that later. The first time he'd shared his traumatic stories with her—stories he'd never told anyone—her heart had broken for him. She'd absorbed his pain as if it were her own, until eventually, she became the glue holding him together. But who was holding *her* together? She sighed, and Baxter jerked his head up, halfway through counting a stack of dollar bills.

"You okay?"

"Me? Oh, yeah." She picked up a child-sized sweater, thinking fast. "There's a hole in the sleeve. I don't think we can sell this."

Baxter gave her a strange look, and for a moment Marceline was terrified he'd somehow sniff out the deception she harbored, but at that moment, Shelby sauntered back over from the far table to which Baxter had banished her. Marceline offered the approaching woman a grateful smile.

Shelby grinned back. "Going for a coffee run. Can I grab you guys anything?"

"That's so nice. Could I have a mocha, if it's not too much trouble? With an extra shot?"

Baxter looked at her like she'd declared a family of dragons had arrived to volunteer. "Since when do you even *like* coffee, Marce?"

She shrugged. "I feel like experimenting."

"You'll be bouncing off the walls, babe, trust me." Baxter turned coolly to Shelby, who continued to smile, though her gaze traveled between them, penciled brows angled in concern. "We'll have two regular coffees."

"You got it." The rhinestones on the back pockets of Shelby's jeans glinted as she walked off toward the double doors.

"A mocha with an extra shot," Baxter repeated, chuckling.

Marceline's lips tightened. "I think I'll browse for a bit, if that's all right."

"Don't miss me too much." Baxter leaned in for yet another kiss—he was so much more demonstrative in public. Marceline complied, brushing her hurried mouth over his as she rose from her folding chair. "Wait." Baxter produced a crumpled ten-dollar bill from his wallet. "Buy yourself a nice dress or something. Oh, and if you see a crib or stroller, tell them to hold it until I can have a look."

The lump in her throat was becoming all too familiar. "Thanks, baby." She wove away through the maze of heaped tables.

The table where Marceline ended up was stacked high with books and about as far from Baxter as she could get. Marceline liked books. She even had a library card—though she rarely went, since Baxter was never in the mood to drive her. It had taken her three months to return the last book she'd borrowed, and Baxter had been furious about the late fees.

The endless boxes of used volumes stretched before her like a banquet. Marceline took in the literary feast, her irritation abating as she fingered the colorful spines.

"Hey, Marcie, good to see you," a high voice said. Baxter's boss, the regional manager. The bald little man presided over the table, his two teenage daughters at his side. Marceline smiled shyly, though she didn't love the nickname.

"Hello, Mr. Patinsky."

"Please, I've told you. Call me Sam."

They chitchatted a bit until a pair of women approached, wanting to pay for their books. Marceline snuck away to the far end of the table. If a book was right for her, she decided, it would jump out at her. Delight stirred in her. Where had this semimystical attitude come from? Was it the café's influence? Slipping the cozy idea on like a favorite sweater, she closed her eyes and felt inside one of the boxes, pulling out a book at random.

Island Paradise: A Photographic Journey Through French Polynesia.

Marceline's smile widened. She could picture the tiny cluster of islands, barely large enough to be visible on her globe lamp. Tahiti was in French Polynesia. Excitement flitting in her stomach, she paged through the book, transfixed by the bright photographs of blue skies and endless stretches of beach, of people who looked like Sylvan. She flipped to a page printed with a map. Tahiti Nui, the largest island. Running her fingers over the squiggling roads and rivers, the green patches of jungle, she imagined his life there.

Marceline tucked the book under her arm. Each one cost a dollar, so she was tempted to grab another, but she wanted to save the change. She headed back toward Mr. Patinsky, who was teaching one of his daughters how to use the cashbox.

"See? It's simple," he squeaked. "Anyone can do it."

Marceline paid for the book and thanked Mr. Patinsky. Across the room, Baxter was busy with a group of customers. He glanced past them and winked at her. Deciding she couldn't bear to go back yet, she meandered to another nearby table, stalling. But by the time her reluctant route brought her back to Baxter, his customers had moved on, and his attention was once again fixed on her.

"What did you get?"

"Just a book." The anxious tremble in her voice stood out to her, so she forced a smile to cover it. The chances that he'd ask to see it were slim, since Baxter wasn't a reader. Even if he were, a random group of islands wouldn't mean anything to him.

Somehow, these perfectly reasonable excuses brought her no peace of mind.

"Special delivery!" Shelby had returned, balancing a quartet of paper cups nestled into a cardboard holder. Pulling one out, she handed it ceremoniously to Marceline. "One regular coffee for you"—she set a second cup in front of Baxter—"and one for you too. Now, where's my tip?" she joked, slapping Marceline lightly on the arm. Marceline giggled, but her shoulders tensed at the spark in her husband's eye. The one thing he hated more than strangers touching him was strangers touching *her*. Even if they'd brought him free coffee.

"Thanks, Shelby," Marceline said, for both of them. She took a sip. When the sweet bite of chocolaty espresso touched her lips, something inside her crumbled. She snuck Shelby a furtive, grateful glance. Blinking back her emotions, she bent her face over her cup. It was only a mocha—nothing to cry over.

"Better head back to my station." Shelby sighed. "That Will is a lot to handle. He asked me how old I am! The nerve..."

Marceline smiled sympathetically. "Good luck."

Not long after Shelby left, a disheveled-looking young woman cradling a baby limped toward their table, accompanied by a high-pitched wail that made everyone nearby turn and stare. A toddler clung to the woman's leg, face grubby with tears and snot as he screamed himself raw.

"Sorry," the flustered woman said, "do you have— *Stop it, Thomas! I will put you in the car if you keep this up!*"

In response, the toddler bit down on his mother's calf. She let out a shriek and jerked her leg, desperate to shake the child off. The motion stirred the baby in her arms, and it too began to cry. Marceline's heart went out to the frantic woman hushing and bouncing the baby in her arms.

"Looks like you've got your hands full," Baxter commented. The distressed woman nodded, eyes widening to acknowledge the understatement. Thomas the toddler had released her leg and begun pawing at a stack of sweaters. Amused, Baxter slid the stack out of reach.

"Sorry. Just wondering if— Thomas, I'm serious!" She bumped the kid away from the table with her hip, prompting another round of earsplitting wails. "Sorry, do you have anything in his size?" She craned her neck to the side, trying to avoid the baby's tiny hands, which grabbed at the loose strands flying around her frazzled face.

"I'm sure we do. Do you need a hand?" Baxter asked. "We'd be happy to hold the baby for you, for a few minutes."

Marceline flinched. She knew what *we* meant. *Calm down*, she told herself. *She's not going to hand her infant over to a stranger.*

The woman looked like she might burst into tears of gratitude. "Oh, would you mind?"

Under the table, Baxter squeezed Marceline's hand. In other circumstances, the gesture would have softened her. Instead, it had the opposite effect.

"Of course not." He rose from his chair, and the woman carefully transferred the bundle over the table. Baxter gazed at the squirming baby in his arms, face softening into an expression so genuine it startled Marceline.

"Thank you so much. I won't be long."

"Take your time." Baxter smiled down at the baby. "How old is he?"

"She. Eight weeks." The woman stretched her back and let out a contented sigh, but her relief was short-lived. "Thomas, no!" The toddler had swiped a permanent marker and was struggling to pull the cap off. She snatched it away, handed the pen over, then wiped her forehead, which sparkled with sweat. "Do you have kids?"

Baxter turned to smile at Marceline with alarming warmth. "Not yet."

"Well, enjoy your freedom while you have it." The woman's laugh rang with an edge of hysteria. "This is a full-time job."

"I bet it's worth it, though." Baxter's eyes shone as he contemplated the baby. "She's perfect. Isn't she, babe?" He turned to Marceline.

"Oh, yes. Totally." She shot the mother a nervous smile. Baxter was about to hand her the baby, she just knew it. Her mind raced in tighter and tighter circles. What should she do? What if she dropped it? Or what if Baxter got one look at her holding the child and was suddenly filled with a yearning so deep and strong that he took her right then and there—

"Here, hold her." Baxter passed the squirming bundle to her. Her panicked thoughts took a nosedive.

"Bax, I don't—I don't know how to—"

"Just make sure you support her head," the woman jumped in.

Marceline did as she was told. The baby lulled in her arms, eyes unfocused. She *was* cute. So what was this feeling of dread brewing inside her?

The relieved young mother gripped her son by the hand and mouthed one more *thank you* before moving farther down the table. Marceline watched her go, a frantic tide rising inside her.

"Look at her." Baxter spoke in a reverent hush, as if he feared his breath might damage the infant. "She's a blank slate, Marce. No pain, no trauma. She has everything. A mother who loves her, a whole life ahead of her, full of possibilities..."

Marceline couldn't answer. She stared after the mother, a ball hardening in her throat. Had this woman accomplished everything she wanted to achieve in her life? Had she traveled, or been to college, or found a job she loved? There were plenty of people who did all those things *and* had children. But her own dreams—of travel, of fulfillment, of living as fully as she could... outside of the café, those dreams already felt so distant, so wretchedly unachievable.

Baxter continued, oblivious to the chaos churning inside his wife. "When we have a child, I'll do everything for that kid. I mean it. I'll give him the best damn life. Everything I never had." He exhaled, his confession floating in the air between them. "It's what I was *meant* to do, Marce."

Marceline looked down at the baby. Baxter's words swirled in her skull at a dizzying speed, making her feel lightheaded, any illusion of choice she'd ever had drifting farther and farther out of her grasp.

"You okay?" Baxter looked at her. "You're white as a sheet."

"What? Yes. Yes, of course." Her voice shook, her arms shook, her entire *body* shook. She felt faint, so faint—

"Jesus, you're going to drop her!" In a flash, Baxter snatched the baby back.

Marceline stammered, thoughts and emotions scrambling inside her heart, stuttering a confused rhythm. She dropped back into her folding chair like a rag doll, watching Baxter cradle the baby, whispering apologies into her tiny ear and stroking the thin hairs covering her head, like she was the only thing in the world that mattered.

When he eventually looked up, the rage in his stormy eyes sliced through her like a scalpel.

Marceline watched her husband's stern reflection melt against the rain-spattered windshield as they drove home from the rummage sale. Usually, their post-sale ritual involved a picnic at the park, but there was no chance of that today—not with such angry gray clouds churning above. Just as well. Baxter was clearly in no mood for a picnic.

The car jerked to a halt in its designated spot.

"Get out," Baxter said. The very words he'd used when he'd abandoned her in the street. Did he realize it? At least this time Marceline was home—not that this dilapidated apartment complex had ever felt like a home to her.

"Aren't you coming?"

The parentheses lining her husband's mouth deepened, eyes cold. She knew that look. He'd go drink somewhere for a couple of hours, maybe less. When he returned later, reeking of liquor, one of two things would happen: either the stony anger would persist for days until it eventually faded, replaced by a fierce avoidance of the subject, or he'd come back brimming with secret pain, desperate to be comforted. In those moments—when Baxter flailed in a sea of his own torment, grasping for her but refusing to explain what he was feeling and why—Marceline felt the immense weight of his unhappiness like a yoke on her shoulders.

She still remembered the first time he'd disappeared.

Marceline's grandmother had died just before she met Baxter, and her grief was still a deep, fresh wound. Quickly, he became her lifeline. The only thing that made sense, an island of calm in the sea of her loss. They'd only been together a few months when he'd proposed.

"You're the one," he'd said. "I just know." It was exactly what Marceline needed to hear. It had been terrible, staying in that trailer surrounded by specters of her previous life. Her father had come back to live with her until she graduated, but even so, she felt alone. He'd never understood her. Baxter was the only cure for her solitude.

"What's wrong with you?" her father had fumed, red-faced beneath his trucker hat. "You just met him. Can't it wait?"

No, Marceline had insisted, through the thick haze of her grief. It couldn't. Their wedding symbolized a fresh start. A new life, hope drifting over a distant horizon. Frankly, it couldn't come soon enough.

"Postpone it," her father had insisted, his stoic face concealing the storm of his own repressed grief. "You're clearly not in a good place."

Of course, Baxter disagreed, restating what Marceline already believed: Married life would distract her from her sadness. He'd take care of her. He'd make it all better.

In the end, the comfort of Baxter's strong arms had won.

But the debate hadn't ended there. Marceline's father hadn't bothered to conceal his suspicion of her future husband. And Baxter, for his part, declared he had no interest in groveling before a man who spent months on end driving trucks across the country instead of raising his daughter.

"We have to invite him," Marceline had argued. "He's the only family I have left."

Baxter had stared back, his face a mask of silent fury she'd never seen before—one that whispered fear into her heart. "What about me? Why get married at all if you're not ready for me to be your family?"

Even as it scared her, his anger softened her too. After all, he wanted her to be his world—he'd said so, down on one knee. He wanted them to have children together, and Marceline was happy to oblige, because wasn't that the natural order of things? She wasn't ready then, but she would be, after they traveled to each continent, discovering the world hand in hand. She'd been more than happy to help fulfill his dream, since he'd promised to help fulfill hers.

Still, she couldn't *not* invite her father to their wedding.

In the end, she hadn't responded to Baxter's question, and the silence expanded between them, fueling Baxter's fury until he'd stormed out of that dingy apartment he'd been renting—one not so different from where they lived now. With a jangle of keys, he'd slammed the door.

She'd stood there, too stunned to cry. It was their first fight. They'd become inseparable so quickly—*too* quickly, her father kept repeating. She'd fallen for his amorous eyes, pale and gray and shining with the light of dreams he wanted her to be a part of. She'd never seen them spark rage like that.

Devastated, she'd sunk into the threadbare sofa. Could she have been more tactful? Parents were a sore spot for him—she didn't know the details yet, and she wouldn't push him to talk about it if he wasn't ready. They had their whole lives to discover those things.

What if he wasn't coming back?

But in the end, Baxter returned.

There he'd stood, a shadow in the doorway. And as he stepped toward her, crossing into the dim light of the murky window, she'd seen the tears glistening over the strong lines of his cheekbones.

They'd killed her, those tears.

She'd run to him and thrown her arms around his shaking shoulders, desperate to absorb his pain with the strength of her love, hardly noticing the faint alcoholic tinge clinging to his collar. His anguish seeped into her heart, mingling with the grief already lodged there, and they'd cried together until the shadows stretched and engulfed them. They'd stumbled to bed, finally, still clutching each other.

Afraid of hurting him again, Marceline avoided the subject from then on. Her father did not come to the wedding.

He'd die of a heart attack a year later. Except for a handful of tense, secretive phone conversations, Marceline never spoke with him again.

CHAPTER 15

Long Ago

As soon as Quill had disappeared into the forest, Bronagh scrambled to her feet, barely taking a moment to stretch her newly healed leg before stalking after her. The chief and druids parted like tall grass before Bronagh, their whispers swelling in her wake as she marched off into the night.

She was sick of wondering what her sister did when she went off by herself. Now, she would find out. And whatever she discovered, she'd use it against her.

Bronagh harnessed her breath into silence as she reached the tree line. In the village, the moon had hung low over the huts, bathing them in silver. But here, dark branches wove a cage overhead, imprisoning shadows, letting through only the faintest slivers of light.

Fearing she'd given Quill too much of a head start, she paused beneath the encroaching canopy, ears straining. A faint crunch of leaves rustled some distance away. Bronagh tensed. Had this been wise? She had no desire to be speared to death by the tusk of a boar. But then she saw it: a shape moving through the trees.

Quill.

Bronagh crept forward, ducking under branches and stepping over roots, following her sister's silhouette through the tangled brush. Right when she thought she'd lost her, Quill reemerged, stepping into a moonlit clearing with a majestic tree in the center.

The sacred oak.

Bronagh inched closer, trembling.

Quill stood alone in the middle of the clearing, scrutinizing the oak's branches. When she did not find what she sought, her shoulders slumped. She waited a moment, kicking at the grass, then traced a large circle in the air with her finger, before stepping through it. Bronagh stifled a gasp as her sister vanished. She reappeared seconds later.

"Ye've improved."

The booming voice had come from a dark shape in the branches above. A shape Quill hadn't noticed either, judging by her startled expression. Even as Bronagh stared at it, the thing began to elongate and shimmer, until it was as radiant as a slice of moon.

Bronagh stepped backward, wincing when her boot crunched over a brittle branch. She ducked behind a thick tree, peering around the trunk. It took several blinks for her eyes to adjust to the shape blazing against the gloom. Bronagh's heart stalled when she realized what it was.

High above, a naked woman perched on a branch, long legs dangling lazily, a twist of a smile playing out upon her face. Her pale skin seemed to absorb all the light around her, in stark contrast to the curling black mane flowing from her head. Blue patterns snaked their way up her arms.

"Mother," Quill whispered, bowing.

Bronagh's heart slammed.

"Well then, Quill," the woman—the goddess—said. "I take it ye've received my vision?"

Even from where she hid, Bronagh could see the glitter in the woman's raven eyes, hear the rough echo of a squawk beneath her words. The goddess twirled a thick length of night-black hair around her fingers, which curved, ending in points sharp as daggers. Bronagh shivered, unable to look away from those sinister talons and the casual way they played with the strand—it wasn't even hair, she realized, but a bundle of long, curling feathers.

A queasy fluttering began in the pit of Bronagh's stomach, something halfway between envy and awe. She'd grown up with stories of the Winged One. Imagined her a thousand times. Fearsome and bloodthirsty, a goddess of battle, of destruction. Of all the things Bronagh wished she could harness when the world turned its back on her, spitting in her face. She'd only half believed the reticent Quill bore any relation to such a fierce, divine warrior. But here, once again, was proof.

Yet the part that stung the most was the simpler truth beneath this fact: Quill *had* a mother.

And Bronagh did not.

"I did receive it, aye." Quill gripped the fur blanket around her. "Ye could have simply *told* me."

Bronagh was shocked at her sister's sullen tone in the face of a divine being.

"Ye *must* practice the art of prophecy. Or would ye prefer to look a fool when there arrives a vision that matters?"

"I've looked a fool already," Quill mumbled. "And what do ye mean, one that matters? An enemy host will soon be upon us! There will be bloodshed, and my people will—"

"*Yer* people? They are not *yer* people. Ye are not a person at all."

"Thank ye for the reminder," Quill said sulkily.

The goddess released a harsh squawk of a laugh. "Ye best get used to it, if ye're to take my place."

"Ye speak as if I have a choice."

"My poor, sweet fledgling." Mockery prickled in the goddess's words. "Do ye nae realize there are mortals who'd kill to be in yer position?"

"I do realize it." All the fight seeped out of Quill's voice in a deep sigh. "Trust me, Mother, I do."

"Then dinnae be cross with me." The goddess extended a muscled arm. Bronagh's fingers dug into the tree behind which she hid. For even as the goddess's arm stretched outward, the swirling blue patterns upon it sprouted more long, glossy feathers, elongating and spreading and multiplying until her arm became a thick, black wing.

Resigned, Quill gripped the goddess's talon and let herself be pulled onto the branch. The goddess wrapped her wing around her. Bronagh's nostrils flared with envy. Her own mother was a distant memory, a collection of images lodged in her heart that now spoke more of dead, empty eyes than affection. What right did Quill have to complain?

"Sorry, Mother," Quill mumbled. There was a long pause in which the only sound was the rustling of leaves stirred by wind—and, for Bronagh, the sound of her own heartbeat pounding in her head like a battle drum. "Why could ye nae have been a goddess of friendship, or of love?"

The goddess released a huff, stirring the branches around them.

"Ye worry me, my fledgling. Sometimes I fear ye dinnae have what it takes to succeed me."

Quill said nothing.

"Ah well, ye'll learn." The goddess removed her wing from around Quill's shoulder, feathers retreating. "Ye have nae choice."

"Could ye nae live forever?" Though said in jest, there was a hopeful, almost desperate lilt to Quill's words.

"I've presided over this green land for more ages than ye could ever count. I'm sick to death of humans. Their offerings bore me. Even their *bloodshed* bores me, if ye can believe it. Nae, Quill, yer turn shall be soon, and ye shan't let me down. Ye'll continue your training, and when the invaders come, ye'll oversee yer first battle, and—"

"And afterward ye'll pull the Eternal Feather from yer heart and put it in mine, and ye'll be able to retire from yer duties and disappear into the Otherworld, forevermore," Quill cut in. "I *know*, Mother."

"If ye know, why are ye so woefully underprepared?"

At this, Quill scowled.

"Ye've nae response. Well, ye best wrap yer head around it, Fledgling. Ye're to fulfill the role of the Great Winged One, whether ye like it or nae."

"Aye, and I'll sprout feathers and talons and become a dark-hearted beast, just like ye are. I know, I know, I know."

At this, the goddess snorted. "Such spite. Perhaps ye'll do me proud after all."

"Dinnae get yer hopes up."

The goddess smirked. "I do love ye, Fledgling. Half-formed and ungrateful as ye are."

Quill sighed and leaned against her mother, feet swinging gently. "Mother, do ye ever think about the mortal who birthed me for ye?"

Bronagh's heart pounded so violently she might not have heard the reply, if not for the jarring screech of the goddesses laugh.

"Nae, Quill. She fulfilled her duty and that was that. Why should I dwell on it?"

"It doesnae seem fair, that humans should suffer for the gods."

"Fair? My poor fledgling. Ye've been around them too long."

A caustic potion of rage, jealousy, and sadness whirled between Bronagh's ribs, consuming her so completely that her fist slammed into the tree of its own volition. A sudden hush swallowed the forest. Realizing what she'd done, Bronagh froze, stomach constricting as the deity's midnight gaze pierced her, arrow sharp.

She'd been caught.

Bronagh turned and fled. Sprinting through the wood, she ducked to avoid branches, weaving her way between the trees. Her shoe hit a root and she stumbled, but within a second she'd sprung back to her feet, darting for the forest's edge. She didn't stop until she arrived panting at the shore of the loch, its dark waters distorting the moon upon its surface.

There, she fell to her knees, gripping the ground as if it could provide solace. Since the day Quill had slid murderously into Bronagh's life, the world had conspired to prove that her sister was special.

That her mother had been expendable.

That *she* was expendable.

She could still feel the goddess's black gaze trailing her. There was power in that frigid stare—more power than Bronagh had ever felt in her life. It buzzed in the air, swelling with such potency, such destruction, such reckless force...

Bronagh tried to rise to her feet but the hateful yearning inside her churned so wickedly she fell back to her knees, retching onto the rocky shore. Quill was part of that power she'd felt. Soon, the whole world would belong to her. Perhaps the Otherworld too. The ground reeled as Bronagh dug her fists into the rocks. The world had passed her over, again and again, and now the injustice of it rumbled, shaking the ground so she couldn't even stand. She wanted what Quill had. She wanted the power to destroy everyone who'd ever wronged her. To wield it against both the goddess and Quill herself.

She crouched low as the world spun around her, the loch rippling in frantic waves, until a thought exploded in her mind.

Some people were born with power.

Others had to take it.

"What do you see?" Quill asked her mother, whose gaze pierced the dark trees before them. "Is someone there?"

"Aye." The goddess hopped down from the branch. A graceful gesture, more of a glide, though her wings had already retracted. "Prying mortal eyes."

"Who was it?" Quill tried to copy the movement, wriggling to the ground much less gracefully. The goddess threw her a side-eye.

"Nae one important, and she has fled now. But we've other things to worry about. The enemy arrives in three days—"

"*Three days?*" That old, familiar panic rose like a swarm of bees in Quill's core—something she experienced more and more often these days. Not that she'd told anyone. The villagers tended to interpret anything she felt as an omen. Once, she'd tripped and cut her knee on a rock, and a gaggle of druids had whisked her away to drain the wound so her blood could be bottled for some useless potion. Quill shook the memory away, trying to breathe, to root her feet to the solid ground. "How will they prepare for battle in *three days*? They've nae had so much as a cattle raid in years!"

"All the more reason to get to work."

"Mother, I…I dinnae think I can do it. I'm nae a warrior, and—" A blazing look from her mother stole her words away.

"There's nae time for debating, Fledgling. Yer destiny is to lead these mortals, as theirs is to die. If ye care for them so much, ye best ensure they dinnae do so before their time. Nae more cowardly protests."

"What do we even know of the enemy?"

"They hail from the north, they're organized, and their gods are strong and unforgiving."

"Grand…" Quill mumbled.

"Cease yer moping, Daughter. 'Tis nae as if ye had to fight yerself. If ye'd rather stand back and let them slaughter each other at random without yer favor, I'll nae stop ye. But dinnae expect the sacrifices to continue if ye dinnae appear and help them at least once."

"I dinnae care about sacrifices." Quill scowled. "I hate the idea of anyone dying on my behalf." She slid her back down the trunk of the oak, her bottom sinking into the mossy ground among the tree's roots. What she wouldn't give to be anchored safely to the earth, like this tree was! To hide away in the depths of the forest, where no one expected anything from her.

The goddess snorted. "Ye say that because ye've never received one. Now, show me what ye remember."

Quill sighed and drew herself up again, raising a trembling finger in front of her and drawing a wide circle in the air. She stepped through it, and the world turned hazy around her, unfocused and wriggling like sunken trinkets at the bottom of a loch.

"I should have known ye'd begin with invisibility," her mother scoffed. "Promise me ye won't hide behind this trick when the time comes. Its purpose is for ambushes and surprises, nae cowardly retreats."

"Aye, Mother," Quill muttered, tracing another circle and stepping out into the crisp lines of the forest.

"Next thing. How does one inspire bloodlust?"

"Two ways. The battle cry for reckless carnage..." She flushed, recalling the incident with the boar's head. It was the only time she'd ever released the cry, and it had been an accident. Would she know how to control it when it counted? She hoped her mother hadn't seen, but what the goddess did and didn't know had always been a mystery.

"And?" her mother prodded. "What's the other way?"

"The harnessing of the warrior's mind, for controlled maneuvers."

"Aye, good. Perhaps if that wretched mortal had stuck around, ye'd have someone to practice on." The goddess frowned at her daughter. "Still, ye'll have yer innate power, for whatever that's worth. That should be more than enough, until I'm ready to give ye the Eternal Feather."

Panic quivered between Quill's ribs. "They're doomed," she croaked, squeezing her eyes shut and steadying herself against the oak. She bore no close relationship with any of the villagers, no thanks to their frustrating reverence, holding her encased like a midge in amber. But home was home. She had no wish to see them perish.

"'Tis certainly possible, given yer attitude. Ye curse yerself with all that cumbersome compassion. Ye'd be better off if ye cared less."

Quill remained tight-lipped. Her mother had been indifferent to her mortal subjects since she'd taken over from her own mother before her, countless ages ago. Why would she begin to care now?

The goddess's gaze shifted, and she smirked, staring into the dark wood. "What's this? More visitors?"

No sooner had she spoken than a pair of fawns trotted out of the brambles to sniff at the goddess's hand, their great, limpid eyes shining with curiosity. The goddess knelt to caress their delicate heads, but when she looked up at her daughter, malice glimmered in her coal-black eyes. "And just as I was lamenting that ye'd nae be able to practice!"

Quill's stomach tightened. "Mother, they're so young," she croaked, gripping the tree's trunk, desperate to ground herself in the rough texture of the bark. "And from the same litter too..."

"Enough, Fledgling! Ye're starting to annoy me." The goddess rose to her full height, moonlight bouncing off her skin like a threat. "Now, show me what ye can do."

"I...I dinnae want to." Quill took a step back as one of the fawns nudged her hand, its great, innocent eyes blinking up at her.

"I'll nae say it again, Quill." The harsh flash of her mother's eyes made her long to burrow into the earth and stay there forever. The goddess only ever used Quill's mortal name when she was very serious, and Quill had no desire to see her mother's wrath unleashed.

She squirmed.

"Now." The goddess glared.

"Fight each other..." Quill muttered, looking anywhere but at the deer.

"With conviction!" the Winged One raged. "Arm yerself with yer invocation! Focus on yer objective. Yer every thought must fuel yer power. Have I taught ye nothing?"

"Fight," Quill repeated, voice wobbling as she forced herself to stare at the fawns.

"Useless!" The goddess's squawk was so furious that Quill's hands shot over her ears. "I am death and blood and pain. Fear my presence and obey my command!" The goddess's skin crackled with blue lightning as she fixed the fawns with a gaze blacker than the sky above. The animals' eyes widened, their thin legs trembling beneath them as the goddess's lips curled into a grin. "Now, fight. To the death!"

The two creatures turned to each other, pawing the ground. Then, all at once, they reared upon their hind legs and locked onto each other. Quill gripped the tree trunk so hard that splinters bit into her fingers. They were such lithe, delicate creatures. It was hard to believe they'd be able to do much damage—but the goddess had said "to the death," and she always got what she wanted.

Sure enough, one of the fawns bucked its hornless head at its sibling, knocking it to the ground. Before the second fawn had a chance to scramble back to its feet, the first one began to trample its face. A piercing wail arose from the injured fawn, as its eyes—those beautiful, shining eyes that had watched Quill with such innocence not a moment before—were mashed to jelly by its sibling's hooves. Quill's stomach constricted. She squeezed her eyes shut, wishing she could block her ears too, against the animal's anguished wail. Silently, she begged for it to end.

And at last, it did. The desperate sound of the dying fawn tapered off into the night.

Still, Quill refused to open her eyes.

"It's over, Fledgling," her mother muttered. A knot the size of a pine cone lodged in Quill's throat.

"Open yer eyes, ye coward," the goddess ordered.

When Quill dared to look, the dead fawn's head had been smashed into an unrecognizable mess of blood and fur, bone and brains. The other stood blinking over it, head cocked at the carnage, as if perplexed about how it had gotten there.

The goddess strode forward and grabbed the surviving fawn. With an unceremonious flick of her talon, she slit its throat.

"Ye best get used to it," she growled.

The knot bobbed in Quill's throat. She dropped her gaze to her feet. "I should go. The chief will be wanting my council..."

"That trembling fool?" the goddess scoffed. "Fine, go. But dinnae come crying to me when ye find yerself floundering mid-battle. I'll be long gone."

Quill's heart stuttered. Her mother might be terrifying and ruthless, but she was the only mother Quill had.

"I love ye, Mother," Quill whispered.

The goddess sighed. "Aye. I love ye too, Fledgling. Even when ye infuriate me."

With that, she sprouted an eruption of feathers and launched herself into the sky.

Neck craned, Quill watched the raven disappear into the inky heavens.

CHAPTER 16

On the first day of her fourth week at the café, Kilda let Marceline inside. "Had yerself a good weekend, did ye, child?"

"Not bad," Marceline lied, letting the café's warmth seep into her bones and soothe her nerves as she traded her coat for an apron. She had no desire to burden Kilda with her drama, nor did she wish to dwell on the stressful silence that had filled the apartment for the rest of the weekend, once Baxter had finally returned from another mysterious drinking binge. "How are you?"

"Well enough, child, as always. Lu's feeling a wee bit tired, though, so she's taking it easy." The cartographer gestured to Lucretia's privacy curtain. Marceline couldn't help but notice the concern creasing the old woman's brow. "She's just feeling a tad anxious. Perhaps tread lightly today, if she emerges."

"Of course." Marceline nodded. She too had observed that Lucretia seemed increasingly stressed last week. She could relate to the feeling, though the reason for *her* stress was entirely Baxter-shaped.

Determined to take her mind off him, Marceline set to work preparing a pot of green tea for an elderly Chinese man who'd shown up for the first time last week. Then, she spent an hour chatting with him as he crafted one paper lantern after another and even attempted a lopsided one of her own. Engrossed in conversation and activity, it was easy to compartmentalize—to put Baxter and their gloomy apartment into a box and close the lid, if only for a few hours.

Once the man had left, Marceline contemplated the storeroom door, fidgeting. There was something she needed to do—a fear she knew she needed to face—but she wasn't ready yet. Shying away from the terrifying idea, she asked Kilda if anything needed doing—which was how she ended up perched atop a wooden ladder armed with a long stick. She prodded the enormous skeleton that hung from the rafters, attempting to remove the thick sheets of cobwebs covering it.

Sylvan had told her the week before that the skeleton had been donated by an Inuit woman a half century ago. The woman had been ostracized from her community and found her way to the café by following a puffin through a snowbank. Apparently, one day she'd managed to drag an entire dead whale through the portal as a gift to Lucretia.

Actually, Sylvan had explained earlier, most of the oddities in the café came from customers. The espresso machine was a gift from the unhappy wife of a Sicilian mobster in the '60s. The Venus flytrap came from a Victorian horticulturalist born in a man's body, for whom the café was the only place she could live freely in women's clothes. These anecdotes fascinated Marceline. Every one of them, she noticed, featured Lucretia. When Marceline asked Sylvan how old the feathered woman was, though, he'd shrugged and confessed that he was just as curious.

But fascinating or not, now that Marceline was witnessing the whale's skeleton up close, and more dauntingly, witnessing the wooden floorboards far below, she wanted nothing more than to finish the job and return both her feet to the ground, where they belonged.

Her outstretched arm trembled as she reached her stick to the farthest rib, where two green lovebirds were canoodling. Her other hand wrapped around the ladder for dear life.

"Marsupial!"

The greeting startled her, and she fumbled. Her heart did a somersault as she flailed to keep her balance, stick dropping from her hand as her foot slipped off the wooden rung. For one terrible moment, she found herself plummeting, and then strong, soft arms wrapped around her, breaking her fall.

A moment later she found herself on the ground, pressed against a bewildered Sylvan, whose arms still enveloped her.

Abruptly, he released her. "Jesus! Are you fine? I did not intend to perturb you."

Marceline scrambled to her feet, cheeks ablaze. "Yes. I'm super fine. I just, I didn't—I mean, I was focused, and— Are *you* okay? Sorry!" She extended her hand to him, helping him hoist himself up with a grunt.

"*You* are sorry? I am the one who toppled you to the ground!"

"Right. No, I mean, *sorry*'s not the word," she babbled, but the cheeky smile on his face—those white teeth and that tiny dimple—broke the tension, and she burst out laughing. "No, I'm not sorry at all."

"You are learning." He smirked, brushing something off her shoulder, then glanced up at the ladder. "You are hard at work, yes? Or do you wish to observe something?"

"A break would be nice," she said, relieved at the excuse not to climb back up the ladder just yet.

"Good." Sylvan beamed. "I was arriving when I realized you still have not met the brick."

"Met the brick?" Marceline grinned back at him, her heartbeat accelerating inexplicably as he led her to a table along the wall. *Calm down*, she chided herself. *You're acting like a silly teenager.*

A hint of mischief glimmered in his espresso eyes as he gestured to the seat across from his. Marceline smiled warily back as she sat, as if half expecting something to jump out at her. The little green birds followed, each settling on one of Sylvan's broad shoulders.

"Do you observe this brick?" He pointed at a spot on the wall about a foot above the table. "Smell it."

Marceline stared at him. "You're asking me to smell the wall?"

Sylvan grinned. "Trust me, you will enjoy it."

However unwise, she *did* trust him. After all, she might have broken her neck if he hadn't been there to catch her only moments before. "Okay..." She leaned in toward the wall and inhaled.

As soon as she did, her caution melted into marvel.

"Snickerdoodles!" she gasped. "Like the ones my grandma would make. The whole trailer smelled like this when she baked them."

Sylvan beamed, sharing in her delight. "Snickerdoodle? That is a breed of dog, yes?"

"That's *labradoodle*," she giggled. "No, it's a cookie. Don't you have them in Tahiti?"

Sylvan shook his head. "I thought it was odd your grandma was baking dogs. To me it exudes like tiaré. It's a flower. They grow in our garden at home."

"A flower that smells like cinnamon?"

"The brick exudes different to each person."

Marceline gazed at the brick. "So, I guess it's like the rest of the café. You step out of your own city and hear people speaking in your own language and smell your own favorite smells."

"I suppose, yes." Sylvan crossed his arms over his belly. "It does not conjure new experiences. Perhaps it is a flawed system. Do you want to inform Lucretia, or shall I?"

Marceline hid her smile with her hand. "Somehow that feels rhetorical."

He snorted. "You have noticed?"

"And so did that." She leaned in and inhaled the brick, savoring the sweet scent and the homey feeling it evoked. Something she hadn't felt for a very long time. "I wonder if tiaré grows in California. I do wish I could smell what you're smelling."

"Maybe it can be arranged," he said. Then he looked down at his lap. Had she said something wrong? The birds on his shoulders twittered and flew away at the same time, and for a moment Marceline wondered if they could read him better than she could. She frowned, replaying the past few minutes. They'd been having such a nice time. Leave it to her to ruin things. Baxter always said— She gritted her teeth, cutting off the thought with a surge of frustration.

"Sylvan, do you think people can change?"

Sylvan's eyes widened at the abruptness of the question. "I think so. With effort. Why do you inquire?"

"I don't know. Sorry, that was probably super random." She fidgeted, watching the lovebirds. "Have you ever had a girlfriend?"

His lips caught halfway between a snort and a laugh. "Um, in the official capacity?" he asked, and she nodded. "Yes, one. But it is not a cheerful story."

"Well, I was wondering—did you guys give each other compliments?"

The crimson hue deepened over the smooth brown of his cheeks. "Um. No. Not really."

"Oh." Marceline's heart dropped, a dead weight. "I guess it's normal, then."

"God, I hope not."

"What do you mean?"

"I mean I would have enjoyed to hear a praise at times. It was more the contrary." He looked away. "Perhaps your eyes are weak, but I am not everyone's perfect prototype. She liked to explain me this. She believed I should consider myself fortunate to be with her."

"She *said* that?"

Sylvan shrugged and looked back down at his lap. She peered at him, this man whose crooked smile could illuminate a room. How had someone as kind as him ended up with someone so cruel? It was hard to fathom.

"She sounds awful. You deserve better." The words startled her as they came out of her mouth. The ghost's own words, drifting like a constant refrain through her mind. She looked at the storeroom door, wondering what other harsh truths lay behind it.

"Thank you, Marce." Sylvan tugged at his shirt. "For the record, I do not believe partners should speak this way to each other. I think it is cruel behavior, in actuality."

Marceline nodded sadly. He was right, and she knew it. After spending five years defending and justifying Baxter's behavior, the exercise was losing its appeal. What happened to compartmentalizing? Shaking the dark thoughts away, she stood suddenly.

"I need to go to the storeroom," she announced.

Sylvan blinked. "Oh? Now?"

She nodded. "Yeah, now." Already her heart was pounding. "Thanks for showing me the brick, Sylvan."

"Of course," he said, clearly baffled. "You are sure? I can go in your place, if you require to fetch something..."

"No. I think this has to be a me thing," she said, despite the trembling in her hands. "Thank you."

Before he could say another word, she propelled herself toward the storeroom, willing one foot in front of the other. The ghost couldn't hurt her. So why was she so afraid? Sweat dampened her brow, collecting in her armpits, resurrecting the streak of icy fear that had chilled her when those ghostly eyes had met hers before. *You deserve better.* Those simple words had wedged like a bullet inside her, blasting her apart.

Yes, she did deserve better. But change wasn't so easy.

Her hand shook so violently she could hardly grip the handle. *Just go in*, she told herself. Just be strong.

The door creaked as she pulled it open and shut herself inside. She was in. Alone in the dark.

Alone, but not alone.

Her ragged breath tore through the space, frantic eyes scanning the darkness, desperate to adjust yet terrified to see. A half second later they found their dreaded target—those eyes, like luminous black pearls peering through the gloom. Attracting hers like a magnet, so she could not look away.

"You're afraid of me," the faint, feminine voice whispered. Within the space of a heartbeat the eyes drifted from the corner, and now Marceline could feel their pull as they floated off to her periphery. A sweep of ice danced up her spine, as ghostly fingers traced her jawbone. Apart from those lingering eyes, she could not make out the rest of the ghost's form. The darkness buzzed with invisible currents. Only her own wavering voice scratched the silence.

"Yes."

A cold breeze on the nape of her neck stunned her, sharpening and dulling her senses at once, overwhelming even the trembling of her limbs until a stillness as pure as death itself consumed her.

"And yet, you came of your own accord, Marceline Sapnis." The stillness poured over her, submerging any emotion she could have had, even her fear. Leaving her open. Raw. "Why?" the ghost purred into the electric silence filling the space around her heart.

Her own breath lingered against the stillness, without marring it. "I need to know what to do. About Baxter. What if he never changes?"

"Then you will be trapped, as you are now." The hushed voice resonated around her, soft and light, a caress transformed into sound. Once again, the stab of truth caught like a barb inside Marceline's chest.

"I can't leave him." She shivered against the unearthly fingertips trailing down her shoulder, the chill blooming across her back. "It would destroy him."

"And what about you, Marceline?" Those eyes, those luminescent black pearls, drifted before her once more—closer, closer still. The slow, invisible choreography of air currents shifting in the dark. Marceline's gaze slid into the ghost's—her own reflection gliding over glassy, unblinking eyes. "What about you?"

A lick of hurt, a pinprick in her heart.

The stillness lifted, evaporating around her as warmth crept its tingling way back into her skin.

The ghost was gone.

Marceline stood alone once more, consumed by a gaping sadness that felt like it had been carved out of her very soul. Not even the embrace of the café's warm light could alleviate the lingering ache of that sadness when she emerged, stunned, from the storeroom.

She had every intention of leaving to go home early—cobweb project be damned— but Lucretia intercepted her on the way to the door.

"Off already?" she asked, peering too closely at Marceline, like she could see something was wrong.

Marceline nodded. She didn't have the heart to mumble an excuse—not right now.

"Well, stay a moment more, I'd like to talk to ye alone." The bird-woman nodded to her private curtain.

Marceline's eyes widened. She'd been made to understand that she wasn't supposed to go into Lucretia's private quarters under any circumstances, yet here she was, suddenly invited. Trying to swallow the mess of feelings inside her, Marceline followed Lucretia through the curtain.

* * *

Much like Lucretia herself, Lucretia's room—hardly larger than the area behind the counter—was draped in scarves. They hung from the stone walls and wafted from the ceilings, a mishmash of hues and patterns. Layer upon layer of woven blankets covered the floor, punctuated by plush ottomans of every color. It felt like the inside of a tiny festive tent, or perhaps an elaborate fort made by a creative child. Mismatched lamps cast pools of color, illuminating the pictures that were pinned everywhere. Charcoal sketches and watercolor paintings depicting sweeping pastoral landscapes, the same cluster of stone huts shown from various angles.

The only stretch of wall not draped with fabric bore a rough, life-size charcoal drawing of a winged woman. Not Lucretia—this woman had sharper features, her eyes deeper set. Marceline fiddled with the hem of her sweater, taking in the portrait.

"Sit." Lucretia patted a paisley ottoman, then sank into the corduroy beanbag chair opposite. "So, ye took it upon yerself to visit the ghost."

Marceline sat, fidgeting. "Should I not have?"

"On the contrary, it means yer learning to face yer fears." Lucretia crossed her legs. "I'm proud of ye."

Marceline glowed, an ember growing warm inside her. *Thank you*, she tried to say, but the lump in her throat wouldn't let her speak.

Lucretia gave a half smirk, and reached out to pat Marceline's knee, like she'd understood the unsaid words. "Now, tell me, Marce, how are ye feeling?"

Marceline swallowed. "I don't know. It's... it's a lot." She paused, trying to gather her thoughts. "Is that why the ghost is there? So people will face their fears?"

Lucretia nodded slowly. "I suspect so, aye."

"You don't know for sure? But this is your café. You created it, didn't you?"

"More like inherited." Lucretia sighed heavily, sinking deeper into the beanbag chair as if fighting gravity required too much effort. Something hid in the birdwoman's jet-black irises. Pain. Rivers of it, flowing so raw its current caught Marceline off guard. It occurred to her that she thought of Lucretia as timeless. And yet, she must have come from somewhere.

Marceline spoke gently, sympathy welling in her heart. "So, does the ghost speak to you too, then?"

Lucretia gave a curt nod, the pain clouding her features like smoke. *Don't push her*, Marceline reminded herself. But much to her surprise, Lucretia spoke of her own volition.

"Kilda thinks I should accept myself, faults and all. She thinks I should be more open about *what I am*." She cringed, like the words tasted bitter on her tongue. "Everyone seems to have an opinion. Kilda, the ghost... Even Sylvan, and he doesnae know the half of it."

"I'm sure you have a good reason for keeping secrets."

"I'm nae so sure anymore," Lucretia mumbled, and Marceline itched to reach out and hug her. She didn't. Lucretia wouldn't have appreciated it. *A pineapple*, Sylvan had called her, *spiky but sweet*. Still, it was hard, seeing this strong woman so dejected. It was the same hopeless glimmer Sylvan had borne moments before when he'd told her about his ex, the same look she'd seen in Baxter after his sudden absences. She'd felt it herself more times than she could count. When her grandmother and father died, when the honeymoon period ended, and she understood how life with Baxter would be... It was everywhere, this pain. Was nobody free of it?

Marceline stood mutely before Lucretia, her entire body humming with compassion she couldn't act upon. "Is there anything I can do?"

"Just act normal, for Nature's sake," Lucretia huffed, then seemed to deflate. "Oh, Marce. Ye mean well, I know ye do. But I dinnae need ye genuflecting before me like I might otherwise smite yer village."

"My... village? I don't understand, Lu... I don't live in a village. I live in San Bruno."

"Aye. So ye do." Lucretia let out a deep sigh. "Sorry. I shouldnae be taking this out on ye."

Marceline bit her lip. "You don't have to apologize. I understand."

Lucretia shook her head, black feathers falling around her face. "Nae, ye dinnae. That's the problem with bloody humans. They cannae understand."

Marceline tested the waters. "So, you're not a human?"

"Have ye ever seen a human with feathers and talons?"

"Well, no. But then, what are you?"

Lucretia sighed. When she spoke, her words were flat: "A goddess."

Marceline blinked. "What?"

"Please dinnae be weird about it."

"Right." She'd thought nothing at the café could surprise her anymore. She was wrong. "No, that's cool. I meet goddesses all the time." It was a silly, flippant thing to say, but Lucretia's hurt was so raw, and Marceline wanted desperately to make her laugh. To make her forget, if only for a moment.

Lucretia did not take the bait. "I'm serious, Marceline. I didn't ask for this."

"So that's why you've been here since, like, the dawn of time? And you never age?"

"Aye."

"And people worship you?"

"They did. Again, 'tis nae the life I wanted, but 'tis the one I got."

"I thought maybe you were a witch," Marceline confessed. "You do that whole map ritual thing. What else can you do? Can you fly? Sylvan said he's seen you go invisible. Is it true?"

Lucretia finally cracked some semblance of a smile. "Ye certainly get excited, don't ye? Aye, here's a party trick for ye." She stood and extended a talon, drawing a circle in the air before her. Then, with a sigh, she stepped through it and vanished.

Marceline gasped. "Lu?"

"Aye, I'm here," her voice said, and she became visible again. She sat back down, with a shrug. "Some abilities I was born with. Others were meant to be passed on to me and developed, but..." Her voice faltered, and she paused, regaining control of herself. "But then my mother died."

The amber spotlight, the one that had heralded Kilda's story weeks before, fell over Lucretia. Panic sparked in her eyes, and she shook her head, waving it away. The beam shut off.

"I'm so sorry, Lu." The loss that wrapped its tendrils around Marceline was so strong it could have been her own. And maybe it was, for she'd lost family too. If she had some way to bring back her grandmother, or even her father—tense as their relationship had been—she'd do it in an instant.

"Nae." Lucretia squeezed her eyes shut, fighting the glimmer dancing on her lashes. "Nae, dinnae be. All mothers die. I just wasnae ready."

"When did it happen?"

A joyless laugh escaped Lucretia's lips. "Centuries ago. More than a millennium, even. But somehow it still feels fresh."

"I get that." Marceline lowered herself to the floor, across from Lucretia. "I have no memories of my mom, but I had my grandma. She always said I could become anything I wanted, but after she was gone, I just... stopped believing it. Then my dad died too. We didn't see eye to eye, but I always figured we'd work through it, and then it was too late."

"I'm sorry," Lucretia said.

"Me too." Even as Marceline spoke, a shock of anger broke through her sadness. Baxter had never given her the time and space to mourn her losses: her old life, the people who had raised her, loved her. She swallowed, holding in her tears. This moment did not belong to her. It belonged to

Lucretia. Lucretia, who had lived lifetimes of pain, and yet welcomed scores of lost souls through the ages, offering them a haven from their own sadness. "You and your mother must have been close."

"'Twas complicated. We were so different. She reveled in her power, causing destruction with nae a second thought. To feed her power she'd even have virgins sacrificed in her name—"

"Sacrificed?" A lump hardened in Marceline's throat. "As in, killed?"

Shame cloaked Lucretia's expression. "Aye. There's nae justification for it. So many sleepless nights I wrestled with it. 'Twas a brutal custom, set by centuries of tradition. And yet, she was my mother, and the one being who never groveled before me, other than—" The lines of her mouth hardened, and she waved her talon, dismissing whatever she was going to say.

Marceline tried to shake away the dismal idea of virgin sacrifices. "I'm sure your mom would be proud of you."

"Nae. That's the thing. She'd ask why I've locked myself away, rather than go forth and rule like the bloody goddess I'm meant to be."

"But you said you couldn't leave."

"Nae one's stopping me but my own fear. The world's a dangerous place. 'Tis full of hate and bloodshed, vengeance and betrayal. And one day I'll have to leave my sanctuary and go face that danger alone. Or worse, I'll be expected to cause it. To cause war, and hate, and rage."

"Expected?" Marceline tread with caution. "But your mother is gone..."

"How can I break a tradition that shaped the foundation of what I am?" Lucretia's lips tightened. "I'm nae ready."

Their eyes met, mutual understanding filling the space, knotting the two women together in their sadness and fear.

When a question prickled her consciousness, Marceline had to ask it, before the opportunity passed into darkness. "Lucretia, when I first arrived, I overheard you telling Sylvan that I had an aura of evil around me..."

Lucretia sighed. "Ye heard that? Aye, 'tis true, I foresaw yer arrival before ye came. Years before, actually. Did ye nae notice the birds at yer grandmother's funeral? Falkirk tried to entice ye then, but ye were too deep in grief to see."

Marceline gasped. "Those were *your* ravens?" She *had* seen them. How different would her life be, had she found the café back then? "Wait, so when you said you'd been expecting me much earlier..."

"Aye, yer catching on. So imagine my surprise when Falkirk came across ye again, half a decade later in that alley? In ye stumbled, all wet and bedraggled, but now ye were cloaked in something dark, a glimmer of malice, or perhaps danger."

"But I've never wanted to hurt anyone in my life."

"Aye, it didnae take me long to realize that. Ye're infuriatingly pure of heart."

Marceline's mouth twitched with bashful pride.

Lucretia continued: "Nae, it must have been a mistake. A bout of bad energy ye picked up somewhere. Perhaps from someone harboring unkind thoughts? Someone ye spend a lot of time with?" Lucretia gave her a knowing look.

Marceline pointedly ignored the comment, swallowing the urge to defend her husband. "So, you don't think I'm evil anymore?"

"Ye wouldnae know evil if it bit yer arse off," Lucretia snorted, wiping at her face with the back of her talons. "Now, leave me be, will ye?"

Marceline heaved herself to her feet. She felt drained, a victim of too many emotions in too little a space. "Lucretia, thanks for talking to me about this."

"Don't ye go soft on me. I cannae bear it."

"Fine, fine." Marceline brushed herself off, turning to go.

"Wait." Lucretia plucked a long, glossy feather from her head. She held it in front of her mouth, blowing lightly upon its tip and all the way down to the end of the stem. The feather quivered between Lucretia's talons as its night-black fibers shifted, taking on a shimmering gilded hue.

She handed the newly golden feather to Marceline, bearing a ghost of a smile despite eyes that still glittered with sadness. "I cannae be bothered to let ye in every bloody time ye arrive. Ye need a key."

Gratitude lodged in Marceline's throat. When she found the right words to express what she felt, she was too choked up to say them. Instead, she whispered a mere "Thank you," though the phrase felt insufficient. For this was more than a feather. More than a key, even.

It was a token of friendship.

CHAPTER 17

Long Ago

In the Hut of the Unclaimed, Bronagh twitched beneath the threadbare blanket, haunted by images of the goddess's piercing eyes, her callous indifference as she'd scoffed at the memory of Bronagh's mother.

With a sharp inhalation, the seedling of a thought sprang into existence. It sprouted, unfurling in black tendrils, multiplying into curling vines of darkness. And in her mind's eye, Bronagh sewed these vines together into a plan. The grand tapestry of her revenge.

Time was of the essence. Quill's prophecy had said the invaders would come soon. But *how* soon? *Perhaps it didn't matter*, Bronagh thought. If Quill was to take over as goddess after the battle, Bronagh had to kill her before then. She had to kill *both* of them before then, and take this feather—the source of the goddess's divine power—for herself.

Bronagh's lip curled. In a way, it was a merciful move. Clearly Quill had no desire to be a goddess. She was only rescuing her from an unwanted fate.

She stared at the thatched ceiling, her plan morphing into a living, breathing thing. The laws of her people dictated that except in the case of divine sacrifice, killing was prohibited. But why follow the laws of a clan who'd never shown her kindness?

The world had given her pain, and now, she would return it.

Her heart pounded out a giddy rhythm as she imagined Quill's despair when she finally learned how it felt to see her mother die at the hand of her sister.

The last feeling she would ever feel.

Bronagh stifled a cackle. She hadn't slept, and her skin was feverish and clammy, yet she felt unburdened and inspired and frightfully alive.

In the morning, when the last of the orphans left the hut, Bronagh pulled on her tunic. She had to bite her lip to mask the manic excitement bubbling within her as she went from hut to hut, collecting soiled garments to be washed, as usual. The villagers eyed her warily, sensing a change in her. Bronagh only leered back. Who cared what they thought? Soon, she'd rule over them—those who survived, anyway. Her fingers tingled with anticipation as she gripped her basket.

It was torturous, this waiting for nightfall.

The sound of a horn blasted Bronagh out of her thoughts, summoning the villagers to converge toward the stump where the worry-crumpled chief perched, surrounded by his druids—solemn and still as a grove of fir trees. On their outskirts stood Quill, misery marring the hateful symmetry of her features.

"My—my people," the chief fumbled, pausing to wipe his brow. "Ye may be wondering why I canceled the Feast of the Goddess's Daughter." He stalled again, worry etching lines into his forehead. "The truth is, war is upon us."

A rumble of fear spread through the crowd.

"The daughter of the Raven Queen has revealed that the enemy shall arrive in three days. Many summers have passed since our village last faced the tumult of war. Now, I call ye to battle once more. Any man fit enough to fight must take up arms. Training begins at once."

The crowd erupted with worry—men putting on brave faces while their wives and mothers wrung their hands, a cacophony of prayers rising in a desperate crescendo as the chief stepped down from the stump.

"Silence!" The High Druid took his place, his booming voice robbing the sound from the villagers' tongues. "Those of ye aged enough to remember our last battle will recall how the Great Goddess demanded a sacrifice." A tremor of terrified murmurs broke out once more, but this time the druid silenced the crowd with a mere look. "On this morn, the bodies of two slain fawns were discovered at the foot of the sacred oak. I read their entrails myself. There was but one conclusion: If we wish to defeat the invading hordes, we must appease the Raven Queen, for she is the Goddess of Battle, the Queen of Bloodlust. And nae with a petty criminal. Ye've heard the bard's tales—in times of desperation, only a true sacrifice will do. A maiden—one who has lain with nae man."

Now the crowd erupted into a panic not even the High Druid could silence. But no one looked as panicked as Quill.

"Nae!" Quill leapt upon the stump, almost knocking over the stern druid as he scrambled out of her way. "There shall be nae sacrifices. Maidens or otherwise! I—" She swallowed, eyes flitting over the crowd. When her gaze crossed her sister's, Bronagh glared. "I have spoken to my mother, and she, uh, forbids it."

The chief and druids exchanged baffled looks.

"Daughter of the Goddess, how is this possible?" Suspicion sparked beneath the High Druid's bushy brows. "The gods have demanded sacrifices since our great green land came to be..."

"Aye." Quill swallowed. "But times have changed. She nae longer believes in bloodshed."

The High Druid did not bother to stifle his scoff. "The Goddess of Death and Battle nae longer believes in bloodshed?"

"Dinnae question me!" Quill's voice rang out, piercingly shrill. Bronagh smirked. She'd never seen such a bad liar in her life. "Dinnae make me bring the wrath of my mother down upon yer heads!" Her voice quivered, but now the druids were grumbling among themselves. Did they truly believe her bluff, obvious as it was? Finally, the chief cleared his throat and set a timid hand on Quill's tensed shoulder. Anxiety marred Quill's face as she stepped down, letting him take her place again.

"They'll be nae maidens sacrificed, if that's what the goddess wills," he announced, careful not to look at the High Druid, who may as well have been launching poisoned spears from his eyes. "Instead, I ask that each family offer their finest animal, be it a sheep or goat or bull." For a moment Quill seemed about to protest, but she held her tongue. "Now, we've nae more time to waste. Let the preparations commence."

He blew one long, blasting note into his horn, signaling the end of the announcement.

The entire village rumbled with frenetic foreboding as the crowd dispersed. The blacksmith scrambled to his forge, already dripping with sweat as he set it alight. Weathered warriors ran to fetch their swords and spears, fear reflected in their shields. Grim-faced women converged, carrying sacks of woad seedpods to grind to a blue pulp with which the warriors would paint themselves.

Only Bronagh stood still, soaking in the atmosphere of panic, thrilling in its jittery wake. Despite the rays of frigid morning sun piercing through the thick fog, the air seemed to crackle with fear.

Bronagh's knife was so battered and dull it could barely slice mutton anymore, but in all the chaos it wasn't difficult to steal a better one. She'd need it. After all, she was a mere mortal—one without battle experience—taking on a goddess of war. Still, she knew the stories. Gods could be outwitted. One only had to be clever—perhaps not even that. Perhaps one only needed to be rash.

When night at last fell, Bronagh slid her pilfered dagger into her belt and crept toward the woods. She wove through the brambles until she found the clearing, then skirted its perimeter. Concealing herself in the foliage, she waited, turning over the plan in her mind, and the blade in her hands.

When the dark shape of a raven passed over the moon, Bronagh crouched low in the brambles, following the bird's trajectory. It crossed the sky three times, coming to a graceful landing on the lowest branch of the sacred oak.

The goddess.

Bronagh's palms began to sweat. What if the Raven Queen remained in bird form, able to fly out of reach? She gripped the dagger's hilt tighter, blood pumping thick with fear and hatred. Part of her ached to strike now and be done with it. But no—Quill had to be here. She had to witness her vengeance, or it would not be as sweet.

If the goddess knew of Bronagh's presence, she didn't show it. She remained on her branch, as if made of stone.

At last, the music of crackling footsteps reached Bronagh's ears. The raven's beak turned, pointing toward her approaching daughter. When Quill slunk into the clearing the leaves stirred, nature's own rustling voice swelling as the raven's wings and legs elongated into human limbs, feathers receding into swirling blue patterns on moonlit skin. Her beak flattened into a delicate nose, feathers uncoiling into a billowing mane.

A whisper of fear leaked into Bronagh's veins. *This* was her opponent. It had been easier to envision defeating her when she was out of sight. She wiped the sweat from her palm and steadied her blade. At least the transformation was slow. At least her foe would not have time to morph back into bird form and fly away the moment Bronagh attacked her.

The sulking Quill hardly glanced at her mother's supernatural display. She approached the oak, worry etched upon her features.

"Take heed or yer face'll stick that way, Fledgling." The goddess smirked, obsidian eyes glittering.

"I cannae help it." Quill tucked her arms beneath her thick cloak. "I've known these people my whole life, Mother, and now, now they're going to be slaughtered—"

"Dinnae start with me. The sooner ye learn to see them as a source of amusement, the better."

"Amusement? Mother, they have lives! They have children and wives and husbands—"

The goddess cut her off with a harsh caw. "Compose yourself. Do ye nae realize we have company?" Her gaze shot through the thickets and brambles, right at Bronagh.

Quivering in her boots, Bronagh shoved the knife into her cloak, hoping against hope the goddess hadn't seen it. She'd meant to sneak up on them, but Quill's talk had distracted her. Quill—whining, ungrateful Quill. Hatred swelled in Bronagh's blood, consuming even her fear as she stepped into the clearing and dipped into a mocking curtsy.

"The orphan returns." The goddess's words rang sharper than the dagger in Bronagh's cloak. "Stand up. What is it ye want?"

"Mother!" Quill gaped in alarm between her mother and sister. "How can ye call her that when ye're the one who—"

"Silence!"

Fear and hatred congealed in Bronagh's throat. She couldn't utter a sound. How foolish she'd been, to think she could kill a divine being.

"I asked ye a question," the goddess screeched.

It was too much.

Bronagh's rage crashed over her, releasing a cry that sent birds scattering from the treetops. She charged, blade flashing with moonlight.

Eyes blazing, the goddess bounded to her feet, feathers detonating from her arms.

"Nae!" Quill screamed, lunging to block the blow.

Bronagh shoved her aside. "Wait yer turn," she snarled.

The goddess cackled, flexing her gleaming talons. "Just when I thought humans could surprise me nae more, here comes one foolish enough to challenge me."

"Bronagh, 'tis nae worth it! She can slay ye a thousand different ways!"

"Shut up, Quill." Bronagh lunged at the Winged One, who spun away, slicing a talon across Bronagh's cheek. Bronagh recoiled, gasping at the pain singeing her from jaw to brow, the hot blood trickling from the fault line of her wound.

"Please go, Sister," Quill begged. "This is but bairn's play for her."

"I said shut up, Motherslayer," Bronagh hissed. Plan be damned! She no longer cared who died first, so long as they both died. Her dagger glinted and plunged, burrowing into the flesh of Quill's shoulder.

Quill's scream shattered the forest, more squawk than human cry.

"Fight, Fledgling!" the Winged One shrilled, wings furling and unfurling with such force the earth shook beneath her feet. "Fight like I've taught ye!" The edges of Bronagh's rage fizzled with pleasure at the note of fear in the goddess's voice. But she had no time to gloat, for the enemy was upon her.

She tried to twist away but the goddess snatched the dagger as if it was nothing, flinging it into the grass. Bronagh lunged after it, but talons sank into her sides, smearing pain across her vision.

"Dinnae touch me," Bronagh screamed, struggling to rip herself free.

"Mother," Quill sobbed. "Please! Unhand her or I'll—I'll nae succeed ye. I'll nae accept the Eternal Feather!"

The goddess spun in a flurry of black wings, jerking Bronagh along. "Quill! Ye cannae refuse—"

"She's my *sister*," Quill screeched, staggering, blood pouring from her wounded shoulder. Bronagh thrashed in the goddess's grip, her dagger taunting her, out of reach.

"She's nae more your sister than this tree is! And she just stabbed ye!"

"Nae, listen to me!" Quill shrilled, voice thick with sobs, with pain. "Ye cannot go around destroying lives just because ye have power! Can ye not blame her for her anger?"

"Ye must let me heal ye before ye bleed out," the Winged One cried, lunging for her daughter. Her grip on Bronagh's sides loosened by a hair. "I'll nae have ye die before—"

One moment of slack was all Bronagh needed. She jerked away from the goddess, lunging for her blade. Propelled by fury, she grabbed it, spinning on her heels. With one desperate motion, she slashed the moonbeam flesh beneath the goddess's breasts.

The goddess staggered backward, her screech tearing the fabric of the world as Bronagh plunged her hand into the wound.

Her frantic fingers probed the tangled web of slick sinew and organs beneath the goddess's ribs. And then the prize was in her grasp. Her entire being shuddered with pure triumph as power shot through her fingertips, sending lightning slicing to her core and crackling through her extremities as she gripped the pulsating stem. She could live forever, destroy anything and anyone in her path. So long as she had the Eternal Feather.

She curled her fist around it as the Winged One writhed, red-faced, choking on her own vomit. With a sickening squelch Bronagh retracted her hand, pulling the dripping black feather from the bloody carnage of the goddess's chest.

"Nae!" Quill screamed.

With barely an instant of shuddering hesitation, Bronagh flipped the blade around and plunged it beneath her own ribs, slicing across like one might gut a stag. The edges of the world began to fade around her as death crept closer—she needed a moment more, just one moment—blood spewed hot from the wound, her own strength seeping into the ground. *One moment*, she pleaded against time. *One moment to show them I am worthy. That I am strong. Please.*

Her hand rose haltingly to her chest, fighting the air around it. And with her one last inkling of consciousness, she drove the feather into her own heart.

CHAPTER 18

After two months of sneaking out in the mornings and returning buzzing with paranoia in the afternoons, Marceline finally let her guard down.

The timing could not have been worse.

Later, she wondered why Baxter had bothered to lock the door. Whether his intention had been to trick her into thinking she was safe, only to terrify her an instant later. But in the moment, as she slipped her key into the apartment's lock and walked inside, then abruptly stopped in her tracks, there was only room for one thought: Baxter.

He was home early.

He sat in the tattered armchair, his ankle crossed lazily over his other knee, watching her. He'd turned the chair 180 degrees so it faced the door, as if he wanted to enjoy the full effect of her reaction. A wicked gleam shone in the stormy gray of his eyes, one she'd rarely seen. *Caught you*, the look said. And he had.

"Hello, Marceline." His voice was cruelly casual, a cheerful melody riding on the enraged baseline of his fury.

She cleared her throat, hands jammed in her pockets to keep them from trembling. "You're... you're here..."

"I am," he agreed. "Someone spilled coffee all over me today at lunch, so I came home for a clean shirt. Now, imagine my surprise when I came back to find the apartment empty. Imagine how it made me feel to wait all afternoon for you, not knowing where you were."

A hundred excuses rushed through the dam of her mind, each more inadequate than the last. "A-a w-walk," she sputtered. "I went for a walk."

"Naturally," Baxter said, then paused. Marceline calcified in the doorway, terrified of what he'd say next. "And did that walk take place in San Francisco, by any chance, or was it just up and down the aisle of the bus?"

So, he'd seen her get off the bus. He must have been watching from the window. She swallowed, acutely aware of the sweat beading her hairline. "I . . ."

It was a small mercy that he didn't wait for her to finish.

"I asked you what you did the other day, Marce. I told you not to lie to me—something I shouldn't even have to say—and you promised you wouldn't. So, I'm going to ask you again. Where have you been going, Marceline?" There was a gleam of triumph in his eyes, as if he'd been waiting for this moment.

Paralyzed in his crosshairs, Marceline sweated, staring and panicking. Was there any excuse he'd buy? Lying by omission was one thing, but she was no actress, and the guilt was already suffocating her—almost as much as the constraints he wound around her. But how could she tell him the truth? What if he forbade her from ever going back? Or worse, from leaving the house at all? She couldn't—no—*wouldn't* give up the café. Not now. It was unfathomable.

But in the end, Baxter made the decision for her. Like he always did.

"This isn't about that ridiculous job idea of yours, is it?"

So, he knew. She stood stock-still, unable to think of a single convincing denial, knowing all the while that her silence was damning her.

She scraped the walls of her brain for an answer, coming away with a one last, pathetic idea. Her go-to. "I just wanted to save money for the baby."

Her words dropped like a bomb, a mushroom cloud of silence expanding in their wake, filling the living room with menace. The last thing Marceline wanted to do was give Baxter the details of her deceit, but the longer she waited without saying anything, the greater her terror grew.

"It's just a few shifts at a café..." She wished she could swallow the words back up. It already felt like too much information. Baxter would want to know how she'd found out about the job, how far it was, how many hours... She struggled, desperate to hide the shallowness of her breaths as she racked her brain for the most inoffensive excuses. The silence only swelled, and she preemptively shrank into herself, bracing for the blow.

If Baxter's unscheduled presence in the apartment had shocked her, it was nothing compared to his reaction now. He sprang from his chair, lunging at her. Marceline cowered, bracing for impact. He'd never hit her before, but then again, she'd never defied him so blatantly. But the blow did not come. Instead, his arms swung around her, encircling her in a hug so fierce her face rammed into his sternum.

"Babe," he growled, voice muffled by her hair. "Why didn't you just tell me? How could I ever resent you for trying to help our family?"

She stiffened in his arms, shell-shocked. Why would he resent her? She thought about how she'd had to ask for his permission, and how he'd instantly refused, even though she'd used the very same excuse. How seconds before he'd called the idea "ridiculous." Was he messing with her? Her head swam, confusion clouding her thoughts. None of it made sense.

Baxter finally released her but continued to stare into her eyes as he gripped her shoulders, the black holes of his irises probing hers. "Here's what we're going to do, babe. You're gonna keep on working. And whenever you get paid, you bring that paycheck to me, and I'll take it straight to the bank and deposit it into our baby fund. Sound good?"

The invisible noose around her neck tightened as she nodded, and he yanked her toward him again, crushing her in another embrace. This was not the time to tell him she was merely volunteering. Money, she thought, desperate. I need money, *quick*. But how was she going to get it? Was there any way Lucretia might agree to pay her?

"We're getting takeout," Baxter announced as he freed her again—the joy in his voice almost enough to convince her that everything would be okay. "I feel like celebrating our future, don't you?"

"Absolutely," she choked, praying she sounded genuine.

This time, the whisper of the storeroom ghost didn't need to needle its way through Marceline's mind, nor did she need Lucretia to serve her another harsh truth. The thought arose all on its own:

This could not go on.

CHAPTER 19

Long Ago

Currents of ecstasy rippled from the feather in Bronagh's chest, dulling the sting of the talons digging into her sides, lifting her body into the air. She teetered on the edge of consciousness, shuddering with the wildest pleasure she'd ever known. Hardly aware of the forest spinning around her, the flurry of black feathers smearing the trees, and the pearlescent moon in the twinkling gemstone sky. All of it seemed so small, so far below, blurring into a distant and nonsensical dance of shapes and impressions.

Even Quill's bloodcurdling scream faded as Bronagh sank into the hypnotic flap of wings. The world peeled away, revealing the whirling emptiness beneath. *The Otherworld*, Bronagh's heart whispered into the chaos. She could almost taste the foreign tang of immortal dirt on her lips.

And then she was plummeting.

With a jolt, it all stopped: the tingling magic of the feather, the dizzying whirl of the universe around her—all of it replaced by the brutal hardness of the ground and the menace of sudden darkness. Bronagh scrambled to her feet, her whole body throbbing from impact, from the violent withdrawal of that sweet power. She blinked, struggling to adjust her eyes without a single glimmer of light.

The goddess's voice filled her head—a weak croak, the sound of suffering: "Ye'll pay, Orphan. Ye'll rot here for eternity, sustained only by grief and darkness."

"Ye forget I have yer power," Bronagh snapped, even as she stumbled, unmoored by the stifling void. "I have yer feather inside of me. Try and take it back, I dare ye." She spun in a clumsy circle, desperate to find her bearings, but her other senses revealed nothing but a cold draft, a faint, rotting smell, and the uneven ground beneath.

"Ye fool!" The goddess's belabored speech reverberated from nowhere and everywhere. "The Eternal Feather will nae obey ye here."

Bronagh's stomach dropped. Not obey? After all she'd done to possess it? "Why nae kill me then, like ye did my mother?" She grasped for a pinprick of hope in the all-consuming darkness.

"That would be mercy, Orphan. And I am nae a merciful goddess..." Her voice waned, a jarring, disjointed whisper. A pale light flickered some paces away. Bronagh spun to face it. The outline of a great wooden door loomed, lit only by a weak, glowing smear limping toward it.

"You cannae contain me," Bronagh screamed, lunging toward the light. But the air thickened around her, viscous as quicksand, tugging her down. "Mark my words, I'll escape. I will!"

She grunted with effort, dread fluttering in her unmoving limbs as the distant light stretched and solidified into the goddess's mostly human form, no longer tall and proud. Instead, she crouched, wings twitching and sticking out at wrong angles as she twisted to pluck a feather from her head. She bent toward the door, hand shaking as it stretched, pointing the feather's stem into the metal mechanism—the *lock*—the word dropped into Bronagh's mind, though she'd never seen such a thing in the village.

The feather's ebony fibers shifted to glinting gold. Then, a resounding *click* shuddered through the darkness.

"Thief," the goddess whispered, and Bronagh cried out as the side of her neck flared with a searing pain. She clapped her hand to it, but unlike her blood-seeping face she could feel no gash. She'd been marked. She couldn't see it, but somehow, she knew.

"May ye remain"—the goddess's voice was naught but a faint squawk now—"in this place..."— Bronagh could hear the words fighting their way out—"forevermore." The sound died, leaving behind only the rustle of jerking wings, a rasping, belabored croak.

The goddess shrank to a mere pinprick. And then she was gone, whisking every trace of light away with her.

Still rooted to the ground, Bronagh clutched at her throbbing neck until the air released its hold on her limbs.

Arms outstretched, she stumbled forward, searching for a wall. Eventually she found its rough surface, following it until splinters raked her fingertips. She pawed at the door until her hands bled. Until nausea wrapped around her. She found nothing.

The lock and handle had vanished.

Bronagh slumped to her knees. The surge of power in her chest had all but disappeared, replaced by a dull ache. She screamed a blood-curdling cry, but all her pain and rage bounced back at her in a mocking echo.

It did not help.

A gaping emptiness opened like a chasm within her. She sat motionless. Numb.

Time passed.

It might have been years, or merely moments, but eventually, the darkness opened itself to Bronagh, and shapes began to emerge from the gloom. The vague outline of something long and flat marred the drafty emptiness—a slab of wood spanning one wall like an elongated table.

Behind it, shelves had been carved into rough stone, laden with rows and rows of strange, dusty jugs.

Mustering a faint glimmer of curiosity out of her despair, she dragged herself upright to examine them. The jugs glinted through strings of cobwebs. She wiped a finger across the dust. They were not made of fired earth like those from the village kiln, but of a transparent, foggy material that looked like the loch's surface on a cloudy day. The word came to her: *glass.*

She grabbed a bottle off the shelf and yanked the stopper out. An acrid-smelling amber liquid sloshed inside. Ale, or something like it. Bringing the bottle to her lips, she gulped down the strange drink, hoping to find solace in its contents.

She tasted nothing. No wetness, no flavor, no sting on the tongue. Nothing at all. Her anger brimmed, overflowing as she smashed the bottle to the ground. Snatching a new one from the shelf she ripped the cork out. Again, nothing traveled down her throat, save bitter emptiness.

Soon all the bottles had been smashed and Bronagh sat hugging her knees, surrounded by jagged shards. This was her life now. And she would never die, thanks to that accursed feather. In a fit of fury, she ripped open her tunic and clawed at her chest, raking deep gashes into her skin—which healed again, seconds later. Glass fragments reflected around her, defying the darkness, flashing her injuries cruelly back to her: The slice of the goddess's talon traced an angry trail from jaw to brow, and an inky black X—the mark of her thievery—marred the side of her neck like a curse.

Bronagh simmered in her rage for hours before resolving to sleep. There were no windows, so she knew not what hour it was. She'd find a solution in the morning, she told herself, if such a thing ever came.

Impervious to the stab of jagged glass shards, she cleared an area to sleep on. But when she closed her eyes, sleep refused to come.

She lay on the floor, glowering.

Slowly, time trickled by.

Slowly.

Slowly.

Quill lay huddled at the foot of the sacred oak, clutching her wounded shoulder when her mother swooped into the dark clearing, careening into the ground mid-transformation. Concern throbbed in Quill's head as she scurried toward the tangle of feathers and bruised human limbs.

"Mother! Are you all right? Where did you go?" She crouched before her, heart twisting with fear at the sight of the writhing goddess, the moonlight glimmering against the carnage of her open chest. "Mother?"

A pathetic half squawk squeezed through the goddess's lips. "I have nae felt pain"—the words were stunted, strained with effort—"in such a long time..."

A sob rose in Quill's throat. "Ye cannae die, Mother. What am I to do without ye? I'm nae fit to be a fierce goddess."

"Ye'll...ye'll have to be, Fledgling..."

"But the feather! I have nae power, nor even wings or talons, and I have so much training left to—"

"Hush, Fledgling." The goddess struggled to push herself up, but her forearms gave out and she crumpled back into the grass. "Ye have my blood. Perhaps 'tis enough..."

"And Bronagh! What happened to her? Did ye—"

"She's contained in a realm of the Otherworld, marked as a thief of power."

"Oh, thank ye, Mother! Thank ye for showing mercy."

"I'd have killed her if I had the strength." The goddess reached for her daughter's cheek. "But listen, Quill. Ye'll always be linked to her. She cannae leave without the key, nor can she simply die, now that she has the Eternal Feather. One day, she'll escape, and 'twill be easy for her to find ye, for the feather will want to return to yer heart, its rightful home. Ye must reclaim it, Quill. When the time comes. Take the feather back…" Her trembling talons stippled her daughter's jaw.

"If only *she'd* been born a goddess of war and death and carnage, and nae I!" Quill whimpered, her despair hardening like a cage around her.

"There's nae use dwelling on such things, Fledgling." The goddess's eyelids slid half closed, breath stuttering.

"Nae, stay with me," Quill pleaded.

The dying goddess's voice was barely a whisper now. "Ah, my Quill… always too sentimental…"

"Please!"

"Aye, I'll take ye away to where ye can mourn," she gasped, every passing second a ragged struggle. "But ye must return…ye must promise ye'll take back yer power, so the Great Winged One does nae disappear from this world…"

Quill bit down against the torrent of tears, sweat, and snot.

"Say it, Quill!"

"I promise," she sobbed, unable to deny her mother her dying wish.

"Come, Fledgling." With her final droplet of strength, the goddess encircled her trembling talons around her daughter.

The mortal world warped, grief blurring the trees and moon, the brambles and grass, curling at the edges of everything Quill had ever known. Like the end of a long sigh, it all faded into oblivion.

When the motion stopped, the world had vanished. The clearing in the forest, the sacred oak, her mother's trembling grip—all of it gone.

Quill was alone.

For a time, she could only sob, clutching her knees as the space around her flashed in tearstained glimpses. She'd never asked to be a goddess. In the past, she'd often wished to be free of the burden of her inheritance. But not like this. Never like this.

When at last her sobs faded to stillness, she lifted her head from her knees, taking in the room around her. Stone walls. Straw-matted floor. Was this truly the Otherworld? Her mother had told her the Otherworld contained a multitude of realms. If this was one of them, it seemed no different from the village huts, save for its lack of windows. The room might have felt like a prison, if not for the soft sourceless light permeating its interior.

She curled into herself, gripped by a silence so complete only her heartbeat punctuated it. The subtle warmth of the place comforted her body, but her mind and heart were beyond reach.

She lost herself in grief.

In solitude.

In time.

And then—hours or days, months or years later—there came a knock. Unable to muster enough energy to raise her head, Quill remained curled on the ground. The second knock succeeded in rousing her from her despondent state. She dragged herself upright and turned toward the door, with its carved patterns of intricate, swirling feathers that made her want to die, so much did they remind her of her mother.

Something sharp scratched at her temple as she wiped her eyes. When she pulled her hand away, she stumbled backward in shock. Talons. Long and black and curling, like her mother's. A natural gift unconnected to the missing feather, it would seem. Her grief erupted again, but now, she waited for it to recede. Running a newly taloned hand through her hair confirmed her suspicion: The texture was all wrong, thick and curling and oddly stiff. She pulled a strand over her shoulders, examining the curl of the jet-black feathers. Her gaze traveled to her arms, where swirling blue patterns snaked past her elbows. Patterns from which more feathers would eventually sprout.

A final knock pulled her away from herself. Cautiously, she crept closer to the door.

She pulled it open, then stumbled backward, startled by the wall of black clouds churning behind it—an expanse of crackling thunder and groaning lightning, scattering the serenity of the silent stone room. Quill clapped her hands over her ears. It was too much. She lunged forward to slam the door shut, when a black shape darted past her into the room.

A thousand panicked thoughts flapped through her mind: Bronagh had escaped! She was going to finish what she'd started. But the panic cleared as Quill's eyes settled on the shape.

The shape of a raven.

Quill began to shake. "Mother?"

With a caw, the bird flapped up to the rafters—rafters that hadn't been present moments before.

"Mother, is that you?"

The bird stuck its beak beneath its wing and began to nibble at some itch. Then it shat. A thick white blob splatted onto the straw-covered floor.

Not Mother, then.

Quill shut the door against the brewing storm, relief swelling within her as she savored the stillness. Above her head, the raven made itself comfortable, as if it were returning home to its perch after a long day.

And perhaps it was.

CHAPTER 20

This truth needled at Marceline as the long, café-less weekend stretched before her. *This could not go on*. It burrowed deep into her skull, shifting the earth beneath every interaction she had with Baxter—who, strangely, did not say another word about the café.

It didn't make sense. She'd thought for sure once the secret was out, Baxter would pester her for every detail. Where was the café located? How had she found it, given that she was mostly housebound? Who were her coworkers, her employers? She was sure he'd insist on driving her there and personally inspecting the place where his wife spent so many hours of her day. But no. Baxter seemed to display no curiosity whatsoever about the secret she'd been harboring for so long.

It's not that she wasn't grateful. The very idea of divulging the café's magic would have felt like the most grievous sin, and any interrogation would have been torturous. But however fortunate, no amount of analysis could help Marceline understand her husband's uncharacteristic behavior.

Something didn't add up.

But there was an even more immediate issue she needed to deal with. Now, she had money to worry about.

The idea of giving her nonexistent paychecks over to Baxter had rattled her. If she told him she wasn't being paid, he would immediately forbid her from ever returning, she was sure of it. She'd never see Lucretia again, or Kilda. Or Sylvan. A tremor of sadness shot through her. No, she thought, handing Baxter his coat as he left the house on Monday morning and pecking him quickly on the cheek. No, she couldn't let that happen. She had to find a solution, and fast.

This could not go on.

She ran to the bedroom to watch his car drive away. Ordinarily at this time, she'd be getting dressed to go to the café. But her time alone was precious, and she couldn't put off this fact-finding mission.

Lamenting that she wouldn't see her friends today, she approached the laptop on the kitchen table, the feather key she'd tucked into her bra—she'd been keeping it there so it would be hidden—radiating courage into her heart. It was impossible not to keep glancing at the door. Mustering the courage, Marceline opened the laptop and typed in Baxter's password with trembling hands.

Not knowing where to begin, she opened a browser window and typed: *Can people change?* Half-holding her breath, she skimmed the topmost articles, skipping past the psychological jargon and overly scientific language until she found a cluster of more relatable blog posts written by a therapist.

She read one article, then another, and another, concluding that yes, people *could* change, but only after a great deal of self-awareness. But informing Baxter that she felt smothered and trapped didn't feel like something he'd react well to, and she had no doubt he'd punish her by tightening her restrictions even more. Or was she being unfair? She thought again about his strange and sudden acceptance of the café. All weekend she'd puzzled over it, trying to make sense of Baxter's abrupt change of heart. The chance that he'd want to work on their relationship was slim, but she didn't want to dismiss it completely. After five years together, he deserved a little more faith than that.

Didn't he?

Feeling suddenly queasy, she kept reading, noticing how certain words continuously popped up. *Gaslighting*, for example. She'd heard the word before on TV talk shows, but she'd never known the exact definition. When she googled it, her heart plummeted to her stomach. *Gaslighting: to psychologically manipulate someone, making them question their own sanity.* She thought of how Baxter had initially shut down the job conversation, then suddenly implied he'd always been fine with it, and how it was silly of her to think otherwise. She'd genuinely wondered if she'd misinterpreted his thoughts on the matter. But no, of course she hadn't. He'd been manipulating her.

This was toxic behavior.

Though the past five years had taught her she was the guilty party in every conflict by default, the testimonials peppering the articles—stories containing achingly familiar details—swam before her eyes, pulsing with relevance.

Realizing she was breathing hard, she tore her eyes from the laptop and went to get herself a glass of cold water. Gulping it down, she tried to clear her thoughts. If she was honest with herself, it seemed unlikely Baxter would ever change. She needed a plan B. She glanced at the door, her heart thundering with betrayal and guilt as she returned to her seat and typed her next question: *How do I leave my husband?*

The nausea spread, a tropical storm of anxiety battering her insides as she scrolled through the advice. Advice telling her to open her own bank account, which was a moot point, since she had no money. Advice telling her to contact friends or family she could stay with—again, she had no one, aside from her café friends. Would Lucretia let her stay there until she got on her feet? She couldn't imagine getting turned away, but the thought of asking made Marceline feel pathetic.

Anxiety roiled, deep in the pit of her stomach. All the advice seemed to apply to people with resources—more specifically, money. Money to save, money for lawyers, money for an apartment... Marceline wanted to cry. She'd already promised Baxter all her future hypothetical paychecks. Could she leave before that became relevant? The thought made her quiver—there was a huge difference between conducting a bit of research and actually going through with a plan.

Even if she did manage to leave and somehow find a miraculously cheap apartment, her potential landlord would still have to run a credit check. And to have a credit score, one needed a credit card—something Baxter wouldn't grant her in a million years. She'd thought her lack of control was a normal part of being a wife. The more she read, the more she realized her situation was anything but normal.

Soon, three hours had slipped by, and any hope she'd managed to gather had melted into thick, sludgy despair.

She closed the search engine and shut the laptop, positioning it exactly where she'd found it. She had zero motivation for chores. Instead, she went back to bed, staring glumly at her globe lamp and wondering what Sylvan, Lucretia, Kilda, and the others were doing right now.

That night Marceline lay in bed, staring at the shifting shadows on the ceiling. Between the deep rumble of Baxter's snores and the looping echo of the ghost's words in her head, she wanted to scream. Instead, she crammed a pair of orange earplugs in her ears, then lay beneath the ratty quilt, thinking herself into a fury.

I'll never leave him. She'd told herself that so many times the truth of it had rusted her brain into paralysis, making any alternative impossible to fathom. Now, she forced herself to fathom it. Could her life truly be different? The café had given her a taste of autonomy, and yet, even now that the truth was out, it seemed like it was only a matter of time before Baxter tightened her bonds. She was flabbergasted he hadn't done it already.

And if that was true, she *had* to leave, didn't she? She'd tolerated her life up until now because she hadn't realized there were other options. Now that she'd experienced freedom, how could she give it up?

She wanted to believe she could make it on her own, even though Baxter thought— No! She flinched, so violent was her refusal of his toxic ideas, then stilled, worrying she'd woken him. Thankfully, he only grunted, repositioning himself in his sleep.

He'd convinced her she couldn't survive without him, but then again, Marceline's grandmother had been a single woman who'd lived on her own terms, answering to no one. Why, then, couldn't she do the same?

Sylvan's gentle smile passed through her mind, and for once, she allowed herself to linger on the warmth spreading through her body. Lucretia had joked more than once that the two of them were peas in a pod. If Marceline was honest, she *did* think of him more than she should, and yes, she sometimes wondered what it would be like to be held by him, enveloped by softness. What did it matter? It was a fantasy. How could she even be thinking about this right now?

Thoughts swam in her mind as—for the first time in her life—she allowed herself to contemplate the possibilities. But beneath the whirlwind, there still hid a truth she could not ignore: Leaving Baxter would devastate him. People had been leaving him all his life. First his drug-addicted mother, then the long string of indifferent foster parents. Could she really leave him too?

Lucretia's cranky retort from the first night they'd met snaked into her mind. *I did nae ask for yer husband's psychological profile. Do ye like yer life?* Marceline had answered yes, but it had been a lie. Now that she realized it, how could she keep lying to herself?

She couldn't. She rolled over to face the window, her back to her husband. She *had* to put herself first.

CHAPTER 21

Long Ago

Bronagh didn't know how long she'd been trapped in her dark stone prison. It might have been hours, or days, or years. It might have even been centuries, perhaps more. She gazed into the gloom, stewing in bitterness as time trickled meaninglessly onward, and no one came to amend her cruel sentence. Solitude settled over her, metastasizing into her bones, congealing her truth into a hardened mass: Anything she did now was justified.

She lay in a heap on the dusty ground, catatonic in her misery, when a shuffling sound snapped her out of her sleepless state.

It came from the door. The realization sliced through her inertia. She'd wasted all her energy screaming herself raw, slamming her body against its planks until her bones ached. Now, she scrambled toward the door again, desperate to seize her chance to escape.

It swung open before she reached it. Bronagh shoved past the man in the doorway, crashing forehead-first into something solid. Pain taunted her skull as she picked herself up, half stunned, and tried again. Another burst of pain confirmed her fear: Some invisible barrier blocked her from the starless, whirling expanse beyond the door. Sick with bitterness, she groped at the empty space, fingertips scraping against a rough surface she couldn't see. Meanwhile, the door itself gaped mockingly open.

Bronagh's furious howl ripped through the empty space. Disgusted, her eyes fell upon the man she'd shoved aside.

Shock gnarled his drooping, wrinkled face as he struggled to pick himself up off the floor, aided by a walking stick tied with jangling bells. He was oddly dressed in a colorful tunic, his knobby, thin legs covered in bright, red britches. On his head flopped a many-pointed hat that jangled with more silver bells.

"Art thou well, maiden?" Despite his eccentric garb, he looked at her as if *she* were the mad one.

Bronagh snarled, "Let me out of here at once."

"Out, mistress? I—I came only for some ale, but I see thou art distraught. I shall leave thee."

"Nae! Dinnae leave." The ferocity of her own cry shocked even her.

The strange old man peered at her as he hobbled to a table. A table that hadn't been there a moment ago—for the cavernous stone room was now furnished with not one, but three rough tables made of dark wood, each with a set of chairs.

"A flagon, maiden, for this old jester be out of spirits."

"Ye'll nae leave?" The edge of a threat rumbled in Bronagh's long-unused voice.

"Nay, mistress, I have nowhere to go."

That, at least, she could relate to. She turned to the wall of bottles. They glinted in a neat row. She'd smashed each one more times than she could count, yet they always reappeared unbroken. A long, high counter now spanned one wall, with rows of various-sized flagons stacked upon it. Choosing a bottle at random, Bronagh filled one for the man, who took a series of long gulps, before setting it back down with a *thud*.

"Another, mistress." He removed his strange hat to rub at his age-spotted scalp. Sparse tufts of gray clung to it like dandelion fluff.

Bronagh frowned. "Who are ye?"

He shook the hat in his hand, making the bells sing. "Why, I am the lord's fool. I dance and sing and make merry for the court. Or I did. My lord hath replaced me but an hour ago, for he claims I be too old." As the crotchety man twisted the hat in his hand, his eyes filled. He slammed his fist into the table with a mocking chorus of bells.

A sudden hankering swelled inside Bronagh as she watched the pathetic trickle of teardrops dribbling down the man's chin. Hunger, she realized, licking her lips. Not the kind that could be satisfied with a cut of mutton or turnip mash. This was different. She wanted—no, *needed*—this man to keep crying, to indulge in the depths of his own misery.

Ye'll rot here for eternity, sustained only by grief and darkness, the goddess had said.

But did it have to be her own?

The fierce, sudden rumbling of her stomach told her otherwise.

"Nae doubt they'll replace ye with someone more suitable," Bronagh said. Her insides palpitated with anticipation as the man sniveled, hurt. His reaction sent a faint rush of tingling satisfaction radiating outward from her heart—from the feather! Bronagh gasped. The goddess had claimed the Eternal Feather's magic would not obey her here, and yet, there was that feeling—subdued, yes, a diluted hit of magic, the ghost of power—but enough.

Enough to tell her the feather was awake.

The sweet shiver receded, replaced by a sharp, nipping fear when she imagined the old man reaching for his stick and leaving. But instead, he only bowed his head, crumpling his hat to the song of jangling bells.

Bronagh grinned as the fear receded. She would have to tread carefully, but she'd always been sly. This new game would fill her empty hours until she found a way out.

Until she was free to test the power of the feather—*her* power—unrestrained.

"Well, go on, fool." Her insides bubbled with the first glimmer of hope since her dark imprisonment. "Unburden yerself. Tell me everything."

By the time the man left, Bronagh was buzzing, drunk on the greedy thrill of his misery, ravenous for more.

The jester was her first customer, but he would not be her last.

Time took on meaning again—still immeasurable, yes—but now filled with anticipation, with the agony of impatience as she waited behind her bar, perpetually polishing glasses that would only be coated in dust again moments later. Sometimes, when time yawned in interminable taunting stretches, she began to lose hope. Other times, customers came in throngs, each one bearing their own unique flavor of misery like an offering.

The Tavern, her customers called this place. They came bearing news of great changes, through a revolving door of new eras and social movements and mind-blowing inventions. Things Bronagh didn't understand but never asked about, for she soon learned that a bartender's job was to listen and bestow sparse glimmers of wisdom. She had to build trust, for without it, her customers' lips spilled no tragic secrets.

Even as the customers changed—their clothing, speech, and mannerisms plummeting forward into the future—so did Bronagh's own clothing, speech, and mannerisms. Tunics fell away, replaced by bustles and corsets, then jeans and T-shirts. Even her speech changed, as if the gaping leagues of time and space separating her from her native village had settled on her tongue, morphing its very composition.

In the face of eternity, change was a relief.

There was entertainment, too. With the advent of the television, boxy appliances appeared on the wall, broadcasting nightmares. A dartboard made of flesh wept with welling blood every time its surface was pierced. A billiard table overtook the center of the dark room, with venomous snakes slithering in every pocket.

The tavern was still her prison, but even prisoners required sustenance. So, she thrived as best she could in this dark place, drinking in the misery of others. Only two things never changed: the heavy black X marring the side of her neck—the same mark all her customers left with after their first visit—and the potency of her own hateful memories. Memories of the goddess, of Quill, of the despicable villagers who had rejected her.

And while time churned outside her tavern door, years drifting away into history's impassive oblivion, her thirst for revenge only continued to grow.

She became the Bartender.

CHAPTER 22

On Monday morning, Marceline hurried along the dirty alley to the café door. Nestling the feather key back into her bra, she removed her exhaustion like a coat, letting the tingling warmth of the café seep into her skin and soothe the anxiety that pulsed inside her—though it did not vanish completely.

"Marsupial! You are here today!" Sylvan greeted her. "Do you wish for coffee?" He handed her an apron. He looked as tired as she felt, but his smile still had the effect of a warm hug. "I was worried when you did not arrive yesterday."

"I just had some things to do. But yes, thank you." She gave him a weak smile, sliding her shoulder bag into a cubby before seating herself at the nearest table with a deep sigh. Maybe what she needed was to sit and decompress for a moment. "Actually, could I maybe have a tea? Something herbal?" She was already feeling jumpy enough without adding caffeine into the mix.

"At your service." Sylvan grinned.

Her nerves slowly calmed as she watched him rummage around behind the counter, chatting as he went. Basking in the warmth of his presence, she let it carry her away, layers of anxiety peeling off as she pushed Baxter to the back of her mind. She gave a little wave to Kilda and Lucretia, both poring over the map together near the fireplace, then took in the handful of customers—one familiar old man reading a book, and a pair of identical twin boys sharing an Italian soda.

Placing the teapot on a silver tray which he held high above his head, Sylvan approached her table. "Your beverage, madame," he said in an overly formal tone as he set it down, bowing like a waiter in a five-star restaurant.

"Why, thank you, sir." Marceline grinned, wishing she could simply never leave the café again.

"So, Marsupial..." Sylvan lingered beside the table. "I, uh, acquired you a thing."

Marceline flushed. "Like a present?" She was getting used to Kilda bringing her little sweets, but *this* was entirely new. Baxter's hypothetical opinion on this scuttled across her mind but she squashed it like the cockroach it was. "For me?"

"Yes. I mean, it is not so monumental. But, well, look."

He sat, pulling a little glass vial from his apron pocket. A transparent liquid sloshed behind the yellow-tinted glass. "Give me your wrist."

The heat in Marceline's cheeks had nothing to do with the blazing fire. "What? Why?"

Sylvan pulled the cap off the vial, chuckling, though she could see he was nervous. "Trust me."

Her skin flared with heat as his hand touched hers, flipping her arm over to expose the blue veins of her wrist. He dabbed a drop of liquid onto her skin.

She blinked. Perfume? Bringing her wrist beneath her nose, she inhaled. A heavenly floral aroma flooded her senses. "Tiaré?"

Sylvan's cheeks turned tomato red. "Because you said you wished to inhale what I inhaled? The day you met the brick? I hope this is okay. I did not wish to appear bizarre, or..." He trailed off.

Marceline stared at her wrist. "No one's ever given me perfume before." It startled her that she had to fight the sudden pull of tears. "Thank you *so* much."

Sylvan's face split into a grin bright enough to power a small city. "You enjoy it? I was going to pluck you a flower, but this has longevity."

"I love it." She beamed, basking in his glow, until a thought dimmed her excitement. "I won't be able to wear it, though. My husband..."

"Oh. Right." Sylvan's smile faded. "You cannot say you purchased it alone?"

Marceline looked down at her hands. "How? I don't have any of my own money, and I'm not even supposed to leave the house without him."

Sylvan looked stunned for a moment, his brow crinkling. "Oh. Wow. I did not realize—"

Marceline couldn't bear his troubled expression. She shrugged, desperate to change the subject. "I do love it, though. I'll smell it in the bottle." She closed her eyes, savoring the aroma. "I hope it wasn't expensive."

"Oh, no. This stuff resides in every shop on the island." His tone was casual, but he looked uncertain, like he was still hung up on Marceline's many restrictions. She needed to talk about something else.

"Tahiti! Oh, Sylvan, I have something for you too. Well, not *for* you, but, well, I'll show you. Hang on!" She launched herself from the table. She'd been carrying the book around for more than a month, waiting for the right moment to show him. She was reaching for her bag, when Lucretia intercepted her.

"Sylvan, lad, grab me some napkins from the storeroom, will ye?" the birdwoman called, banishing him to the far side of the room. She bent down, whispering in Marceline's ear. "Ye all right, there, Marce? Looks like the two of ye were having a moment."

"What? No, we were just talking." Marceline straightened, hating the blush creeping into her cheeks.

Lucretia put a talon on her shoulder, her flint eyes boring into Marceline's in a way that held far more meaning than she liked. "Just dinnae lead him on."

Marceline's eyes widened. "Lead him on? What do you mean?"

Lucretia sighed, releasing her. "Ye know what I mean. When ye're free of that husband of yers, ye can do what ye please, but Sylvan's been through enough. Dinnae toy with his heart."

Marceline swallowed. She wanted to protest, to tell her Sylvan was the one who'd given *her* a gift, and that she had them all wrong.

It would have been a lie.

Instead, she only nodded, feeling ashamed. Lucretia turned to go.

"I am going to leave him, though."

Marceline had only mumbled the words, but Lucretia whipped around. "Pardon?"

Marceline breathed deeply, keenly aware that she was finally giving voice to the feelings that had been lurking inside her for weeks now. Months. Maybe even years—the concept had been so long suppressed it was hard to say. "Yes, I've decided. I'm going to leave him." Tears stirred in her eyes without warning. She squeezed them back, confused by the jumbled rush of emotions.

For a moment, silence reigned. Then Lucretia released a *whoop* loud enough to scatter the birds above, and clapping Marceline on the back with such force she almost fell out of her chair. "About bloody time!" She ran to the storeroom door, knocking loudly. "Sylvan, come back here! 'Tis time for a family meeting." Within the span of a second, she'd swooped back and looped her arm through Marceline's. "Come now, we've got things to discuss!"

"I did not encounter napkins," Sylvan said, emerging from the storeroom.

"Because we dinnae have any," Lucretia hooted joyfully, tugging Marceline over to Kilda's table. "Did ye hear? She's finally going to leave the bastard!"

"*Lucretia!*" Kilda scolded, setting down her magnifying glass. "Be a wee bit more sensitive!"

"I'm proud of her! Can I nae be proud? Why the long face, Marce? 'Tis cracking news."

Sylvan approached with caution, eyes brimming with concern but edged with a glimmer of hope that made her want to throw herself into his arms and weep—in fact, the want of it compressed her from all sides—but of course, she couldn't.

Not yet.

"Congratulations, child." Kilda handed over a celebratory bar of chocolate from her pocket, like she'd been saving it for the occasion. "Ye're doing the right thing, 'tis quite unanimous. Ye're about to go through a big transition, but we'll be with ye every step of the way."

Again, Marceline had to fight to hold in her tears. What had she ever done to deserve such compassion? She looked at her feet. "The thing is, I don't know *how* to leave him."

Sylvan cleared his throat, obviously uncomfortable. "You ladies have a seat," he said, his smile heartbreakingly kind. "I will concoct more tea."

A moment later, with the smell of cinnamon tea wafting in steaming curls over their table, Marceline explained how Baxter had toyed with her, and what she dared research, and—timidly—the financial bind she was in.

"Well, if it makes ye feel better, I've never had a credit card either," Lucretia said.

Kilda shot her a look. "Nae helpful, love. Ye've been hiding away in an Otherworldly realm for centuries."

"Aye, true. But 'tis similar. Marce's husband has trapped her in her own realm too, away from the world."

Marceline shrugged glumly. Lucretia wasn't wrong.

"Perhaps you all are losing the point," Sylvan interjected.

"Well, what's the point, then?" Lucretia shot back.

"Clearly she needs funds, bird face!"

Lucretia huffed. "Someone ought to teach you some manners."

"What will you do, fire me?"

"Dinnae tempt me." She ruffled the black mop of his hair with her talons.

"Jesus! You could skewer an eyeball with those."

"Focus, the two of ye," Kilda chided. "Ye're a brave girl, Marce, asking for what ye want. That must have been hard for ye." Marceline nodded. Kilda had no idea. "The fact is, while the café has nae income to speak of, I daresay we're quite fond of ye. I've got some savings of my own, tucked away. Perhaps we can come to an arrangement." She glanced at Lucretia. "What do ye think, love?"

Shocked, Marceline held her breath. Lucretia was gazing at her wife, and their sudden silence made Marceline wonder whether they were telepathically communicating again.

"Aye," Lucretia agreed at last. "Perhaps we should. These are exceptional circumstances, after all." She glanced at Sylvan. "We cannae pay everyone, obviously..."

He waved the idea aside with his hand. "Marceline requires it more than I."

Marceline swallowed, touched beyond words, but not without a dash of shame. How had she managed to become a charity case? "I don't know if I could accept—"

"Consider it a personal loan from yers truly, if ye prefer," Kilda said. "One ye dinnae have to pay back until ye're ready."

"Oh, Kilda! Are you sure? I mean, that's so, so—"

Lucretia cut her off. "Good, 'tis settled."

The folds around Kilda's mouth arranged themselves into a cheerful smile. "Don't ye bother arguing, lass. Ye'll get naewhere." She pulled something out of her sweater pocket, setting it on the table before her. "Here, have another chocolate."

"This calls for a celebration," Lucretia announced, standing abruptly, a blue teacup in hand. "I believe I have something a tad stronger back here somewhere..." She sprang up and bolted toward her curtain, then stopped short. From the back, it looked like she had stiffened, as if suddenly remembering something urgent. And then she was plummeting.

Lucretia crashed to the ground, the teacup shattering beside her.

The birds took off. They dove from the rafters, a blur of feathers and color all flocking at once to where Lucretia lay as her body began to spasm and jerk, limbs and feathers flailing over the hardwood floor.

With a scrape of chairs, Marceline, Sylvan, and Kilda bounded toward her.

"What's happening?" Marceline knelt before Lucretia, shaking with fear as she shooed the birds away.

"A prophecy," Kilda gasped, hobbling after them on her cane. "An important one."

"Quick! Grab her!" Sylvan anchored a hand around Lucretia's ankle. Marceline reached for one of the birdwoman's arms as the other flew at her head. She shrieked and dodged, narrowly avoiding the curled talon that almost slashed her across the cheek. It batted the air, then swiped against Lucretia's other arm, slicing the top layer of blue-swirled flesh. The black beads of her eyes rolled back into her head. Marceline grabbed Lucretia's wrists, cuffing her into submission.

"She's speaking," Kilda wailed over the chaos. "Can ye hear what she's saying?"

Marceline pushed down on Lucretia's wrists, pinning her with all her weight—but the feathered woman was ropy and lean, her movements unpredictable. Her lips moved feverishly.

"I can't hear anything," Marceline shouted above the din of concerned birds—screeching owls and cooing pigeons, the manic chirp of sparrows. A heron dove toward Lucretia, its beak missing Marceline's face by mere inches. "Why are they doing this?"

"They are worried for her," Sylvan panted, struggling to anchor Lucretia's jerking legs. "Like us."

"How do we stop it?" Marceline cried. Falkirk swooped past her head, flying in low circles.

Then all at once, with a violent, full-body shudder, Lucretia went limp. The birds instantly settled. A ringing silence replaced the chaos.

"Lu?" Worry distorted Sylvan's voice. "Lu? You are fine?"

The same worry gripped Marceline as she let go of her friend's wrists.

"Can ye hear us, love?" Kilda trembled.

A taut silence filled the café—then at last, Lucretia shuddered, eyes shifting into focus. Falkirk landed on her collarbone, peering into her face. A collective sigh of relief rose in the air, but no sooner had Lucretia blinked than another shiver gripped her.

"Danger," she muttered, her panicked eyes shooting toward Kilda's. "It's coming."

"What do you intend, Lu?" Sylvan shot Marceline a worried look, before bending over Lucretia's arm to inspect the long scratch marring the blue patterns on her skin, inflicted by her own talon.

"We must prepare ourselves." Lucretia brushed Sylvan off and attempted to stand, but stumbled, weakened by her outburst. All three of them lunged forward to catch her, but it was Sylvan's hand that steadied her.

"Prepare ourselves for what?" Marceline prodded, heart racing. "Lu, are you okay?"

Falkirk landed on Sylvan's shoulder as Lucretia gained her footing, swaying on unsteady legs. She gawked at her surroundings, as if the very walls were inscribed with messages of doom. Her gaze found Kilda's again. Jaw clenched, her eyes transmitted some wordless message. The cartographer gasped.

"What is it? What's happening?" Marceline asked.

"After all this time . . ." Kilda whispered.

"After all this time *what*?" Sylvan interjected.

Neither Lucretia nor Kilda answered. Both appeared locked in silent communication, oblivious to anyone else, until Lucretia jolted, spinning frantically toward Sylvan and Marceline.

"The keys! Do ye all have them?"

Marceline's hand flew to her bra where she kept her feather pressed against her heart, while Sylvan's gravitated to his pocket. Kilda, too, showed hers, hanging from a chain around her neck.

"Good." Lucretia exhaled. "Dinnae let them out of your sights. Nae under *any* circumstances."

"Can someone explain me what is occurring?" Sylvan pleaded. No one responded. "Or should we just observe your panic?"

"This is nae time for sass," Lucretia snapped.

"Come now, love," Kilda interjected. "Ye cannae expect him to understand the gravity of it, if ye dinnae explain."

Marceline shot Sylvan a look, but he didn't return it. He seemed to have withdrawn into his own thoughts. She couldn't blame him. There was no mistaking the thick currents of fear passing between the two Scots: Whatever Lucretia had seen, the threat of it hung over them, sinister and dark and real. She watched as Kilda rolled up her map and hobbled wordlessly after Lucretia into her private lair.

“I suppose we should clean up,” Sylvan muttered, gesturing at the mess of feathers. The teacup Lucretia had been carrying when the seizure had begun lay in pieces, sharp blue pottery shards peppering the floor.

An eerie stillness dusted the café like snow. Sylvan and Marceline cleaned in unbearable silence.

A silence that lasted until it was time to go.

Quietly, she bade Sylvan goodbye and trudged down the rain-drenched alley to the bus stop. Gone was the tingling joy she’d felt when Sylvan had given her the perfume, the grateful relief the prospect of a loan from Kilda had inspired. All of it was now overshadowed by a dark, creeping dread.

A dread Marceline could not explain.

CHAPTER 23

Long Ago

In the solitude of Quill's hiding place, the raven followed her like a shadow. Its presence was both a blessing and a curse. An eternal reminder of the mother she'd lost, but also a companion, and a living memento of her village, where birds had often visited her with messages from the goddess, or simply to chat. Tulla, Quill called her, after the loch beside which the village had stood.

Within the windowless walls of her refuge, days strung into nights without distinction. Each time Quill willed herself to open the door, a different scene greeted her. The windswept top of a barren mountain, a frozen tundra, the dry heat of a savannah dotted with strange, striped horses, the white-capped waves of some distant sea, with no solid land on which the door might stand—yet still, it stood.

Quill weighed the security of her hideaway against the interminable oppression of her grief, opting every time to remain within the safety of those Otherworldly stone walls. There was no reason to leave—when she shivered with cold, a fireplace appeared. When she longed for a comforting brew, she turned to see a cauldron bubbling over the fire. If she craved meat—a frivolous luxury, for like her mother she had no use for sustenance—she found it already carved and smoking above the hearth.

Except to let Tulla out for her daily wanderings, Quill soon stopped opening the door altogether. The thought of stepping through it filled her with trembling dread, for who knew what dangers lay beyond? She'd spent her entire life longing to be human, believing in people's goodness, only to be betrayed. If that was the world, Quill had no desire to inhabit it.

Worst of all, somewhere out there, her greatest foe lurked. Contained, yes, but alive. And wielding a power that did not belong to her.

Quill passed the time idly. When Tulla was there, Quill told her stories of the village. When she was not, she sketched images of her mother onto the stone wall with bits of charcoal from the fire. Learning to hold anything between her talons was no easy feat, but time yawned on, and Quill found herself desperate to fill it.

Eventually, Quill's reluctance to leave the safety of her hideaway began to matter less, for the world began coming to her.

Tulla brought in twigs and bits of straw, building herself a nest in the rafters, within which to lay her speckled blue eggs. When the eggs hatched, Quill felt the first glimmer of joy she'd experienced in years. When the raven grew clumsy and slow, a milky film dulling her eyes, grief crept into Quill's bones, and she lost herself to it once more. Again and again, the chicks hatched and grew and died, and Quill rejoiced and wept, weathering a new tide of emotions with each generation, the painful and endless cycle of mortal life.

When the grief became too much, and Quill could do nothing but huddle on the floor and cry, a gentle whisper would startle her out of her own thoughts. *Go outside*, it murmured, cold breath icing her ear like frost upon a leaf. *Reclaim yer power and hide nae more.* Quill was no stranger to spirits—the woods around her village had teemed with mischievous fae folk—yet the possibility within those words filled her with dread.

"I dinnae need yer council, Spirit," Quill snapped, the first time the ghost whispered to her. Still, it continued to whisper, its unwanted words worming their way into Quill's thoughts.

She longed to entrap it so she could grieve in peace. And when at last another door appeared, cornering the spirit in its own small room, Quill exhaled her relief.

One day—or perhaps one night, one could never be sure—there came yet another knock. Quill paused, halfway through shading in her mother's charcoal profile. Her arms prickled, feathers stiffening in alarm beneath her skin. Her current raven companion, Oban, dozed on the mantel, basking in the rising warmth of the fire. Who, then, was knocking?

She set down her charcoal and tiptoed toward the door, talons stuttering warily against the handle. The door opened upon a sun-filled pasture, but her relief was short-lived. The gentle breeze carried a rancid odor. One Quill had smelled many times on her mother's plumage, when she returned quivering with bloodlust from some distant battle.

The stink of death.

Shivering, Quill moved to shut the door again.

"Wait!"

She froze at the shrill voice. Her gaze traveled downward to where a small girl stood in the doorway.

She looked about five, maybe six, but her haunted eyes loomed over sunken cheeks, giving her a skeletal appearance. On her shoulder perched a tiny brown-and-white sparrow.

"Mummy has the sickness," the girl said.

"Pardon?" Quill croaked, eyes flitting from the girl to the sparrow.

"Daddy had it too. And my brothers. They stopped moving and the priest said they went to heaven. I'm hungry."

Quill stared blankly at the child. Her heart already burned with its own grief. How could she take on more? But the girl was so small, so wretched...

"Come in." She stepped aside, letting the child amble past her. The tiny bird took flight and settled on the mantel beside the dozing Oban.

Quill shut the door. While her back was turned, a large table had appeared, on top of which stood an earthenware jug and two small mugs. Cautiously, she dipped her talon, tasting the substance. Sheep's milk.

She filled both mugs. "Come, lassie," Quill said, patting a chair. Instead, the feeble girl climbed into Quill's lap. This startled Quill. Rarely had anyone in the village dared act so familiar. She held the mug to the child's lips, and the girl drank eagerly, reviving a little more with each sip. When she finished the contents of the mug, Quill gave her the second one, and she drank that too. Once the entire jug had emptied, the girl drifted off to sleep, satiated in Quill's lap.

Quill sat unmoving, lulled into a trance by the child's soft, contented snores. Perhaps this tiny mortal could fill the void of her loss, mending the threads of her old life. But even as the thought sprouted, the child jerked awake.

"Mummy," she said in alarm. "I must go back to Mummy."

Emptiness consumed Quill when the child slid off her lap. "Come back when ye wish," she called. The girl was already halfway to the door when she paused.

"Who's that?" She pointed at the half-finished sketch of the goddess upon the wall. The question slapped Quill in the face.

"My mother," she whispered. "She's gone. Like yer daddy and yer brothers." Her supply of tears had refilled, and they began to tumble anew.

"Is she in heaven too?"

Quill wiped her eyes, heart squeezing. "I know nae." She had never heard of this "heaven" place. Perhaps it was another realm of the

Otherworld. The girl brooded for a moment, then scurried toward the door, and was gone.

Again and again, the girl returned to Quill's refuge. She always left satisfied and grateful, even as her body revealed weakness and broke out in great pus-filled sores.

Until she came no more.

Quill, who thought she'd shed enough tears for a lifetime, cried for the girl. She wondered how many lifetimes of grief she'd have to hold within her, and if it would ever end.

The girl had been Quill's first human visitor, but she was not the last.

After the sick child, a dark-skinned man with shackles around his feet followed a peacock through her door. He was a tribesman from Ghana, a distant land on a continent Quill had never heard of. She'd naively assumed the whole world resembled her own village—which, her birds told her, had long been destroyed.

The tribesman had been captured by slavers and brought to a place called Portugal. He longed for a haven from which to honor the gods of his native land, to sing prayers for the family from which he'd been stolen. Wooden masks from his homeland appeared above the mantel.

Soon after came an Aztec boy from yet another continent previously unknown to Quill, seeking refuge from conquistadors. Then, an Ottoman girl forced to marry a man twice her age, a failed Florentine painter, a reluctant geisha, a mistreated servant from India, a Polish housewife who longed to leave her shtetl. Each of them accompanied by a different bird, until the room rang with hoots and trills and squawks. These birds—every size, color, and species—crowded the rafters, and splotches of white dotted the wooden planks that had appeared over the floor.

The world continued to change—new countries and continents, wars and social movements swelling like ocean waves. Only Quill stayed the same, watching the progression of it all, gathering information and seeking patterns, striving to learn as much of the world as she could, without actually inhabiting it.

Her mother had said as long as there were humans, there would be suffering. She'd said it smugly, implying that as a goddess of destruction, she would always remain relevant. But humans didn't need gods to create wars. So, as time spun forward, Quill crafted herself a new purpose: to provide a haven for those who suffered.

Soon Quill began to shed the past like a skin. She let her name slither away from her, whipping off in ribbons into the distant past. She spent a century nameless, until one day, when an Italian soldier in Mussolini's army—a secret pacifist, forced to fight—told her a heartfelt tale about his lost love, a woman named Lucretia. As soon as he spoke it, the nameless woman shivered, watching the Latin sounds curl like smoke in the air before her. She reached out and tried it on.

It fit.

And so it was that the immortal Quill died, and Lucretia rose like a phoenix from her ashes. But there was one piece in the sprawling puzzle of the past that could not transform into something new: The scar her dead mother had burned into her soul, the fear inscribed there by her own sister, who no doubt pined for revenge. Lucretia buried the wound in swathes of time and history, but in moments of quietude it still throbbed, the fear still searing across her heart.

One after another the guests came, seeking what the mortal world had deprived them of. Lucretia kept her guests satiated while they explored corners of their hearts they'd thought unreachable. She brought them whatever beverage they craved, until what was once an empty hut had become a vibrant café, teeming with relics of every mortal age.

Without ever leaving the confines of those walls, Lucretia had managed to gather her flock. A flock dependent on neither geography nor ancestry, as it might have been in the days of her mother's rule. No—this flock welcomed anyone who found it within their heart to follow a bird through a doorway.

Still, contented as Lucretia told herself she was, an itch niggled under her skin, for she could never shake the creeping dread that her murderous sister lurked outside, waiting for revenge.

She gathered her birds and told them of her fears. The birds cawed and cooed among themselves, and after much deliberation, they agreed. They would allow her to peer into their minds, to look for signs of danger and ensure every entrance to her haven remained protected.

But she still needed help.

Though she'd developed a knack for anticipating new flock members, no true prophecy had come to her since that fateful day by the loch. So when her vision began to blur, in the middle of brewing a pot of tea for a dying Jordanian man, that old, familiar panic swelled. Her heart stuttered fear as colors and shapes bled together, sound fading in her ears.

Then, all at once, the world dimmed to black.

When she awoke, a handful of worried customers knelt around her, and Lucretia herself buzzed with the absolute certainty that in her own ancestral lands, a child named Kilda MacMander had been born. That in a couple of decades, this child would grow into an astute and gifted woman. And that this woman would somehow become as indispensable to Lucretia as air itself.

CHAPTER 24

An anxious tide pushed down on Lucretia's lungs, the prophecy still bombarding her with residual images: a dark, filthy tavern, crawling with cockroaches and cobwebs. Despair—clouds of it, filling her lungs with toxic fumes as the dizzying void jolted around her. Bronagh, in black, modern-day clothes, smirking as she polished a glass.

Her tiny room spun around her, a dizzying storm of colors and patterns. She ripped a wall hanging aside, laying her cheek against the stone. Something solid, steady, real. Her café, her haven, her self-imposed prison.

The curtain swished and Kilda hobbled in after her, tossing her rolled-up map aside. She grasped Lucretia's shoulders, kneading the muscles underneath. "I'm here." The warble of Kilda's voice smoothed itself, ringing with a low sweetness. "Ye'll nae have to face her alone."

"I knew this day would come eventually," Lucretia croaked, craning her neck to watch Kilda's wrinkles tighten and disappear, in response to her touch. "I just… I thought I still had time."

"Dinnae panic, love. We've been preparing for years. Do ye know how long we have?"

"Nae long," Lucretia whimpered. "She could arrive at any moment. I need to reinforce our defenses, or she'll destroy us all, Kilda. Just like she murdered my mother." She turned—grasping Kilda's hand to maintain the connection—and searched her wife's now youthful face. *Focus*, Lucretia tried to order herself. *Be in the present.* As long as she was here, her skin touching Kilda's, nothing could hurt her. She was protected, safe, and seen. But even as she held on to the thought, worries slithered up her spine, sinking their teeth into her soul.

They could not stay this way forever. Eventually they'd have to let go—danger would creep up and mortality would ravage the face of her love, death lurking just beyond, waiting. Lucretia ran a talon over the silver wedding band on Kilda's finger. Hopefully, the ring would protect her from injury. But even if Bronagh never attacked, Kilda would still die. Time would take her, the way it took all mortals. There was no escaping it, not even with magic.

"We'll fight her, love. Ye're so much stronger than ye know."

"I'm a coward."

"Nae. Ye suffered trauma. 'Tis nae the same."

"What if I cannae protect them? Sylvan and Marceline—the rest of my flock. What if I cannae protect *ye*?"

"Ye're already protecting me." Kilda caressed the silver band on her finger.

"And what if it makes nae difference? Without the Eternal Feather I've nae idea how strong my power is."

"Love, have I ever injured myself, since the day we exchanged vows and ye slipped this ring on my finger?"

"Well, nae, but—"

"Ye're a goddess, Lucretia. My Quill." Lucretia shuddered as the name splintered her soul, tracing a fissure across her fragile composure. Her original name, the one only Kilda knew—for no one else could see the trembling girl who still lived within her, terrified by the cruel power lurking in her blood. "The stem of yer powers has been stolen, aye, but by someone with nae idea how to wield it. She's human, yer sister. A mere thief. Besides, ye've still got the strength that lives in yer blood—naebody can take that away."

"What use is power if I cannae muster enough bravery to step through my front door?"

"Hush! Ye'll find courage when the time is right. I know ye will."

One of Kilda's thick ginger locks had escaped from the clip holding it in place. Lucretia reached for it, winding it around her talon. Seeing her wife age broke her heart a thousand times over, every time. Her mother's voice resounded in her head: *Ye try my patience with yer endless sentimentality.* But Lucretia couldn't help it. She *did* care about mortals. They were complicated and damaged, flawed and grateful. Yes, they could be cruel, but who was she to judge? She who'd been birthed for the mere purpose of sparking wars and bloodlust and pain. At least humans could learn. At least they could change. Could she?

She wasn't so sure.

"Breathe," Kilda whispered, pulling Lucretia close, entwining her fingers in the feathers of her hair. They sank together into the sea of cushions, clinging to each other like shipwrecked survivors.

"Would ye still love me if I were nae a goddess?"

The warmth of Kilda's low chortle grazed her ear, conjuring summer breezes—stalks of purple heather waving along the loch. "I've told ye a million times. Ye called me to assist ye, to help ye protect the café. But I chose to love ye all on my own."

"'Tis nae what I asked."

"I'd love ye if ye were a midge biting me in the arse."

Lucretia snorted, her panic at last receding, its final traces lingering like dampness in the sand.

"And ye?" Kilda nuzzled Lucretia's neck even as sadness crept into her whisper. "Do ye miss the days when I was young and bonny, even when ye were nae touching me?"

Lucretia's heart clenched like a fist. "I'd think ye were beautiful nae matter what." And it was true—the wrinkles spanning her wife's face were mere details, a superficial covering for the beauty and truth shining within. It was what they represented that scared her. "I cannae believe I survived over a thousand years before ye came into my life." Desperation bared its sharp teeth as Lucretia pulled her wife close. Could she survive a thousand years more, after Kilda was gone?

They held each other for a long while, until Kilda disentangled herself with a sigh. "I could stay like this forever, but we've got a café to protect. Ye said yerself she'd be here soon, and it's been ages since we practiced swordplay."

"Kilda, love, do you really think—"

Kilda silenced her with a look, and Lucretia knew better than to finish. They'd discussed it countless times, yet Kilda always insisted she could still wield a sword if she had to, that the wedding band would protect her in combat.

Lucretia was less certain. She sighed, sadness filling her soul. "Aye, ye're right, there's nae time to lose." Even as she pried her talons away from Kilda, she longed for an excuse to keep them there. And as Kilda's skin puckered and aged before her, the spray of freckles giving way to liver spots, Lucretia felt the cruel hands of time encircling her own neck—squeezing just enough to hurt, yet with no promise of death's sweet mercy.

CHAPTER 25

A Little Less Long Ago

Bronagh's sense of betrayal never dulled, remaining ever as lethal as a freshly sharpened blade, though sometimes now the blade was mislaid, set aside temporarily while a particularly miserable patron unloaded their sorrows and stole her attention. It was the 1970s now, the boxy little televisions festooning her walls showing flickering nightmares of dirty warfare, student protestors being beaten by the police, and bloody political coups by the dozen. If good things were happening too, Bronagh did not know—nor did she care. She cared only for the delicious distress that abounded, the self-pitying customers that kept her comfortably drunk on her own malice.

On the day the raven entered the tavern, however, her wrath returned to her in a torrent so fierce it almost knocked her over.

Back in the village, she'd constantly felt the shadows of ravens passing overhead, their presence a relentless reminder of the mother she'd lost, the sister she envied, the divinity she lacked. She had not thought of the birds and their taunting black eyes, judging beaks, and beating wings for over a millennium—locked away as she was.

There was no time for rational thought. No decision was made, no calculated plan began its meticulous unfolding. Instead, Bronagh sprang into action, and the bird hardly had time to hop its way across the floor before she lunged, wrapping her fingers around its neck.

How she was able to catch the creature, she did not know. Perhaps the tavern had dulled its senses—its curse threatening complacency, a sluggishness Bronagh herself constantly struggled against. Regardless of the reason, she caught it.

The impulse to throttle the struggling raven was strong, and yet, she did not, for something stopped her. A memory. Stories circulating in the village, about how the druids found prophecy nestled within the entrails of animals, turning carnage into knowledge.

Bronagh was no druid, but she had achieved the impossible. She'd wounded a goddess—perhaps mortally. And somewhere, beneath the pervasive murk and lethargy the tavern imposed on her, the Eternal Feather she'd stolen still pulsed steadily inside her heart.

She held the raven aloft, indifferent to the panicked movement of its eyes, the helpless flapping of its wings. Was there perhaps a way to learn whether the goddess had truly died, and what had become of her sister?

Only one way to find out.

It took one swift gesture to snap the bird's neck. Immediately afterward, Bronagh wished she'd savored the moment, slowly tortured the bird for what it represented. It was a lost opportunity, she thought, witnessing the last struggling jerk of its feathered body, but an opportunity gained, too. Clutching the dead bird like one of her sullied rags, she trudged back behind the bar. Only a few ragged souls straggled in the tavern, all too preoccupied with their own misfortunes to even notice a minor instance of avian murder. Still, Bronagh found herself longing for a private space from which to conduct her business, for she suspected what she was about to do would require concentration.

Her pulse quickened as she laid the corpse on the counter, the anger at the bird's appearance temporarily smothered by the glee of killing it.

She spread its wings so its undercarriage lay exposed, but as soon as she let go it flopped to the side, so she trod to the dartboard and plucked a handful of darts from its fleshy, blood-encrusted surface. The dartboard released a small sigh of relief with the removal of each dart.

Bronagh returned to the counter and pinned the creature's wings down. Wielding a small knife used for cutting lemons, she slit its body down the center, then used the remaining darts to pin the feathered flesh aside so the raven's insides lay glistening and exposed. She dabbed at the blood with a dishrag, then peered at the wreckage, keenly aware of the manic twitching of the feather in her own heart. The sensation filled her with a palpitating anticipation akin to nausea, telling her she was on to something.

Still, despite this hunch, gazing at the bird's innards revealed nothing but a stomach-churning stench. How did the druids do it? Was there some trick, some obscure, ancient knowledge she did not possess? It was the twitching in her heart, coupled with the low groan of her empty, never-satisfied stomach, that revealed an answer. And then, she did not hesitate.

Digging the bird's tiny heart out from between its ribs with one finger—it was roughly the size of a strawberry—she popped it in her mouth and swallowed, without even chewing.

The result was immediate, the image in her mind so vivid that she toppled backward into the wall of bottles. She did not hear the crash, nor did she see the bottles fall and shatter, nor feel the crunch of shards beneath her boots. Instead, she saw only a roaring fire in a hearth, a scattering of tables, a few figures sipping from mugs, a dozen mismatched birds twittering in the rafters. And in the foreground, staring into the fire, directly in front of Bronagh, a tall, pale woman with feathers for hair sat wringing her hands—no, talons.

Bronagh's heart pounded, the feather in her heart thrashing like a fish on land as she stared at the face before her.

Quill, the motherslayer.

She was alive.

The vision dissolved as quickly as it had come, and Bronagh stumbled in its aftermath, clutching the counter's edge as she tried to hang on to each small detail. Her head had begun pounding alongside her heart, stomach churning with queasy vigor. She retched, the raven's heart coming back up and spewing onto the floor in an eruption of bile. Spinning away from the mess, she tugged at her own hair, trying desperately to think.

Quill was alive. Alive and well, enjoying a roaring hearth, in—what was that place? Not the village, of that she was sure, for there had been modern accoutrements in the background, and the feeling pulsing up and down her body was screaming that something uncanny was afoot. The X on her neck throbbed furiously, recognizing the magic that had spawned it. The magic of the goddess.

This was a realm of the Otherworld.

The Bartender paced among the tables of her own miserable realm, digging her sharp nails into her fists. Yes, yes, it had to be part of the Otherworld. And if the rules there were the same as the rules here, then there were various ways to enter. Various portals, created by need.

Bronagh's own patrons came from all over. When their resentment—or spite, or self-pity, or merely their need to wallow—became unbearable, an entrance materialized and then existed in that place forevermore. Could Quill's realm be accessed in the same way? Could she plant someone to infiltrate and finish the job? No, no, that wouldn't work. The need had to be true, not fabricated, or the portal would never open. And besides, she wanted to—had to—kill Quill herself.

Another thought struck, reverberating feverishly through her shivering body. She'd long given up hope of ever leaving this accursed tavern, but this new knowledge ripped the old wound open, exposing it to the elements. The goddess had locked her in here with a key created of her own feathers. Quill was her daughter. And she, too, had feathers...

The ember of a plan sparked, spreading in flames across her mind as she trudged back to her counter. Now that she knew Quill was alive, it couldn't be a coincidence that this raven had swooped right into her tavern... Likely, it had come here because her sister was looking for her too. Quill would likely send more birds to spy on her—birds with hearts full of knowledge, ripe for the plucking. Not that Bronagh could pluck them—not unless another bird was foolish enough to stumble across her threshold. But her customers, they were free to come and go as they pleased...

Yes, that was it. She'd enlist her customers—pathetic and vile and eager to please—to catch her any ravens lurking around the tavern's portals. Then, once she learned her sister's whereabouts, she'd find a way to get one of her feathers and unlock this filthy prison. She would finally break free.

Inspired, Bronagh swept the raven's corpse from the counter, darts and all. It might take years for the pieces to fall into place, but Bronagh had nothing but time.

She perched on a stool, the storm in her body at last settling, thunderclouds moving aside to make room for something long forgotten: hope. Someday in the future, Bronagh would break out of this vile place. She'd taste freedom and finally wield the Eternal Feather's full power. She would release her rage upon the entire miserable human race, exacting dominion over a world that had always spat in her face. She would become a goddess.

At last.

CHAPTER 26

In the weeks following Lucretia's prophecy, the café darkened. Marceline felt it in the way the masks above the mantel stopped smiling, the eerie rattling of the skeleton, the record player that mysteriously slowed, distorting even the peppiest of songs into minor-key dirges, and in the literal darkening of the café's sourceless light, previously ember warm, now casting long, somber shadows across the floorboards.

She wasn't the only one who felt the change. Sylvan seemed to have retired into himself, his good-natured jokes becoming more and more forced, as if he was fighting some dark tide within himself. She wished she could hold a light out to him, but lately, her own situation had felt equally bleak.

Kilda's preoccupation with her map had acquired an urgent quality too. And Lucretia—well, where to even begin? When she dared to emerge from behind her curtain, which wasn't often, her eyes remained locked on the door, her movements becoming rushed and stilted. She began conducting her kettle ritual more frequently, and not a day went by that she didn't sweep the entire perimeter of the café with her feathers, muttering protection spells under her breath.

Customers still came, but they were subdued, somehow. Even the birds in the rafters had gone still and quiet.

Marceline, for her part, became increasingly paranoid as she rode the bus to the café, half convincing herself every glimpse of a gray Honda was Baxter following her. He had hardly brought up the café since Marceline's forced confession—a fact that still reverberated confused nausea into her gut every time she thought of it.

On one such morning, maybe five minutes after she'd unlocked the portal and let herself in, a fierce pecking sounded at the door. It was Falkirk—feathers disheveled and franticly cawing. Alarmed, Marceline called for Lucretia. In the amount of time it took for the kettle to be ready, Lucretia and Kilda had set up their ritual, anxious to peer into the panicked raven's mind.

Having gulped down the memories, Lucretia's eyes shot open, lightning fizzling over the swirling blue patterns of her arms. "Some bloody bastard tried to catch him," she spat. "Just outside, in a dirty brick alleyway." She stared at Kilda, aghast. "Of all the portals to the café, which one does that sound like?"

As Kilda listed the possibilities, Marceline's mind raced, picturing the derelict passage she'd just come through. When she managed to utter a sound—interrupting Kilda's theorizing—her voice cracked. "What did he look like?"

"Pardon, child?" Kilda asked.

"The man who tried to catch Falkirk. What did he look like?"

Lucretia's arrowhead eyes speared her. "Tall, sandy-haired. Strong jaw, cold eyes." She paused, gasping. "And that same shadowed aura I first saw clinging to ye."

Marceline exhaled, frost spreading from her spine. "That would be my husband."

Sure enough, when Baxter returned home from work, hours later, Marceline saw that his arms and face were covered in scratches.

She hadn't been paranoid. He really had followed her.

* * *

It was impossible not to panic. The café had become Marceline's safe place, and she needed her safe place to remain—well, safe. Even though there was no question whether she should leave Baxter now, and Kilda had promised that her "paycheck" would be coming soon, the prospect of actually *acting* on the plan was becoming more terrifying by the day. She was both afraid to go home and afraid not to go home, for fear of the consequences. Baxter's act of senseless violence against Falkirk had petrified her, and she could not fathom the reason for it. The café was the only place she could breathe. If things here weren't okay, then they weren't okay anywhere.

Sylvan, she could tell, was not okay either.

"Hey," she said, sliding the Tahiti book across the counter to him after they'd finished restocking the syrups in sober silence. The uncharacteristic somberness of his mood was scaring her almost as badly as her own anxieties. "I was going to show you this, before . . . well, you know." She didn't know why she couldn't utter the word *prophecy*, as if mentioning it would draw the danger Lucretia had predicted—the danger every single one of them could sense—even closer.

Sylvan snapped out of whatever dark daydream had clouded his face, looking briefly disoriented, as if he'd genuinely forgotten where he was. He looked down at the book. "'*Island Paradise: A Photographic Journey Through French Polynesia*.'" He gave a distracted, forced smile. "You know, Marceline, it is not all shining beaches and fruitful jungles. There is also poverty, and unemployment, and in parts of Papeete, women renting their bodies . . ."

"I'm trying to cheer you up," Marceline blurted. "Just let me, all right?"

The honesty of the statement seemed to reach him, and for a moment a genuine smile broke through the fog of his distraction. "Thank you. I am a grump today. It is not your fault. You are very thoughtful." He flipped the book open on the counter.

Immediately, his face fell again.

Unnerved, Marceline looked over his shoulder to see a photograph of a sickly, old, white man she swore hadn't been there before. She furrowed her brow, trying to figure out where the photo had come from, when Sylvan let out a shaky breath. On his face was a look of unmistakable panic.

"Sylvan? Are you okay?"

He swallowed, fiddling with his apron and tugging his T-shirt down on the sides. "Damn café magic," he muttered, shaking his head and shooting Marceline a look halfway between shame and terror. "It is like the ghost. You are minding your business, and suddenly it spits upon you a thing like this."

She tightened her fingers on the edge of the table. It was all she could do to stop from hugging him.

"Do you know that man?" she asked gently, fingers brushing over the photo.

Sylvan snorted. "Unfortunately. He is my father."

Marceline's heart stuttered. "You don't have to talk about it."

He put his hand over his face for a moment. She watched him, burning with empathy, until he dropped it again. His eyes were damp at the corners. "No. I want to." He heaved a sigh, his shoulders slumping. "Maybe it will help."

Sylvan and Marceline moved to the table near the scented brick—the table Marceline had begun to think of as theirs. When Sylvan sat, he drew in a shaky breath. Then, after a long, tense silence, he began: "My father hailed from continental France."

With these words the already dim café lights darkened almost completely, the yellow beam of the enchanted spotlight falling over him, like when Kilda had told her story. The light held a sickly, sallow quality this time, as if it, too, had been poisoned by the prophecy. Swallowing,

Sylvan hesitated, only relaxing when it became clear the other customers were oblivious.

"He had studied tourism, back in Marseilles," he continued. "After his studies finalized, he voyaged to Tahiti for a resort internship, and that is where he met Maman." Sylvan's hand gravitated to the book, tapping nervously at the cover. "Maman sold souvenirs at the gift shop—puka necklaces, painted shells, similar trinkets...she used to tell stories about how he would chat to her until both would become in trouble with the manager."

Sylvan's hand trembled as he flipped to the next page, where the same fair-skinned man leaned over a counter—only this time he was in his prime. Strong, tall, and muscular. A young Tahitian woman sat behind the cash register, lips quirked on the verge of laughter. Both wore the same uniform: a polo with a palm tree embroidered on the pocket.

"*C'était le coup de foudre*, she used to swear. A strike of lightning—love at the first viewing. Hard to believe, but I hypothesize he was then different. On the last day of his internship, the night before his returning flight to France, my father met Maman one last time, behind the snorkel and wakeboards shack on the beach. She arrived with a hand on her belly, shaking with worry. For days she had wondered how to tell him. When finally she did, he cried. That is even harder for me to believe. I never saw my father cry, ever. He thought emotions belonged to women only. But regardless, the facts are these: My father remained on the island, and my sister Eva was born after six months. Three years after that, I followed."

Sylvan flipped the page, his expression becoming unreadable as he stared down at the new image. A class photo—fifteen or twenty children, most of them Polynesian, arranged into three rows. Marceline leaned in to observe the photo. Sylvan wasn't hard to find. He stood at the end of the back row looking shyly at the camera, the largest of his classmates.

"My father had multiple ideas about how men should exist, but none could fit me," Sylvan said. "I was not good in sports, I enjoyed more to draw and paint. But let us not forget my greatest failing: my weight. *How did your son become so fat?* he would shout at Maman. *Your* son. Like he did not contribute to making me. From age four I was on a diet, ingesting only lettuce and protein drinks while the rest of my family enjoyed yams and breadfruit. I was always starving. *Chéri, it is not his fault*, Maman would say when Father raged over the scale during my daily weighings. *Not everyone is built the same*."

Sylvan turned the page like he was ripping off a Band-Aid, and there he was again, a few years older. The family sat around a cramped but tidy kitchen table, parents captured mid-argument—arms in the air, faces pinched with rage—a still life of dysfunction. Sylvan bore a stony expression, Eva glowering beside him.

"Things escalated, worse and worse. *What girl will want him?* Father would say. *Look at him!* Maman would come to my rescue, but it could not help. What twelve-year-old boy wishes to be saved by his mother? And then, he left us."

A flip of the page: the same kitchen table, though the tablecloth was now stained, family pictures conspicuously missing from the wall. Sylvan at thirteen or so, bent over his mother, who buried her face in her hands.

"I remember returning from school one day and encountering Maman this way." His fingers lingered over the image. "He had met a woman. A travel agent from Normandy. He was sick of island life, rageful that Maman had trapped him there. Trapped! After sixteen years! Remember, she had not ever asked him to stay in the first place. But those were his words, and then he was gone. Back to France without even sharing a goodbye to me and Eva.

"Life improved away from him. We held each other together, the three of us, and we had support from others too. You know, in Tahiti you cannot chuck a rock without hitting a cousin or aunt or uncle. Family is always nearby." He gave a soft chuckle. "They say on the island if you admire a girl, you must always first inquire of her family, to check she is not a relation. Anyway... later, Eva fell into pregnancy. With Maia—my niece, not the plant—in our house we were four again. I never could silence my father's voice in my head, but after a while, it became quieter."

Another page, another image. A smiling Sylvan leaning against a palm tree, glossy black hair hanging in his eyes. Laughing friends clustered on the sand around him, passing around a bottle in a paper bag. Marceline smiled, recognizing the paint-splattered vest, the one Sylvan had described the day they'd met.

"When I finally realized no tortures could change my body, things became improved. I discovered something amazing: When you like yourself, other people will like you too. It sounds so clear, but when you grow up thinking you are *une ordure*—a piece of trash—an idea like this feels like a revolution. I started to relax myself, attract friends, and cease worrying so frequently about girls. After years of stifling it, I even hugged my creativity and started painting again.

"After I graduated, I joined a job at the postal office. I continued to paint, spent time with Maman, and supervised Maia after work. By then I had finally learned to bury my father's voice. It took over a decade, but I decided to forgive him, even if only within my head, for my own peace. At last, things were good..."

Sylvan swallowed. Things were good *but*... the word lingered unspoken. This was it—the thing hurting him so deeply. The reason he needed the café.

"Two years ago, a letter arrived from France. The travel agent from Normandy. They had become married and made a whole life together—she spared the details to us and wrote to the point: My father had lung cancer. His days were numbered.

"That night, Maman and Eva and I debated. Neither of them could allow themselves to see him, but I believed it a sign. I had worked enough on myself to face him and forgive him for abandoning us and killing my confidence those numerous years. I told myself I had to go, so I bought a ticket and flew to Marseilles, where Father lived now."

Sylvan turned the page again, and the image showed him looking much like he did now, sitting in a chair beside a bed, discomfort tugging at the corners of his mouth. In the bed lay his father, shrunken and unrecognizable with his sallow skin and faded pajamas. Scowling.

"I thought everything would be different, here at the end. I thought he would regret hurting us. But this shriveled man tucked into the bed, surrounded by photographs of strangers, was still the bitter one who had left us. Even though he could only croak, when he saw me, his only words were: *You are even fatter than I remembered.* Not one question about Maman, or Eva. I do not even believe he knew of Maia. I had come so far—literally, yes, but emotionally also—but his words sliced deeper than ever.

"I searched to defend myself but found nothing. By the time I could even look to him once more, he had become asleep—a corpse already, but one still fighting with ragged breaths. I had to leave there, Marce. So, I bolted. I was halfway down the stairs when I saw *him*."

A final flip of the page, and here was Sylvan from the back, hand on the wooden railing, facing a stoic figure at the bottom of the staircase. A teenage boy, lean and strapping, with a soccer ball under his arm.

"I wish I could forget the confusion his face showed when he observed me—a fat, foreign stranger in his house. *Who are you?* he asked. *Why were you in* mon papa's *room?* My brain turned to blank. This boy, this perfect example of how my father believed a man should be—my half brother—had no awareness I existed.

"I took the next flight back to Papeete. After a day and a half of travel, Eva took me from the airport to home, where I dragged to my room. For weeks, I remained there. You have to understand—on the island we do not do that. When you are home, you help. You do not isolate. Some people do not even have a door on the bedroom. I hated myself for it, but I could not remember how to pretend I was fine. I even ceased to go to work. Maman was so worried—she constantly would burst into my room, begging me to converse. She would leave meals on my nightstand, looking worried. Eva took a different approach: She screamed that I must get better before Maia forgot her uncle's face. She was always a tough one, Eva. Nobody could understand what was happening to me. Not even me.

"Then, one day, a bird tapped its beak to my window. A sandpiper, I think. I rolled over in bed, but I could feel it watching me. Eventually I dragged to the window, wishing to shoo it off. Only then it was looking straight at me, and I felt the most odd sensation—like flipping upside down from a surfboard. Somehow, I knew I had to follow that bird.

"For the first time in numerous weeks, I crept outside. There was the bird, waiting in the yard. The warm breeze slapped me awake when I tiptoed after it, but it hopped away toward the shack I used for my art studio. And when I opened the door, I was here."

Sylvan's eyes glimmered with unshed tears as he tore them from the book, slamming it shut.

"And you've been coming here ever since?" Marceline could hardly bear the lost look upon his face.

He sighed. "It's the one place I feel I am myself again."

"And what happens when you go home?"

"The feeling fades and the world paints itself gray, and I have energy only for sleep."

"And your family?"

"They worry. I hate to observe them upset about me, but I cannot mend it. I do not know how to cease my sadness."

"What if you tried painting what you felt?"

He sighed. "I do not know, Marce."

"What if—"

"Listen, I know you are meaning well, but I beg you—please do not offer me advices."

"Sorry." She looked helplessly at him, understanding how his family must feel. She wanted so badly to help, to tell him he was worthy, and handsome, and kind. That he deserved happiness.

But it was clear he wasn't ready to hear it.

CHAPTER 27

A Little Less Long Ago

Bronagh hadn't had a customer in ages when the heavy door creaked open, pulling her focus from her mindless polishing. The sound jolted the feather in her chest, its rustle reverberating through her. Still as a corpse, she watched the boy linger in the doorway, his eyes glued to the floorboards beneath his threadbare sneakers. He had a scrappy look about him, scrawny and pale, face half smashed into a purpling welt. Far too young to be drinking, but the Bartender had no qualms about that, for she recognized him as a regular—or at least, someone who would be soon.

"What can I get you, kid?"

"Ain't got no money," the boy mumbled to his shoes. Mismatched socks showed through the holes in the mesh, one lace replaced with a grubby string.

"Join the club," the Bartender smirked, wiping her wet hands on her ripped black jeans. She'd become intimately familiar with the kinds of clichés patrons responded to. "What'll it be? Milk? Soda? Tequila?"

The boy hesitated, scanning the rows of crude, unlabeled bottles. "That one." He pointed to a bottle on the edge of the shelf.

"Whisky?" The Bartender reached for it, flipping it in the air and catching it again. "If you say so. Rocks?"

The boy's brow furrowed as he clambered awkwardly onto a stool. Despite his gangly frame, it was too tall for him, and his legs dangled above the floor.

"It means do you want ice."

"Oh." He looked dubiously at the bottle, as if he didn't quite believe it was real.

"Neat it is." She poured a muddy stream into a glass. It clattered against the scratched wood of the bar as she slid it toward him.

He reached both hands around the glass. Several of his fingers were swollen, battered the same rotting-eggplant shade as the welt spanning his forehead and eye. Something flickered in her chest. She pressed her black-painted lips together against the saliva gathering at the back of her mouth.

Not yet, she told herself. *Wait*.

The boy sniffed the liquid. His nose wrinkled, and bitterness flashed across his pale face, aging him for a moment. Then he grabbed the glass and downed the drink in a series of desperate gulps, like someone gasping for air. He set it down with a *clang* and stared at it.

Between the glass and his eyes, it was hard to say which was emptier.

"Another?" Bronagh didn't wait for a response. She reached for the bottle again, sharpened tips of her nails clinking against the glass. "What's your name, kid?"

"Baxter Grone." He glowered down at his lap, as if his name were a thing to be ashamed of. The Bartender smiled to herself.

He was perfect.

"What happened to your face, Baxter Grone?"

The pain that knit into the boy's brow speared pleasure in the pit of the Bartender's stomach, sparking an idea.

In the two decades since she'd eaten that first raven's heart, the Bartender had been able to successfully replicate the ritual four more times, to say nothing of the dozens of useless dead ravens who'd turned out to have nothing to do with Quill, and left Bronagh retching and furious. But four regulars—desperate and quick enough to catch a raven—had proven useful.

One: a corrupt banker who could never have enough money. She'd convinced him she could manipulate the stock market.

Two: a lecherous priest, preying on the teenage girls of his congregation. She'd promised to make the evidence disappear.

Three: a jealous actress who wanted revenge on her competition. She'd offered to curse the other actresses with disfiguring diseases.

Four: a compulsive cheater. She'd claimed she could wipe his wife's memory.

Each of them had found the ravens loitering near their respective portals. Each of them had felt the sudden, searing burn of the X marking their bodies as they'd approached the birds.

For Bronagh, the wait had been worth it. Each raven's heart had yielded another vision: She understood Quill's realm was a café now. She'd identified two entrances: one in a Kyoto sewer, and one in a Bavarian wine cellar. She'd witnessed Quill performing a ritual with a kettle, looking for other realms.

Looking for Bronagh.

Yes, it had been more than worth it—not that she'd bothered to reward the loyal customers who'd done her bidding. All of them were loathsome and shallow and flawed, and even the most self-pitying of them believed the world owed them something. They'd been furious, of course, though each of them deserved every lick of misfortune that befell them. Misfortune that the Bartender so loved to feed on. Why would she diminish her own pleasure source? Each of them had cursed her name, but Bronagh wasn't worried. There would always be more customers. And anyways, adults were fickle.

But here was a child. A blank slate who needed a friend.

And as luck would have it, Bronagh needed a friend too.

Perhaps there was a way they could help each other.

"Do you like ravens, Baxter? You look like you can move fast. I'll whip you up something nice if you can catch me one." The Bartender smiled invitingly.

She hadn't realized how hungry she was.

CHAPTER 28

"What's wrong with Maia?" Marceline asked, peering at the Venus flytrap. The plant was drooping, hardly showing an interest in the handful of dead flies she'd just sprinkled over it. Usually, Maia's many heads battled against each other, bloodthirsty for sustenance. Now, only the largest of them even bothered to tilt upward and open its jagged jaws.

Sylvan looked over, tapping the ceramic pot with the toe of his sneaker. "Perhaps she is tired." He'd been increasingly sullen since his spotlight confession, though she sometimes caught him looking at her, his lost gaze somehow fierce and tender and sorrowful, all at once. She hadn't brought up his story again and neither had he, yet it lingered between them like a secret, an invisible bridge built of pain and trust, silently uniting them.

Sylvan took the tongs from Marceline and sprinkled another pinch of flies onto the pot, but the plant's heads remained immobile and disinterested. Worried, Marceline looked down at the plant, almost missing the way its various heads used to snap and snarl at each other. Clearly, the prophecy's gloom had gotten to them too.

It seemed no one could escape it. Even the child from the Mexican orphanage kept crumpling her drawings and snapping crayons in frustration. Usually, the little girl sang along to whatever record was playing, but all the records were distorted now, their notes stretched long and ominous, chords sliding into an eerie minor register at will. At another table, a skeletal man clad in rags glared down at a crossword puzzle, an equally skeletal Great Dane slumbering fitfully at his feet.

"Sylvan?" Marceline set the now-empty saucer on the counter, turning to him. She wanted to talk about what was happening, but the look in his dark-coffee eyes pinned her in place. There was something in that look, like he was searching for something, or trying to send her a wordless message. A message about what? Was he yearning for something he couldn't have?

Her thoughts stalled in her brain as her gaze shifted to his lips, wondering what it might feel like to press them against hers.

"Marce, child," Kilda called from across the room, and Marceline snapped to attention, spine suddenly ramrod straight. "Could ye bring me a chamomile?"

"Coming up," Marceline shouted too loudly, spinning away from Sylvan. "Be right back," she muttered to him. What had she been about to do? She might be planning to leave Baxter, but he was still her husband!

Marceline scurried off to boil some water, trying valiantly *not* to wonder what Sylvan was thinking, whether they'd shared a moment just then, or whether it was all in her head.

When the tea goblins had been shooed away and the pot had been rinsed and filled, Marceline brought it to Kilda's table on a tray. She set it down, hesitating to speak. Given the current mood, the map and kettle ritual was starting to feel like a taboo topic, but being kept in the dark only amplified Marceline's anxiety.

"How are things progressing with your project?" More than half the map's surface was covered in dark shading now.

"Hard to say, lass," Kilda sighed, dark circles underlining her eyes.

Concerned, Marceline pulled up a chair. "Are things going to be okay?"

"Who's to say, child? I'm nae the one who makes prophecies around here." Kilda's brow furrowed as she paused, before her shriveled lips shifted into a grin that was too deliberate. "Come now, lass, let us nae trouble ourselves with things beyond our control. Anyway, I've got a present for ye."

"Oh no, you don't need to give me anything." Marceline blinked, trying hard not to linger on the evasive nature of Kilda's ominous non-answer. She watched the cartographer rummage through her flowered tote, expecting chocolate, or a cookie, or some other treat.

Instead, the old woman produced a white porcelain piggy bank, painted with delicate bluebells. Marceline's heart swelled. This was the kind of gift her own grandmother would have given her.

"For yer earnings." Kilda's kind eyes crinkled. "There's a fair bit in there already. Lucretia can keep it in her private quarters until ye need it."

"Why are you so generous?" Marceline blurted. "I haven't done anything special, except serve you drinks."

"Would ye rather I were nae?"

"No! I love it. You remind me so much of my grandma—" The words stopped in her throat, held there by an unexpected knot.

"Oh, child, dinnae fret." Kilda laid a veiny hand upon her shoulder. "Hush now."

Marceline choked. Lately, this place had been slowly excavating all her old wounds, one by one. "Sometimes I remember how much I miss her."

The old cartographer stroked Marceline's hair. "Sweet lass. I've nae intention of replacing anyone, but I'd be happy to be yer grandmother, should ye be needing one. 'Tis something I believe I might have a knack for."

At this, tears trickled down Marceline's cheeks. "Really?"

"Aye, of course. Consider yerself adopted."

Touched, Marceline smiled through her tears. "Okay," she sniffled. "It's a deal."

"Lovely. Now ye've nae choice but to accept my gift. After all, 'tis yer inheritance."

"If you insist." Marceline wiped the tears with her sleeve. Rising from the table, she picked up the piggy bank, cradling it. "I'm going to pay every penny back, though, Kilda. As soon as I can, I promise."

The corners of Kilda's eyes crinkled. "I'm nae worried."

Marceline wished Lucretia would come out from behind her curtain so she could thank her too, but it seemed unlikely, since the feathered woman hadn't emerged all day. Still, despite the low howl of the record player and the inexplicable tinge of rot in the air, Marceline's mood was considerably brighter as she returned to the counter.

"They're paying me," she told Sylvan, setting the piggy bank on the counter.

"That is good. I am glad it will assist your needs," Sylvan said, and Marceline could see he was indeed happy for her, despite everything else he was dealing with. Her eyes slid to his lips again, mind jolting her back to the previous moment.

In a sudden burst of bravery, Marceline thought, why not? Before she could lose courage, she reached for his hand. She held her breath as she waited—statue-still—to see if he would let go.

Sylvan stared down at their intertwined hands. "Marce, what . . . ?"

She didn't let him finish. The world seemed to be crumbling around her, the only place that felt like home becoming dark and full of shadows. She was tired of waiting around for things to get better. She was ready *now.*

Leaning in, she pressed her lips against his, heart pounding so hard it threatened to break through her ribs.

He pulled away.

Mortified, Marceline sprang back. "I'm so sorry. I—"

An earth-shattering scream erupted from behind them. Marceline whipped around in time to see Lucretia clutching a dead owl in her arms.

But there was no time to process what she was seeing.

The café fell into chaos. Birds dove from their branches in a chorus of dissonant squawks. The coloring child hurled her pencils across the room, ripping the pages from her coloring book in a screaming frenzy. The Great Dane that had been slumbering under his master's table sprang up and dove after a swooping cockatiel, barking and knocking over tables as he bounded after it. The dog's owner tore after him, shouting a string of swears.

Was this another prophecy? The thought evaporated, the world blurring into a muddied slush of shapes as Marceline spun, a primal wail erupting from somewhere deep inside her. She needed to destroy something. Hardly registering Sylvan's fist thrusting into the wall nearby, she propelled herself at him. A frenzied horde of hummingbirds fell upon her, and she batted at them as she charged into Sylvan. The force sent her bouncing back, toppling to the ground. He lunged for her, his face twisted in fury.

The air thickened, slowing all motion. Immediately, the screeching died down as the birds settled back on their rafters. The dog backed off from the cockatiel with a confused whimper. His owner straightened, bewildered.

Marceline blinked, realizing she was sprawled on the ground. Sylvan lay pressed against her, clutching her shoulders.

He released her, a look of shock on his face. "Oh God, did I harm you?"

"I—I'm okay..." Marceline scampered backward, yanking her eyes away from him as her mind skipped like a record to the moment before, where she'd tried to— No! Marceline flinched, confusion heightening her mortification. They each clambered to their feet, shocked by the blood slowing in their veins, the receding tide of their heartbeats. The Mexican child stooped, pouting as she retrieved the scattered pages of her sketchbook.

Only Kilda had remained at her table—though she'd bent forward in her seat, body thrown over her map like a shield.

A gasp rang out behind her. Lucretia stood rooted to the ground, her face drained of color. She let out a strangled sound, before bolting behind her curtain.

Stunned, Marceline stared after her. The café lay in tatters: tables and chairs overturned, mugs broken, feathers and bird droppings covering every surface. Bewildered, she looked to Kilda, who shook her head sadly.

"Give her a moment alone, child. Come." The old woman beckoned Marceline back to her table.

Marceline plopped into the chair. "What just happened? It wasn't another prophecy, I know that. It felt different, like I was losing my mind…"

"Nae, child, it wasnae. In short, she found one of her birds dead, she screamed in horror, and all hell broke loose."

"But *why*?"

"'Tis something that happens with her. Have ye nae noticed the calming effect of this place? 'Tis good for her flock, but also for herself, so she does nae get overstimulated. Because when she does, well…" She gestured to the mess around them.

"But, Kilda, I could feel my blood boiling. One moment everything was normal, and then I lost control."

"Aye. 'Tis the scream that triggers anyone who hears it. A family trait. One she's terribly ashamed of, for she cannae control it."

Marceline reached over and squeezed Kilda's hand. "You're worried about her, aren't you."

"Aye, lass, I'll nae deny that. She's been my one and only for half a century—more than twice yer lifetime. She can be a stubborn old crow—well, raven—but underneath those ruffled feathers she has the kindest heart ye ever saw. She's done more good for the world than any one of us could ever hope to. I cannae stand to see her in pain."

Marceline understood. She'd seen Lucretia's harshness, and she'd seen her gentleness too. Maybe that was what love was—accepting the good and bad in a person and choosing them anyway.

Her stomach constricted as she thought about Baxter. It was when the bad outweighed the good that you had to leave.

She changed the subject. "Kilda, how come you didn't freak out when Lu screamed? Everyone else lost control, but you, you were protecting your map."

"Ah. A complicated bit of magic." Her eyes twinkled with mischief as she reached into the side of her white cloud of hair. Her hand reappeared gripping a beige piece of plastic the size of a jelly bean. "I often remove my hearing aid to better concentrate. Seems there are advantages to being nearly deaf." She manipulated the hearing aid back into her ear.

When a throat cleared behind her, Marceline twisted in her chair. Sylvan approached the table timidly, carrying a newly brewed cup of tea for Kilda. He set it down. "Hey, Marce. You are sure I did not harm you?"

"I'm okay." She cast her eyes downward, trying not to remember the electric pressure of his bulk on top of her, the proximity of their lips only moments before that. "We better sweep up this mess."

Marceline cleaned in a daze, acutely aware of Sylvan's movements as he gathered feathers from the floor. Once the damage had been swept away, she went to gather her things, thinking now would be a good time to leave, since any further interaction with Sylvan seemed like it would only lead to more embarrassment.

Apparently, Sylvan had other ideas.

"We can converse, yes?" he asked her, dumping a handful of crumpled papers into the garbage.

"I'd rather pretend it never happened," Marceline mumbled. "I misread the signs. You brought me that perfume the other day, and I thought…I mean, in my defense, it's been a while since I felt…it doesn't matter. Let's not—"

"Wait, Marce." He caught her hand, contorting himself so she couldn't look away. "Let me say this, and then I will drop it, yes?"

Humiliation pooled in her gut. She nodded.

"You did not misread the signs. I have wished to kiss you since the first time you trampled inside here like a drowned rat. But you are *married*. I know you plan to leave him, but you still have not, and neither of us are in a nice place. I cannot become involved until everything has resolved. It would not be fair for either of us."

Marceline swallowed. The relief that he'd wanted to kiss her back was tempered by all the reasons he couldn't. Reasons that—as much as she hated them—made undeniable sense.

"You're right," she mumbled, untying her apron and trading it for her coat. "I'm sorry."

"Hey." He offered her a gentle smile. "You know my opinion on your apologies, Marsupial."

She nodded, forcing a half-hearted laugh. "Yeah, I do." She shrugged, looking anywhere but his beautiful, dark eyes, as words spilled too quickly from her lips, betraying her shame. "I have to run, I'm probably late. See you tomorrow, Sylvan."

She left, not waiting for a reply.

CHAPTER 29

When Baxter slunk through the tavern door, emotions roiled over him in a cloud so black it made Bronagh salivate. He was smeared head to toe in foul-smelling sludge, as if he'd slipped in something vile on the way in. Sweet, delicious Baxter. Did he have any news for her? Though she burned with the desire to ask, she kept her cool. Let him come to you, she reminded herself, even as her insides writhed in anticipation.

He stormed over to the counter, collapsing onto his regular stool. The Bartender eyed him, feather tingling inside her chest as Baxter banged his fist on the counter. "Whisky!"

"With pleasure," she purred, already reaching for the bottle of pungent brown liquor that remained eternally half empty, no matter how much she poured out. She slid a smudged glass across the counter with a grating scrape and filled it to the brim. Baxter emptied it mechanically down his throat.

Look at me, Bronagh urged him silently. It was through the eyes that she could access the pain most directly.

"She's hiding something from me." For a fraction of a second his eyes flickered toward her, and she had to fight to hide the rush of pleasure twisting inside her with an intensity that was almost sexual. "Marceline. I knew she was, and now I have proof."

"Oh, my sweet Bax. What did she do now?" The Bartender struggled to keep her voice soothing as her stomach fluttered in anticipation. His torment hung sweet in the air, a succulent, familiar flavor tinged with the suspicion of infidelity.

Baxter was *always* convinced his wife was cheating on him, and the Bartender never tired of hearing about it.

"They're really all the same, aren't they?" Baxter spat. Triumph bloomed in the Bartender's gut as she realized he was already fighting back tears. It usually took at least an hour to get him to this point. He shoved his glass forward. He'd been an absolute mess since the waiter incident at his anniversary dinner, about a week ago.

"It would appear so." Bronagh took his glass to refill it, but a cockroach scuttled across the bar, so instead she smashed the insect with it.

"And she thinks I don't know, but I can tell! I'm not an idiot." Rage sparked in the sandy slant of his brows. "She's been different lately. All distracted, like she's thinking about someone."

"Oh, my sweet Bax. You sure know how to pick 'em." She lifted the glass, cringing at the mess of cockroach guts, then turned and tossed it into the sink, where it shattered, making Baxter flinch. "It breaks my heart," the Bartender continued, wiping the counter with a rag. She grabbed a new glass, filled it, and set it down in front of the sniveling man. "And the worst part is, the problem isn't *just* women. You've been through more hardship than most, and trust me, I've seen some wretched characters pass through my door." She inclined her head toward a muttering man down the counter whose face was covered in pustules, one of the few other customers present. "You deserve so much more." She laid a hand on his shoulder, massaging the tantalizing tension.

"I know. I know I do. It just isn't fair."

Toying with him was simply too easy.

"At least you have me," she said, releasing him. "At least you know *I'd* never lead you astray. Unlike everyone else in your life, haven't I always been here for you? I mean, when you told me not even your own mother wanted you..." She sighed, hand on her heart, watching Baxter's knuckles whiten around his glass. "There has to be something seriously wrong with someone who chooses to bask in a heroin-soaked stupor, instead of taking care of their own child."

Baxter made a sound—a dejected half snort—before downing his drink once more. He pushed the glass away, burying his head in his hands. The Bartender thrilled, wondering how far she could push him.

"Not to mention all those foster families," she went on, grabbing her rag—cockroach innards and all—so she could polish yet another glass. Knowing he hated when her attention was split, she glanced at the TV mounted in the corner, where someone's nightmare was projecting a blood-crusted guillotine. "All that neglect, that indifference. And there you were, this poor, scrappy kid, getting into fights and acting out."

"Not all of them." Muffled by his hands, his voice was a near whimper. "The Murphys almost adopted me."

She had to turn to hide her grin. He was making this far too easy. "Right, the Murphys." Her rag squeaked against the glass. "Remind me what happened with them again?"

Had Baxter been on the floor instead of at the counter, he might have rolled into the fetal position.

"Mrs. Murphy got pregnant," he mumbled. "Their fucking rainbow baby, they called it. Fucking bastards." A sob escaped his lips, and a burst of ecstasy sent fireworks through the Bartender's extremities.

"Cruel," she murmured, bliss fizzing inside of her. "Just cruel. As if they couldn't have kept you anyways. Yes, I remember it now. You threw a fit and trashed the house, didn't you? But who could blame you, after all you'd been through?"

Baxter hung his head. "The worst part is Marceline knows all of this. How can she fucking lie to me, knowing everything I've been through?"

On the screen behind him, a severed head toppled into a straw basket.

"Right," the Bartender agreed, offering him a sympathetic smile. The trauma of his past seemed to have sobered him up. "And it's not like you've never been cheated on. You *know* the signs. You may be unlucky, but you're sure as hell not stupid." The Bartender set her rag down and leaned over the counter, so close she could smell his putrid, alcoholic breath—the same odor that clung to everything in her miserable tavern, but even more concentrated. "God, Baxter, what did you do to deserve all that?"

He slammed his fist onto the bar again, this time with a sickening crunch that made him whimper and clutch his wrist. "It just. Isn't. Fair," he repeated.

The Bartender watched Baxter's tears stream down his angular jaw. "Why don't you tell me about it?" She reached to tilt his chin up, her black lacquered nails tracing his stubbled jaw, his prominent cheekbones. "What exactly did the bitch do this time?" Pleasure danced up her spine as he squinted through his tears, expression momentarily glazed with a sheen of wonder. She held him there for a moment, both revolted by the blind adoration in his bloodshot eyes and delighted by his pathetic hypocrisy. It wasn't the first time she'd seen it, but it had been a while. Once, before his wedding, he'd even tried to kiss her.

Sniffling, he began. "So, I come home from work just now, and I'm about to enter the building and I see a goddamn raven fly into the kitchen window."

The Bartender inhaled sharply.

She jolted, the pleasure of his delicious torment immediately eclipsed by something far greater, far more important. Slowly, she repeated the word, as if needing him to confirm he'd really said it. "A raven?"

"Yeah. I would've caught it for you, but I couldn't. It had something in its beak. So, I'm watching it from the parking lot, and it goes in, stays a while, then flies off again, without whatever it was holding before." He glowered, picking at splinters on the bar's grimy surface.

Triumph zinged up the Bartender's spine. Quill! Whatever his cheating wife was up to, it had to do with her sister. Her zeal was quickly marred by anger. Had the bastard really let the bird go? It took all her self-control not to shake the man out of his self-pitying stupor. "What have I told you about ravens, Baxter? What are you supposed to do when you see one?"

He was too preoccupied with his own insignificant drama to catch onto her threatening tone. "I told you, it got away. It landed on the hood of a car for a second, and I was going to ambush it, but then my tattoo starts pulsing like someone set it on fire, and when I look up again it's already flying away. So I run inside, and she's just cooking, acting like nothing happened. The lying bitch."

His tattoo! Her own X—the one at the nape of her neck—began to pulsate. Each of the four regulars who'd caught ravens for her had described the exact same sensation. Bronagh thrilled. So, Quill's realm had a portal in San Francisco, and Baxter's wife had access to it. That was what it all meant—it had to be! If she didn't know any better, she'd call it an enormous coincidence. But no. Her magic had been taken from her sister's. Of course they would attract each other. She refilled Baxter's glass, practically shaking with the effort of masking the excitement frothing between her ribs. "And then what?"

"Then I came straight here."

"Tell me more. You really didn't see what the raven was holding?"

"I don't know. A piece of paper or cardboard, probably a note from some lover, like it's the fucking Middle Ages. Who does that?"

She let out a high, shrill laugh, setting the bottle down with a *bang.* "Find out."

"What?" Baxter balked, truly looking at her for the first time since he'd come in, but now, the Bartender was too distracted to taste his agitation.

"Find out what it gave her. Ask her—or don't, actually. Best keep a low profile. Find out without asking…"

He gripped his glass like a lifeline. "Do you know something I don't, Bartender?" It was the only name he knew her by—an inadequate moniker, masking her true identity. "This is something to do with your raven vendetta. Are you ever going to tell me?"

"Of course, Baxter. One day, when the time is right. But not yet. So, about Marcella—"

"Marceline."

"Yes. About Marceline—does she go out, when you're at work? Can you follow her?"

"Jesus, you think she's sneaking out too? You think she's going out to meet him?"

"You know what women are like. It was always going to happen."

He downed the rest of the drink. "Fuck. You're right. Fuck!"

Now the Bartender set a tender hand on his shoulder. She felt him shudder beneath the thin fabric of his shirt. "Don't despair, Bax. Find out all you can, and then come back and tell me. And if you see that raven again, try to catch it. We'll find out what that worthless wife of yours is up to, and we'll make her pay, you mark my words. I'm here for you. She'll be sorry she ever betrayed you. My sweet, sweet Baxter."

Baxter set his glass down, reaching pathetically to lay his hand over hers. "Do you mean that?"

The Bartender grinned, glee surging through every vein as she imagined herself ripping Quill's feathers out, one by one. "With all my heart."

CHAPTER 30

Marceline fidgeted in the hard plastic chair of the OB-GYN's waiting room, listening to the sounds of flipping magazine pages, the *tap-tap-tap* of the secretary's acrylic nails on her keyboard. Usually, Baxter would be here with her, leaning over her shoulder and supervising each interaction. But not today.

Today, she was here alone.

Without his knowledge.

She swallowed, looking at the clock on the wall. She was missing out on café time to be here, but if everything worked out, it would be worth it.

She ran her finger over the edge of the golden feather, trying not to think of what Baxter would do if he learned what she was planning.

"Marceline Grone?" The nurse's voice pulled her from her anxious thoughts.

Marceline sprang to her feet, tucking the feather back into her purse. "Yes, I'm here." She smiled at the nurse, perhaps too brightly, judging by the girl's puzzled reaction.

"This way, please."

They arrived in an examination room and the nurse shut the door. With a side of uninvested small talk, she began checking Marceline's blood pressure and weight. "The doctor will be with you shortly." She left the room, clipboard in hand.

Now alone, Marceline sat on the paper-covered exam table and pulled the feather out again, desperate to focus on the sensation of its smooth fibers against her cheek as she willed her heartbeat to slow. When the door opened again, she jumped, half expecting Baxter to burst in. Instead, a tall, older woman stepped into the exam room.

"Dr. Santiago."

"Marceline, nice to see you. No husband today?" Her black ponytail was streaked with gray; lines etched deep around her mouth like parentheses.

"Yes, no, he had a—a thing." She shrugged, plastering a manic grin on her face.

"I see." The doctor's keen eyes swept over her, no doubt noting Marceline's nervousness. "What's that you've got?"

"Oh, I just found it outside." She set the feather down with trembling fingers.

"Ah." The doctor shot her a perplexed smile. "So, what brings you in today?" She checked her chart, flipping a page to read the other side. "Looks like you were trying to get pregnant, last time I saw you. How has that process been for you?"

"Great," she said automatically, before remembering her plan. Biting her lip, she stared at Dr. Santiago, struggling to untangle her thoughts. "I mean, not great. I mean . . ." She trailed off, feeling helpless.

The gynecologist's eyebrows furrowed. "Many women struggle to conceive, Marceline. It's nothing to be ashamed of."

Again, words eluded her. She stared back at the doctor. Why was she stalling? What she'd come here to say was right there, on the tip of her tongue.

"Why don't we have a chat." The way Dr. Santiago's eyes bored into Marceline's contrasted starkly with her casual tone. There was no question she could tell something was off. "When were you and your husband last intimate?"

Marceline swallowed. This is it, she realized, her courage waning thinner by the second. This is the moment. Somehow, the feather had made its way back into her hand. She pressed it between her palms, praying for a sliver of Lucretia's confidence.

Then the dam broke, all her words bursting through. "We did it earlier this week but I already took a test and I'm not pregnant and actually I was hoping I could get some birth control—" She halted, heat rushing to her cheeks as awareness dropped through her like an anvil.

She'd said it.

Out loud.

For the first time.

Marceline's worried gaze shifted toward the door. She could imagine Baxter lurking just outside, listening through the layers of wood and paint.

Dr. Santiago scrutinized her, and Marceline was sure she saw pity lurking in the crow's feet around her eyes. "It's no coincidence your husband isn't here with you today, is it?"

Marceline only looked down at her hands.

"Right." The doctor frowned. "Marceline, I'm afraid I must get straight to the point. This is a question I ask all my patients, but it's important: Do you feel safe at home?"

She stared at Dr. Santiago. *Safe* was a strange word. It came in so many different shades. She was sure Baxter would never hit her, so when had this creeping sense of dread first appeared?

"Whatever you say will not leave this room," the doctor pushed. "It'll be one hundred percent confidential. You have my word."

Rejecting the urge to defend him, Marceline bit her lip. "No, he's not violent. He just doesn't want what I want..."

The gynecologist nodded, unfazed. "I see. Well, there's no shame in not wanting children. They're a big commitment. You shouldn't have them if you aren't sure. And if you do decide you'd like access to resources, regarding the situation with your husband"—she paused, her eyes boring into Marceline's—"then I can give you a phone number and some pamphlets."

Marceline shook her head vigorously, as if admitting she was a victim would be an act of great shame. "Just the birth control, please."

"Of course. I'd be happy to discuss the options with you."

"Really?" Marceline clamped her hands together to hide the shaking, channeling silent gratitude to the feather still tucked in her grip.

"Yes, really."

"Oh, thank you!" She leapt from the exam table, wanting to hug the doctor, but that glimmer of pity stopped her in her tracks. Ashamed, she sat back down. Here she was, a woman too afraid to tell her husband she didn't want to have his child. That she was leaving him. The adrenaline of the previous moment evaporated. Maybe she *was* a victim.

"All right," Dr. Santiago said. "Before we begin, let's start with a routine pregnancy test. After I examine you, we can discuss contraception methods. How does that sound?"

Marceline nodded, shaking away the confusing jumble of emotions. This was good. It was what she wanted. As long as Baxter didn't find out...

The doctor gave her a cup to pee in and sent her to the bathroom. In the stall, she managed to fill the cup with minimal splashing. Who would have thought her first step toward freedom would consist of filling a cup with urine? Lucretia and Kilda would be proud of her. And Sylvan, he'd be proud too—not that she'd tell him about the pee, specifically. She pictured his face, that warm glow spreading inside of her. Was it wrong to think of him at a time like this? Especially since he'd rejected her kiss? Maybe, but she couldn't help it.

When she returned to the exam room, the doctor unwrapped the test stick and set it in the cup.

"It'll be negative," Marceline said. "We did a test three days ago, after we . . . well, you know."

"Still, it's a precaution I like to take. Putting you on a birth control program could be dangerous to an existing fetus if you are already pregnant." Dr. Santiago checked her watch. "It'll just be a minute."

Marceline made a half-hearted attempt at small talk while they waited, before falling silent again. The thought of a human being growing inside her made her stomach squirm. She shivered. Despite the lurking fog of guilt, this was the right thing. The discomfort she felt at the thought of pregnancy spoke volumes: No part of her was ready for motherhood.

Relax, she told herself. *You're out of danger now.* It was time to focus on the next step. She didn't know how much money she'd accumulated from the café yet, but she doubted it would be enough for an apartment. That age-old urge to travel still tugged at her mind. Could she visit Sylvan in Tahiti? No, no, she was getting ahead of herself. Perhaps she should lie low at the café and figure out her next move. Although first, she had to do the actual leaving—the thought tied her stomach in knots. And yet, it had to be done.

"Oh . . ."

The two whispered words jolted Marceline out of her planning. "What?"

"I'm afraid it's positive. You're pregnant."

Her stomach dropped—a broken elevator plummeting twenty stories down. "No, I'm not."

The glimmer of pity had spread, engulfing the doctor's entire face as she showed Marceline the plastic stick with its two glaring pink lines. "I'm afraid so."

"I can't be. I tested negative, remember?" Her hands shook, pulse revving like an engine.

"It's not unheard of. That's why it's best to do two tests, to be sure."

"Well, do another one. How do you know this one isn't wrong? Besides, you're supposed to feel sick. I didn't—I don't feel sick..."

"Well, typically morning sickness doesn't start until roughly six weeks in, but we can do another test if—"

"Please," Marceline gasped. "Please do another test."

"Of course."

The few minutes it took for Dr. Santiago to retrieve another test stick felt like a lifetime. The following minutes—in which they waited for the second result—could have been six more lifetimes.

The doctor pulled out the second stick and peered at the display, brow wrinkling. "I'm sorry."

Marceline's mind went blank. Her shock enclosed her in a cocoon, filling her ears with white noise and blurring her vision. Through the static, the doctor's voice sounded like a distant call.

"Marceline? Do you need a glass of water?"

The cold, clammy touch of a plastic cup in her hand brought her back to planet Earth. She stared at the doctor, grasping for an explanation. She'd misheard. It was all an elaborate prank. She'd imagined the whole thing.

"It's not the end of the world, Marceline, I promise you. You can put the child up for adoption. Or you can choose to terminate the pregnancy altogether—"

"Like an abortion?"

"Yes. We don't do it here, but if you need an address, I can give you one."

"I don't know." She hadn't been raised to be particularly religious or political, and she didn't think she believed a collection of cells could have thoughts or feelings. She tried to imagine what it might look like at this stage, but all she could conjure were colorful 3D images from her high school biology textbook. That, and Baxter's face, twisted with betrayal.

"You don't have to decide today. But it should be soon. Assuming you conceived the last time you had intercourse, you have eleven weeks. After that things become more complicated. I'll give you the clinic information, and then it's up to you. Okay?"

The static returned to her ears, the blurriness to her eyes. This couldn't be happening.

And yet, it was.

"Okay." The voice that responded sounded like it came from miles away. As if her own lips, her own tongue, belonged to someone else. Because they did.

Her body was no longer her own.

Perhaps it never had been.

CHAPTER 31

The thought of returning to her cold, dark apartment after her appointment was unfathomable. Marceline studied the bus routes posted at the stop outside the medical complex, stomach roiling and constricting—with what? The fetus growing inside her, or just stress? When her bus came, she couldn't bring herself to climb aboard. So what if a detour to the café would mean getting home late? Baxter would just have to make his own damn dinner.

She doubled back to the clinic and asked to borrow the receptionist's phone. Thankful Baxter was still at work, she left a hurried message on the house phone saying she would be working late, forcing herself to sound bright and cheerful despite the vicious churning in her gut. Fizzing with barely contained emotions, she went back outside, crossed the street, and waited for a different bus—one that would take her to San Francisco.

On the bus, she pressed her forehead against the cool glass of the window, willing herself not to vomit. She disembarked at her stop, clutching her stomach as she trudged down the alley and let herself into the café using her feather key.

Lucretia startled, almost dropping the three-tiered pastry stand she was carrying, but when she saw who it was, her panic evaporated. "Marce? Where were ye, earlier? Sylvan was just about ready to call Interpol."

Sylvan's head snapped up. He'd been folding origami cranes with a customer at the center table, the white chicken pecking at a saucer of crumbs beside him.

Marceline opened her mouth to respond. Instead, she burst into tears.

In an instant, her friends surrounded her.

"What is it, child?" Kilda cooed as Marceline sobbed. "What did he say to ye?" The old woman took Marceline in her frail arms.

Marceline couldn't answer. Telling them would make it real.

"You are here now," Sylvan said. "You are safe." Red-eyed, Marceline peeked over Kilda's shoulder to where he hung back, the smooth skin of his forehead contorted in sympathy. He made a move forward, as if he was going to hug her too, then stalled, a helpless expression falling over him. An expression that only made Marceline cry harder.

In response, Lucretia's muscular arms wrapped around both Marceline and Kilda. "Whatever it is he did, I know a final straw when I see one," the feathered woman murmured, her talons brushing lightly up and down Marceline's back. And meanwhile, all Marceline could do was sob—for the life she'd wanted, for the years she'd wasted, for the awkward distance Sylvan now kept, and for the cluster of cells growing inside her. She sobbed until Lucretia's gauzy tunic was soaked, until she felt depleted.

Marceline cried herself dry.

"Surely ye cannae be going back to him now." Lucretia's voice was uncharacteristically gentle.

Marceline sniffled. "I have nowhere else to go."

"What are we, bloody chopped liver?"

Marceline pulled away to look at her, feeling as small and vulnerable as a child. "Could I?"

"Ye dinnae need to ask permission." Compassion glinted from the inky depths of the goddess's eyes. "This place is for anyone who needs it, and trust me, Marce, ye need it. Why don't ye stay a night or two?"

“Could I stay longer? I mean, just long enough for Baxter to give up on me? Maybe a few months?”

“I’m afraid that will nae be possible, child,” Kilda said gently, exchanging a glance with Lucretia. “The café is a haven for yearning souls, aye, but it cannae replace the ‘real’ world. ’Tis meant for temporary solace, nae for hiding away forever. Problems must be faced. If ye stay too long, ye risk losing yer mind. It’s happened before.”

“But Lucretia never leaves.”

“I’m a goddess, Marce. ’Tis different for me.”

Marceline swallowed. She hated to admit it, but they were right. Simply running away from her problems wasn’t the answer. She looked at Sylvan, who lingered off to the side, listening but saying nothing. He gave her a small smile, brown eyes shining with concern.

“Dinnae despair, child. We have something for ye,” Kilda said.

Marceline swiped at her cheeks again. “You already gave me a present last week.”

Lucretia rolled her eyes. “We had a feeling ye’d be needing a little extra help soon.”

Kilda dug a little velvet sack from her sweater pocket and plopped it into Marceline’s hand.

“But—”

“Aye, I know, ’tis nae yer birthday,” Lucretia said. “Just open it before I do it for ye.”

Marceline loosened the drawstring, peering inside. She gasped. “How much money is in here?”

“Significantly less than I gave the teller,” Kilda lamented. “’Tis a right scandal, the commission they take on top of the exchange rate.”

“A thousand dollars, roughly,” Lucretia announced. “I understand there’s nae getting by without money these days. A shame it’s come to that, but there ’tis.”

Marceline pulled the bag shut again. "This is what I've earned?"

"Nae, consider it a bonus." Kilda raised a gnarled finger, cutting off Marceline's protest. "Indulge me, child. I'm an old lady with a house full of more wee knickknacks and heirlooms than I can keep track of. Besides, it pleases me, knowing I'm helping ye."

"But—"

"Nae," Lucretia cut in. "Nae buts. Ye've suffered enough."

Choked up, Marceline cradled the pouch. "It's just... it's so kind..."

"Well, I'm proud of ye." Lucretia shrugged.

Marceline smiled through her tears. "Wow, Lu, I didn't think you were the sentimental type."

"Believe it or nae, Mother used to say I was *too* sentimental," Lucretia admitted. "'Twas nae fitting for a goddess, she'd say."

"Well, I wouldn't know about that, but I do think you'd make an exceptional human," Marceline said gently.

"All right, all right," Lucretia retorted, hiding the telltale shine glazing in her obsidian eyes. "I like ye, and ye like me. Let's stop this nonsense before it gets out of hand. And if ye tell anyone I've gone soft, I'll have ye murdered."

"Of course." Marceline smiled, willing herself not to cry again. "That's totally fair."

Lucretia brewed a scalding tea of fragrant herbs, which Marceline sipped in silence beside the fire, minutes stretching into hours. Kilda and Lucretia took turns sitting with her in silent support. All the while, Marceline clutched her bag, the address of the free clinic radiating through the canvas, triggering nauseous spasms from the deepest parts of her anatomy. Leaving Baxter was only step one. She could escape halfway across the earth, but part of him would remain inside her, a ticking time bomb wrought of their mingled DNA. Unless.

Time meandered, waning past the hour she usually went home. Baxter must be furious, she thought, dread pooling in her gut, yet she couldn't bring herself to leave. Around her, the café went to sleep. The masks slumbered upon the mantel, and the birds dozed in the rafters. Even Maia the plant emitted a chorus of tinny rumbles from each of her snoring heads.

Kilda and Lucretia retired to bed, and then there was only Sylvan, sitting quietly beside her. Where a moment ago exhaustion had tugged at her eyelids, now every part of her came alive. She stole a sideways glance at him, the whole miserable episode of the failed kiss replaying in her mind. God, he was right. She truly was a mess. She squeezed her eyes shut, bile rising in her throat—a timely reminder that she had bigger problems to worry about than silly infatuations.

But when she opened her eyes again, Sylvan was watching her.

Her breath snagged. She gazed back, daring to hope he'd changed his mind, that he'd lean toward her and tell her he'd been wrong to reject her—even if it was a terrible idea. The dancing flames brushed his pensive face with a golden shimmer.

"I should go," he sighed, voice barely breaking the electric silence that had fallen over the room like a fine dusting of powdery snow.

"Yeah," Marceline said, hating the words coming out of her mouth. "Me too."

He hesitated, and for a moment their shared reluctance hung heavy in the air, and she thought he might relent. Instead, he reached out and squeezed her hand, his touch light as air. Electricity sparked between them as she moved to entangle her fingers in his. "I'm sorry," he said. Then he pulled his hand free, heaved himself out of his chair, and walked away.

Sylvan's departure left a gaping hole in the empty café. Marceline stared at the dying embers in the hearth, trying to kindle some semblance of hope. Wishing she were a goddess so she could stay here forever, hiding from her problems like Lucretia.

But she couldn't. She knew she couldn't. And as tempting as it was to spend the night, she knew she had to get this over with.

Gathering her courage, she clutched her feather key in her hand and headed for the door.

As it turned out, Baxter was not home when Marceline returned to the apartment. It didn't take a genius to guess what had happened. More than likely, he'd arrived home, found her gone, and waited for her to return, growing increasingly angry until he'd finally left to drown his fury in liquor.

Like he always did.

Marceline couldn't have been more relieved.

CHAPTER 32

If the Bartender had looked forward to Baxter's visits before, now she practically salivated at the thought of him walking through the door, and every customer who wasn't him sent thunderous rage rolling through her body. In the two months since he'd mentioned the raven, he'd returned a dozen times. Each time, the Bartender hung on his every word, desperate for a sliver of information, for something she could actually *use*. She was getting awfully tired of pretending to care about his relationship drama.

Now, he was back again, raging drunk and sick with jealousy.

"I can't do this anymore." His glass clattered onto its side, rolling back and forth across the scratched counter with a discordant scrape. "I can't keep pretending everything's fine. She deserves to be punished! She blatantly defied our agreement, admitted she was going off to work, and I'm not even allowed to ask her about it? It doesn't make sense."

"Just be patient," the Bartender sighed, pulling away again, though in truth she wanted to slap him. Marceline could fuck anyone she wanted, for all Bronagh cared. She just needed to know about Quill. Why was Baxter so bloody useless? She reined in her rage, controlling her voice.

"You know what they say: Good things come to those who wait. You have to trust me."

"But I feel like a wet blanket! The bitch is walking all over me! Whatever happens in that café of hers, it *means* something to her. She's even been sleeping with a feather tucked under her pillow. This big, golden thing. She thinks I don't know—as if I don't sleep right next to her! What am I supposed to make of that?"

For the first time in an endless vortex of indistinguishable years, the Bartender dropped a glass. Sharp projectiles burst in all directions.

Baxter jerked his head up in alarm.

The Bartender did not move a muscle. The information dug its claws—no, *talons*—deep into the dusty remnants of the past, down through layer upon layer of sediment. Sifting through the silt of memory, she grasped for artifacts. Something ancient unfurled inside her, murderous and angry, triumphant and sweet. She could see it now, clear as the night it had happened: the dying goddess, locking Bronagh away. A smear of gold, glinting in the dark. A feather that was also a key.

This was it. Her ticket out of this crumbling tavern.

The X on her neck crackled with electricity.

Baxter almost fell off his stool. Drunkenly, he stumbled to his feet, nearly falling backward into the billiards table and disturbing the snakes writhing on its surface. "Bartender?"

The details of her plan careened into place, fragments of memory sharpening the past into a fresh, bleeding wound. Trembling with furious celebration, she lunged for another glass and hurled it across the tavern. It shattered against the dartboard. Shards stabbed the board's fleshy surface, blood bubbling up from the lacerations and dripping down the wall.

Baxter recoiled. "Wh-what's happ—"

She cut him off with a resounding screech. "Get me that feather."

The pathetic human stumbled over another stool, flailing to catch his balance. "I don't under—"

She lunged over the counter, wrapping both hands around Baxter's neck. His veins throbbed and pulsed beneath her thumbs.

"Stop!" he choked out. "What— Why—?"

"That feather." Her whole body clenched with rampant need. "The gold one. Get it for me."

"Please let—let go," he pleaded, his voice a stifled mewl. "I'll—get it," he gasped. "I promise."

She released him so violently he almost lost his footing again.

"Go now," she growled, "then return immediately. Do you hear me?"

He gulped, staggering. But even after he'd regained his balance, he made no move to leave.

"Did I stutter?"

Baxter gave her a wide-eyed look, head shaking vigorously. "No, no. It's just, we're trying to start a family, and with my wife lying to me, well, I have a lot on my plate—"

"Bax." She willed herself to calm down, reining in her frantic energy and redirecting it at Baxter so that he flinched beneath her gaze. "We've known each other a long time, haven't we?"

The human nodded, his Adam's apple sailing up and down his throat. "Over twenty years." His eyes dropped to the floor. "You're my only friend."

"Well," she purred, lips curling into the most compassionate smile she could muster. "Now it's time to do me a little favor. Believe me, Bax, you won't regret it. I may seem like I'm just some washed-up goth stuck behind a dingy bar, but when I get out of here, I'll be more powerful than you can imagine. And if you stick with me, you can be powerful too. You may be the unluckiest bastard I've ever met, but if you help me out of here, I can do great things for you, Baxter. I can turn your sorry life around—make you the happiest man alive. I can bring your little wife running back to you, begging you to impregnate her." She inched closer to him, cupping his face in her hands, her voice dipping to a low, intimate register. "It's what you deserve. What you've always deserved."

"Promise?" The human trembled from head to toe, his voice cracking. Just the effect she'd intended.

"Promise," she murmured.

"But... I just don't understand how it's possible."

"Oh, Bax. My sweet, naive Bax. I've been hanging around in this goddamn dump of a tavern since you were a child—and have I aged by even a day?"

"Well, no."

"Exactly. You've witnessed impossible things. It's time to accept the world for what it is."

"But—about Marceline. What if she refuses?"

"I wouldn't worry about that." Bronagh smiled, a dark malice bubbling inside her. "I can be quite persuasive."

"If you can fix my wife and give me a son..." He trailed off, as if this idea only existed far beyond the scope of his limited imagination. "Well, I'd do anything for that."

Bronagh's lip curled in triumph. She had him in her pocket.

With one sensual finger, she reached out, tracing his chiseled jawbone. "Deal. I'll make your wildest dreams come true, in exchange for one simple favor."

The human glistened with sweat, mouth twisting as he fought some internal battle. For a moment, Bronagh feared his cowardice would return, that he'd refuse, and walk away forever.

But then, he looked at her, the resolve in his eyes hard as steel. "I'll do it."

After he left, the Bartender paced back and forth behind the counter. Determination bubbled within her as each detail resurfaced from the hurricane of memories: The despicable villagers and their gossip. Reeking baskets of soiled washing. The chief fawning over her sister. *Everyone* fawning over her sister.

Quill would pay for how they'd treated Bronagh. They would *all* pay.

The X on her neck still pulsed, but now another even stronger sensation was taking over: Her chest throbbed. In her rib cage, something twitched. The Eternal Feather, the one she'd rightfully taken—the key to the goddess's power.

Itching to be unleashed.

CHAPTER 33

When Marceline woke up in her bed, after too few hours of fitful sleep, she found that Baxter still hadn't returned. A distant part of her wondered if something had happened to him, but the truth was, his absence was a relief.

Rising from the bed and peering nervously out the window to make sure his car was really gone, she pulled the feather from under her pillow and held it to her chest as if it might bring her courage. Her stomach lurched, reminding her that even if she packed up and left immediately, her most pressing issue remained unsolved, right there in her womb.

She knew what she had to do.

Her insides constricted, the near-constant turmoil spiking as she staggered toward the somber living room where they still kept a house phone attached to the wall—the one she'd left the message on the day before. The landlord had planned to remove it, but Baxter had asked to keep it so he could check in on Marceline from work. Check in on her, or surveil her? She whimpered, every interaction from the last five years shifting into a more sinister light. How had she let him do this to her?

Her fingers shook as she pulled the slip of paper from her pocket and dialed the number. When the chipper voice of a receptionist greeted her, she almost lost her nerve. Instead, she forced herself to speak.

"Hello, I'd like to schedule"—she took a shaky breath—"an abortion. My doctor told me to call here..."

The receptionist took down her details, her light, cheery voice a stark contrast to the worries churning in Marceline's gut as she stared at the golden fibers of her feather.

"You're in luck," the woman chirped. "We just had a cancellation. If you can get here today, we can fit you in at twelve thirty."

"Twelve thirty?" Marceline swallowed, looking at the clock on the wall. It was 10:47 now. She took in the shabby living room, searching for an answer she already knew. "I'll be there."

The receptionist gave Marceline directions, and Marceline thanked her, ending the call. Less than two hours. Less than that, even, with travel time. Such a tiny window for such a life-changing decision. She hadn't even started packing her things...But perhaps that was a blessing. After all, she didn't want to spend a minute more than she had to in this depressing apartment, with its rusting fixtures and chipping paint, its faint, moldy odor that clung to the walls and permeated her dreams.

Perhaps she'd leave not only Baxter, but California altogether. Perhaps she'd even find a way to leave the country. How long could she last with only the money Lucretia and Kilda had given her? It had been such a generous act, but Marceline couldn't expect them to pay her indefinitely. Sooner or later, she'd need a real job. She gripped her feather tighter.

Let's make this fast, she thought, heading back into the bedroom. She set the feather on her pillow and made a beeline for the closet. When she dug out her ancient duffel bag, a flood of memories assaulted her. She'd used the same bag to pack her overnight things when she and Baxter were dating, against her father's wishes. What if she'd listened to him? How would her life have been different? She began pulling clothes from the closet and throwing them haphazardly into the bag, regret and anger making her reckless as she tossed coat hangers aside, clanging around and muttering to herself.

"Marce."

She froze, dropping the winter coat she'd been clenching. Baxter was not at work. Baxter was right here.

A clammy sweat broke out over her brow. She'd been too absorbed in her task to pay attention to the rattle of his keys in the door, to his softly approaching footsteps. With agonizing slowness, she willed her body to turn and face him.

He loomed in the doorway, his laser-beam gaze boring into her. "You can't leave me."

His voice rang with authority, the statement unnerving in its directness. An order? A simple fact? She braced herself, trying to muster courage. Excuses flitted around her head: *Who said I'm leaving? I'm just cleaning out the closet.* Could she deflect instead? Confront him about where he'd spent the night? All the possible responses clamored inside her, making her dizzy. But deception wouldn't do anymore.

"I have to," she said, as gently as she could.

His voice broke, features twisting into rage. "You think anyone else will take care of you like I do? Stupid bitch! You won't survive without me."

The insult only hardened her resolve. "I will."

"No, you won't." Without warning, his tone turned pleading. It was only then she realized how disheveled he looked. "You don't know anything about the world. It's hard out there. Hard and cruel, and—and dirty." He gripped her arms, like he was trying to anchor her to himself, his storm-gray eyes begging her. As if he hadn't called her a bitch seconds before. "Women get attacked—abused and raped and murdered—every single day. You need me to protect you, Marce." The alcoholic stench on his breath made her cringe.

She wriggled out of his grasp and turned back to the closet. "I can take care of myself."

"No, you can't! I know what I'm talking about. You *know* my story. I had no one to count on. You don't wanna know what that's like."

"I won't be alone." She crammed another sweater into her bag and grabbed a shirt off a hanger.

In the blink of an eye, his rage returned, sharper than ever. "Oh yeah?" he growled, yanking the shirt out of her hand and tossing it aside. "You think your fucking workplace takes in refugees? Or do you have a boyfriend there? Is that who you were with last night?"

"Don't." Her nails dug into her palms, nerves jangling. She knew each of her husband's moods by heart, but the way he switched erratically between them now rattled her down to the marrow of her bones. What if he hit her? Would she be able to dodge him?

He seethed, taking a step closer. "Don't lie to me, Marce. Who the fuck is he? What does he have that I don't?"

"Drop it, Baxter." She turned back to the closet, pulling clothes off hangers with determination.

"Answer the question!" His voice rose. A ripple of fear scurried down her back as she jammed fistfuls of clothing into the duffel. "Don't you dare ignore me. I'm still your husband."

She wheeled around. "He's *nice* to me," she snapped, then froze. She hadn't meant to say that.

Panic rising, her gaze shot to the door, plotting an escape route.

But Baxter didn't lunge for her. Instead, he jolted, like he'd been punched in the stomach.

Slowly, he made his way to the bed, sinking onto its edge, gray eyes swimming with hurt. Marceline watched him, unconvinced the danger had passed. She was distantly aware that just a few months before, her instinct would have been to throw herself to her knees before him and apologize. To grovel. Now, she couldn't fathom doing such a thing. All she wanted was to get away from him, as quickly as she was able.

"So it's me," Baxter whispered.

Marceline said nothing.

"I don't deserve love."

She held fast to the closet door, saying nothing, bracing herself for a tide of sympathy that never came.

"It's true." His face crumpled, mouth distorted. "She's wrong—I don't deserve better. I'm worthless."

"She? Who's she, Baxter?"

"It's why my mother didn't want me—and all of those families—none of them wanted me—"

She gritted her teeth, bracing herself against the urge to reassure him, against five years of desperate dependence. She was stronger than that now. She had to be.

His gaze speared her, blazing with pure anger that twisted his handsome face into something deeply ugly. "If you leave me, I'll kill myself."

She looked away. This was manipulation. The realization set off fireworks in her brain as her mind raced to all those articles she'd read online about toxic relationships. He was using her compassion against her, trying to bully her into staying. She felt sick to her stomach. Would he actually do it? She swallowed.

"I can't be responsible for your mental health anymore. I have to be responsible for me."

"You're saying you don't care if I die?" In an explosion of motion, he sprang from the bed and lunged at her. "After everything I've done for you?"

She bounded backward, hands raised to protect her face. Adrenaline sang through her veins as she grasped for something—anything—to use as a weapon, but all she could reach was another measly coat hanger.

Baxter sneered at the flimsy piece of plastic but dropped his hands. "You'll come crawling back as soon as he realizes he doesn't want you," he murmured into her ear, his voice all venom.

With that, he spun on his heels, stalking out of the room.

The slam of the door reverberated through the apartment as Marceline gripped the closet door, desperate to soothe the hurricane of her fear. He was gone.

It was over.

CHAPTER 34

The moment Bronagh saw Baxter stumble into the tavern, she tore toward him, knocking over tables as she went. "Well?"

Panting, Baxter stopped short, an uncertain look clouding his eyes. Bronagh took a step back. She was scaring him, she realized, breathing deeply before slipping him a reassuring smile. She couldn't afford to lose his trust—not until she was out.

"I have it," he said finally.

The Bartender's pulse began to rush again, the feather twitching so violently in her chest she could scarcely focus on anything else.

"The bitch just left it lying on her pillow," Baxter continued, his voice growing stronger as spite overtook his uneasiness. "Almost like she *wanted* me to take it."

"Let's see it then." It took everything Bronagh had to harness the usual silkiness of her voice while her heart thundered inside her. Baxter reached into his jacket, revealing the feather. Despite having been crammed in his pocket, it still looked intact, long and graceful and curling, glinting with a golden shimmer.

At long last, her key had arrived.

Bronagh exhaled, reaching out with trembling fingers.

Baxter stepped back. "First I want to revise our agreement."

The Bartender barely restrained herself from wringing his neck. The world stalled as the feather's graceful tip waved in the air, rocked by Bronagh's own heaving breath, consuming her every thought. "Go on."

"Marceline betrayed me." He clenched his fists, crumpling the feather's delicate fibers. "She was supposed to be there for me, but she was planning to leave me all along. I need you to make her suffer."

Bronagh's obsidian lips curled. Perhaps he was not as spineless as she thought. "Done."

"And not just her, either," Baxter continued, his voice growing stronger, gathering speed. "I want everyone who's ever fucked with me to suffer." He was almost shouting now. "I want them to be sorry they ever met me."

"Deal." Bronagh's grin was genuine now. "Oh, Bax. We are going to have so much fun."

At last, Baxter handed over the feather. It touched her skin, and the entire tavern shuddered in response—floorboards groaning and creaking—the whole place awakening from some comatose state. The glasses and bottles rattled on their shelves, the dartboard expelled bloody trickles from its many perforations, and the snakes slithered hurriedly back into the pockets of the billiard table. Bronagh trembled with wolfish pleasure as she brought the golden feather to her face.

"This is it." She turned it over in her palm, skin flaring with heat. "This is the one!" Her voice crackled with joy.

Her gaze shifted to the door behind Baxter—that infernal door that had so long remained shut to her. Now, its surface wavered, shifting from rough to smooth, from wood to metal until the unmistakable form of a lock materialized.

Bronagh bolted for it, shoving the feather's stem toward the lock. The feather's tip resisted the metal like the wrong end of a magnet, but she fought against it, grunting, every part of her tensed with the rippling strain of long-dormant muscles coming alive—until at last, she managed to maneuver the stem into the hole.

The lock clicked.

Ecstasy exploded within her as the door groaned open. A flash of light illuminated the world beyond, before disappearing just as quickly. Beside her, Baxter staggered, thrown off balance by the turbulent void behind the door.

Gasping, Bronagh stared into the churning emptiness. She felt herself soften. With a burbling rush of affection, she turned to Baxter, extending her hand. "Come now," she purred. "Take me to your world."

"Bartender—" Baxter started to say, but she stopped him with a medusan stare, a giddy grin tearing her black-painted lips apart.

"My name," she rasped, "is Bronagh."

She felt him tense as he wrapped his fingers around hers, the world jolting around them. They stepped forward in unison, the void whirling away with a sickening motion that made her stomach rise into her throat.

A split second later, the two of them landed knees-first in sludge.

Bronagh blinked the dizziness away, rising to her feet. It was daytime—the air crisp and gray and cold...and utterly foul-smelling. She swiveled her head, taking it all in. They'd landed in the mud outside of a decrepit blue-plastic structure, disguised with layers of graffiti. Some kind of outhouse.

Bronagh gave a sharp laugh. "*This* is my front door? No wonder you always smell of shit when you visit!" Baxter looked affronted, but Bronagh couldn't bring herself to care. She stumbled away from the structure, throwing her hands to the sky and inhaling. "The air's different outside. I'd forgotten."

"Bartender?" Baxter half slipped in the mud as he stumbled after her. They appeared to be in some sort of empty lot, in the center of a patchy green space surrounded by trees. "What are we—"

"What part of 'my name is Bronagh' didn't you hear?" she snapped, before morphing her lips back into a smile that made the mortal visibly flinch. His vulnerability softened her as she took in his disheveled, mud-and-probably-shit-slathered appearance. *Oh, Bax*, she thought, reaching out to ruffle his hair. *I can't wait until we find out what I'm capable of...*

She turned and took off, stomping over the half-torn-down chain-link fence toward where towering trees reached into the gloomy, overcast sky.

Baxter cleared his throat, trailing after her. "Um, how long were you stuck in the tavern?"

Her laugh rang sharper than glass. "Hell if I know. Too long. Now. How did you get here?"

"I drove—"

"In a car?" She grinned. She'd learned all about the outside world from her customers, and gleaned snippets from the nightmares on her mounted television screens, but she'd never actually believed she'd be able to come out and play. "How charming. Why don't you show me?"

It wasn't really a question.

Baxter made a strangled sound. She could practically hear his gears turning, questioning whether he could trust her, whether this was all a terrible idea. Poor, pathetic Baxter. He was growing more entertaining by the minute.

When they came to his rusty gray car, parked at the edge of the grass, she couldn't help but cackle. Baxter shot her an uncertain glance, his hand trembling as he opened the passenger's-side door for her.

"So, uh, where to?"

She grinned at him, reveling in the tension of his clenched jaw. "Tell me, Baxter, what's the most miserable place you can think of? I'd like to run some experiments."

CHAPTER 35

Marceline sat on the bed, hands still shaking, though Baxter had been gone for at least ten minutes. Her stomach roiled as she replayed their interaction. *You'll come crawling back as soon as he realizes he doesn't want you.* His words carved into her mind, amplifying the pain in her stomach with their cruelty. *He doesn't know me*, she told herself. *I have plenty to offer.* Still, she couldn't shake the fear she'd felt when he'd leapt toward her.

The interaction had left her sweat-drenched, and she felt desperate to cleanse her body and spirit of the grime of this sad life—the insecurity, the fear, the submission. She wanted to scrub it all off, to let every memory swirl away down the drain. *Yes, that was it*, she told herself, standing. She would shower, gather the last of her things, and head to her appointment, where the doctors would banish the final, terrifying thread of potential linking her to him.

Then she would be free.

In the bathroom, she threw back the shower curtain and turned the faucet to nearly scalding. Steam sank into her pores as she contemplated the cracked tiles, the showerhead that shot sporadic streams in the wrong direction. She wouldn't miss it.

Squeezing out a blob of shampoo, she began to massage her scalp. But then a thought struck her: Where was her feather?

She screwed her eyes against a stream of suds, mentally tiptoeing through the emotional minefield of the past half hour. She knew she'd been holding it during the phone call, so she must have set it somewhere when she was packing. In her duffel, maybe? The events of the last hour made it hard to focus.

Don't panic just yet, Marceline told herself. *One thing at a time*. She'd probably left it somewhere in the bedroom.

She dried off and unearthed a pair of jeans she hadn't yet packed and a powder-blue sweatshirt with a kitten on the front—another garage sale treasure Baxter had mocked. Once dressed, she dumped the contents of the duffel out on the bed. She didn't see the feather right away, but then again, she'd stuffed a lot of things in the bag all at once. She rummaged around the pile, dispersing the items over the bedspread.

Nothing.

Relax, she told herself. If it wasn't in the bag, it had to be somewhere else in the house. Probably somewhere obvious, like the closet floor. Still barefoot, she plunged to her hands and knees, searching. And when she didn't find it there, she scrambled down the hall, checking the side table near the wall phone, then returning to ransack the bedroom once more. Peering under furniture, Marceline upended everything she encountered.

The feather was nowhere to be found.

Hope began to fade. No, Marceline thought. No, no, this isn't possible. Lucretia's frantic words echoed in her mind: *Dinnae let them out of your sights under* any *circumstances.* She was no closer to knowing which mysterious threat loomed on the horizon, but whatever it was, it had Lucretia—strong, no-nonsense Lucretia—trembling with fear.

She would not be pleased.

Marceline doubled over, queasy with preemptive guilt. And after she and Kilda had given her all that money, too... What a way to repay them.

Could Baxter have taken it? No, no. He had no interest in shiny trinkets, and he didn't even know what it did. Even if he somehow did know, she couldn't imagine someone as serious as Baxter believing in enchanted objects.

She slipped on her sneakers and repacked her duffel, anxiety churning. She needed to hurry if she wanted to get to her appointment in time. Slinging the bag over her shoulder, she threw one last look around the bedroom—remembering to stuff her globe lamp into a plastic shopping bag—then slunk into the hallway and through the shabby living room toward the door, slamming it shut behind her.

In the confines of the elevator, Marceline fought the dizzying spiral. She'd already made a colossal mess of things with Sylvan, and now Lucretia would likely be furious. But she'd find a way to fix it. She had to.

She stopped in front of the mailboxes, slipping the apartment key into the slot for Baxter to find later. At least one thing was certain: She and Baxter were done.

CHAPTER 36

Baxter gripped the steering wheel, his discomfort drilling that familiar fizzle of anticipation into Bronagh's stomach, already multiplied a thousandfold by her sudden freedom. She grinned as the boxy metal-and-glass facade of the hospital's ER came into view.

They were going to have so much fun.

As soon as they parked, Bronagh tore from the vehicle and marched through the hospital's double doors. Inside, a handful of sullen patients populated the lines of attached plastic chairs—a woman filling out a form on a clipboard, a man with a bloody cloth around his thumb, a child doubled over in pain while her mother stroked her back.

"Can I help you?" A young, bespectacled receptionist frowned at Bronagh, like she might be a hallucination.

"Oh, I'm sure you can." Glee palpitated like trapped flies in Bronagh's chest. "I thought it would be all chaos and carnage in here, but it seems you're having a slow day." She leaned over the reception desk, rejoicing at the way the girl recoiled.

"Um, are you here because of an emergency?"

"Yes, indeed." Bronagh's sharp black nails drummed against the counter. "The emergency is I'm terribly bored."

Somewhere behind them, a patient muttered into a phone.

The girl's glasses magnified her unease as she drew back, her rolling chair squeaking against the linoleum. "Are you here to visit someone?"

"Oh yes. Everyone."

The girl swallowed, voice cracking. "I'm going to need a specific name."

Anxiety churned in the stale air of the waiting room, making Bronagh's heart race. A feeling she could easily get drunk on.

"Come on now"—Bronagh glanced at the receptionist's name tag—"Kelly. Don't tell me you'd rather watch the hours tick away than see me shake things up." She reached over the counter, tucking a limp strand of the girl's hair behind her ear, like a cat toying with a mouse.

The receptionist stood so abruptly she almost tripped. "If you aren't injured or checking in on someone, I'm afraid—"

"Relax, Kelly!" Bronagh laughed. "Indulge me. What would float your boat? Heart attack, maybe? Gun wound? Ooh, how about a freak accident? Like, you're climbing a ladder reaching for a light bulb..."

A tremor rose in the girl's voice. "I'm calling security." Her hand was already wrapped around the corded phone receiver. "Hello, this is—"

Bronagh reached over the desk and pressed the button on the phone cradle, ending the call. "No, you're not." She rounded the counter and grabbed the girl's chin, forcing her to look into her eyes. "You're going to give us a tour."

The alarm on the receptionist's face vanished, and her mouth went slack. Triumph detonated in Bronagh's chest, the feather inside it twitching, alive and well. The phone receiver dropped from Kelly's hand, clattering onto the desk. When she spoke, the tremor in her voice had been replaced by a steady monotone. "Okay."

Bronagh turned to shoot Baxter a grin. "See what I mean, Bax? Stick with me, and the world's your fucking oyster."

Baxter's expression—like he might be sick—made her laugh out loud.

The receptionist floated toward a set of doors, her face blank. "Wait," Bronagh ordered, grabbing Baxter's hand. She called over her shoulder, addressing everyone in the waiting room: "You're all coming too."

She thrilled as the patients and guests rose from their chairs in unison, that same glazed look falling over their features.

Her entire mortal life, Bronagh had been insignificant. Then, in the tavern, she'd been little more than a parasite. Now, as the clustered patients followed the receptionist through the doors without question, she felt powerful.

Powerful, like a goddess.

I deserve this, she thought, triumph singing through her veins.

The muffled wail of sirens crescendoed behind them as they made their way down the glaring-white hospital hallway. Bronagh knew the sound well, for she'd often heard it in the nightmares that endlessly played on her tavern's boxy televisions.

"Stop!" she commanded her followers, pulse quickening, relishing the impending confrontation. She spun to face the double doors they'd just traversed, her skin sizzling with delight as—sure enough—a pair of armed cops burst through.

"Hands in the air," a policewoman shouted, aiming a gun at Bronagh. The pack of expressionless patients merely stalled.

"Oh, hello." Bronagh leered. "Are you here for the tour?"

"I said hands in the air, goth girl," the policewoman growled.

"Such a lack of manners," Bronagh lamented. "Put the guns down, kids, before you hurt yourselves."

The police officers' eyes glazed over. They set their guns on the ground, the intensity fading from their faces.

It was almost too easy, Bronagh mused, turning back to the receptionist. "Now, Kelly, I'd love to take this party into one of the wards."

"Okay," the receptionist complied, voice flat. She led the group around a corner.

Bronagh addressed the pair of cops with a sly wink. "Follow the leader." The officers joined the procession, a stiff military precision to their coordinated gait.

Beside her, Baxter had to lope to keep up. "Bar—Bronagh. What are you going to do?" He looked sickly and pale as a plague victim.

"I told you, I'm experimenting."

"And you're sure we can't get in trouble?"

When she halted, the cops and patients plowed into her like a traffic pileup. "*Get in trouble?*" she scoffed. Inside the tavern she'd craved his misery, but now that she was free and surrounded by countless malleable humans, something strange was happening: He was starting to annoy her. He'd always been spineless, but that spinelessness tasted different now that she was out.

She sighed, shooting him a withering look. "You truly are the most pathetic variety of chickenshit."

Baxter colored, glancing around the group as if worried the others had heard, but their gazes were empty. A small mercy for him, Bronagh reflected, noting the hurt in Baxter's eyes with dispassion. *Peculiar*, she thought, ordering the receptionist to keep it moving. Perhaps she'd only been fond of Baxter because she'd had so little else. Perhaps now— The burgeoning theory was interrupted as they crossed paths with a nurse pushing a bandaged man on a gurney.

"Oh, how fun!" Bronagh exclaimed, lunging toward the gurney. "This is mine now."

"Okay," the nurse agreed and floated aimlessly off in the other direction.

Bronagh tilted the gurney, and the injured man gave a shocked groan as he crashed to the ground in a tangle of limbs. Grinning down at him, she climbed onto the gurney's upholstered pad. Even the village chief had had to walk on his own two feet. "Push me, Bax!"

Baxter gaped at the writhing patient. "But—"

"I could *make* you do it, you know."

Baxter swallowed and gripped the gurney's metal handles, a whole host of emotions playing across his face—emotions that Bronagh had no interest in analyzing at present.

"Pick a door, Kelly," she said, and the receptionist opened the first door to the right, where a predictably sickly woman lay in a bed. Panicked, the woman lifted her tired head, gawking at Bronagh and her posse as they crowded into the small room. Bronagh giggled, dangling her legs over her mobile throne. "What're you in for?"

"Who are—"

"*Tell me* what you're in for," she repeated, rolling her eyes toward Baxter. "Semantics."

"I'm getting a liver transplant." Dark circles ringed the woman's eyes, skin sallow against the fluorescent lights.

"Well, it's your lucky day." Bronagh beamed, twisting to look at the duo of blank-faced cops. "Who here's an organ donor? Come on, don't make me check IDs."

Both cops raised their hands, expressionless.

"Bax." Bronagh nudged him. "You wanted power, right? I'll let you choose."

"My—my surgery is tomorrow," the woman in the bed sputtered.

"We're able to take you early." Bronagh dismissed her. "Baxter. Choose!"

"You're a nightmare," the woman uttered. "This . . . this can't be real." But even as she spoke, Baxter's arm rose, his finger pointing at the male cop. He gaped in horror at his traitorous finger.

The policeman—a gangly, ruddy-faced man, began unbuttoning his uniform top automatically. Beside him, Baxter grew paler and paler.

"Chop-chop, officer, this isn't a bachelorette party." She nudged Baxter in the ribs, cackling, before pointing to the other cop. "You. Assist him."

The female cop gripped either side of her colleague's shirt. With a rip of fabric, she tore the garment right off his body.

"You've done this before," Bronagh quipped, hopping off the gurney and sauntering across the room, where a small cart displayed an array of surgical instruments. She snatched up a shiny scalpel.

"Catch!"

The male cop's hand shot into the air. He moaned as the blade cut into his palm, blood seeping through his fingers. Baxter twisted away toward the wall, trying to hide from the squelch and stench of flesh and sinew. "It's okay," Bronagh heard him mutter to himself. "It's okay, it's okay, it's okay—"

She was almost relieved when he passed out. Her affection for him was fading by the minute. But she still needed him, she reminded herself. He was her driver, and more importantly, he knew where her sister lurked. She needed him to serve his purpose.

Perhaps after that, she'd kill him.

Bronagh hummed tunelessly to herself, reveling in the joy of freedom. She winked at the dying policeman clutching his own blood-smeared liver in his hand.

No more holding back.

CHAPTER 37

"All done."

Marceline blinked at the blurred shape of the nurse's smile floating above her. Her thoughts swam dreamily through her mind as she tried to make sense of the woman's face, obstructed as it was by colorful flashes from the light fixtures on the ceiling.

"You were very brave. We're going to bring you to another room to let you rest, but I'll be checking in on you. You should be good to go in about an hour."

Dazed, Marceline basked in the light, an airy feeling drifting over her like a cozy blanket. "Drugs are great," she giggled, and the lights blinked in agreement.

The nurse chuckled. "Come on, you."

The room shifted as the nurse helped her up, guiding her into another room. Marceline let herself be led, melting into peaceful bliss as she climbed into a bed with clean, white sheets. The sedatives blurred the details around her. She let herself sink into the feeling of calm as she gazed at a hazy print of a sailboat drifting into the horizon on the opposite wall.

* * *

Later, Marceline left the clinic and boarded a bus to the city, lugging her duffel bag behind her, the plastic bag with the globe lamp clutched in her hand. The anesthesia had worn off, exposing her to a world that felt harsh and sharp around the edges.

She plopped herself onto a hard plastic seat, nudging her things under her feet, and lay her cheek against the cool window. She couldn't believe it was over. Not counting her consultation with the doctor, her ultrasound—during which she'd kept her eyes firmly shut—and the time she'd rested afterward, the operation itself had only lasted ten minutes.

"You might have some light bleeding and some cramping," the nurse had told her before she left, smiling kindly. "I'd take it easy today if I were you, but you should be good to go back to work tomorrow."

Now, Marceline slumped in her seat, wondering if she should regret it. She couldn't bring herself to. It had been necessary to her freedom—a freedom that now stretched before her, vast and daunting. Still, she could not deny the thin veil of sadness that had drifted over her. The thing inside her had represented a new beginning, yes, but its absence did so even more.

Besides, she could still be a mother one day, if she ever felt ready.

She gazed at the light drizzle splattering against the window, trying to subdue the dizzying vertigo that gripped her as a multitude of tiny raindrops slid down the glass. The freedom she'd so longed for gaped ahead, a canyon so vast and deep she couldn't see the bottom.

This morning, she'd been trapped in her marriage, subject to the rules Baxter imposed on her. This morning, she'd been pregnant. How could such a life-changing dilemma have disappeared so quickly? It was so hard to fathom she half expected that now-familiar churning in her stomach to return. Save for an occasional dull cramping, nothing came.

It was truly done.

CHAPTER 38

"You missed everything!" Bronagh accused, slapping Baxter hard in the face. She'd ordered the remaining cop to wheel him to the car in a stolen wheelchair, then dump him in the front seat.

The mortal winced at the impact but kept his eyes squeezed shut, as if he could convince her he was still unconscious. Bronagh wasn't buying it.

"Some sidekick you are." She slapped him again, nails scraping his stubbled jaw.

"Stop it," he whimpered, ending the ruse. "You're hurting me."

"Don't be such a wimp." She slapped him a third time, so hard that his head wobbled with the impact.

"What the hell? I'm awake!" he protested, clutching his face.

"Oh, grow up," Bronagh hissed. "And get your shit together. I need you to drive again."

Baxter groaned, tugging his seat belt on. His fingers shook as they tightened against the steering wheel, his face pink with—what? Anger? Shame? He paused, gaze sliding down to a warm, damp spot on his crotch. He gasped, his complexion deepening further still. Bronagh grinned. She'd been waiting for him to notice.

"What happened?" he asked through gritted teeth.

"You wet yourself," she replied gleefully.

"Besides that." His face was so red, Bronagh could imagine it exploding—a delightful image, to be sure.

"So many things! A blood fight, a couple of spontaneous amputations, then we took turns scaring patients in the cardiac ward—"

"Okay, okay!" Baxter clapped his hands over his ears. "And this . . . this was all for fun?"

"You absolute chickenshit." The Bartender swatted him. "It *was* wildly amusing, yes, but it also served a purpose. My experiment was a success." She leered, gripping Baxter's shoulder so hard her nails dug through his shirt. "Quill doesn't stand a fucking chance."

Baxter nodded with a tad too much emphasis. "Great. Well, I'm actually supposed to be at work, so—"

"Not so fast." Bronagh slapped the car key into his hand, sliding her fingers sensually along his palm as she did. "You'll leave when I say you can."

"I can call you a taxi," Baxter countered, his voice cracking. "I'll even—"

"Shut up," Bronagh interrupted. She was on the brink of compelling him, when he exhaled shakily and stuck the key in the ignition of his own accord. "That's the spirit. Now, can you guess where we're going?"

He shook his head, clearly afraid to speculate.

"We're off to visit your dear wife's place of work."

He swallowed. "Excuse me?"

She grinned. "You want her to suffer, right?"

Baxter said nothing.

"Well? Don't you?"

He mumbled something under his breath.

"Speak up."

"I'm good, actually."

The Bartender howled. "You should see the look on your face. Relax, Bax! Before you wet yourself again."

"I'd rather not see my bitch of a wife right now. She's leaving me, remember?" He glanced in the rearview mirror, tensing when he noticed the ragtag group of vacant-eyed patients and staff piling into an ambulance behind them.

"All the more reason to show her who's boss. Now step on it, before I force you."

With a pathetic whimper, Baxter did as he was told.

Twenty-five minutes later, they peered down the desolate alley. Pregnant storm clouds churned high above, casting shadows that concealed the door at the alley's far end. So this was where her sister had ended up. For all the cozy, crackling fireside vibes in her vision, the place sure looked like a shithole. Bronagh gave a low chuckle. Oh, how the mighty had fallen. And now, she'd fall farther still.

Right into oblivion.

Bronagh strode down the alley, the feather tingling inside her as she stopped before the great oak door with its raven-shaped knocker. Yes, this was it, all right. A pulse of power thrummed in her heart.

Tracing her finger in a circle in the air before her, as she'd seen the goddess do over a thousand years ago, she triumphantly stepped into invisibility, tugging Baxter along with her. Then she climbed the stoop and planted herself in front of the door, inspecting the keyhole beneath the knocker. Could the golden feather that had freed her be used on all Otherworldly realms? She extended a finger, brushing it against the wood—

"Argh!" A white-hot migraine sliced through her skull as she retreated.

"Bronagh?" Baxter called from behind her.

"Shh!" She clutched her head, wincing in pain. "Let me focus."

When at last the ache receded, rage simmered in its place. Quill had accounted for her. Had she given herself away? She scowled at the knocker, this brass replica of the goddess in bird form. The goddess whom she'd fought and injured, possibly killed. Was it smirking at her?

Perhaps this ambush would not be so easy.

A moment of stillness passed as Bronagh glared at the door, ruminating to the sounds of Baxter shivering beside her. When nothing happened, she guessed her intrusion had gone unnoticed.

Good.

She reached her hand out again, careful this time not to touch the wood. She closed her eyes, inexpertly trying to determine the quality of the magic.

There was *something* there. Subtle currents, a certain static—strong enough to raise the hairs on her arms, but not enough to shock her again. Her good humor returned when she felt it. How many times had she wished she could ban a patron whose flavor she had grown tired of? She'd been powerless to keep anyone out before. But now, things were different.

Now, she was out.

Baxter interrupted her scheming. "If you don't need me here anymore, I might—"

Bronagh whipped around. "Didn't I tell you to shut up?" She turned back to the door, and inhaling, focused her attention on the feather in her heart, willing it to pulse its way to her fingertip. It twitched within her, resisting. Did it know she was not its intended mistress? She doubled her efforts, silently commanding the feather to obey.

A moment later, a tingling rush told her she'd succeeded.

Buzzing with triumph, yet determined not to break concentration, Bronagh reached for the door, bracing herself against the pain that would follow.

This time, when her fingertip touched the wood and her head flashed with blinding pain, she was ready for it. *Hold strong*, she told herself, summoning every ounce of self-control so as not to break contact. A moan escaped her, low and anguished, as she dragged her finger over the surface of the door. The druids in the village had always invoked the gods, but Bronagh would do no such thing. Regardless of where it had come from, the power she bore now belonged to her, and her alone. "I hereby block all entrances except this one, calling on no deity save myself," she whispered through the searing chaos in her brain.

The force of the door's own magic thrust Bronagh backward, toppling into Baxter, who broke her fall as they both tumbled to the trash-strewn concrete. For a moment they lay there, stunned. Then, Bronagh released a piercing cackle. She scurried back to her feet, triumph sparking into fireworks as she stared at the door.

A bold, black X had appeared where she'd dragged her finger.

It had worked.

"What does it mean?" Baxter scrambled to his feet, voice cracking. Bronagh only continued to laugh, her manic glee soothing the final pulses of pain singing through her head. Her gaze drifted to the alley's entrance where the ambulance was parked. Inside, her soldiers awaited her orders.

She laid a hand upon her mortal companion's shoulder. "It means, sweet Baxter, there's nowhere left to run."

CHAPTER 39

Have ye thought of any other ways we might fortify the place? Lucretia reached for one of the many bird feeders hanging from the rafters. She was perched on a ladder, talons gripping a bucket of seed.

Nae, love. Nae since five minutes ago. Kilda dipped her quill into an inkpot, looking pointedly at her wife before making an adjustment to her map. *Yer frantic mood is nae helping.*

"I can tell you two are conversing," Sylvan called up. He was holding the base of the ladder steady. "You think you are wily, but I can literally observe your eyes moving to each other."

Ye see? Kilda thought. *Even Sylvan can tell how tense ye are. Ye must relax.*

Relax? How can I relax when everyone I love is in danger of dying, yerself included?

"Hello? I know Kilda is ear-impaired, but, Lu, you possess no excuses! Did you make me invisible?"

"Lucretia's a bit stressed, lad," Kilda apologized.

"Yes, I observed this. Has she considered a massage?"

"Mind yer own bloody business, Sylvan," Lucretia warned. "I swear to bloody Nature, I love ye, but I am nae joking." She flung a handful of birdseed down at Sylvan's head.

"Rude!" He ducked as a flock of canaries dove at him, pecking the seeds from his hair.

"Lucretia!" Kilda chided out loud. In her mind she said: *If ye cannae keep a level head, we'll all be in trouble.*

"We're already all in danger," Lucretia snapped back, forgetting to confine the words to her mind. Bloody humans! At times she could convince herself she was one of them, despite her endless years and the powers pulsing like mysteries beneath her skin. But then there were moments like these. Could they not sense the looming threat, the ominous buzz saturating the air? She scowled, pouring more seed into the feeders. This sense of foreboding wasn't new, but now it seeped to the forefront of her mind, a toxic fog so thick she could almost see it. How did no one else notice?

Even Kilda, who understood the danger Bronagh posed, wasn't treating the threat with the magnitude it deserved. She seemed so certain that Lucretia's instinct would kick in and save them all. Was it the protection of the wedding band that infused her with such confidence? Lucretia scowled, licking a couple of stray seeds off her talon before beginning her descent down the ladder, shooing Sylvan out of the way.

Before she could step down, a jolt of unease struck her heart like a gong. She gripped the ladder's sides, keeping her balance despite the cold shiver rippling down to her tailbone. Fear twinged inside her as the feeder she'd been filling began to tremble.

"Did ye feel that?" Lucretia croaked.

"I did." Sylvan glanced nervously at Kilda, who'd turned her attention to the surface of her teacup, where a turbulent brown storm brewed. "Is it an earthshake?" Sylvan's features twisted in concern.

"There are nae fault lines in the Otherworld." Lucretia scrambled to the ground, searching for Kilda's gaze. *'Tis her. It must be.*

Stay calm, love. We'll fight against her. Ye're nae alone.

"So, what is it?" Sylvan glanced between the two women.

Neither responded. Instead, Lucretia put a talon to her lips, crossing over to Kilda's table. The icy chill down her back drew her shoulders tight as she strained to hear beyond the chatter of birds, the crackling of the fire. *Kilda, what if the ring and the protections I laid down are nae strong enough?*

'Tis nae use worrying about that now, love.

And the weapons! We've nae had time to train Syl—

Sylvan cleared his throat. "Um, what is precisely happening?"

"Ye should go home," Lucretia whispered to him, her tone urgent, her eyes pleading. "'Tis nae safe here."

"I cannot leave you if there lacks safety..."

Lucretia nudged him toward the door. "I'll nae put ye in harm's way."

"But you two will still have danger—"

"Ye're right. Kilda should go as well," she realized. "'Tis my fight." As much as her wife's presence calmed her, she could not risk her getting hurt. Regardless of Kilda's appearance when they touched, she wasn't young. She wouldn't stand a chance.

"I'll nae go anywhere," Kilda huffed.

"Do I have nae authority in my own bloody café?"

"Someone is taking a power vacation," Sylvan mumbled.

Lucretia gripped the edge of Kilda's table so as not to throttle him. "I'm trying to protect ye both," she hissed. "Why does naebody understand?"

Sylvan was about to protest, but she threw him her darkest look. "Fine, whatever. I will just depart, I guess." He shook his head in frustration, marching off to hang his apron.

Exasperated, Lucretia turned back to Kilda. "The map. Do ye see anything strange? Anything different?"

Kilda frowned, adjusting her spectacles over her nose as she peered down at the parchment. "Nae, I dinnae think— Oh." She paused, her wiry brows furrowing. "Oh, wait." Her face slipped into confusion as she pointed to the shifting clouds of ink scrawled across her map, toward a cluster of circles, each now crossed out with a thick, black X.

"Bye," Sylvan shouted. "I am truly leaving."

Lucretia looked down at the map, thrumming with tension. "What? What does it mean?"

"Our portals are closed. All but San Francisco."

Gasping, Lucretia whipped around in a whirl of feathers, her fear flaring as Sylvan reached for the door handle. "Dinnae open that door," she shrieked.

Sylvan froze, dropping his hand. "But you just told me—"

Panic clogged Lucretia's throat. She pushed through it, forcing herself to speak. "Ye cannae go home now, 'tis too late."

Sylvan's brown eyes swam with the same fear they all felt. "Wait, so we are trapped? We cannot return home?"

His question hung in the air like a storm cloud, crackling with the threat of imminent lightning.

"Aye," Lucretia whispered, her blood fizzing with terror. "It seems she's found us at last."

I am death and blood and pain. Stand down or feel my wrath.

Lucretia dragged her feather along the perimeter of the floor, muttering feverishly to herself as she went.

"Do you intend to explain me what is going on?" Sylvan pleaded, tossing another chair onto the growing pile of furniture barricading the door. Lucretia gritted her teeth and redoubled her concentration. The place had to be impenetrable.

"Let her concentrate, Sylvan," Kilda warned.

I am death and blood and pain. Stand down or—

"But if someone plans to attack us, we all should know what we expect, no?" He grabbed another chair, tossing it onto the pile with a clatter.

"Silence!" Lucretia snapped. "For Nature's sake, Kilda, tell him what he needs to know!"

"Me? 'Tis *your* story, Lu!"

"Please, love! There's nae time!" *Breathe*, she told herself. *I am death and blood and pain. Stand down or feel my wrath.* You cannae lose control now. She inhaled, desperate to rein in her frazzled energy, the thoughts swooping like frenzied birds inside her head. She'd spent millennia strengthening the defenses of her realm. The words she whispered to herself—a self-invocation pilfered from her mother—had become second nature, yet she stumbled over them, unable to manifest any conviction.

Ye're right, love. I'm sorry. Ye leave the worrying to me, Kilda whispered in her mind. *Ye just focus on keeping yerself—and all of us—safe.*

"Could someone respond to my query one day?" Sylvan fumed.

Hurriedly, Kilda filled Sylvan in, provoking increasingly distressed noises on his part. Tuning them out, Lucretia crouched back down, swiping her feather to the bottom of the wall. *I am death and blood and pain. Stand down...*

Her confidence wavered. Frustrated, she squeezed her eyes shut and started again. *I am death and blood and pain.* A fearsome claim, but based on what evidence? Without the feather in her heart, Lucretia's mother had been no stronger than a mortal. Why should things be different for Lucretia? Would Bronagh slaughter her the same way?

The entire café reverberated with dread as a heavy knock sounded at the door. Bronagh's cold eyes flashed through Lucretia's mind—a face that had haunted her nightmares for over a thousand years. A shameful whimper escaped her lips, revealing the lie in the incantation. How could she claim such fierceness when her soul cowered in fear? Her sister was far more bloodthirsty than she'd ever be.

"We're doomed," she whispered.

"Nae." Kilda shook her head, fingering her wedding band. "Nae, we must hold out hope."

"Thank God Marceline is not present," Sylvan muttered. The masks on the mantel trembled, and the potted plant burrowed its heads in the soil.

An army of worries crowded Lucretia's mind. Had she spent all these years hiding, only to be ruthlessly slaughtered in the very haven she'd built for herself, for all the suffering people of the world? What would become of them if—

The three of them jolted as another knock resounded. The bird feeders trembled, the hanging whale skeleton clattering like a macabre wind chime. The birds clustered together, dead silent, their beaks turned toward the door.

"Sylvan," Kilda whispered. "Go fetch the bundle of swords from behind Lu's curtain. They're in a flowered tote."

"*A bundle of swords?*" Sylvan repeated, mouth hanging open. "Truly? I lacerate myself when I trim my nails!"

"Ye swing the sharp end at your target," Kilda said. "I'd hoped to get ye trained up but 'tis too late now."

"You are claiming *you* know how to use a sword?"

"I'm nae soldier, but I've been practicing all my life. There's a lot ye dinnae know about me, lad."

Sylvan remained rooted to the spot. "Where even does one acquire a bundle of swords?"

"Well, there's this lovely wholesaler in Glasgow—"

"Sylvan, get the bloody swords!" Lucretia hissed, sending him scurrying. The sourceless glow of the room flickered, plunging them into momentary darkness.

We're going to die, aren't we, Kilda? Lucretia trembled as Sylvan hurried back, lugging Kilda's ludicrously cheerful shopping tote over his shoulder.

Nae. I will nae let that happen. Kilda continued aloud: "We've got three good heads between us, and ye've got yer power—dinnae forget it." She clutched the bag, removing the swatch of tartan fabric covering the swords, and pulled one out.

Sylvan's voice was rife with panic. "I believed swords were longer than that."

"'Tis a gladius." Kilda swished the blade in a figure eight before her, though she leaned heavily on her cane as she did. "They're easier to wield. Lighter."

A shock of terror jolted through Lucretia as she imagined Kilda attempting to fight the way she used to. She'd done well enough when they'd sparred for practice, but Lucretia had gone easy on her, terrified the ring would be ineffective, that *she'd* be the one to injure her aging wife. If the ring failed—and the chances seemed high, given she'd enchanted it with an improvised spell, for lack of any proven example—what were the chances Kilda could withstand physical battle against a malicious enemy? *Nae, stop it. Stop!* Lucretia chased the poisonous thoughts away.

She turned to Kilda, voice trembling. "If it does turn badly, know that I love ye dearly."

"Hush, love. 'Tisn't the end. Ye'll show her what yer made of." Kilda gripped Lucretia's talon, youth flickering over her face as she squeezed it, before thrusting a sword into her grip.

"I'm serious. Ye too, Sylvan. Ye've been a good friend, kind and loyal even in my darkest moods—"

A third knock reverberated, plunging them into darkness yet again. A great *crack* rang out, shaking the floor beneath them. The light returned in time for Lucretia to throw herself in front of her friends, shielding them from the assault of ribs flying every which way as the whale skeleton exploded above them.

Breathe, love, Kilda's voice echoed in her skull. *Stay calm and remember who ye are.*

Lucretia trembled. *But I dinnae know who I am.*

A cackling voice engulfed the room—muffled, and yet intimately close, as if emanating from the walls themselves: "Hello, Quill. I see you've changed the locks. Is this how you treat family?"

Bronagh had found her at last.

A whimper escaped Lucretia's lips as her sister's low, purring voice triggered a torrent of painful memories. Her entire body trembled as Kilda squeezed her talon. She turned to look into the eyes of her now-young wife, grappling to pull courage from their depths. Sylvan stepped forward beside them, tightening his grip on his sword.

"Well, fine," the enemy called through the hole in the door. "I wasn't going to resort to this, but you leave me no choice."

CHAPTER 40

The raven-shaped knocker glared at Bronagh as she forced the stem of the golden feather toward the lock, despite the repellent force radiating from the keyhole. She could feel Baxter's eyes trailing on her from his hiding place behind the dumpster, sense the two-dozen deliciously empty vessels of her hidden hordes, waiting to be filled with bloodlust.

While the door had been protected to repel Bronagh, it was enchanted to accept Quill's key. A key now in Bronagh's possession. She couldn't be sure what would happen when the two items collided.

Triumph sang through her veins as she managed to finagle the stem into the hole. She braced herself for another searing headache, but this time, none came.

Instead, a strange, numbing tingle emanated from the feather in her heart as sparks began to fly, golden flecks filling the air around the lock like tiny fireworks. The feather key vibrated in Bronagh's hand, begging her to let go.

She held tight. She would not give up. Not while Quill stood a mere few feet away.

The lock exploded.

Shrapnel shot in all directions, sparking a hysterical *whoop* from Bronagh. Fizzing with anticipation, she peered through the jagged hole where the opposing forces had blown up the wood. A mountain of furniture barred her vision, but she sensed movement beyond it. The Eternal Feather tugged at her heart, twinging as if determined to draw her forward. Bronagh thrilled at the pulling sensation, willing her legs to follow suit—but when she tried to climb through the hole, her knee collided with some invisible barrier. A hot bolt of irritation dampened her joy.

Perhaps it would not be so easy.

"Stand down!"

When Quill's willowy shape emerged from behind the furniture barricade, Bronagh's zeal returned tenfold, ripping murderously through her. There she was. Her sister, a frazzled flurry of black feathers, tiptoeing forward with a comically short sword clutched in her talons. Bronagh stifled the pinprick of menace her sister's claws inspired, though she'd already been aware of Quill's evolution. *So what if she looks just like the goddess?* I'm *the one with the Eternal Feather*, she reminded herself, focusing on its sweet vibrations and rhythmic pulse.

Bronagh twisted her lips into a grin. "Well, well. Reunited at last."

"Stand down!" Quill shouted again, a wall of black feathers erupting from her arms. "I am death and blood and pain. Stand down or feel my wrath."

"You?" Bronagh tittered. The warble in her sister's cry had betrayed her. "You're death and blood and pain? Little miss 'please don't treat me like I'm special'? There must be some mistake."

"Be gone!" Quill screeched. "Be gone, lest I smite ye where ye stand!"

"Aw, come on, sis," Bronagh sneered. "It's been ages since I saw you. Literally. Let's catch up."

"We'll do no such thing." Quill waved the sword, stumbling as though she were not used to it. "Out with ye! And dinnae show yer murderous face here again."

"Murderous? That's quite the accusation."

"Ye killed my mother. Dinnae play the fool with me!"

A tremor of pride danced under Bronagh's skin. That confirmed it. The so-called Great Winged One had indeed died of her injuries.

"And may she rest in peace," Bronagh quipped. "Now, if you refuse to let me in, I'll have to bring you out."

"And how do ye suppose—"

"Attack!" Bronagh raised her fist, feather beating in her chest like a drum. She leapt out of the way, springing across the alley and onto the dumpster for a better vantage point from which to watch the thunderous mob of possessed patients, doctors, and nurses—each propelled by unstoppable bloodthirst.

Quill's shocked gasp merely multiplied Bronagh's delight. If only they had horses, Bronagh mused as her soldiers rushed past her, bodies bashing against the splintered door and its gaping hole. And weapons. Still, it wasn't bad for her first war. There would be many more in the future.

Bronagh glanced down at Baxter, who was cowering behind the dumpster. *Did you expect this from me, my little pet? Did you know what I was capable of?* He looked every bit the small, unhappy boy he'd been when she'd met him. She turned away from him, anxious not to miss a second of the action.

Bodies clashed against each other with a sickening crack of bones as all her soldiers dove for the hole in the door at the same time. They tore at its splintered edges, trampling each other as they fought to clamber through. When the first soldier—a dark-skinned young man in scrubs—managed to push his way inside, Bronagh twitched with delight.

They were in.

"Grab her!" Bronagh commanded from atop the dumpster, pride trilling inside her. A bruised woman in a pale pink hospital gown clawed her way in, closely followed by a half-dozen more soldiers. "Go on! Grab Quill and pull her out!"

But when her soldiers slowed, doubt crept into her heart. Something was wrong. Their *faces* were wrong.

"Where am I?" a doctor slurred, bewilderment softening the anger that had distorted her face moments before. Her question melted into a swell of similar sounds—sounds of confusion, as two dozen humans awoke from their bloodthirsty stupor.

Shit, Bronagh hissed to herself. Shit, shit. She leapt down, scurrying back to the door. Of course. The building was protected against her, and these soldiers were under her influence. It seemed crossing the threshold nullified her power over them. A riptide of anger crashed over her as the dazed mortals turned to gawk at her.

One of them—the policewoman—whispered something to a man next to her, and soon a current of murmurs spread through the group.

One voice rose above the din—"She did this to us!"—sparking a chorus of fear and disbelief.

A memory flashed through Bronagh's mind: the shocked villagers following the accusatory finger of the boy who'd seen her steal the boar's head.

Quill's voice rang out as she pushed through the crowd. "Ye have nae power here, Bronagh!" She addressed the confused mob milling around her: "The rest of ye are all safe within these walls. I can offer ye shelter from her as long as ye need it."

Ever the hero, her dear divine sister. If she hadn't been barred from entering herself, Bronagh would have rushed in and murdered Quill on the spot.

Some things never changed.

But then, inspiration struck. "I'd gladly leave," Bronagh snarled over the crowd. "However, I've got a friend of yours back at my place. I thought you'd want to ensure I didn't hurt her—I know how protective you are of your beloved humans."

"What are ye talking about?" Quill demanded.

"Marceline. You do know her, don't you?" She winked down at Baxter, who slumped against the filthy brick wall like he longed to merge with it.

Horror distorted Quill's face. "Ye've got Marceline?"

"I do. She's delightful. A bit naive, no sense of style, but so very polite." Bronagh grinned, pleased with her ability to recall the various details Baxter had shared about his wife.

When fear flashed through Quill's eyes, Bronagh triumphed. Once again, she had the advantage.

Her sister seemed about to act when a corpulent young man pushed to the front of the crowd, brandishing a sword above his head. "Where is she?" he demanded. "If you harm her, I will—"

Bronagh erupted with a delighted howl. "You like her, do you? Oh, this is far too good! Baxter, I think we've found your culprit." She peered at her sidekick, whose face had turned beet red, eyes sparking with fury.

"Where is she?" the big man demanded again, practically quivering with worry.

"At my headquarters. You're welcome to come visit and bring dear Quill along."

"Who is Quill?"

"I am." Quill's black eyes smoldered. "'Tis a trap, Sylvan."

"And what if it is not?" he protested. "She did not arrive today like she usually does."

"Don't be stupid!" Quill shrieked. "Can't ye see she's trying to lure—" The words dropped from her mouth. It was too late. He'd already pushed through the gap where the door had stood.

He was over the threshold.

"Come here, big guy," Bronagh purred, and his determination fell away to blind obedience. Sylvan lumbered forward, a vacant look clouding his irises. The sword hung loosely at his side.

"Sylvan!" Quill's scream rattled what remained of the door. "What have ye done?"

"Don't you worry, dear sister," Bronagh cackled. "I'll take good care of him. Until, shall we say, midnight? After that, he dies, along with the girl. If you'd like to see them again, you best come before then."

"Ye monster!"

"Oh, Quill, you flatter me." She chortled, feather pulsing through her limbs. "I'm feeling generous, so I'll even give you the address. Bax, tell her where you live." She stared down at the human, compelling him to speak, loud and clear.

Despite the tempest in his eyes, he complied.

"Got that, sweet sister? Good. See you soon." With that, Bronagh traced a circle in the air and stepped into invisibility, tugging her prisoner along with her.

"Come on now, Baxter," she hissed.

The mortal fumed as he followed her through the circle, glowering at the back of the hostage's head. Bronagh smirked. No, things hadn't gone according to plan. But this would be so much more fun.

CHAPTER 41

The bus dropped Marceline off along Folsom Street. Weighed down by her cumbersome duffel and the globe in the bag that kept banging into her leg, she pulled her hood up against the drizzle, dodging puddles as she trudged toward the alley. Anxiety rumbled in her now-empty womb, and she tried to gather courage, feeling the absence of her feather key keenly. Perhaps Lucretia would understand. People misplaced things all the time—it was careless, yes, but what were the chances the key could have gotten into the wrong hands? Baxter might be a manipulative predator, but his world was not one of magic feathers and goddesses and enchanted maps.

A squawk sounded above, and Marceline shrieked in surprise as an enormous black bird dove at her. She gasped, recovering. "Falkirk?"

The bird circled around her, squawking frantically. Had Baxter tried to catch him again?

"Whoa, calm down!" Alarmed, Marceline doubled her pace, turning into the alley's entrance. But when she set eyes on the door—or what used to be a door—she froze.

Only a splintered fringe of jagged planks remained, as if the rest had been blasted away.

"Lucretia?" she called, heart hammering as Falkirk swooped through the gaping hole. She peered after the raven. "Kilda? Sylvan?" A dozen stunned faces turned toward her—faces she didn't recognize. Had these people broken the door down? No, she didn't think so. They huddled in groups, some sipping drinks, some wrapped in blankets, others gazing into the fire. All looking as lost and frightened as Marceline felt.

She stepped over the debris, anxiety growing. What had happened to her beloved café? And where were her friends? The place looked like it had been ransacked, tables and chairs thrust into a haphazard pile. When someone clutched her from behind, she screamed, alarming a cluster of tense newcomers—but when she spun around, she saw it was Kilda.

"Thank God ye're okay, lass." She hugged Marceline with surprising force for one so frail. "She said she had ye. We figured she was bluffing, but—"

"Who? Who said that, Kilda?"

"The sister." Kilda said, trembling. "Lucretia's sister, Bronagh. She attacked us."

Marceline's eyes widened. "She has a sister? But how—"

"Seems she got ahold of a key."

The words landed. Marceline covered her face with her hands. "Oh, Kilda, it's all my fault. I misplaced it, and—"

"Hush now. 'Tis done. We cannae waste time blaming ourselves. We must do something."

"Where's Lucretia? Is she safe? And who are all these people?" She swallowed, fear amassing into a thick ball in her throat. "Is Sylvan all right?"

The look in Kilda's weathered eyes made her heart plummet. Marceline groped for a wall to steady herself against, her stomach cramping with pain and guilt. She tried to focus on Kilda's frantic explanation. The sister had used Marceline as bait. Sylvan had fallen for it. He'd run out, thinking he could rescue her. Sylvan had cared enough to— Oh! Marceline's anguish leapt out of her, twisting her voice in desperation. "Where did they take him?"

When Kilda recited the address, it felt like a blast of frigid water to Marceline's face. "But that's my apartment." A lump hardened in her throat. "This sister…she didn't happen to be with a man, did she? Tall, blond hair, gray eyes…"

"Aye, aye, she was." Kilda wrung her hands.

"Baxter…" The anxiety in Marceline's stomach spiked. So he *had* taken the feather.

"Yer husband? But how—"

Every last bit of warmth drained from her body. "I don't know." Yes, *bait* was the right word. She'd been a pawn in a game she wasn't even aware of. And if Baxter was in cahoots with Lucretia's sister, that meant the two of them must have somehow used her to get to the café.

She tensed, her gut rebelling so she feared she might vomit.

Betrayal was too weak a word.

"Marce, child." Kilda gripped her arm. "We cannae dwell on this now. Bronagh and Baxter took Sylvan and disappeared, and Lu was too distraught to follow. 'Twas a mere ten minutes ago. Maybe less. Oh, Marce. She's in such a state."

"Where is she?" Marceline's heart was galloping, bucking like a crazed horse.

Kilda pointed to Lucretia's curtain, just as another gut-wrenching cramp hit Marceline deep in her core. She doubled over, moaning.

"Are ye all right, lass?"

Marceline bit down against the pain. "Yes, I'm fine." Shoving the agony—both physical and emotional—to the back of her mind, she took off toward Lucretia's lair. But when she passed two women huddled together, she halted.

The women were bloodied and bruised—one with a black eye and a sling, wearing a faded hospital gown. But what caught Marceline's eye was the woman's tattoo: a messy black X inked onto her bicep.

Marceline gasped, her gaze sweeping over the second woman, who wore a tattered police uniform, one pant leg torn off at the knee. There, on the front of her leg, was yet another X.

"How did you get that?" Marceline demanded, pointing at the policewoman's leg.

"Get what?" The stranger looked down, brow furrowed. "Oh. I... I don't know..."

Marceline tore away from the pair, scrutinizing each newcomer. Here was an X on someone's hand, and another marking someone's cheek. And another, and another. They all had them.

"That must be Bronagh's mark. It was all over my map," Kilda whispered. "Why are ye making that face?"

"Baxter has that same tattoo." Marceline braced herself against the cramp clenching her insides as the cartographer's eyes grew saucer-wide. "He's had it even longer than I've known him. I have to talk to Lu." With that, she bolted behind the curtain.

Lucretia lay huddled in the corner of her lair, buried in pillows. "Marce," she gasped. Her face glistened with tears. "Marce! I knew it was a lie! I knew ye were safe! I told him nae to step outside, but he—"

"I'm so, so sorry. This is all my fault. Baxter confronted me when I was leaving, and I think he stole my key. If I'd known he was working with your sister—"

"I knew I recognized him, the sniveling bastard. I saw him in Falkirk's mind, after the brute tried to catch him."

Marceline nodded, feeling queasy. "I would have told you immediately if I'd known. I never, ever wanted to put you in danger."

Lucretia fell back into violent sobs, burying her face in her arms. "I should have gone after him. I should have followed. 'Twas all so fast, and I—I'm so afraid. I couldnae cross the threshold. Bronagh killed my mother, and now she's going to kill my friend too."

"No!" The fury in Marceline's voice was so fierce it surprised even her. "No, I won't let that happen. We're going to get him back." She rushed to her friend, tugging at her wrists. "We can't just wallow when we're in a bad situation! You're the one who taught me that. Are you coming?"

Terror rose in the feathered woman's coal-black eyes. Marceline grasped her trembling talons, desperate to squeeze the torment out of them despite the fear that swirled inside her own stomach, mingling with post-op pain.

It worked. Lucretia's sobs died down, her breath at last steadying.

"Ye're right. 'Tis time for me to face my fears." Her quivering lips locked into a resolute line as she picked herself off the ground. Every part of her shook, and fear cowered in her eyes, but she drew herself to her full height, all the same. "I'm ready."

CHAPTER 42

Bronagh twisted in the passenger's seat, chatting away with the near-catatonic hostage taking up most of the back seat. Beside her, Baxter glowered. She could feel his rage brewing like a storm, filling the battered car as he navigated them toward the interstate. It made her want to dance. A few hours ago, his cowardice had begun to bore her. Now, things were becoming interesting again.

"You comfy back there?" She grinned over her shoulder. "We're going to have *such fun*, the three of us."

"Why do we have to go to my place?" Baxter mumbled. "Why not the tavern?"

Bronagh snorted. "I've seen enough of that shithole for *several* lifetimes."

When they pulled into the apartment complex, her attention shifted. Much like Baxter's car, the cluster of matching buildings had seen better days. *How appropriate*, she thought, remembering the way he'd complained about his life. A stale, uninspired block of peeling paint and cluttered concrete balconies.

Baxter jerked the gearshift into park and threw his door open, wrenching his long legs out of the driver's seat before loping off toward the building's entrance.

"Don't mind him. His people skills are lacking." Bronagh let herself out and ushered the hostage from the back seat, looping an arm over his massive shoulders like they were the best of friends.

She stood between the two men in the elevator, reveling in a tension so heavy she was surprised the whole mechanism didn't plummet to the ground. As soon as the doors opened Baxter pushed forward, marching toward his apartment.

Bronagh snatched the key from his hand, pushing him aside to open the door herself.

"And just like that, we're roommates." She grinned as a black X slashed itself onto the door's surface in response to her touch. She tugged the prisoner inside, leaving Baxter to trail after them, still glowering.

"My, what a gloomy vibe." She locked the door behind them. "Luckily, I'm used to that."

The hostage gazed around absently, making no move to resist as Bronagh tugged the short sword still dangling from his hand. "We won't be needing this yet."

She sauntered into the kitchen, setting the sword on the counter. So *this* was where Baxter lived his sad little life. She began opening cupboards and browsing the contents of the fridge, before striding to the battered corduroy couch and flopping down with a satisfied sigh. Baxter watched from the hallway, seething.

"Oh, cheer up, you grouch." She winked at him, before turning to the hostage, who stood in the corner, a blank canvas. "And you! You can relax now, big guy. Take a load off your feet. Be yourself. What was your name—Simon?"

The hostage snapped out of his stupor, brow furrowing as his consciousness returned. "*Elle est où?*" His neck swiveled as he took in the room.

"Excuse you?" Bronagh raised a brow. Of course there would be some ridiculous loophole. Somehow, she'd always been able to understand her tavern customers regardless of where they came from. Now, she suspected Quill's café was the same.

Unfortunately for her, the world of humans contained no such magic.

"I don't suppose you speak French, Baxter?" she asked sardonically. Baxter only glared back at her.

The hostage implored with wild eyes, "*Où est-ce qu'elle est?*" When his panic yielded only a bemused smirk, he screwed up his face as if thinking hard. "Marceline... she... where?"

Bronagh responded with an exaggerated shrug. It was interesting that her commands still affected him, as if they bypassed the language section of his brain, aiming straight for his body.

Understanding that the apparent object of his affection wasn't present, the hostage's shoulders relaxed. Then, his searching gaze landed on a framed photo of Marceline and Baxter. His eyes widened. He turned to stare at Baxter. "*C'est toi son mari?*"

"Don't look at her," Baxter hissed, the first words he'd spoken to the hostage.

Whether the big man understood or not, there was no mistaking the tone, and he shot Baxter a withering look in return.

Bronagh smirked, observing the vein throbbing on the side of Baxter's neck, then turned back to the hostage, who'd picked up the frame. Had the fool not realized who Baxter was? What a way to find out. Bronagh leaned over to look at the photo, in which the couple posed in front of a turquoise hotel pool. Their honeymoon in Palm Springs, she suspected. Baxter had complained for weeks about how much that trip had cost him.

The hostage tried speaking again. "*Elle est vraiment pas là?*"

"This is going to get old really quickly," Bronagh sighed. "Baxter, don't you have some sort of translation device?"

Scowling, he gestured to a flat, metal rectangle on the table. The tavern had provided Bronagh with adequate knowledge of the outside world, so she recognized it as a laptop, but she had no idea how to use it.

"Well, go on then, Bax. Do your thing."

Seething, Baxter opened the laptop.

"Tell him Marceline isn't here and he's incredibly stupid to have fallen for that," Bronagh ordered, and Baxter clicked around a bit before typing. "Say that I've never even met the bitch, and she looks frumpier than I'd imagined." Baxter scowled but continued to type.

When he was finished, the Bartender gestured for the hostage to come forward and read what had appeared in the box beside where Baxter had typed. He did, and the anguish in his eyes melted into relief. Sylvan backed away, letting himself sink into the couch, which groaned beneath his weight. "*Tant qu'elle est en sécurité.*"

"Go sit next to him, and bring the laptop," Bronagh told Baxter. "This conversation isn't over."

"I'd rather shoot myself in the head," Baxter muttered.

"There'll be plenty of time for that later. Ooh, also, ask him about when he first met Marceline. Like, did he know he wanted to fuck her immediately, or was it more gradual?"

Baxter looked sharply up at her. "I'm not writing that."

"Sweet Bax. You know if you don't comply, I can simply compel you, right?"

The vein in Baxter's neck pulsed so hard, it looked like a worm trying to escape his skin, but he picked up his device, shooting the hostage a loathsome look as he sat beside him on the couch.

Clearly unnerved by this move, the hostage looked over at the screen, his expression hardening, as if Baxter's hostility was contagious. He took the laptop and typed out a reply.

Delighted by the delicious tension in the room, Bronagh rounded the couch, leaning over the edge so she could read. It seemed Baxter had embellished the text with several insults pertaining to the hostage's size. Now, the hostage responded: She's a person, not a blow-up doll. And say what you want about me. I don't care, as long as she's safe.

"How very noble," Bronagh scoffed, covering her disappointment in his lack of a reaction with amusement. She leaned forward, speaking softly into Baxter's ear. "You know, Bax, you two have more in common than meets the eye. This little chat could be quite transformative. What do you say?"

Baxter's jaw tightened, and Bronagh felt the feather in her heart twitch with glee. What was a bartender if not a therapist?

"Go on." She nudged him, lip curling. "Ask him if he knew she was married."

"Don't," Baxter interjected, but the objection only made Bronagh more eager.

"Don't make me compel you," she chided, inspecting her black-lacquered nails. She shivered with pleasure at the cloud of white-hot rage radiating off him.

He turned to her, craning his neck to look at her face. "Why are you doing this? I thought you were my friend."

The hostage typed something into the laptop and shoved it onto Baxter's lap, gesturing at the Bartender. I don't like how you treat your wife, but this woman is clearly manipulating you.

"How I treat my wife is none of your business," Baxter snarled.

"Oh, this is good stuff! We're getting somewhere now, boys."

Baxter went to type a venomous reply, but his fingers stalled. The pause sent a tremor through Bronagh, only this time, it wasn't one of pleasure.

Slowly, Baxter stood and turned to face the Bartender.

He was so transparent, usually, but now she felt a disconnect. His gray eyes flickered, swimming with something like confusion. All his life, Bronagh had been there for him. Sure, her behavior in the hospital might have surprised him, but certainly twenty-two years of support deserved *some* form of loyalty. Besides, she'd made him a promise—not that she intended to keep it. She said she'd make him powerful. Wasn't that the one thing he'd always wanted?

Bronagh's stomach lurched as she felt something break in Baxter. The cramped apartment seemed to shudder, tinged with the taste of betrayal—his or hers? Either way, it tasted sour.

"You're gonna let some fat loser get to you?" Bronagh scoffed. Could they tell she'd been thrown off-kilter? "Come on, Bax, you're smarter than that. Haven't I always said you were a smart guy? That you deserve better?" She softened her eyes at him in a desperate attempt to rekindle two decades' worth of devotion.

Baxter swallowed, crossing his arms. But the moment his gaze dropped away from hers, Bronagh felt the change. He realized what he'd always been to her: a pawn, a plaything. And now he was turning against her.

The annoyance she'd felt for him all day sparked into rage.

CHAPTER 43

Lucretia stood rooted to the spot, paralyzed before the pile of rubble separating her from the world outside. She'd been the mistress of her own little realm for so long. Stepping through this door—the spot that had been a door—meant surrendering that control. And what if Bronagh returned? What if she was lurking around the corner, waiting for her?

Ye can do it, love. Kilda arrived at her side, wrinkles fading momentarily as she squeezed Lucretia's shoulder.

Where were ye?

Taking care of some business. Now take a deep breath and step outside. I'm right beside ye.

Falkirk landed on Kilda's shoulder, squawking agreement.

Marceline was already waiting in the alley, pale and anxious. "Come on, Lu! The longer we take, the more chances Sylvan—"

"Aye, I know." The wobble in Lucretia's voice betrayed her. Marceline was right. She could no longer put off the inevitable—not when her friends were in danger.

Her heart spasmed as she slid a foot over the threshold.

Nothing leapt out to kill her.

She moved the other foot.

She was out.

"Come on!" Marceline urged, disrupting Lucretia's relief as the wind chilled her skin—something she hadn't felt in a long time. Gulping, she took another step forward. The outside world was vast, and her fear was not limited to the threshold. But they had to get moving, for Sylvan's sake.

Beside her, Kilda fiddled with a tiny, flat phone, the tote bag full of swords weighing her shoulder down. "Bloody roaming fees. Right, I'm calling a car. What's the address?"

Marceline gave it to her, eyeing the phone with visible surprise as she tugged Lucretia down the alley and toward the bustling street, Falkirk swooping beside them.

The world had changed in a innumerable ways since Lucretia had inhabited it. She thought she'd known it all—from books, from her human clientele, from the memories her birds shared with her. But being out here was different. Almost exhilarating, if she could get over the dizzying fear that gripped her—the fear of a thousand new concepts bombarding her at once. And, more than that, the fear of getting to Sylvan too late. Of finally facing Bronagh. Had her sister evolved with the times? Would it give her an advantage?

A moment later a car pulled up in front of them. Lucretia leapt back, making a grab for one of the hilts sticking out from Kilda's tote bag.

"Don't!" Marceline hissed. "It's just our taxi."

"Fly overhead," Lucretia muttered to Falkirk, fear overtaking her embarrassment as she wedged herself into the car beside Kilda. Marceline helped her with her seat belt—as if she were a child—before sliding in on her other side.

"Who are these for anyway?" Marceline nudged Kilda's colorful tote. "I don't know how to use a *sword*." She whispered the last word, glancing at the back of the driver's head.

"There's nae question, lass," Kilda sighed. "The two of ye are made for each other."

Lucretia tuned the conversation out, distracted by the driver's eyes watching her in his little mirror, and the way they widened when she pushed her mane of feathers from her face with her talon. She glared back. Bronagh could have allies anywhere. But when the car pulled out into traffic, the motion jerked her from her thoughts. She gripped Kilda's cardigan sleeve, heart palpitating at a dangerous speed as streets and buildings sped by. Kilda filled Marceline in about Bronagh's stolen power of compulsion, apparently unbothered by the motion.

When an enormous truck sped past them, Lucretia yelped. "Is this normal?"

"Yes." Marceline squeezed her forearm. "You're okay. You're fine." She groaned, clutching her middle.

"But are *ye* fine, child?" Kilda squinted at her. "Ye dinnae seem well."

"I'm good." Marceline wiped the sweat off her clammy forehead. "Give me one of those." Keeping it low so as not to alarm the driver, she tugged a sword out of Kilda's tote and rested it on her lap.

Eventually the car wove off the freeway and turned into a cluster of matching, run-down buildings. "Here I was hoping I'd never have to see this place again," Marceline muttered. "This way." She threw open the car door, practically tumbling out. Kilda exited, too, urging Lucretia to follow.

The car sped away, leaving Lucretia rooted to the concrete as Marceline ran across the parking lot toward one of the buildings.

"Hurry." Kilda tugged at her tunic sleeve. "Sylvan needs us!"

Lucretia stared after Marceline. "I've never killed anyone before."

"If it makes ye feel better, neither have I. Nor has Marceline, I'm willing to wager," Kilda said. "Now come on!"

CHAPTER 44

Bronagh's voice teetered on the edge of a snarl. "That's enough chit-chat for today." With an exaggerated yawn, she rose to her feet and sauntered into the kitchen. "I'm ready for a bit of action. Aren't you?" She stalked to the kitchen area and leaned against the counter, plucking up the sword.

Baxter and the hostage tensed but did not look at each other.

The hostage typed something into the laptop and stood, trying to show her, but Bronagh had lost interest.

"What are you doing? Barten—Bronagh?" A small spasm racked Baxter's shoulders as Bronagh ran her nails against the blade, like she was filing them. The hostage nudged him, and Baxter glared at him, then looked at the laptop. Surely they weren't going to ally against her, were they? "He says you can't do anything. You gave Lucretia until midnight."

"Her name is Quill," the Bartender growled. "And do I strike you as the kind of person who cares about promises?"

"But—"

She silenced him with an acrid look, jabbing a finger toward the hostage. "You. Come get the sword." She had no idea whether the compulsion spell would still work given the language barrier, but the glazed look fell over the hostage's face, as if his muscles understood even what his brain did not. But no sooner had he reached for the weapon, than Baxter shot forward, snatching the sword from Bronagh's hand.

He chucked it out the open window.

The hostage gazed at the window, advancing toward it like a zombie. He stuck his head out, searching for the prize he'd been ordered to obtain.

"You idiot." The Bartender lunged at Baxter. He dodged her, scouring his surroundings for another potential weapon. "This is how you repay me for my years of friendship? After everything I promised you—"

"You don't strike me as a person who cares about promises," Baxter parroted back to her.

"Very clever," Bronagh sneered, her rage bubbling over as she lunged for his neck. She had every intention of ending his sorry life then and there, but Baxter bolted sideways, putting the kitchen table between them. "And yet very stupid. I wasn't going to do this, but you leave me no choice." She pointed at him. "The two of you are going to fight. To the death."

Baxter opened his mouth to shout something, but the sound never made it out. A storm brewed in his gray eyes as he fought for control. He didn't stand a chance. The blank look descended like a curtain. Without emotion, he turned toward Sylvan, who still leaned halfway out the window, gazing at the discarded sword.

Bronagh crossed her arms, betrayal amplifying her thirst for violence. *Your miserable little life ends today, Baxter Grone*, she thought.

Good fucking riddance.

CHAPTER 45

Doubling her pace, Marceline begged her cramping insides to cooperate as she hurried for the building's entrance. She'd made it halfway across the parking lot when something dropped from the sky, flashing as it clattered where her body had been a half second before. She gasped.

Another sword. Exactly like the one she was clutching.

"Kilda, 'tis one of yours!" Lucretia croaked.

Marceline craned her neck, heart screaming with relief at the face gazing down at her.

"Sylvan! Hold tight, we're coming!" Without waiting for a reaction, she broke into a full sprint toward the door, forgetting her pain. Remembering she'd discarded her key in the mailbox earlier she stopped short, but before she could even open her mouth, Lucretia sprinted up behind her, pointing at the lock. It exploded with a puff of silver smoke. Marceline thrust the door open, barreling through.

"I'll meet ye there," Kilda called, panting after her. "Which floor?"

"Third!" Marceline bolted for the stairs—there was no time to wait for the elevator. Lucretia kept stride beside her, Falkirk soaring overhead. Marceline's breath was ragged by the time her unit came into sight. Hardly noticing the messy black X burned into the door, she ripped it open.

There was Sylvan.

And there, crouched like a predator across from him, was Baxter.

Both in the same place.

And a woman—tall, bone-white, dressed all in black, down to her heavy combat boots—pointing at both men like some mad conductor, as she snarled "The two of you are going to fight. To the death."

Bronagh, Lucretia's murderous sister.

Marceline reeled, gaze falling upon her husband's face: He looked like a rabid dog as he seethed at Sylvan, whose own face burned hot with an alien hatred that doubled the pain in Marceline's gut. It was all wrong. Kilda's rushed explanation of Bronagh's powers skidded through her mind. She hardly had time to scream before the two men hurtled toward each other, fists raised.

"Stop!" Marceline brandished her sword the way she'd seen done in movies. "Make it stop, please!"

Bronagh swiveled, mouth curling into a ghastly smile. "Marceline. I've been dying to meet you. Do you see, boys? It's the object of your shared affec—FUCK!" She dove sideways as Marceline chucked the blade at her. It soared across the room, its hilt striking her forehead. Bronagh growled, lunging for the discarded weapon.

"Nae so fast!" Kilda burst in, brandishing her own sword as she hobbled forward on her cane, panting.

Bronagh emitted a sharp bark of a laugh. "Looking for the retirement home? Give me the sword, you crusty old—" Kilda's cane crashed down upon Bronagh's head before she could finish. The villain spasmed, tottered, and fell slack-faced onto the ground. Baxter and Sylvan blinked, releasing each other's necks in confusion.

"Rule number one, lass. Dinnae throw yer weapon to the enemy!" Kilda wheezed as she bent to pick up Marceline's sword, handing it back to her.

Marceline blinked. "I panicked. Wait, you had a cane and a sword, and you chose the cane?"

"Hmm?" Kilda lifted a tuft of cloud-white hair and winked, pointing to her ear, sans hearing aide. An idea flashed through Marceline's mind. Bronagh could only control people if they heard her. She held up a finger, mouthing *I'll be right back* before sprinting to the bedroom.

The room looked exactly how she'd left it, ransacked and full of overturned furniture from her frenzied search for the feather. She'd pulled the nightstand drawer out, but a dozen plastic packets still lay scattered inside, each containing a pair of orange foam earplugs. Stuffing her pockets with them, she ran back out to the living room.

"Catch!" She lobbed one of the packets at Sylvan and another at Baxter. "Put them in, quick, before she wakes."

Both men stared at her: Baxter, suspicious, and Sylvan, bewildered.

"We'll talk after. Hurry!"

Already Bronagh was groaning, fury awakening upon her face as she lifted herself from the floor. Marceline shoved the plugs into her ears, the men following suit. The sounds of the world muffled, leaving only the rapid thump of her own pulse in her ears. She clutched her sword, palms slick with nerves. Where was Lucretia? And Falkirk, for that matter?

Quite suddenly, the lights flickered, and gale force winds whipped into the living room, slamming the door on its hinges.

Lucretia's body rebelled against her as she watched Kilda disappear into the apartment after Marceline. Her head spun, dread carbonating her very blood as her thoughts scattered like leaves. The door stood ajar, her friends just beyond it. Her *sister* just beyond it. In the flesh, ready to kill. The longer she stayed planted here, the graver the peril.

Falkirk pecked her earlobe, urging her to move. She had to go in. She couldn't let her friends die at her expense. The knowledge overwhelmed her, rife with urgency—yet her feet had once again sprouted invisible roots, anchoring her to the concrete.

Breathe. Her mother's instructions echoed in her head. *Arm yerself with yer invocation! Focus on yer objective. Yer every thought must fuel yer power.* Battling her own lungs, she squeezed out a shaky breath. And another, and another. At last, the tide of panic began to subside—just in time for Marceline's frantic cry of "Stop! Make it stop. Please!"

How could she wait outside at a time like this?

Drawing a hasty circle in the air, Lucretia stepped into invisibility, bringing Falkirk with her. Her mother would have called her cowardly for approaching an enemy while concealed. Right now, she didn't care. Invisibility meant protection. She needed all the help she could get.

At least now no one could see her shaking as she slipped into the apartment.

But discretion was not in the cards. The moment she crossed the threshold, something within her jolted to life, extinguishing all the lights around her. The force almost bowled her over, transfiguring her panic into something hot and alive. For one irrational second, she feared her heart would explode and obliterate everything in its path. Then the light flared back, illuminating her target.

The feather. Lucretia's rightful inheritance—the power her sister had stolen.

It was here, in this room.

Inside of Bronagh's chest.

Marceline's breath thundered in her plugged ears as the lights returned, temporarily blinding her. Bursts of color were still blooming over her vision when the dark shape advanced on her.

She stumbled as she raised her sword, desperate to fend off Bronagh's reaching hands, but she'd never been athletic, and she was too slow.

Bronagh plucked the weapon away like it was nothing. She raised the blade above her head.

The sword glinted in the dull light of the apartment. *Shit. This is how I go. This—* The thought became a scream as strong arms wrapped around Marceline's torso, lifting her into the air. She kicked, flailing, but already the thing holding her was setting her down several paces away. It was as if some invisible— Oh! The realization came a split second before her earplug popped out of her ear, allowing Lucretia to hiss: "'Tis me, ye daft lass!"

"Don't fucking touch my wife," Baxter protested, but there was a weak warble to his voice, and he didn't move, not even by an inch. An instant later, Bronagh backhanded him in the face.

Marceline winced as Baxter staggered into the wall, but she had no time to detangle her feelings about it, because Bronagh then rounded on *her*. Instinctively, Marceline cowered, but the blow did not come. Instead, Bronagh plucked the levitating earplug that Lucretia had been about to stuff back in Marceline's ear.

"Don't be a coward, Quill, show yourself!" Bronagh growled, chucking the plug over her shoulder. The pinprick of orange landed in the hallway, beyond reach.

Realizing she was exposed, Marceline bounded after the plug—only Bronagh tripped her. She landed hard, ramming into the edge of the coffee table. Gasping in pain, she hardly managed to struggle back onto her feet before Bronagh came flying at her again.

"I order you to—" The words were snatched from her when, out of nowhere, Kilda swung her sword at Bronagh, who spasmed with an enraged howl, pawing at her shoulder where a shallow scrape was starting to ooze crimson.

Sylvan, Marceline thought suddenly. *Where was Sylvan?* He'd been poised to fight in the kitchen when she'd arrived.

The answer came seconds later, when a plate whizzed by, exploding into porcelain fireworks against Bronagh's ribs. Marceline whipped around in time to see him grab something from the cupboard and dip behind the refrigerator. His arm shot out, sending another plate zooming by like a Frisbee, hitting Bronagh square in the neck.

Batting aside the swell of pride—no time for that—Marceline took advantage of the distraction and scrambled into the hallway. Her side throbbed as she stumbled awkwardly, palm pressed flat against her ear. The ugly brown-and-orange pattern of the carpet just happened to match the foam plugs perfectly. Fucking fabulous. A shape loped past her and down the hall—Baxter, bruised and limping, barricading himself in the bathroom. Clenching her teeth, she ignored him, scanning the ground. She'd just spotted the rogue plug under a side table, when a hand wrapped around her ankle.

"Get off me," she screamed, trying to kick Bronagh away. A coffee mug sailed toward them, and Bronagh let go, screeching as it shattered against her lower back. At the same time, her sword escaped her hand, levitating several feet until the hilt knocked against Marceline's fist. "Take it," Lucretia's voice rang ragged in her unplugged ear. "Ye need to protect yerself!"

Marceline panted in the direction of Lu's voice. "Haven't we established I'm useless with these?"

A teacup flew by, exploding against Bronagh's leg, and she half buckled before catching herself, snarling. "Wrong move, you fat son of a—" The words disintegrated in a furious howl as a ceramic fruit bowl—one of Marceline's garage sale finds—shattered against her shoulder.

"*Merde*," Sylvan muttered. He'd run out of plates—and glasses, bowls, and saucers. The cupboard he'd been using as an arsenal was now empty. Marceline's stomach twisted in fear.

Bronagh advanced on him.

"Sylvan!" Marceline shouted, lunging to intervene, but Bronagh drew a circle in the air with her finger—and vanished. Something white flashed across the living room. Kilda's hair. Cane raised, the cartographer stumbled toward where the villain had stood. She began whacking her cane at the empty space. A loud crack resounded. She'd hit her mark.

A half second later, Kilda's frail body crashed into the side of the couch.

"Kilda!" Lucretia's disembodied scream shook the room.

Marceline's heart buckled, her entire body reverberating with fear. Kilda was still breathing, but she looked rattled and pale, her body crumpled over the armrest. Marceline made to run for her, but a hand wrapped around her bicep, pointed nails digging into her flesh.

She didn't need to see the madness glittering in Bronagh's gaze, or witness her obsidian lips twitching, the venomous words forming through her sneer. The realization had already dawned on her. Her earplug was still missing.

She was still exposed.

"Kill Sylvan," Bronagh hissed.

Marceline tried to scream, to drown out the words. The sound never escaped her lungs. Instead, the world slowed around her, air thickening into a heavy soup as a curtain of lethargy dropped over her mind.

No, she thought, struggling to stay present. *Don't*— A hazy film obscured the concept. Don't what? What was she resisting? Bronagh's voice echoed through the last of her desperately clinging thoughts. *Kill Sylvan*. Her mind throbbed, everything else slipping away into the ether.

Her empty gaze fell on Sylvan, and a surge of inexplicable rage bubbled in her gut as her entire history with him vanished. He was nothing more than a target—a target rifling through the cupboards, searching for something to throw at an enemy he could no longer see. He stopped, his eyes meeting hers. Something scalding burbled in her throat, blotting out any awareness of the panic warping his face.

Kill Sylvan. Sword swinging, Marceline advanced toward her target. *Kill Sylvan.*

"Marceline? Qu'est-ce que tu fais?"

She heard herself snarl in response, violence surging in her veins as she took a slow step toward him, triggering a string of expletives from him as he looked frantically around. His gaze landed on a ceramic cactus pot, and he grasped it, holding it in front of him like a shield.

"Arrête! Résiste!"

Marceline rammed her fist into the pot, indifferent to the crunch of her fingers against the hard terra-cotta. Dirt flew as the pot shattered. The target lurched to the side. She jabbed her blade toward him, slicing flesh. He gasped, clutching at his stomach, where a red stain was rapidly spreading across his white shirt.

She raised her hand to finish the job.

Groaning, the target lunged aside and reached for her, fighting to remove the weapon from her clutches. She held tight, jabbing her elbows into him. *Kill Sylvan*, her mind echoed. *Kill Sylvan. Kill Sylvan.* There was no fear anymore, only grim, bloodthirsty determination.

But mind control or no, Marceline was still smaller than the target. Managing to knock the sword from her grasp, Sylvan clobbered her against the counter and wrenched her hands behind her back. "*Je veux pas te faire de mal*," he grunted, struggling against her thrashing. She bared her teeth, intending to bite his face, but he twisted his neck away. His eyes landed on Marceline's cleaning apron, hanging from a peg. An instant later he'd wrangled it around her wrists, binding them behind her.

She jerked and wriggled and fought, but she was nothing without the use of her arms. Enveloping her in a crushing bear hug, the target wrestled her to the ground, pinning her down with his weight. Blood seeped from his wound. He faltered, the ever-growing stain dripping down his shirt and onto her in rivulets.

"Je suis désolé, Marce," he groaned, wincing as his hands disappeared beneath his stomach and tugged his belt off. With the last of his strength he shifted, battling her thrashing body until he'd managed to wrap the belt several times around her legs. *"J'espère que tu me pardonneras."* He gasped as he tightened the belt, unable to look her in the eye.

When he'd finished, he heaved a deep, shuddering breath, and slumped over her.

Lucretia quivered with fear and wrath as the room rippled with static, whirling around her sister's snarling face as it came into focus. Both were invisible to the world now, but not to each other.

"You thought you could sneak up on me, did you?" Bronagh's black nails curled around the hilt of Kilda's discarded blade. It glinted, promising pain as the sisters circled each other.

Lucretia struggled to control the simmering rage, the caustic fear brewing inside her as she gripped her own sword. The feather in her sister's chest pulsed, calling to her. "Why are ye here, Bronagh?"

Bronagh took a step closer, eyes burning with vengeance, and yet oozing an eerie calm, a snake about to strike. "I want you dead. Just like your dear mother."

"Why?" The question that had plagued Lucretia for over a thousand years tumbled out. "Why did ye kill her?" Falkirk punctuated the question with a threatening caw.

"You killed mine."

"I didnae! 'Twas nae my fault she died. Women die in childbirth all the time. I never asked to be a goddess. All I ever wanted to be was yer sister!"

A puff of white moved in the corner of Lucretia's eye. She willed herself not to shift her gaze as, in her peripheral vision, Kilda pulled herself upright, shaking as she retrieved her discarded sword and her cane. She crept forward, blade raised.

Three steps forward, Lucretia urged her silently. *A tad to yer right.* Her wife followed the instructions, hobbling against her cane, her sword arm trembling with effort.

Bronagh's eyes darted to the side.

Kilda! Lucretia thrust her sword at her sister. *She knows ye're—* Bronagh spun away, knocking Kilda's sword from her hand. Falkirk swooped at Bronagh's face, but she batted him away. She seized Kilda with both hands, flinging her against the wall with all her might.

Panic squeezed Lucretia's chest as her wife crumpled to the floor. *Love! Love, are you all right?* Her mind rushed in anguished circles, desperate to run to Kilda and yet knowing she could not let her guard down.

I'm fine, love. Just in shock. 'Tis nae as bad as it looks.

Lucretia tried to calm herself. Kilda was okay. A blow like that should have done serious damage, and yet she was alive. Perhaps the wedding ring held more power than she'd thought.

Feathers ruffled, Falkirk swooped at Bronagh's head again—only to be batted away a second time.

"What do you think, sis? Shall I finish her off?" Bronagh's grin flashed in her sword's surface, pulling a memory from Lucretia's terror: Bronagh had slashed the goddess across the ribs and stolen the feather while Lucretia watched, powerless as she felt now.

Lucretia's heart clenched. This was it—the moment she'd avoided all these long years, now barreling toward her, inevitable. What could she do?

The sound in the room amplified, exacerbating the manic thumping of her heart in her ears. The creak of a door: the terrified face of Marceline's husband peeking out from a room down the hall. A groan: Sylvan, slumped on the kitchen floor, shirt stained with a mess of blood.

A thrashing Marceline half pinned under him, her wrists and ankles bound. And Kilda's ragged breaths— Oh, Kilda!

Lucretia's nerves submerged her thoughts once more, deflecting her concentration so her invisibility melted away. When the world flared into focus with all its harsh, crisp lines, a lost look had fallen over her wife's eyes.

Kilda, she thought, desperate not to cry. *Kilda, ye said ye were fine!*

I am, love. The reply rang in her head. *I am. The ring keeps me safe. Yer power is strong, love.*

Without her own cover of invisibility, Lucretia could no longer see Bronagh. Falkirk must have sensed this. He released a determined screech, his battered form making an ungainly swoop at the empty space before her—an empty space that fought back.

"Falkirk!" A scream tore from Lucretia's throat as one of her raven's wings dropped clean off with an ear-splitting squawk. Bronagh's bloodthirsty form materialized, blade dripping with the bird's blood. Dumbstruck, Lucretia watched her feathered companion plummet to the floor after his bloody, severed wing. Would she be able to heal him later? Would there *be* a later? There was not a single trick up her sleeve. What good was being a goddess when she didn't know how to use her own power? Magic only led to pain. *If I were human none of this would have happened.*

If ye were human, ye'd already be long dead, love. Kilda's faint whisper echoed in her head.

Bronagh leered, her face a mess of scratches. Sword held high, she pounced at Lucretia. The weapon whizzed past her ear, barely missing her.

Arm yerself with yer invocation, love, just like yer mother taught ye. Remember?

Lucretia's voice warbled as she blocked the next thrust. "I am death and blood and pain. Stand down or feel my wrath." She went in for an unconvincing jab of her sword.

"You? Please," Bronagh scoffed. "You don't have what it takes to be a goddess. You never did."

Dinnae listen to her, love. Ye can do this.

"I am death and blood and pain. Stand down or feel my wrath," she repeated, louder now, trying to ignore the taunt of her sister's words as the latter blocked her thrust effortlessly, dancing to the side to attack from a new angle.

"I bet you've never killed anything in your whole, long, miserable life."

Her distress rose, hot and fierce. It was true. She'd never killed anyone. She'd hoped she'd never have to.

I dinnae know how to fight her, Kilda. Lucretia's shoulders clenched as she blocked another blow.

Lucretia, my love. Quill. Ye can do this. Ye dinnae know what yer capable of. But I do.

As she blocked yet another thrust, something glimmered in her periphery. Falkirk, dragging himself toward Kilda, nestling against her shaking hand. The wedding band winked as Kilda fingered it.

Nae! What are ye doing?

I always said I'd do anything to help ye. Kilda tugged at the band, slipping it off her gnarled finger. *Now's my chance.*

The ring rolled onto the floor.

Nae!

I'm going now, my love. Dinnae look at me as I go, for ye must not break concentration. Ye must accept this gift from me.

Gift? Kilda, love— What gift? She slashed at the enemy, her fear fueling her as she whipped toward her wife. Kilda's hand groped beside her, landing on a long shard of glass—part of a broken photo frame. She gripped it, trembling.

Lucretia gasped. *What are ye—*

The words that interrupted her were not in her head. They rang out, ragged and desperate, yet clear as the shard Kilda gripped between her frail and bloodied fingers. "I sacrifice myself—a virgin, having been touched by nae man—in the name of the Great Winged One. May my spirit join her spirit. May my blood join her blood. May my love join her love."

With these words, Kilda brought the shard to her neck. Her eyes widened as the point pierced her flesh, a crimson stain blooming, dripping down her cardigan as she dragged the shard across the skin. It fell from her fingers.

Kilda sputtered, gasping. Lucretia screamed, all her shock and pain erupting out of her like lava, spilling hot magic into the room so the very floor trembled.

Kilda's sacrifice flooded Lucretia's veins, her lungs, the bones inside of her. The walls shook as she spread her arms, feathers sprouting forth at her command. *I will wield this power. Kilda will nae have died in vain.*

"Give me a break," Bronagh snarled, though alarm flared through her pupils. "As if some little old granny can..." Her words died away as the power of Lucretia's scream sucked the sound from the room, spinning it out again, endowing it with a life of its own. With a shocked grunt, Bronagh fell convulsing to the floor.

Lucretia slashed the air with her talons, her voice ringing out, taking the place of the scream: "I am life and healing and love. And I will not be stifled."

Fear spiked Bronagh's pupils as she tried to scramble to her feet. Even as she faltered and fell again, she struggled to recover her bravado, sputtering: "Life? Healing? Is that the best you can—"

Before the words had escaped her lips, Lucretia flung her sword aside and swooped forward, a tingling thrill overtaking her body as she morphed into bird form, air rushing beneath her wings. So this was what it was like to fly. Her heart soared at the sensation as she pointed her beak toward her target, diving straight at her, talons out.

Bronagh scurried backward to dodge the swooping raven. Rage rose in her throat, flaring into fear, blocking her airways. She hadn't anticipated this.

Quill's talons swiped at her cheek with a sharp sting. *Do something!* Bronagh screamed silently at the feather inside of her. *Obey me!* The feather twinged and tugged in her chest, like it longed to escape its throbbing prison. *You're mine!* she seethed. *I claimed you!*

But the feather only seared hotter.

With an enraged caw, Lucretia swooped again, talons ripping Bronagh's shirt from her skin—right where the feather was trying to push through to the surface. Bile rose in Bronagh's throat. She could see its glow beneath her vulnerable flesh.

Ye have something of mine, Lucretia's voice rang in her head, screeching vowels distorted. Bronagh flailed, but someone had grabbed her shoulders, holding her fast. She twisted to see who dared lay hands on her, and a rip of betrayal shot beneath her ribs. Baxter glowered, trembling, his breath hot against her neck.

"I wish I'd never met you," he hissed, wrenching her arms backward. Lucretia dove. Her talons tore at Bronagh's flesh. Bronagh released a cry. Blinding pain spewed forth from her chest.

"You loathsome—"

"Shut up." Baxter gave her a violent shake, unmoved by the spray of hot blood and viscera. "All my life you've been mocking my pain. It's over."

"You ungrateful piece of shit," she gasped, staggering as another swipe of talon widened the gash in her chest. The Eternal Feather burned, a cattle brand inside her skin.

"It's over," he repeated, jerking her violently as Lucretia's beak tore away a great strip of flesh. All the hurt and trauma the mortal had ever shared with her bubbled out of him, turning against her. Thrashing to the ground, she collapsed, her cry wrenching the fabric of the world as the feather lifted from her chest. It sang in Lucretia's talons as she swooped high into the air.

Morphing back into human form, Lucretia landed. A look of pure ecstasy shone like moonlight upon her face as she gripped the feather against her, eyes shut in triumph. And then, with a hiss, the Eternal Feather vanished—absorbed into her heart.

Lucretia's wings receded into their blue swirls as she opened her eyes.

She turned back to Bronagh.

"I'm sorry ye felt such pain." Lucretia's voice was hoarse, yet it filled the destroyed living room with enough compassion to kill Bronagh on the spot. She writhed beneath its weight, as all the misery of her life—her mortal life, so long ago—came crashing down upon her. The weight of the villagers sneering, the sting of being forgotten, of being overlooked. "And I'm sorry ye inflicted pain in return." Lucretia gestured her talon toward Bronagh—a gentle stroking motion, a fissure cracking her soul down the center. "Be at rest."

A blanket of warmth draped over Bronagh—strong arms wrapped around her body—soft, sweet. The quiet croon of a lullaby filled her ears. Her mother's voice, lulling her to sleep.

At last, she'd see her again.

CHAPTER 46

The fog of the enchantment lifted just in time for Marceline to watch Bronagh's body crumble into ash and scatter over the musty carpet. A shape stood over the vanishing remnants, still as a statue. Baxter.

Marceline blinked drowsily, unsure of what she was seeing. She twitched, trying to push herself upright, only to find that both her arms and legs were bound, and that the heaviness of her body was due to someone lying half draped over her. The warmth of his skin pumped adrenaline to her heart. Sylvan. Was he all right? His arm draped over her, his shallow breaths stunted and irregular against the shell of her ear. Something wet and sticky pressed between his body and hers.

"Sylvan?" She gasped, trying to lift herself up—which proved impossible with her wrists bound together as they were.

His eyes fluttered in the liminal state between open and closed, his voice a faint croak. "*Marceline*..." She could feel his body shift, but the effort seemed too great, and he merely groaned, eyes squeezing shut.

An instant later, Lucretia was by their side, pulling Sylvan onto his back. He coughed, and Marceline's eyes fell on the slash across his torso, the deep red stain overtaking most of his shirt and exposing the damaged flesh beneath. Had she done that? Distraught, she racked her foggy mind, the horrible truth flickering like a distant memory.

Lucretia lay her talon over the wound. "Hold on, ye great fool. Ye cannae leave us now." She began muttering, and Marceline could scarcely hear the words over the pounding of blood in her ears: *I am life and healing and love. I am life and healing and love...* She repeated it, over and over.

Relief surged as the light of consciousness returned to Sylvan's eyes, and the blood began to recede, seeping back into the gash, until it too disappeared, leaving his skin smooth and unmarked. The walls of the apartment seemed to exhale a relief so vivid that Marceline hardly noticed when Lucretia bent to unbind her. Her gaze locked onto Sylvan's, and as soon as she was free, she gripped his hands and disintegrated into tears. "Oh, Sylvan! I'm so sorry..."

"*T'inquiète pas pour moi*," he said, his voice still weak. "*Tout va bien*."

She gave a strangled half laugh, realizing he couldn't speak English outside of the café. But the words didn't matter. It was enough to see that he was breathing more easily, that there was no resentment in his eyes—only relief. She threw her arms around his neck, pulling him close, no longer caring that Baxter was watching. She only cared that Sylvan was okay.

But then her eyes met Lucretia's over Sylvan's shoulder, and the naked grief on her friend's face hit her. Marceline didn't need to ask what had happened. Her eyes fell on Kilda's body—slumped against the wall, a ribbon of blood spanning her neck. Her heart seized, breaking a thousand times over.

Poor, sweet Kilda. Marceline's self-proclaimed grandmother and dear friend, true to the last moment.

Sadness rolled over her, flattening her. They'd won, but not without a cost.

Lucretia sank to the ground before Kilda's body. Falkirk lay in her lap, mangled and bloodied, missing a wing. Clenching her jaw, Lucretia picked up the severed appendage, hugging the raven's butchered body close and muttering to herself until the wing fused back where it belonged.

"'Tis the best I can do," she whispered to the bird. "I fear ye may nae fly again, my friend. I am sorry."

Falkirk twitched, croaking in pain as he moved the stiff, awkward wing. Then Lucretia turned back to Kilda, and all at once she collapsed into anguish, moaning and cradling the white cloud of Kilda's head against her chest.

Marceline watched them, steeped in grief. She wanted to wrap her arms around her friend, to express how sorry she was for her loss—though truly, it was a loss for all of them. But words were insufficient, and this moment was a private one.

A throat cleared, and Marceline turned, wiping her tear-stained face. Baxter stood awkwardly before her, arms dangling at his sides—both were pale and smooth, save for a smattering of blond hair. As if his tattoo had never been there at all. "Let's just get this over with," he said gruffly, not looking at her. "Send me the paperwork once you have it."

"Baxter," Marceline said, her voice gentle. "I'm sorry—" She paused, her eyes darting to Sylvan, who was watching closely, though she didn't know how much he could understand. She started over. "I'm *not* sorry I'm leaving. I have to do what's right for me."

Baxter's jaw tightened. "You think he'll take better care of you than I did?" The spite in his tone was dampened by dejection.

"You never gave me the chance to take care of myself. You always told me I couldn't, and I believed it."

"I was trying to—"

"Please let me speak." She shut her eyes, breathing deeply, then opened them and tried again. "I know you thought you were helping. But I needed respect, Baxter. Not protection."

She could almost see the shame sweeping its pink fingers across his face. Yes, respect. Baxter had expected it from her, but it had to be a two-way street. She hoped he understood that. But even if he didn't, it didn't matter.

It wasn't her problem anymore.

For a moment he only looked at her, his jaw tight. And then he spoke again. "You never wanted to have a baby with me, did you?"

She swallowed, trying to suppress the guilt, to stifle the hand flying to her stomach. "That was your dream, Baxter. Not mine."

His storm-gray eyes fell back to the floor, gazing at the last remnants of dust at his feet. Then, without a word more, he strode through the ruined apartment, grabbed his keys from the hook by the door, and left.

Marceline watched him go. She didn't regret her decision to keep the pregnancy to herself. There was no point in making things worse by taunting him with a dream that would not come true.

A part of her still worried how he'd cope with the separation, but it was only a small part—one she'd have to learn to let go of. She'd spent enough of her life worrying about Baxter, and now it was time to worry about herself.

Alongside Sylvan, Marceline cleaned the apartment in silence, keeping a respectful distance from Lucretia as she wept over her wife's body. When all the damage had been swept into garbage bags, Lucretia swaddled the suffering Falkirk in a dish towel and tucked him into Kilda's lifeless arms before scooping her up like a child. "I'll meet ye at the café," she whispered. Tracing a circle in the air, she stepped into invisibility.

Sylvan and Marceline hailed a taxi and rode back to the café in silence, seated on opposite sides in the back of the cab. Marceline glanced at Sylvan, memorizing his profile as he gazed out the window and took in this unfamiliar city, thousands of miles from the home he'd left that morning. Probably thinking of Kilda. Like she was.

The driver dropped them off at the entrance of the alley.

"Sylvan—" she began, unsure of how to express the stampede of feelings galloping inside her, and whether he'd even understand her when she did find the words. When he slipped his hand into hers, she understood perhaps the best thing to say was nothing at all.

Together, they stepped over the wreckage of the doorway. The last of the hospital patients and personnel had gone, leaving a pile of overturned furniture in their wake. Marceline wondered if it had been hard for them to leave the café. If so, she could relate.

Several tables had been pushed together in the corner by the fireplace, and Kilda's body had been lain atop them. One of Lucretia's vibrant scarves draped over her—an unlikely death shroud—surrounded by the fallen ribs of the whale skeleton that had once hung overhead. Birds gathered around, perching on the mantel and on the backs of chairs, paying their silent respects. Even the masks upon the walls wept. Two ravens guarded either side of Kilda's head like sentinels—Falkirk's crooked wing sticking out at an awkward angle. When Marceline and Sylvan approached, the other raven took flight, sweeping in a circle over the room before materializing in human form before them.

Grief glimmered from the depths of Lucretia's coal-black eyes. When she opened her mouth to speak, no sound came out. Marceline hugged her devastated friend, and Sylvan moved in, enveloping them both in his warmth. They stayed like that for an eternity, until at last, Lucretia began to squirm, and Sylvan released them.

"I believe she planned to save us all along," Lucretia whispered. "She did nae tell me, for she knew I'd never consent to losing her."

"If not for her, we would all have expired." Sylvan's voice grazed the silence, his English having been recovered upon entry to the café.

The finality of their friend's death resonated across each of their minds. Then, after a long while, Lucretia spoke again. "My dear, generous

Kilda left some things behind, knowing she'd nae be back. I found them laid out in my room, with a letter explaining it all…" She gestured at a small wooden chest that lay among the sea of pillows and rugs. Lucretia reached inside, retrieving a thin scroll of parchment and a tiny parcel, flat and rectangular. She handed them to Marceline, whose heart seized with sadness.

Of *course* Kilda would leave one last gift.

Marceline unwrapped the parcel carefully. Inside was a thin, burgundy book. She flipped open to the first page, where her own picture smiled back at her, along with details about her birthday, her maiden name, her place of birth. "A passport?"

"Aye. From the United Kingdom."

"But I'm not British."

"Nae. Ye're Scottish. Ye are now, anyway. Open the scroll."

In shock, Marceline obeyed. The scroll felt heavier than it should, and when she unfurled it, she found a small metal key taped inside. Her eyes widened, scanning the looped scrawl of Kilda's handwriting.

> To my dear friend Marceline, the granddaughter I never had, I leave my home in Fort William, along with all my possessions therein. In exchange, I ask only that she maintain my garden and feed the orange cat that visits from time to time.

Marceline gasped, her hands beginning to shake as her heart leapt into her throat. Kilda's house? The family home she'd grown up in and lived in all her life? In Scotland, no less?

It was too much. She'd never so much as left California.

"Lucretia, I can't possibly—"

"'Twas her dying wish, Marce. She knew ye'd be feeling lost after all this, and it gave her such joy to know she could help. Besides, we all know how ye long to travel."

"But…" She looked at Sylvan, whose neck was craned, reading the letter over her shoulder.

"Lu is right. You must accept."

Marceline nodded, a lump in her throat. She wished she had a way to thank the old cartographer who'd been so kind to her.

They cleaned up the café, putting the furniture back in order. Maia the plant had been overturned but was still alive and angrier than ever, and the masks smiled sadly at Marceline as she straightened them upon the wall.

When Marceline's stomach constricted with a residual cramp, she groaned, causing both Sylvan and Lucretia to turn in concern. Marceline looked back at them. She hadn't told a soul about her pregnancy, or the decision she'd made. But why not? Sylvan and Lucretia only wanted the best for her. If anything, they'd be proud of her for finally making an important choice for herself. *I want to tell them*, Marceline realized. *Why should I carry this alone?*

"I had an abortion today," she said.

Sylvan dropped his mop with a clatter. "What? Today?"

It occurred to Marceline she could have introduced this more smoothly. "A few hours ago. I couldn't have a baby. Not right now, and not with him."

Lucretia rushed forward and pulled Marceline into her arms. "How long have ye been dragging this secret around with ye? And why? Ye know we would nae have judged."

Marceline sank into Lucretia's embrace. "I don't know," she admitted. "I guess announcing it would have made it feel real."

Sylvan still hadn't moved a muscle. He stared at her. "And you tossed yourself into a supernatural battle? Directly after your operation?"

"You were in trouble. What else could I have done?"

He exhaled, shaking his head in wonder. "My God, Marce. You must be the strongest woman I have met. And trust me, I was reared by strong women."

Strong. Marceline smiled, as the word burrowed into the center of her being, spreading warmth. Yes. She *was* strong.

When the café was intact once more, the splintered hole in the door reconstructed by a muttered spell from Lucretia, the three of them united in solemn silence around Kilda's body.

"This place won't be the same without her," Marceline said.

"Nae. And it willnae be the same without me, either. For before the day's done, I intend to bring Kilda back to her native soil. Our soil. It scares me to think how it'll have changed, but 'tis where I belong."

"You are departing?" Sylvan leaned his mop against the wall. "Who will nourish Maia?" He nudged the potted plant with the toe of his sneaker.

"I'll be back soon." Lucretia set her talon on Sylvan's shoulder. "After all, I've still got to train my successor. Provided he accepts the job." Her brow raised into a question.

"Me?"

"Aye. I know ye've got responsibilities on your island, but perhaps part-time? This realm existed long before I came along, but I'm quite proud of what I made of it. 'Twould be a shame for it to be abandoned."

Marceline squeezed Sylvan's arm. "You should do it." Her life had changed in a thousand ways since she'd first stumbled, soaking and injured, into this sanctuary. She wanted others to have that too.

"Could my family visit on occasions?" Sylvan asked.

"Dinnae ask me. Yer the boss now. I mean, if ye're saying yes."

"Are you jesting?" Sylvan grinned. "Of course I am saying yes. We will miss you, though."

"Ye dinnae need me anymore," she said, a broken edge to her smile. "My true responsibilities lie in my homeland. 'Tis high time I returned. I promised Kilda I would, and I intend to keep that promise."

"You're going to be a goddess again?" A warm current of awe rose through Marceline as she contemplated all her friend might be capable of.

Lucretia smiled, black eyes glittering with tears. "I was always a goddess. My mistake was believing I was the wrong kind. But come." She curled a talon, beckoning them. "If ye wish to pay your respects to Kilda, now is the time, for we must be going. I'll nae wait a thousand years more."

They made their way to the table, to Kilda's body, unmoving beneath its colorful shroud. Lucretia hooked her talons over the fabric and drew it away. Kilda looked so serene, as if she were merely napping.

Lucretia instructed them to take one of Kilda's hands in each of theirs, while she set her own talons over her wife's shoulders. Marceline and Sylvan closed their eyes, plunged into their separate minds.

Thank you for being my friend, Marceline thought, heart splintering. *Thank you for being so kind and generous.*

When she'd said all she had to say, she peeked. The years had vanished from Kilda's face—not just for a flickering instant this time. Her skin was smooth, her hair a vibrant red, a spray of freckles across her rosy cheeks.

When Lucretia leaned in to kiss her, Marceline shut her eyes again, pretending she hadn't seen.

She couldn't say when she stopped feeling the weight of Kilda's cold hand in hers, but when Lucretia whispered for them to open their eyes, there remained no body at all.

Only a tiny blue egg, speckled and delicate, lay at the center of the table.

"I must be going now." Lucretia gazed tenderly down at the egg. "Sylvan, will ye take care of Falkirk for me?"

"Of course." Sylvan's brown eyes glimmered with emotion as he stroked the wounded raven. Lucretia bent to kiss the bird.

"Marceline, when ye're ready, the door should lead ye straight to the thicket in Kilda's garden. 'Tis your home now, after all. Dinnae lose your key this time." She winked even as tears slid down her face, moving around the table to wrap her friends in one final embrace. "I'm proud of ye both," she whispered.

A moment later she swooped into the air in bird form, looping three times around the room before diving to scoop up the delicate egg in her talons. Carrying it with her, she soared out the door.

And then she was gone.

Marceline watched her disappear, heart thrumming with pride, sadness, and awe. When at last she turned back to Sylvan, the intensity of his gaze crackled like static on her skin.

"Scotland, hmm?" His voice was a murmur. "I suppose you do not require this place anymore."

Marceline reached for him, taking his big, warm hands in her own. "Sylvan—" The yellow glow of a spotlight fell over her as soon as she said his name. Of course. Marceline soothed her pounding heart. "I know you said things were too complicated." She made herself smile, though tears tugged at her eyes. "But I want you to know I wasn't just looking for comfort. I care about you."

His eyes shone, face bathed in the golden glow of the spotlight. The touch of his hand against hers made her heart swoop, and a warm, tingling feeling flooded her entire body as his fingers traveled up her arms, tugging her closer. "I know," he whispered. "You are a gust of clean air, Marce. You have reminded me of what is good in the world, and what is good about *me*. How I can ever thank you?"

"I know how you can thank me," she whispered, rising onto her tiptoes.

This time, he didn't back away. Instead, he leaned into her, his soft lips connecting with hers and setting off a euphoric explosion. She sank into the kiss, reveling in its sweetness, the most delicious sensation she'd ever experienced. And when their lips parted, she let herself lean into him, savoring the comfort of his arms as she lay her cheek against his soft chest, listening to the rapid beat of his heart—a beat that matched her own.

Home. The word pumped in her veins, singing throughout her entire body. This was what home felt like.

"You know," she said, the kiss still tingling on her lips, "even if I don't technically need the café anymore, I don't mind sticking around a bit. If only to help you out."

She could feel his smile without even looking. "That would be nice," he murmured.

As they melted into each other, the warm, sourceless glow of the café enveloped them, vibrant with possibility.

ACKNOWLEDGMENTS

Writing a book may be solitary, but revising one and having it published is anything but! There are so many people I'd like to thank for helping me realize my lifelong dream of becoming a published author, so without further ado, and in no particular order, here are some people I'm immensely grateful for...

My dad, for accepting and supporting my impractical career aspirations. (At least I never joined the circus!) The disgustingly talented and deeply silly women of the Telepathic Critique Group: Amber Sötemann, Belinda McCauley, and Celina Poole. (Porpoise of acknowledgments! Porpoise of this is totally an inside joke and I deeply apologize to all those who are confused by it!) Kai from Reddit for her generous and detailed answers to my questions regarding Tahitian culture. My professors at the University of Edinburgh for encouraging me to take myself seriously as a writer. The people of the Writing Warriors Facebook Group, especially Elizabeth Daly, who beta read an early version of this book. My sweet pup, Dobby, who cannot read but still deserves to be immortalized in print. The team at Jill Grinberg Literary Management, for first seeing the potential in my story. My fabulous new agent, Kim Carson, for jumping in as my advocate at the drop of a hat. The organizers of the Southern

California Writer's Conference, with a special shoutout to the unstoppable night owls of the late-night Rogue critique workshop. My brilliant editor, Barbara Berger, for her attention to detail and enthusiasm—without her you would not be reading this. The rest of the team at Union Square & Co., including project editor Alison Skrabek, creative director Lisa Forde, jacket art director Patrick Sullivan, cover designer Jared Oriel, interior designer Marie Mundaca, production manager Sandy Noman, and copyeditor Diane Joao.

And finally, my husband, Ash, who has been supportive of my dreams since we met, even though there are exactly zero explosions or car chases in this novel, and not even a single mention of fishing. (Maybe next one . . . but probably not.) You're my soup.

QUESTIONS AND TOPICS FOR DISCUSSION

1. How does Marceline's backstory influence her present relationship? What assumptions do you make about her based on her past?

2. What methods does Baxter use to keep Marceline from leaving him? Does this constitute abuse, in your opinion? Why do you think she stays with him for so long?

3. The ghost in the storeroom gives voice to the difficult truths that café patrons are not ready to accept. What does it say about Marceline's mindset that she eventually chooses to visit the ghost of her own accord?

4. How does the community Marceline discovers in the café help her find empowerment?

5. Though both Bronagh and Lucretia are trapped in separate realms of the Otherworld, they follow parallel character journeys. How are their experiences different? How are they similar? What does the way they evolve say about them as characters?

6. Motherhood is portrayed in various ways throughout the novel. How do these various portrayals influence the characters? Is there a unified message about motherhood?

7. The café is a haven for lost souls, and its portals appear based on need. The tavern also serves a similar purpose. What separates the people who end up at the café from the people who end up at the tavern? Do you think it's an innate character trait, something more circumstantial, or completely random?

8. What is the symbolism of the whale skeleton hanging from the rafters? How about the swirling black void outside the café's portal?

9. How does society's restrictive standards of men's bodies factor into your perception of Sylvan's character?

10. What criteria constitute a "strong" female character? Are there different types of strength, and if so, what are they? Do some get more visibility than others?

11. In the book, gods and goddesses are not necessarily immortal. Instead, they pass on their role to their heirs when they choose to retire. What are the implications of this?

12. What role does sacrifice play in the book? How many instances of sacrifice can you identify?

13. How does colonialism influence Sylvan's backstory?

14. How do you reconcile Baxter's desire to do good in his career, when weighed against how he treats Marceline? What is the difference between justifying and excusing trauma?

15. The two fawns from the same litter who are forced to fight each other to the death in chapter 15 foreshadow the deadly fight between the two sisters at the end of the novel. What other instances of foreshadowing did you notice?

16. Kilda's body is replaced by a small blue egg at the end of the novel. What are the implications of this? How might this tie back into the novel's opening scene?

17. What do you think happened to the tavern after Bronagh dies? What do you imagine the other realms of the Otherworld might be like?

18. Think of the various characters in the book. What do you imagine happens next in each of their lives, after the events of the novel?

ABOUT THE AUTHOR

ZARA MARIELLE hails from two worlds: a Northern Californian hippy town and a rustic village high in the French Alps. A former ESL teacher, she loves to travel and has lived in Canada, Venezuela, England, and Scotland. Zara earned a master's in creative writing from the University of Edinburgh in 2015.